Other Titles by

The DEAD Series:

DEAD: The Ugly Beginning
DEAD: Revelations
DEAD: Fortunes & Failures
DEAD: Winter
DEAD: Siege & Survival
DEAD: Confrontation
DEAD: Reborn
DEAD: Darkness Before Dawn
DEAD: Spring
DEAD: The Reclamation
DEAD: End

DEAD Special Edition

DEAD: Perspectives Story (Vols. 1 - 4)
DEAD: Vignettes (Vols. 1 - 4)
DEAD: The Geeks (Vols. 1 - 4)

Zomblog

Zomblog
Zomblog II
Zomblog: The Final Entry
Zomblog: Snoe
Zomblog: Snoe's War
Zomblog: Snoe's Journey

That Ghoul Ava

That Ghoul Ava: Her First Adventures
That Ghoul Ava & The Queen of the Zombies
That Ghoul Ava Kick Some Faerie A**
Next, on a very special That Ghoul Ava
That Ghoul Ava on the Lam

The World of the *DEAD* expands with:

Snapshot—**Las Vegas, Nevada**
(Coming Summer of 2016)

ISBN 978-1-940734-53-8

A moment with the author...

Welcome to the third installment of the **DEAD: Snapshot—{insert town here}** series. This is one of those stories that I am very excited about. Now, no spoilers, but this is another time I got to put a different spin on the normal zombie tale. So often, the destruction is total and complete. But what if a small town banded together to stand against the walking dead? That is part of the idea behind this tale. Also, I get to drop a bit of a morality story on you. I hope it plays out as well on paper as it did in my head.

I will say that, as a fan of the original *Dawn of the Dead*, I am of the belief that endings in a zombie story can often be a bit open and ambiguous. While there is certainly a lot to be said about a hard or solid conclusion, the zombie genre is not always best served by that approach.

I am a fan of how Fran and Peter are lifting off from that mall in the WGON chopper as the zombies pour out onto the roof. (Forget how they managed to suddenly learn to climb ladders.) I walked out of the theater and spent hours wondering what happened next. Did they find someplace safe? Did Fran crash when they ran out of fuel?

To that end, I want to give my readers a conclusion, but I also like them to be able to ponder the fate of the characters they have come to love or hate in the pages of this book. When reach the last page of this particular tale, I hope the story remains with you for a while. No, this is not the start of another series. This is a stand-alone title; just like all my other *Snapshot* books. However, I think we all know that "life goes on" so to speak after the story ends. Just like real life. Just something to ponder.

I do want to extend my thanks to the good men and women of Liberty, South Carolina. As this book came together, I was blessed to have a few of her fine citizens offer me some helpful tips. For instance...Liberty has a chief of police. Not a sheriff. That was an error that might seem small, but I bet to the people of Liberty, it would make a big difference.

I must say here that I have fictionalized the town to make it fit my story. All errors are my own doing. I had to create a few creeps, and that in no way reflects on the actual people of this little town in Palmetto State. So, if you from Liberty, please don't be offended. This is, after all, a work of fiction.

I want to thank the real Stephen Deese for offering his town up to the apocalypse. I also want to thank Jamie Burns for her time early in the creation of this project. I would be remiss if I did not thank Sarah Gilstrap for her help getting a few of the facts straight and Jonathan Patterson for throwing his name in the ring to be used at my discretion.

To my Beta readers: Sarah, Jonathan, Miranda, Debra, Sophie, Heather, Tammy, Hope, Donna, Lynne, Todd and Amy, this book would not be nearly as good without you. I started with forty, and you were the hardy crew that lasted to the end. I thank you sincerely for your help, hard work, and constant input.

To those of you who are not aware, this is a spinoff of my 12 book *DEAD* series. Each of these is a self-contained story and yes, I do realize that each could become its own series, but that is the idea of a "snapshot" as the title suggests. It is one look into one location during the zombie apocalypse that lives in depth in my proper series. I sometimes drop teasers or Easter eggs that fans of the series will understand, but you don't need to have read the series to enjoy these individual stories. (And I do hope that you enjoy them.)

As always, I do hope that you will leave a review (good or bad, don't worry, I can take constructive criticism) after you read this book. Believe it or not, they do matter. Some people dismiss it, but I have seen a difference in the exposure of my titles with 50 or more reviews. So please, just take a moment when you're done. You have my eternal gratitude.

Where neighbors become friends.
TW Brown
February 2016

For Stephen, Jamie, and the wonderful REAL
people of Liberty, South Carolina

Contents

1

Welcome to Liberty, South Carolina

Bruce Gibbs started to bring his big rig to a stop. The car just ahead was only partway off the highway and had its hazard lights flashing. Sure, he could have just drifted over to the left lane and shot past, but that simply was no longer in his nature.

Two months ago, Bruce had come to the Lord. After over a decade of drug and alcohol abuse, his sister had staged an intervention. It was then that she revealed she had been diagnosed with breast cancer and needed her big brother's shoulder to lean on in the trying times that lie ahead. He'd started attending church with her every time he was in town, and was starting to feel better about himself than he had in years.

The big rig shuddered as it came to a complete stop and Bruce engaged the brakes before opening his door. The cool night air made his skin erupt in goose bumps, and he got a funny feeling that sent him to his favorite verse of scripture. It was the first bit he had ever memorized and it always calmed him when Satan tried to unsettle him, to lure him back to the bottle or the women.

"The Lord is my shepherd, I lack nothing. He makes me lie down in green pastures…" he whispered as he approached the beat up old Buick. There was something peculiar about the rear window. As a car zoomed by, coming from behind him on the

Calhoun Memorial Highway, better known to passing truckers simply as Highway 123, the rear window looked like it was melting.

"...You prepare a table before me in the presence of my enemies. You anoint my head with oil..." Bruce continued as he reached the rear bumper.

Almost immediately, there was a horrific smell that was foul and gagging. It was like feces mixed with spoiled chicken. This had to be serious. He finished his recital of *Psalms Twenty-three* and switched over to simply praying for the poor souls in that vehicle. He fished his cell phone from his pocket and hit the emergency button as he reached for the recessed handle of the front, driver's side door.

"Nine-one-one...police, fire, or medical," a bored sounding voice answered.

"I think all of them," Bruce gasped as he gave the door handle a tug. "Oh, my God."

In the front bench seat, a male was sprawled over and lying on his side. Crouched in the floor well on the passenger's side was a child. He couldn't have been older than seven. His face was a dark mask. But Bruce knew that the moment that face came into the light, the black stain would morph to red.

The man's throat had been torn open and blood had sprayed all over the interior of the car. A good jet of it must have hit the back window; explaining why it had looked like it was melting. Bruce staggered back and dropped his phone. The tinny voice on the other end was now unintelligible.

Losing his footing, Bruce fell backwards—directly into the path of one of his fellow truck drivers. This particular eighteen-wheeler was hauling a full bed of thirty-foot poles and moving at just over sixty-eight miles per hour when it slammed into Bruce, killing him instantly. The impact was so great that there was very little of the poor man other than what dripped from the front grill of the semi.

The newly arriving big rig began to squeal as the brakes

were applied much too hastily to be safe. The trailer heaved around and the rear end began to catch up with the cab. It drifted into the median and began to destroy the high-tension cable line that so many people in the area had complained was completely useless and needed to be replaced with an actual concrete divider that separated the east and westbound lanes.

An oncoming SUV with a family returning from a trip to Greenville after checking out the upstate campus of the University of South Carolina was coming east at that unfortunate moment. The oldest daughter was planning on attending USC next year if everything went well.

The family was cruising along at just over seventy when a dark shadow filled the entire lane directly ahead in the blink of an eye. All plans ended abruptly when the rear trailer full of poles smashed into the front of the SUV and sent the engine block all the way through the rear of the car, killing the mother, father, and oldest daughter, as well as seriously injuring the fourteen-year-old sister who was thrown out the rear of the SUV.

Nobody would know that her body lay broken and bleeding in the tall roadside grass. The living were so occupied with the terrible scene of the accident that nobody saw the three figures coming out of the trees as they paused and suddenly changed direction. Almost as one, they dropped to their knees and began clawing, biting, and tearing at the helpless girl who was fortunate to never actually regain consciousness.

Cars from both directions began to stop and people emerged from their vehicles; some to see if they might be able to help, others just to be able to get a better look. One boy ignored his mother's reprimands and emerged from his parent's car with his cell phone in hand. He felt his heart race as he neared the carnage. This was the first time he'd even used the new cell phone and he had to fumble a few seconds to get the camera function to start recording.

He approached a body that lay sprawled on the ground. There was a dark pool on the asphalt that he knew had to be blood. Another person was crouched over the body and twelve-year-old Ben Jones zoomed in on his screen so that he could see a little better. He expected to hear crying or maybe the crouched person trying to communicate with the individual lying flat on his back, but what he heard was a strange sound that reminded him of how his cousin Jenny ate spaghetti. There was a loud slurping noise and then what he thought to be open-mouthed chewing.

The long hair that hung down from the head of the crouched person prevented him from really seeing what was going on and so he took a few more steps closer. *This is going to blow everybody away at school on Monday*, he thought. A smell hit his nose as he took those final steps that put him in arm's reach of the scene. It was possibly the nastiest thing he had ever smelt in his life. It was worse than going into the bathroom after his dad in the mornings.

"Is he dead?" Ben breathed as he got to within a few steps of the man who stared straight up with eyes that looked sort of strange. Ben noticed that they looked clouded over like the blind man who sat in the front row every Sunday at church; only…different.

The person who was crouched over the body paused whatever it was doing. For a moment, there was no movement, then the head began to crank around in slow, jerky, bird-like fits.

Young Ben Jones did not even realize that his phone slipped from his fingers. He was in shock as his brain struggled to make sense of what he was seeing. The man's face was a dark mask around the mouth and something long and stringy dangled from one corner. The man's long hair was dripping from where it had been dragged through the horrible and bloody open gash in the belly of the man on the ground.

The crouching figure began to move towards Ben, hands reaching and mouth opening in a low moan. That sound was the last straw for Ben's bladder although he no more registered that fact than he had dropping his phone. He stood frozen in terror as the long-haired man stumble-crawled towards him. A hand grabbed his ankle and he simply watched the bloody face come to his leg. The stained mouth opened and then clamped down on the outside of his right calf. Now his bowels joined his bladder, but Ben registered nothing. He had already gone into shock and continued to stand unmoving as a piece of his leg was torn free.

At last, pain registered in his brain, but Ben did not scream, he simply let out a feeble whimper. His eyes had now fixed on the second man who had been sprawled on the ground; this person was sitting up with his insides spilling out onto the highway; and now he was coming for Ben as well.

Ben's mother had jerked away from his father and stood outside the passenger's side door. Much like her son, she could not believe what she was seeing. However, she did not freeze in shock, instead, her motherly instincts took control and she charged the two terrible men who looked to be attacking her son.

"Shondra!" Clarence Jones shouted as he now emerged from the car as well.

He heard a sound behind him and turned to see a child standing just a few feet away. The boy couldn't be any older than seven or eight, and he was covered in blood and gore. The stink rolling off the child was enough to make Clarence take an involuntary step back. What began as a reaction to the smell changed to fear as a man came stumbling up behind the child with pieces of his face looking like they'd been chewed off.

His first thought was dog attack, but then his eyes returned to the child who had stopped advancing and was cocking its head first to one side then the other. The man behind the child made no attempt to slow and stumbled past the little boy, sending him sort of careening off the side of Clarence Jones' car.

"You just stop right there," Clarence warned.

At that same instant, his wife screamed their son's name. Clarence turned his head to see Shondra lit up by the headlights of his car. She was on her knees trying to pull Ben free from two men. She didn't even see the woman stumbling up behind her due to the blue-white glare of all the headlights. This creature was limping horribly from what looked like the left foot having been turned completely backwards and dragging along with a scratching sound as exposed bone scraped asphalt.

Clarence's head whipped around when a strangely cold hand swiped down his face and landed on his shoulder where it grabbed hold with a peculiar firmness. He tried to jerk away but his feet tangled in those of his attacker and the two fell down with Clarence landing flat on his back and the strange, foul smelling man on top. The impact knocked the wind from him. In the end, he was only able to emit a feeble squeak as teeth tore into the flesh of his throat.

Pain slammed into him and he was almost certain that he saw a dark jet that had to be his own blood spray across his vision. He blinked once and opened his eyes to see the darkly stained face of the child leaning down over him. Its tiny mouth was open wide and came down to fasten on the bridge of his nose.

Clarence's screams were just one of many as the unsuspecting living emerged from their cars and made for easy prey. Not one person in the midst of the carnage could fathom what was taking place. Nobody could force themselves to believe that the dead were getting up and attacking the living.

It was simply too ridiculous, a thing of pop fiction.

***

Mayor Jamie Burns sat at her desk and allowed her eyes to shut as she rolled her head in circles to try and ease the tension in her neck. She looked out the window of the tiny room where she had set up her office in the old Rosewood Center. The headlights of a car passing by on Main Street flashed in her window and then were gone. She pulled her headphones off and set them on her desk, the tinny sound of her iPod continued to play a song by The Judds until she hit the stop button and flicked off the power.

"Glad to see I'm not the only person awake at this hour," she mumbled as she glanced up at the clock on the wall. It read just past three in the morning.

She hit the save button on her open spreadsheet file and started closing down her computer. She paused on her email and was about to close that as well when something caught her attention on the muted television sitting on the shelf to the right of the coffee pot. Opening her top drawer, she grabbed the remote and increased the volume.

There was a man holding a microphone with a large military truck as his background. The man looked nervous and kept glancing to his right, wincing from time to time as he spoke words she could not yet hear. That alone had not been enough to grab her attention. It was the banner at the bottom of the screen that had done the job. The banner read: *Multiple fatalities at the junction of Highway 178 and 123 closes major route to all traffic*. That was just a mile or so south of town.

"…have set up a perimeter just south of what I am told is 5 Forks Road near the town of Liberty. We are on the western side of the overpass, but military vehicles have just rolled in and an Army National Guard unit has joined with elements of the State Police to ensure that nobody gets past and enters what we have been told is a scene of unimaginable carnage." There was a distant popping sound that Jamie heard on the television and then from somewhere outside just a split second later.

She walked to the door and paused to look in the full length mirror that she'd hung on it. It wasn't often that she had to do anything in an "official" capacity when she was here at the center doing paperwork, but it never hurt to be prepared. It wouldn't do to go out and look a mess.

Her long, sandy colored hair was only a little disheveled. She ran her fingers through it and it fell straight and at least presentable as it cascaded past her shoulders and came to rest on her dark blue blouse; the blouse made her light blue eyes almost look like smoky gray. Her makeup had held up nicely and all she would need to do is touch up her lipstick.

As she exited the office and stepped into the mostly dark hallway, the main doors to the center opened. She recognized the outline of the figure coming in—Chief Adam Gilstrap. His six and a half foot, two hundred and fifty pound frame made her just barely over five feet tall seem even smaller.

"Trouble out on the highway," Adam said by way of greeting.

"I just saw it on the news." Jamie patted her pocket for her keys. "We should head over there and see if there is anything we can do to help."

"Army is shutting things down. I just came from out that way and the sumbitches turned me around. Told me to go back to town." The undisguised anger in the large man's voice was unmistakable.

Adam had been the Chief of Police in Liberty, South Carolina for as long as Jamie could recall. He had to be on the downhill side of fifty and she could remember him coming to her grade school for various functions and assemblies when she was a child. Still, for as old as the man was, he had kept himself in remarkable shape and seldom had to do little more than step out of his car if he arrived at any sort of disturbance.

"Yes, well perhaps if we go together?" Jamie hated that her voice sounded so frail and weak. She'd meant that to be a statement, but it had come out squeaky and ended up sounding like a question.

"Mayor Burns, I don't like what I was seeing, and think it best that perhaps we sit tight like they said," the fatherly tone in his voice was at war with the fact that he'd actually addressed her by her title.

At only twenty-nine, Jamie Burns was not the usual choice for mayor in a town like Liberty. As much as the world had changed and supposedly moved forward, Liberty still had a foot in the past; as did many towns in the South.

Jamie had gone away to the University of South Carolina, in the state's capital of Columbia. That had not been a very popular choice in her home where everybody else bled Clemson orange, but she'd wanted to major in political science. She'd been fascinated with politics since she'd been just a girl of nine years old. Of course that had all started back in 1990 when her family had taken a vacation to Washington, D.C.

The family had been on a guided tour of the White House when a commotion up ahead had caused everybody to buzz with excitement. A group of men in suits with dark glasses had rounded the corner and the tour guide had stopped in her tracks.

"Ladies and gentlemen, we are in for a rare treat...that is President Bush and his secret service detail," the older woman had spoken in a hushed tone that had been very unlike her loud and grating tour guide voice.

The entourage had suddenly changed course like a flock of birds and was now coming directly at them! For Jamie, everything after that had been a blur, but she still had the picture on her desk of President Bush kneeling beside her with a huge smile on his face.

When she had returned to Liberty after earning her bachelor's degree, she started attending city council meetings. Her face became a fixture and it was not long before she had taken a seat at that same council. Still, she had not even considered running for mayor. Howard "Skip" Merchant had been the mayor of Liberty for over sixteen years. He was loved by everybody; so much so that he'd run unopposed the last three terms.

Then came the cancer. It hit hard and fast; reducing the large, robust man to a sickly shadow of his former self within weeks. It had surprised just about everybody when he'd requested that she be his successor from his death bed. That had been just over four months ago and she still was not used to being called Madame Mayor or Mayor Burns when walking around in public.

"I think we should take your car and go see if there is anything that our town can do to offer assistance," Jamie said as she struggled to maintain eye contact and stare up at the chief.

"I agree, it's just…" Chief Gilstrap started, but his voice faded and he suddenly seemed unsure of what to say or how to say it.

"Is there a problem?" Jamie fought the urge to plant her hands on her hips. This was a time to be as professional as possible and prove that she had been the right choice for this job. If there was a terrible tragedy unfolding on their doorstep, the good men and women of Liberty were by-God going to help in any way possible.

"I saw something that I can't explain," Sherriff Gilstrap stated. He pressed his lips together tight and ran a hand through the gray stubble of his crew-cut. "There was a body…I made it out in the lights of one of the trucks. It was just lying there in the road, but it was missing an arm, and it looked like…" Again he paused and his face screwed up tight as if he had just swallowed something foul. "I can't be sure, but it looked like the body was sitting up as the soldiers were sort of herding me back to my car. A second later, I heard a single gunshot."

"But I could have sworn that I heard several," Jamie finally spoke when it was clear that the chief was done talking.

"Yeah, me too." The man nodded. "But those came just as I was pulling into the parking lot out front."

"You aren't saying what I think you are?"

"If what you think I am saying is that the army shot and killed an injured man, then yes, that's exactly what I'm saying."

"Then we have a duty to go and see just exactly what is happening this close to our town."

Jamie edged past the large man and headed out the door. She heard his heavy steps follow and inwardly breathed a sigh of relief. Hurrying down the steps she went to the front passenger side door and waited for the chief to get in his car and unlock her side. She climbed in and glanced out her window as the engine turned over. She was startled by the crackle of voices on the radio.

"...falling back..."

"...where are they coming from...God there are six more..."

"...can't stop them..."

A hiss of very loud static erupted from the speaker. A second later there was a bright flash in the sky to the south along with a ground shaking rumble and boom.

Sherriff Adam Gilstrap threw the police car into reverse, stomped on the gas, and sent the car backwards in a jolt. Just as suddenly, he slammed on the brakes and cranked the steering wheel, spinning the vehicle in a near-perfect hundred and eighty degree turn before flooring it again and rocketing out of the Rosewood Center parking lot.

In moments, they were cruising down Moorefield Memorial Highway; the road that was at the junction with Highway 123, and the scene of this terrible accident.

The television in Jamie Burns' office had been left on. The image now playing was that of a pair of newscasters in the actual newsroom. They were staring back at the camera with looks of horror and astonishment at what had just played out a moment before, ending with a bright flash of light and then static as the feed from the field reporter had ended abruptly.

***

Ricky Porter tapped away on the keyboard of his computer. His parents would tan his hide if they knew he was up at this hour and on the computer, but he hadn't been able to sleep and the lure of his favorite video game was simply just too strong. He'd been so close to beating the final boss on the last level that he'd absolutely had to give it just one try...then another...and another.

Thirty-seven tries later, he'd done it! He had eradicated the zombie king and beaten the game. Of course, now, he was bored out of his mind. His allowance would not let him buy another game for his computer for at least another three weeks. By then, he knew that jerk Mitch Henry would not only already own it, but would have beaten it and bragged to everybody how easy it had been for him to do so.

A pop-up in the lower right hand corner of his screen got his attention. It was his best friend, Lawrence Martin. Lawrence was a shoe-in to be the captain of the baseball team this year. That was already ruffling some feathers since Lawrence was two things Mitch Henry was not; first, Lawrence was not Coach Henry's son. Second…and this was only a problem for some of the families that had called Liberty their home for generations going back a couple of hundred years—Lawrence Martin was not white.

What are you doing up so late? the message read.

Just beat Zombie Menace, *then I couldn't sleep*, Ricky typed back. *What about you? Try outs are tomorrow. You need to be on your game.*

Dad got called away, something bad is going down over on the highway. I think it has something to do with that news report out of Kentucky three days ago.

How could something on the highway here have anything to do with that crazy story out of Kentucky?

Turn on the news.

That message was followed with a link. Ricky clicked on it and had to plug in his headphones so that he could actually hear what the reporter was saying. He recognized the man's face, but it was not normal for any of the local stations to have local news on the air at this hour.

"Elements of the National Guard have set up a perimeter just south of what I am told is 5 Forks Road near the town of Liberty. We are on the western side of the overpass, but military vehicles have just rolled in and an Army National Guard unit has joined with elements of the State Police to ensure that nobody gets past and enters what we have been told is a scene of unimaginable carnage."

A sound that Ricky was pretty certain had to be gunfire could be heard. First it came in a few sporadic bursts, then a barrage. The reporter on the screen flinched and turned his head, obviously in the direction of the sound.

WTF? Ricky typed. There was a long pause with no reply, so he hit the "question mark" and "Enter" keys a few more times. At last, Lawrence replied.

Sorry, phone just rang. Mom answered it. She sounded really upset and then she took off out the house. Didn't even stick her head in to check on me or say anything.

Ricky was trying to think of what to say to his friend when the next message popped up on his screen.

I'm hopping on my bike and heading over to see what's going on.

WAIT! Ricky responded. After a few seconds, he added, *Lawrence?* Six times he repeated his friend's name, but there was no reply. He knew he would be in a whole mess of trouble, but Lawrence was his best friend. There was no way he could just sit here at his desk and wait.

Slipping out of his bedroom, Ricky pulled on his heavy coat and slipped out the back door. He made it down the stairs and to the garage. This was where it would be tricky. The side door to the garage needed some serious WD-40 on the hinges. Even worse, his parent's bedroom window was on this side of the house and his dad always slept with the window open. It didn't matter what time of year it was, he claimed that his body ran hotter than normal.

Turning the knob, he pulled the door about an inch before he froze with the first sounds of the high-pitched creak. He swallowed his heart that had somehow managed to reach his throat, and then opened the door another inch. It felt like it took an hour to get the door open enough so that he would be able to slip in and then exit with his bicycle, but at last he'd managed his goal.

Moments later, he was pedaling as fast as he could down

South Peachtree Street, also known as 5 Forks Road. He could already feel his legs burning as he pedaled the long and gradual incline. The darkness made the ride even worse. His tiny headlight did very little to keep the dark at bay as he strained to reach the top of the shallow hill. He never ceased to be amazed at how such an easy hill as this that seemed like nothing in his parents' car or truck felt like he was going up the side of a sheer mountain when he took it on his bicycle.

It felt like forever, but at last he reached the top and now began the trip on the downhill side. His hands kept squeezing the brake handle grips as he rode. On the uphill side, he'd run no risk of riding so fast that he could not see something and react well before he was close enough for it to matter, but going downhill was an entirely different matter.

Plus, for the first several minutes of his ride, he'd heard the sounds of continued and sporadic gunfire coming from the highway. He just realized that, at some point, the noise had ceased. For whatever reason, that did not leave him even the slightest bit comforted. If anything, the ominous silence only made things that much worse.

He was pedaling downhill as fast as he dared. Apparently that was still much too fast because he never spotted the person on the road until it was too late. Ricky jerked his handlebars to the right out of reflex, but he still collided with the figure and went sailing as his bike stopped suddenly.

He was momentarily grateful that he landed on the side of the road in the brush until the pain shot through his body, emanating from his left shoulder. He tried to move that arm but stopped when the jolt of agony threatened to make him sick.

Rolling onto his back, Ricky looked up to see…nothing. His tiny headlight had gone out. Its only power came from the bicycle being pedaled and now he was in the pitch black on an empty road.

But he was not alone!

Ricky heard the shuffle of feet in the blackness and thought that he could see an even darker outline silhouetted against the night sky. He was about to open his mouth. Was the person okay? Had he injured him or her? But then the smell hit Ricky and before he could stop himself, he leaned over and vomited.

A low moan sounded in response. Now Ricky was sure that he'd hurt whomever he'd hit with his bicycle. Had he made the person mess their pants...or was that him? He tried to get his mind off his pain enough to be sure that he hadn't been the one to have the stinky accident.

After a split second of self-assurance, Ricky called out, "Hey? Are you okay?" There were a few heartbeats of silence and then another moan. This one was just a bit louder as whomever it was in the darkness turned to orient on the sound of his voice.

"Hey," Ricky hissed again, sensing that something was in fact very wrong with this individual. "How bad are you hurt?"

Maybe this was one of those people from the highway. Maybe they'd been hurt before and had wandered into the woods. Only, from what little he had learned from the news report, the military had been called to deal with whatever was going on. Even Ricky knew that was not the usual way a traffic accident was dealt with.

Lawrence had mentioned Kentucky. Just the other day, there had been a story about some small town being totally quarantined due to what some folks were calling the "Blue Plague" or something to that effect; he hadn't really paid it that much attention. Only, apparently Lawrence had because he had come to school the next day talking about how the entire news story had simply vanished. He had been unable to find anything online about it, and none of the news media had spoken of it since the initial report.

"The government is trying to hide something," Lawrence had confided to Ricky that afternoon as they rode home from school.

"You watch too much television," Ricky had laughed.

15

Another moan snapped him out of his thoughts. The sounds of shuffling were closer now. Ricky tried to sit up and scoot back; but only being able to use the one arm made that task next to impossible. He managed a few inches at best. He tried to get up and was struggling to his knees when something cool and peculiar feeling swiped across his face.

That had felt like a hand!

"What the—" was all Ricky managed before something collapsed on top of him, sending him falling backwards.

He was bent at a very awkward and painful manner since he had been on his knees when this stranger had attacked him. It had sent his body collapsing flat onto his back, but his legs were now folded underneath him and the pain was incredible.

He felt hands clawing at him, ripping at his jacket. There was the sound of cloth being torn and Ricky's only thought was just how angry his mom and dad would be at him for ruining his best coat.

Cold hands found his skin as his shirt was torn away. Now Ricky was thrashing and screaming. He had no idea what this person was trying to do, but he'd watched the news. He knew about those creepy sorts who did terrible things to children.

Well, that was not going to be his fate. He brought his right fist up and punched the crazy person in the side of the head. He swung again and again, but it did not seem to be having any effect. The person wasn't crying out or nothing. Ricky Porter might not be the biggest or toughest kid in town, but he knew how to throw a punch. This should be having more of an effect.

Something clamped down on his shoulder and once more he heard the sound of cloth being ripped.

This lunatic was trying to bite him!

Ricky opened his mouth to scream and felt fingers force themselves into his mouth. He gagged, and then a new pain came. It felt as if his cheek was being ripped away. Blood filled his mouth and Ricky choked on it. The warm, salty, coppery fluid filled his throat and went down the wrong pipe. Ricky started

16

to choke and shudder as he began to drown on his own blood.

The next sensation he felt was that of teeth digging into the meaty part of his already injured left shoulder. He'd thought breaking his collar bone was painful; that didn't hold a candle to the feeling of his flesh being ripped away from his body by hungry teeth as those hands that had torn at his clothing now began to rip open his belly.

As he faded out of consciousness, he felt a second and third set of hands begin to claw at his middle. His last thought was an impossible realization.

Zombies?

***

Stephen Deese put his truck in park, turned the key, and let the peace and quiet wash over him. The porch light still needed to be replaced. He kept meaning to get around to that, but he'd been working his butt off lately. With the seasons changing and spring right around the corner, folks were starting to put in orders for new windows and doors.

His gaze flicked to the patch of ground that ran alongside the house. The nice neat rows with stakes at each end were all Terri's doing. His wife had an amazingly green thumb. He thought she could probably get flowers to grow in the middle of the desert.

He opened the driver's side door and cocked his head to one side. He knew the sounds of gunshots when he heard them. An occasional pop or burst was one thing, but this was different. There was a barrage and then it dwindled to just a shot here and there. It lasted a long time and that had Stephen very concerned. There was simply no reason for that sort of thing to be happening; especially at this hour. Then the boom came.

He glanced at his watch and saw that it read just past three in the morning. He debated just brushing it away and going inside, but with the stuff that had been in the news the past few days, he could not dismiss the possibility that something serious might be happening just a few miles from his front door.

The sound of a car approaching fast was the last straw; he watched as Sherriff Gilstrap's car rocketed down the road. He also thought that he saw somebody in the passenger's seat.

Stephen hopped back in his truck, turned the key, and took off in pursuit of Sherriff Gilstrap. He switched on the radio and punched the button that ejected the CD he'd been listening to on his drive home.

"…expected to activate local National Guard units this morning," a woman's voice reported. There was a brief pause and what sounded like the microphone being bumped. "Are you sure?" the woman finally spoke as Stephen sped up to close the distance between himself and the taillights of the chief's vehicle.

"We have just received this bulletin and I need to inform you that the emergency broadcasting network is set to assume control of the airwaves for more information and an important announcement within the hour. As for the bulletin, it has been reported that as of 3:27 AM Eastern Standard Time or 1:27 PM yesterday which would be the time difference between the East Coast and Tokyo, the entire island of Japan has gone silent. No communications have come from or been answered by Japan or any of its citizens.

"The same holds true for most population centers of Indonesia, both North and South Korea and China. The White House has not commented and we here at WTGR are trying to confirm the accuracy of these reports. Keep your radio here for further updates as well as the previously mentioned upcoming announcement from the Emergency Broadcasting System…"

Stephen turned the radio down as he came up on the chief's car that had stopped short of where Hardee's and the Spinx station cast their bright lights to guide passing motorists in from the Calhoun Memorial Highway for some fast food or gasoline. However, he was no longer paying attention to the chief's car; his eyes had been drawn to the huge spotlights mounted on the back of what looked like a pair of drab tan military trucks.

The overpass showed signs of what looked like people moving about, but there was something odd about them besides the fact that they were apparently wandering around on a major highway. As he watched, a figure approached the guard rail and then simply toppled over it, landing hard in the middle of Moorefield Memorial Highway—the road he was on behind Sherriff Gilstrap and what he was now able to identify as Mayor Burns.

Both had emerged from the car just ahead of him and were apparently just as horrified at seeing the person do a belly flop on the asphalt. Stephen got out of his truck as well and rubbed at his eyes as the figure on the ground looked to be getting to his or her feet. *That is impossible*, he thought.

His gaze drifted to the grassy slope that came down from Calhoun Highway in the open space where the long on- and off-ramps ran. There were a handful of dark figures moving down those hills and heading his way.

He was having a tough time making sense of just what he was seeing. Taking a deep breath to clear his head, Stephen took a better look around at his surroundings. It was then that he realized that none of the establishments were occupied. There was no sign of movement coming from within or without any of them. Then his eyes stopped on something else: a body.

He wasn't sure why, but he now felt that he needed to reach in and pull the shotgun down from the rack mounted on the window at the rear of the cab of his pickup. He absently hit the button that released the safety. He already knew that the weapon was loaded and gave it a pump to slam a round into the chamber.

"That you, Deese?" Sherriff Gilstrap's voice called.

"Yep," Stephen replied as he started towards the figure sprawled on the ground by the outermost island of pumps beside a white compact car. The hose and nozzle was on the ground as well. There was a dark stain around the body, but it was not gasoline; that he was certain of just by observing.

19

"This is Sherriff Gilstrap. I need you to stop where you are," Stephen heard the chief call.

Stephen glanced over to see that Sherriff Gilstrap had come around to the front of his car. The mayor had wisely stayed behind the passenger door and was looking back and forth between him and the scene unfolding in front of her with the approaching group of people that all looked like they might be just a bit drunk. Their pace was slow and unsteady and they kept pausing, their heads twitching as they seemed to need to re-orient and consider where to take the next step. A couple had fallen as they came down the hill and were having a hell of a time trying to get back to their feet.

Stephen was now just a few feet away from the body sprawled on the ground. The harsh lights from the awning over the gas pumps cast everything in a brilliant light. His guess as to the stain around that body was now confirmed. A bloody handprint ran down the front of the closest pump and was obviously made by the outstretched arm of the inert figure lying face down.

He only turned his head for a moment to once again check on the situation between the chief and the figures stumbling down the hill in his direction. They did not seem to be inclined to heed the warnings being given. He turned back just in time to see the figure that he'd assumed to be dead start to move and struggle as if wanting to roll over.

Slinging the shotgun over his shoulder and trusting that Sherriff Gilstrap would soon have the situation under control, he knelt beside the body on the ground.

A nasty smell rolled off the man who was making a weak mewling and gurgling noise that sounded like he might be having trouble breathing. Recalling his first aid training from his days in the USMC, Stephen inspected the body and did not yet see the source of the bleeding.

"I'm going to help you onto your back, fella," he said in a rush. "I know I probably shouldn't move you at all with all the blood loss, but maybe if I get you on your back I can see what the problem might be."

Gripping one shoulder and placing his other hand behind the man's neck for support, Stephen took a deep breath through his mouth and hauled the man onto his back. He was at least five feet away and scooting on his butt before he even realized how instinct had caused him to react at what he'd seen.

The man's throat was torn out, but he was still managing to move his mouth like he was trying to speak. If that was not bad enough, the man was now trying to sit up when, by all rights, he should be dead.

"There is no way that you are getting any breath," Stephen gasped as the man turned his head in Stephen's direction and regarded him with eyes that were unlike anything that he had ever seen, and during his time overseas, he'd actually seen more than a few dead bodies.

The man's eyes were glazed over with a putrid, pus-colored film and they were shot full of black tracers. The man opened his mouth and a weak moan came, but it was what followed that made the hair on Stephen's arms and the back of his neck stand straight up.

It was almost like a baby cry. In fact, if he were not staring directly at this man and hearing that sound come out of his mouth, he would be searching for the actual baby that had to be the source of that plaintive wail.

Pulling his shotgun back around in front of him, Stephen stood up and backed away from the man who was slowly gaining his feet. He was still trying to decide what to do when he heard a commotion from behind him.

"This is your last warning!" Sherriff Gilstrap barked with all the authority he could muster around what sounded like the man gagging. There was a pause and then a single shot.

Stephen looked and noticed the chief's gun hand pointing skyward. The man had almost retreated the entire distance back to his car. The several figures stumbling towards the chief and the mayor made no sign that they heard and just kept shambling closer, arms outstretched and hands opening and closing as they drew nearer by the second.

Stephen returned his attention to his own problem and saw that the improbable man was advancing in bird-like fits and starts. It cried once more and Stephen brought his Browning 12-guage up to his shoulder and aimed for the center mass of his target. As soon as he heard the chief fire again—he knew Sherriff Gilstrap well enough to know that the man only gave one warning—he squeezed the trigger.

There was a flash from the muzzle and the round of buckshot slammed into the man's chest causing him to stagger backwards and almost topple. Stephen could not believe his eyes. He knew his weapon well enough to know that there would be a hole at least the size of his fist at the exit wound on the man's back. His insides would be jelly, and there was simply no way to survive a nearly pointblank round to the chest from a shotgun. Yet, the man took another step forward and reached for Stephen as that awful cry spewed from its mouth again.

Taking two steps backwards, Stephen brought his weapon back to his shoulder as he jacked another round into the chamber. He adjusted up slightly and gritted his teeth.

"Let's see you survive this," he whispered as he pulled the trigger.

The man's head practically disintegrated. The body still managed to take one more step before realizing that it was now dead. It fell with a meaty slap, but Stephen was already turning to help the chief and the mayor.

The mayor had retreated inside the vehicle; for that, Stephen was grateful. The chief was just now finishing up firing the last round of his Beretta M9A1's fifteen round magazine into the chest of the closest of the oncoming mob.

"The head," Stephen called as he jacked another round and stepped up beside the man who had been the best man at his father's wedding. The man who had met him at the airport the day he returned home from his tour.

Two minutes later, silence once again fell over the area. Bodies littered the ground and Stephen was sitting on the hood of the chief's car passing him his lighter so that the man could light the cigarette dangling from his lips.

"Nasty little gash on your left hand," Stephen said to Sherriff Gilstrap.

"Yeah, one of them damned things bit me while I was reloading."

Dead: Snapshot—Liberty, South Carolina

2

Impossible Things

Jamie sat in the front seat of the chief's patrol car and could not believe what she was witnessing. One part of her mind screamed that this was all so terribly wrong. However, there was another part of her that tried to see things as they truly were.

The people that were converging on Chief Gilstrap and Mr. Deese all had a variety of terrible injuries. A few had bits of their insides hanging out. That was too much for her to understand and reconcile. Those people should not be alive, much less up and walking.

A still smaller voice in the back of her mind was doing everything in its power to be heard. *That could not be possible*, Jamie thought as she dismissed the nagging idea that was really trying to get her to listen.

"Zombies?" she whispered as she watched a bullet slam into the chest of one of the approaching figures. That person made no outward registration that he'd just been shot. When the second round caught him in the forehead, the man dropped in an instant. "No," Jamie shook her head, "that is fiction…the kind of crap you see in bad movies."

She'd seen a few zombie films over the years. She hadn't ever actually sought one out; her having seen them was more of an accident. She thought she'd seen a couple at a Halloween party or with some friends during a Netflix movie binge after finals week. That was often when everybody took turns picking the next flick while a good deal of alcohol was being shared.

She knew a few of her friends who had really been into watching horror movies. Personally, she would much rather watch Tom Hanks and Meg Ryan.

She saw Mr. Deese step up beside Chief Gilstrap as a pair of those things closed in with their slow, awkward steps. The chief was reloading and basically defenseless. She looked down in surprise at her hand. It had actually started to open the passenger side door of the patrol car.

"And what exactly would you do?" she mocked herself. "Give them a stern talking to?"

The loud report of the shotgun brought her attention back to the men. Mr. Deese had apparently shot one of the attackers and was bringing the butt of his shotgun up and slamming it into the face of the second one. The woman had stumbled back a few steps, but that was all. She did not react like a person was supposed to when a large man crushed your nose.

At last, the final members of the mob had been dealt with and the two men sort of backed up and sat down on the hood of the car. She scowled as they each apparently felt that this was the perfect time to have a smoke.

She reached over and turned the radio back up. It had gone silent just before they had arrived, but she thought that she'd just heard something. As the seconds ticked by with a terminal slowness, she began to lean forward as if being closer might inspire the radio to come back to life.

There was a hiss and a crackle, and then a weak voice spoke. "Anybody?"

Jamie threw the door open causing both men to jump, bringing up their weapons and spinning in her direction. She flinched, throwing up her hands.

"Sorry...somebody is on the radio. They sound like they need help."

26

Chief Gilstrap holstered his pistol and came to the car, opening the driver's side door. He snatched the mic from the holder and spoke, "This is Chief Adam Gilstrap of the Liberty Police Department. Is there somebody on this frequency?"

After a hiss, some more static, and then a loud pop, a voice came back sounding like he was speaking through clenched teeth. "This is Private Dan Cronin...umm...I can't remember our unit designator. I've only been with this group since this morning. I am up on the highway near an overpass. There was a lot of shooting a moment ago and it made a bunch of those things go away, but there are still five of them outside my truck...and my weapon is on the ground with them." He revealed that last bit after a brief pause and with obvious embarrassment.

"Stay put, young man," the chief said, suddenly sounding very different from his normal gruff tone. "We are coming up. It will be me and another man. I want you to just be still until we get there."

"I'm scared, sir," the soldier blurted, sounding like he was on the verge of tears. "One of those things got a good piece of me. I think I got whatever it is that is wrong with them."

"Last I checked, none of them was speaking," Chief Gilstrap soothed. "You're still talking. I am gonna take that as a good sign."

"Yeah, but I looked in the rearview mirror and my eyes are already looking different."

Jamie saw the chief glance at his hand. That was when she noticed that the man had been hurt. The light wasn't the best, but it was enough for her to make out the clear outline of a mouth print. Had one of those people bitten him?

"I need you to just hang on, you hear me?" Chief Gilstrap dropped the mic onto his seat and glanced over at Jamie. "You keep talking to him, you hear? I will let you know when we have him and are heading back." He leaned down and unlocked the pistol-grip shotgun that was secured between the driver and passenger seats. "You take this. Anybody comes, you give them one

27

warning to stop and get on their knees. If they don't comply, I want you to drop them."

"But—" she started to protest.

"No time for this, Jamie…err, I mean…" the chief seemed to get a bit flustered.

"I know what you meant," Jamie said with a nod. "Go on, y'all, see if you can help that poor man."

She watched Mr. Deese and the chief take off at a jog. They crested the embankment at the edge of the highway and came to a sudden stop for a few seconds. They were nothing more than black outlines due to the lights up on the highway, but she could tell they were discussing something.

"Hello?" the voice came back on the radio; the query ended in a series of wracking coughs. "Are you still there?"

"Help is coming, Private Cronin," Jamie replied. "Just hang in there."

"They shouldn't waste their time, ma'am," the soldier wheezed. "I'm pretty sure it is over for me."

"Don't talk that way," she scolded. Still, she could already hear a definite deterioration in his condition in just the few minutes since he'd last spoken.

"Trust me…I don't want to die." That reply ended in another series of horrible and oddly wet coughs that sounded as if he might be practically hacking up a lung. "It's them things, ma'am. You can't let 'em bite you."

Jamie listened, but what he was saying didn't make sense. How could a person's bite cause another person to become so violently ill…and with such suddenness? Once again her mind drifted to those scary movies.

"It's worse than the folks in charge are letting people know. Just before we got here, somebody said that places like Tokyo are already gone. It's worse than those movies…spreads fast."

That comment made Jamie's head snap up. He couldn't possibly be saying…

"Zombies, ma'am. Plain and simple, that is what people are turning into. Just promise me that you won't let me become one of them things. I don't want to be a..." There was a pause and then another series of coughs that ended in a choking rasp.

"Private?" Jamie keyed the mic after a few seconds of silence. "Private Cronin, answer me," she implored.

Silence.

Outside and in the direction that the chief and Mr. Deese had vanished there came a few pops as well as the deep booming reports of a shotgun. It was over in just a few seconds and then silence fell once again.

Another single pop.

"Mayor Burns," the deep voice of Mr. Deese came over the radio. "He didn't make it."

She dropped the mic and sat back. The only consolation she could find at the moment was in knowing that the young private's last request had been granted.

"What in the hell is happening?" she whispered as she stared out the window. She perked up at the sight of a set of headlights coming her way from town.

***

Sophie Martin rounded the corner and slowed. She saw a squad car sitting in front of the Hardee's. She also saw a white pickup just parked in the middle of the road in front of the Spinx. Neither one of these vehicles belonged to her husband.

She edged around the pickup and came to a stop beside the police car. It was a little surprising to see the mayor sitting in the passenger seat staring out at her. It looked like the woman had been crying.

She parked her own vehicle beside the chief's and opened her door. Right away she could smell something foul on the night breeze. Her eyes paused on several shapes scattered about just past the intersection. They looked like...bodies?

29

She heard the door open and the mayor calling her name as she approached the closest unmoving figure. It was a woman. She was on her back, her dead eyes were staring straight up, but there was something peculiar about them beyond just the fact that the woman was dead. A nasty wound just to the left from the middle of her forehead was visible; but it was the horrendous rip on her forearm that looked much more sinister.

As a nurse, Sophie had seen a few nasty dog attack injuries. This almost resembled a dog attack, but there was something different. She looked closer and saw an imprint of a bite mark on the right bicep that definitely did not belong to a dog. It was human!

"Sophie, is that you?" a voice called from behind her.

"Yes." Tearing her eyes away from the terrible scene, she turned to discover the mayor just a few feet away.

"Jamie, what in the world is going on here?" Sophie Martin asked and then hurriedly added. "I mean, Mayor Burns."

"We've been friends way too long for that." Jamie came to stand beside her and look down at the corpse.

"Then can I count on you to give me a straight answer to my questions?"

"If I know anything, you bet. I came with Chief Gilstrap to see what was going on. There was a newscast about some sort of terrible accident. We came to see if there was anything that we could do to help...the citizens of Liberty I mean. We got here and then it got crazy in a hurry. These people came at the chief and Mr. Deese. Some of them were torn up so bad that there is no way they should have been walking, and I saw some take a few bullets without even slowing down." The mayor paused and seemed to weigh her next words carefully. "You are going to think I'm crazy, but it was like those zombie movies...swear to God. The only thing that stopped these people from tearing apart the chief and Mr. Deese was a bullet to the head."

"Clifton got a call about twenty minutes ago and hurried out here, I guess all the units from up in Pickens and over in Easley were dispatched," Sophie explained. "He wasn't gone five minutes before the hospital called me. Only, the nurse who called was Sharon Meyers and she told me that I might be helping more if I went to the scene instead of coming in like they were having everybody else do right now. Also, I guess the first ambulance that arrived had some sort of problem with the person they were transporting. At first the lady flat-lined, but the machines must have been on the fritz because she came to and attacked one of the paramedics."

"I haven't seen your husband, but then I haven't been up to the highway. The chief and Mr. Deese went up there a few minutes ago. One of the soldiers was on the radio."

Jamie seemed to pause for a moment as if she was debating on what she should say or how much to reveal. Apparently she decided to spill everything. She went on to give as much of a detailed account about the ordeal including what the poor private had said on the radio.

"My God," Sophie breathed as the account concluded. She was about to suggest going up to the highway. Part of her wanted to see what all had gone on up there, but another part of her simply wanted to find her husband. However, just as she was about to open her mouth, a voice cut her off.

"Mom?" her son's voice called from behind where she and Jamie stood.

Sophie Martin turned to see her son pedaling up. Her initial reaction was to give him a good scolding, but then she realized that she'd rushed out of the house without even saying anything to him or leaving a note. Still, how he knew to come here was a bit of a mystery.

"Lawrence, you should be asleep," Sophie said with just a hint of motherly disapproval in her tone.

"I woke up when Dad got called. The television says that there is something terrible happening out here." Lawrence brought his bicycle to a stop in front of her and gave a polite nod to Jamie. "Mayor Burns."

31

At least she now knew how her son had figured out where to go, but that still did not totally get him off the hook for riding all the way out here at such a late hour. She glanced at her watch. Early hour? It was coming up on four in the morning.

"You still shouldn't have come out here. It's a school day. And don't you have baseball tryouts this afternoon?"

The boy was about to open his mouth when a yell from up on the highway cut him off.

"Get in the car…we need to go right now!" It was the chief and Mr. Deese. They had both hopped the guardrail and were running down the hill for all they were worth.

***

Stephen moved along down the emergency lane. About a hundred yards away or so was the scene of a terrible accident involving a semi and what was left of a newer model SUV. But that was actually not the worst thing up here on this small stretch of highway in the middle of the South Carolina countryside.

Scattered around on the ground were at least fifty bodies. Some of those bodies had small clusters of what Stephen was now ready to call zombies. People were being ripped open and fed upon. Most of those being eaten were in uniform and were obviously part of the military support that had been sent to the scene.

He spied five South Carolina Highway Patrol vehicles parked in the eastbound lane. All of them had their lights on and doors open, but not one trooper was in sight.

There were two news vans parked just past the military roadblock, but, like the police, there was no sign of anybody in or around the vans. Just beyond the news vans was a military truck that was still ablaze. Something had caused the truck to catch fire, but it would be impossible at this point to even begin to guess as to what exactly had happened. He guessed that to be the source of the loud explosion that he'd heard and actually felt

32

a touch of relief. His fear that some sort of heavy military ordinance had been brought into play could now be discarded.

"Deese, over here," Chief Gilstrap called.

That caused a few heads to turn their direction, but the mobile bodies in the area were pretty well spread out and not of much concern yet. They seemed slow and uncoordinated. It should be no problem to take care of any that might come after him or the chief. He also noted that the ones feeding merely glanced up and then went back to their grisly tasks.

Stephen walked over to the military truck where the chief was standing. He'd already dispatched a handful of the walking dead that had been clustered around the cab of the truck. Inside, a single face stared out at them. The figure inside had skin that was a bluish-gray, and once again he was drawn to the eyes. They were glossed over with a milky, pus-colored film and shot full of black tracers.

The figure inside the cab reached up and slapped at the window and seemed to be trying to gnaw on the glass that separated it from him and the chief standing outside. The name on the shirt came into view. It read: Cronin.

"Damn," Stephen sighed. "We can't leave him like that."

"Why not?" the chief asked as he stepped back and peered up the highway towards where the state troopers had all parked.

"It just doesn't feel right."

"He's dead, Stephen."

"He was a soldier. He deserves better. Wouldn't you want me to put you down if you became one of these things?" He threw his hands up to indicate the dozen or so dark figures moving in their direction. He could not help but glance down at the chief's hand. If this was in fact like the old zombie movies, then the chief was a goner. The bite was a guaranteed death sentence.

"I guess," Chief Gilstrap agreed. He stepped back and shaded his eyes from the glare of the assorted headlights, spotlights, and the flaming truck. "But I think we need to hurry up and then get the hell out of here."

"Why?" Stephen asked as he turned to see what the chief might be so interested in. "Holy crap."

To the south of them, coming up the east and westbound lanes were perhaps a hundred or so dark shapes. Since they were walking along the highway, it was a pretty good guess that they weren't just a bunch of folks out for an early morning stroll.

"How do you want to do this?" Chief Gilstrap asked, snapping Stephen back to the situation at hand.

"How about I open the door and you pop him."

"Sounds like as good of an idea as any."

"On three." Stephen grabbed the door handle and looked up at the slack face of Private Cronin who stared out at him with those creepy eyes. The black tracers added an especially eerie factor to the man's face, beyond the way that the skin seemed to sag and was now a gruesome shade of pale gray with just a hint of blue. Also, the man's tongue was an even darker shade of gray to the point where it almost looked black.

"One...two...three!" He jerked the door open and was hit by another wave of stench as well as the body of Private Cronin tumbling out awkwardly to the pavement.

He could have sworn that he heard the sound of a bone snapping. When the thing that was no longer Private Cronin rolled over, the odd angle that his right arm hung confirmed Stephen's suspicion.

The mic was dangling down to the floorboard and he stepped around the struggling body of the private. He could hear the voice of Mayor Burns saying something and reached in to pick it up.

Chief Gilstrap stepped forward and put his pistol just a few inches from the man's left temple. He mumbled something and then pulled the trigger. A splash of black blood sprayed the side of the truck and the body collapsed in a heap.

"Mayor Burns," Stephen said as he looked back to watch the chief end it for the young soldier, "he didn't make it."

Looking back up the highway, the mob was approaching and now he could hear an assortment of moans and possibly even a few of those pitiful cries. The two men took off at a run back for where they'd left the mayor. He only had a moment to register the fact that another car had arrived along with what looked like a kid on a bicycle. He and the chief cleared the guard rail and hurried down the slope towards the bright lights of the roadside oasis.

"Get in the car...we need to go right now!" Chief Gilstrap bellowed.

***

Jonathan Patterson sat up and slapped the top of his alarm clock. Four in the morning was not his normal wake-up time. Last night had been a freaking disaster at work. One of the pipes had burst and flooded out the Domino's Pizza store.

He'd been the shift manager that night and was tasked with the less-than-pleasant job of calling the actual manager with the bad news. He'd had to shut down for the evening and clean up a bunch of water. It wasn't just any normal water line. Nope, it had been the damn sewer line. They would be throwing out a whole bunch of product today.

That was why he had to get up at this ungodly hour. He and the manager would be going over the store with a fine tooth comb before the sanitation inspectors arrived. The only good thing about this whole clusterfuck was that he'd been approved for overtime. He had been saving since his eighteenth birthday for that trip to Las Vegas he'd always dreamed of taking. If everything went right, he would be waiting for Santa in a suite at the Bellagio.

Throwing off the blankets, he sat up and stretched. The room was cold and he scurried to the bathroom and turned on the shower so that it would get nice and warm while he emptied his bladder.

"Nothing quite beats that first piss of the day," Jonathan mumbled. He flushed and then leaned over and turned on his tiny portable radio.

He was just getting lathered up and howling along with Van Halen when the tones of the Emergency Broadcasting System blared. He hated those stupid screeching bleats. Why did they need to ruin a good song to interrupt with another stupid test? He was about to lean out of the shower and punch the button to change stations when the announcement began.

"A state of emergency is being declared on a national level. The CDC has called for curfews to be executed. State and local officials are to stand by for instructions and all members of the military reserves are to report to the nearest depot for assignment.

"The president will be addressing the nation later on, but has asked that all citizens remain home for the time being as emergency protocols are prepared. In addition, a representative from the CDC has asked that if you or somebody you know has come into contact with a person who is acting irrationally and either appears bitten or scratched, you or somebody that you know needs to please bring them to the nearest medical facility.

"All hospitals are instructed to set up a quarantine area for anybody brought in suffering from a bite wound inflicted by another person. Military units will be arriving at major metropolitan medical centers as soon as possible to assist—"

Jonathan turned the radio off and ran to the bedroom to get his phone, punching his mother's number in haste. As it rang, he turned on the television and muted the sound. The scene being played on the local news was that of a reporter standing in front of a large military looking truck. The words "Recorded Earlier" were in the upper left hand corner of the screen.

"Hello?" a frail voice answered.

"Mom?" Jonathan struggled not to sound agitated.

"Johnny Cakes," the woman said, suddenly sounding cheerful. That nickname had been his since he'd been a baby. He hated it, and she'd stopped using it in public when he reached high school, but in private, that was her normal greeting.

"Good, you haven't gone on your walk yet," he sighed.

His mother went for a walk first thing in the morning no matter the weather. Her advanced age had not curtailed that activity one bit.

"I was just getting my coat on."

"Yeah, well do me a favor. Can you hold off until I get there? I want to go with you," he lied.

"But that will throw off the rest of my day," Mildred Patterson groaned.

"I will be there in five minutes, just wait for me."

"Fine," the elderly woman huffed. "But I don't understand. You never come with me on my morning walk. What's going on, Johnny Cakes?"

"It's just been a while since I've seen you and I have a busy next few weeks. I figured I could suck it up. Besides," he glanced over at the mirror and turned sideways, "I can use a little exercise."

That part was absolutely true. Ever since he'd gotten that job at Domino's Pizza, he'd been putting on a bit of weight. He'd never been skinny. In high school he had been the anchor of the defensive line on the football team. He'd had dreams of being scouted and getting a scholarship to Clemson, but he hadn't even merited a glance from a small college.

At just a shade over six feet tall and more than a shade over two hundred and seventy pounds, Jonathan had somehow let himself slip into the worst shape of his life. His eyes flicked to the three empty beer bottles on the nightstand next to his bed and the pizza box on the dresser.

He kept meaning to do something about the weight, but at the end of the day after a shift dealing with delivery drivers who could not find their own asses with both hands and a map as well as customers who thought the "30 minutes or its free" campaign still existed, all he wanted to do at the end of the evening was come home, turn on Sports Center, log onto his computer to get in some gaming, toss down a few cold ones, eat a few slices, and then fall asleep.

Something told him that he was going to regret not being in better shape in a very short time. He bumped his mouse to wake up his computer.

"Just promise me that you will wait for me," Jonathan insisted.

"I won't go any farther than the corner," his mother said, sounding extremely inconvenienced and put out by the request.

"NO!" he barked. "I want you to wait inside the house."

"But—" she started to protest.

"I mean it, Mom."

"Fine." The sigh at the other end of the line was overly dramatic.

"Promise."

"I said—" she began but he cut her off.

"I said promise."

"I promise, Johnny Cakes."

He didn't wait for her to say anything else. He hung up and stared at his screen. Sure enough, he had two emails waiting for him. Both were from the same person.

"Okay, Fumio, whadda ya got for me."

One of Jonathan's gaming buddies turned out to be a fourteen-year-old from Tokyo. He'd been blown away when he'd learned that the guy he'd been going into the arena with for over six months was almost half his age.

One day after his ass had been pulled out of the fire no less than a dozen times by this one person, he'd sent him a message of thanks and added his personal email. The next day he'd received a reply and learned the identity of his battlefield savior.

Thirteen-year-old (at the time they'd met) Fumio Koguchi from Tokyo, Japan. The two became the modern-day equivalent to pen pals. It didn't hurt that Fumio was oddly impressed that Jonathan was a manager at a pizza place.

Last week, Fumio had missed their regular gaming session. The next day, there was an email from him with a file attached. It was a video that took his computer forever to download, but when he finally played it, he was initially confused. Why was Fumio sending him a clip from a Japanese horror movie?

The video was taken in the hallway of what looked like a hotel to Jonathan. A man was on his knees in the middle of the hall and ripping the insides out of a young Japanese girl who was kicking and screaming her head off. Jonathan thought she might be overacting a bit.

After a few seconds, the camera jerked around and a young boy's face filled the screen. Jonathan recognized him instantly. Was Fumio in a movie? If so, that was more than a little cool. The boy began to speak in halted and very heavily accented English.

"Jonathan-san, something very terrible is happening. They have tried to hide it, but it is now out of control." The camera jerked again and things were blurry for a moment until the hand holding it steadied once more. The scene now was a long street. It looked like hundreds of people were wandering aimlessly. They did not seem to have any direction or actual destination and often changed their paths on a whim. The camera jerked again and Fumio's face filled the picture once more. "I am afraid. It is impossible to leave my home. My parents have not returned in three days."

The sounds of screams could be heard in the background. A few were just like that one girl in that they were unlike anything Jonathan had ever heard before. Not even the old classic movie "scream queens" could match these poor souls. That was when it sunk in. These were the screams of real people being ripped apart.

Once more the camera jerked around and the hallway came back into focus. The person that had been hunched over the poor girl had gotten to his feet and was staggering towards Fumio.

"Get out of there," Jonathan had whispered impotently.

He breathed a sigh of relief when it was obvious that the boy was moving away. He paused, and the sound of a door being jostled could be heard. The creak of hinges almost seemed comical if not for the fact that this was really happening and not the trick of some foley artist to add tension to the scene. Just before the camera jerked away again, Jonathan had seen the girl on the floor begin to stir.

The rest of the video consisted of scenes outside the high rise apartment that Fumio Koguchi called home. There were plumes of smoke rising into the sky in every direction. The streets were packed with people wandering about. Having no knowledge of Tokyo, Japan other than what he saw on television, he would have not seen anything out of the ordinary. Only, there was one thing that nagged at him about what he was seeing; he simply could not place it. After the third replay, it struck him.

There was not one single motor vehicle moving in the streets below. The only traffic was that of pedestrians milling about.

He had not known what to do with this footage. He was considering trying to sell it to one of those tabloid television shows. Then Kentucky happened.

The government had to believe that the American public was nothing more than a bunch of idiots. Unfortunately, that turned out to be a fairly accurate assessment.

When the first reports of the quarantine broke, it was not greeted with an overwhelming degree of alarm. After all, unless you lived in whatever the name of that Podunk town was, then it wasn't your problem. In fact, Jonathan remembered his own reaction.

"Sucks to be them," he'd said when he had pulled into work that evening. And then he'd shut off his engine and walked in to start his shift.

He had thought nothing of it until one of his drivers mentioned the next day that nothing further had been reported about

40

that small town that had been quarantined. Even then he'd just brushed the comment aside. But that night as he watched Fumio's video once more and debated between a tabloid and one of the big cable news networks, he had remembered.

A quick search revealed absolutely nothing. There was not one single mention of a town in Kentucky or anyplace else in the United States having been quarantined. He popped into the lobby of his favorite game and typed in a single word: Kentucky.

There were over a hundred rooms with Kentucky mentioned. He popped into one after another and read line after line of nutjob conspiracy theory crap. Only...maybe this wasn't all a bunch of crazy talk.

He'd finally weighed in and started recounting what he'd seen on Fumio's video. He was deep into it when an instant message popped up on his screen. Whoever this user had been, he was obviously more than just some casual gamer, his user name was nothing more than a scrambled batch of bizarre symbols. The message was very direct.

SHUT UP. IF THE GOVERNMENT SEES THIS, THEY WILL COME FOR YOU.

Jonathan waited for anything else but nothing came. A feeling of paranoia crept over him and he logged off, shut down his computer, and turned off all the lights...as if that might help.

"Yeah, Jonathan, that would stop a team of covert operatives. Just shut off the lights...that way they won't be able to see you."

That had been two days ago.

He opened on the first email from Fumio and clicked on the attached file. The second email did not have anything attached and so he opened it while he waited for his computer to do its thing.

Jonathan-san, I apologize for how short this will be, but I know I don't have long. They have been outside my door for the past day and I fear it will not hold up much longer. Plus, power has been going off and on the past several hours and I fear it will not last more than an hour or so. I hope my video reaches you. You must tell somebody. Do not let your country hide this as mine has.

Fumio

He looked at the bar that indicated the status of his download. The countdown timer declared that he still had over ten minutes. He knew very well that his mother would not wait that long. He would simply have to watch it after he went and picked up his mother.

"And then what?" he asked himself out loud.

He didn't have the slightest idea, but he knew that he had to go get her. Once she was safe inside his home, he would figure out his next move.

Grabbing his keys from the kitchen table, he hurried out the front door, locking it behind him and then hurrying to his beat up Toyota wagon. He paused and sniffed. Taking a look at first the sole of one shoe and then the other, he sighed in relief that wherever the nasty pile of dog shit might be, he hadn't stepped in it.

As he pulled away and sped down the street towards his mother's house, something moved in the bushes beside his porch.

3

The Dead Come

Jamie stared out the window of her modest two-bedroom home on Clay Street. She was trying to remember the happiness that she'd felt the day she'd been handed the keys to her house. The green roof had been what first caught her eye.

The fenced yard was just waiting for her to get a dog. She'd been meaning to look for a puppy, but she was always too busy and had kept putting it off. The chief and Mr. Deese were still out on her porch. They looked to be involved in a pretty serious conversation. If not for the night she'd already had, she might be curious. As it stood, all she really wanted to do was stumble into her bedroom and flop down on the bed.

"Instant coffee all you got?" Sophie called from her kitchen.

"Yeah, I ran out of the regular stuff yesterday. I keep the instant for emergency situations." Jamie turned and headed into the kitchen to join Sophie and her son Lawrence.

The boy was at the back door staring outside much like she'd been doing out the front. Surely there couldn't be any of those things in town. Could there?

"I have tried the hospital at least four times," Sophie said softly as the two women took their cups and walked back out into the living room leaving Lawrence to continue his silent vigil.

Jamie hadn't seen Sophie in a few months. It seemed odd for that to happen in such a small town, but with her hectic schedule as she tried to get a grip on being a mayor as well as the office manager for a land developer based in Greenville that was now expanding out towards Liberty coupled with Sophie's shifts as an RN over in Pickens at Cannon Memorial Hospital, the stars had just not lined up.

Sophie looked better than ever. She'd always been beautiful, but there was something else. Her light brown skin was absolutely radiant and her hazel eyes practically glowed. Her tall, athletic body had a grace that Jamie had always envied. The two years that they'd played on the high school basketball team together had been the thing that built their friendship. Sophie was everything on the court that Jamie was not. In fact, after the first day of practice, Jamie had considered dropping out. It had been Sophie that sat beside her in the locker room and told her that she needed to use her speed and forget about how tall anybody else on the court might be in comparison.

Her thoughts were broken up by the sound of Sophie's phone ringing. She snatched it from the counter and thrust it out at Jamie.

"It's Clifton's partner, Terry Gibbs. I can't…" Sophie's voice trailed off and the tears welled up in her eyes making them even shinier.

Jamie took the phone and answered. "Hello?"

"Sophie?" a voice said, sounding confused.

"No, Cliff, it's Jamie Burns." She knew the man's deep, rich voice and let out a breath that she hadn't realized she'd been holding. "She's right here, hold on a sec." She handed the phone to her friend and stepped back as Lawrence hurried in and put his head next to his mother's so that he could hear.

"I went to the highway. You weren't there…I thought that was where they sent you…no…uh-huh…WHAT? Don't you dare!…No, I can't."

There was a long pause and Jamie could see tears start to

well up in Lawrence's eyes as well. She had no idea what was being said, but it was obviously not good news. She recalled her radio conversation with Private Cronin and how his voice had sounded so bad. It had been clear that he was sick. Clifton had sounded fine.

"Clifton? Hello?" Sophie pulled her hand back and stared at her phone like it had committed the ultimate act of betrayal.

"What is it?" Jamie asked. "Is he okay?"

"No." Sophie set her phone down on the counter and lifted an arm to allow her son to nestle in for a hug. The two stood clutching each other. Jamie wanted to know what was going on, but she didn't dare ask and break up this moment for the mother and son.

"He's at Cannon Memorial," Sophie finally said through a throat that sounded tight like she was fighting back a flood of tears.

"Is he hurt?" Jamie asked as delicately as she could manage.

"No. The big dummy is fine. They transported an injured girl who seemed to code just before they arrived at the hospital. Just as they pulled in, she started trying to get free from her restraints. She managed to bite Terry. That is why Clifton called on his partner's phone. The army had already arrived at the hospital and I guess they grabbed the girl from the bay and then insisted that Terry go to some special quarantine wing that was being set up. Terry gave Clifton his phone and asked him to call his wife and let her know that he was okay."

Sophie was quiet for a moment and Jamie started to fidget. There was obviously more going on. Cliff had said something at the end of the call that had upset both Sophie and Lawrence.

"He is apparently helping in the emergency room. I guess they are already so overwhelmed with people being brought in that he felt it was important to stay and help," Sophie said at last.

"How did this get so bad so fast?" Jamie asked nobody in particular.

The front door opened and Mr. Deese stuck his head inside. "Mayor Burns, you need to come out here."

Jamie heard the tone in the man's voice and her stomach twisted into a knot. Taking a deep breath to steady herself for whatever fresh hell was about to ruin her morning just a bit more, she walked to the front door. The large man stepped back and she joined him and the chief on her porch.

"Oh, my God," Jamie gasped.

***

Stephen kept looking at the chief. He seemed as healthy as always. He wasn't sounding tired or sick in any way, shape, or form. In fact, that run had reminded him that this was the year he'd promised Terri that he would quit smoking. And so what had been the first thing he'd done after they had taken down all those people (he kept going back and forth on completely accepting them as zombies)? He'd lit up. And then after they had run from that mob that was coming up the highway, he'd had a smoke in his mouth before the truck had even left the lights of the Spinx station behind.

"I don't see how this has gotten so out of control so quickly," the chief was saying.

"Easy," Stephen replied with a shrug, crushing out the half-smoked cigarette he'd been dragging on, "nobody wants to believe it. I just saw it with my own two eyes and already my brain is trying to find something that will help me make logical sense of it."

"But there is no way a person can take a magazine full of .45 caliber slugs to the chest and keep walking. And while not all of them were torn up, I saw a few that had their insides dragging on the ground or hanging out." Chief Gilstrap took off his hat and rubbed his stubbled head. He jammed the hat back on and then glanced down at his hand. "You think I'm gonna turn into one of them sumbitches, don'tcha?"

Stephen looked away and pressed his lips together tightly. That had been almost exactly what he'd been thinking. Still, he

46

wasn't going to say it; no way in hell. Then his eyes lit on something and he stood up a bit straighter.

Coming up the road was a single figure. That alone wasn't a big deal, but he'd seen that limping drag-step walk before. It was one of *them*. He stepped down off the porch and felt his skin pebble for what seemed like the hundredth time that morning.

From the direction of the water tower he could make out at least twenty or so more shadowy figures. It was like a scene from an actual horror movie. The sun was rising at his back and the shadows were being chased away; the morning mist that swirled a few feet above the ground was winding around the knees of these horrific individuals.

For a moment, he had to wonder if perhaps he'd driven past some of these things on the way home from work. Southern Vinyl Window was not far past the trees. He'd driven right by the water tower on his way home. As slow as these things moved, they couldn't have come from all that far away.

He sighed and reached for his shotgun which had been set on the rail of Mayor Burns' porch. The chief put a hand on his shoulder.

"Let's try not to use our guns. We don't really know what is bringing them. If they are attracted to sound, we will just be ringing the dinner bell." He looked around and then pointed back to the house. "Go ask the mayor to come out here."

Stephen did as he was asked and escorted the mayor out to her porch. She seemed confused until he pointed.

"Oh, my God," she gasped.

"Yeah, well, we need weapons to go and deal with them. The chief thinks it would be best if we tried to avoid using our guns." He wasn't entirely enthusiastic about that idea. At the moment, his top priority was staying alive and getting home to his wife.

He'd called her on the way to the mayor's house. Apparently she was already up. She had been watching the television and was less than pleased that he had gone out to the highway. Considering what he knew now, he saw her point. When he'd asked if he should hurry home, she told him that she would be fine as long as he didn't take too long. She had access to his wide selection of pistols, rifles, and shotguns, and said that she was more than capable of holding down the fort.

"What sorts of things do you need?" Mayor Burns asked.

"Well, since it looks like we have to go for the head like in the movies, something that will bust a skull would be nice." He noticed that the mayor got a funny look on her face when he'd mentioned the thing about this being sort of like the movies. He wondered briefly if perhaps she had come up with the same idea.

The mayor pinched her lower lip for a moment and then her face brightened. She bounded off the porch and ran to the small metal shed beside the house. She fiddled with the combination lock and then threw the doors open wide with a clang.

Stephen was right behind her and following her in when the chief called out, "I think we can safely assume they are drawn to sound."

"What?" He turned to regard the older man who had come down the first step of the porch and would not take his eyes from the approaching danger.

"As soon as young Miss Burns threw open those doors, they all seemed to re-orientate on this location."

Stephen backed up and craned his neck so that he could see better. Sure enough, he watched as a few of the stragglers were altering their course just a bit to bring them towards the mayor's house. The only problem that that would present for several of the undead was that many would run into the cyclone fence. On the plus side, many were now being split away by a long wooden fence that sectioned off the back yard of the corner house one block over on Jackson Street.

He turned back to look inside the shed and a smile twitched at the corners of his mouth. "What the hell?" was all he could manage to say as he counted a dozen machetes hanging on one wall, two large splitting mauls, three hand axes, five picks of varying sizes, a short-handled and long-handled sledge hammer;

and a bundle of what appeared to be fiberglass replacement handles for the mauls, picks, and the long-handled sledge.

"I was storing these for the scout troop. They were going to help clear some of the grounds on the far side of the football field next month," Jamie said as she cut the twine that held together the bundle of spare handles.

Stephen grabbed one of the heavier machetes as well as one of the spare handles. He hefted it and was happy with the way it felt in his hands. He stepped aside as Chief Gilstrap moved in and selected the short-handled sledge.

The two men turned to start for the oncoming group of undead. Mayor Burns caught up brandishing her long, yellow fiberglass handle.

"Umm…" Stephen began, but the look the mayor shot him made it clear that there was not going to be a discussion.

The three of them spread out and Stephen was the first to reach one of the zombies. This one had been a very skinny man in his fifties or sixties. His gray hair had been pulled back in a long ponytail that was coming undone. It looked like whatever had attacked him had grabbed him by his long hair; a large flap of scalp hung down the left side of the man's face and a dark stain ran down that side. Stephen had to swallow a bit of rising bile as he realized that he could actually see a bit of the man's skull. He quickly recovered and chose that area as his target.

He swung the large handle-turned-bludgeon and felt a horrendous stinging in his hands. It was so bad that he lost his grip on the handle. To add to his misery, the skull had not shattered or appeared to have even cracked from that first heavy blow. The old man had tumbled, but that was a shallow victory as two more of the things were closing in.

Drawing the machete, Stephen hacked down hard, cutting into the man's temple. He had to step down on the now lifeless corpse to jerk the weapon free and did so just in time to spin and swing wildly at the first and closest of the pair of walking dead. He took a hand off just above the wrist and stumbled back a few steps to get some room between himself and these zombies that were suddenly a lot scarier now that he wasn't holding his shotgun.

He thought he heard somebody yell something and risked a look either way. Both of his companions had paused as well and the mayor actually looked as if she might cut out and run back to her house, but then another zombie stumbled up to her and she returned to the grim task at hand. Chief Gilstrap barely seemed to break stride and was right back to dealing with the situation in front of them.

Stephen turned his attention back as well and drove the tip of his machete into the eye socket of the one-handed zombie, jerked back much easier this time, and repeated the move on the other one. With three down, he scanned the scene and made certain that neither the mayor nor the chief was in trouble. He felt a bit embarrassed to see that it looked as if they were having no problems whatsoever. Returning his mind to the task at hand, he stepped in and dropped two more with almost no effort. He was feeling a little better until he turned to face the owner of the long shadow that was coming at him from the left.

Stephen Deese froze and staggered back a step. The little girl was perhaps no older than four or five. Her blond hair was hanging down past her shoulders and he imagined her to have once had blue eyes; but now, only those glazed over, tracer riddled orbs stared back. Her left leg dragged behind her and he could see that she'd had a nasty chunk torn from it as well as a hideous bite on her left hip where her shirt was shredded and stiff from the dried blood.

"No way," he gasped, not noticing that his machete had slipped from his grasp and fallen point down to stick into the ground.

***

Sophie drained the cup of instant coffee and grimaced. She watched Jamie follow that Deese fellow down the stairs of the porch and vanish around the corner of the house. She recognized the man, but hadn't ever really gotten to know him. She laughed sometimes when she would speak to a friend or relative from one of the larger cities like Greenville or Charleston. They assumed that everybody in a small town knew each other. They had this idea that with only three thousand or so residents, the entire population of Liberty was on a first name basis with everyone else.

She might have seen him in the hospital. She did know that he had been in the Marines. She also was pretty sure that he was a member of the volunteer fire department.

She went to the porch to see what they might be doing when a sound from the kitchen made her spin on her heel and rush through the house. The kitchen door was wide open and her son was gone.

She hurried out onto the back stoop and saw her son sprinting across the yard. She thought she saw something emerging from some of the trees and hedges. Like Jamie's house, the one that bordered the back yard had a fence. However, it was obvious that a section had been knocked down.

Then she saw them.

They were mostly obscured by the greenery, but she thought she could see at least two people kneeling on the ground. Coming off the porch, she moved so that she could better see. Her son had stopped at the fence and was now gripping it, his head dropping. Even from here, she could see his body shudder. Her son was crying. Whatever he was witnessing, it had to be terrible to make a fifteen-year-old boy actually cry.

At last she had moved enough so that she could see, and her hand came to her mouth to stifle a gasp. There were, in fact, five people on the ground. They were all clustered around a furry figure. She saw the rear legs still twitching and thought she might have heard a small whimper. She recognized the tail as belonging to what she was almost certain had to be a Golden Retriever.

Suddenly, Lawrence vaulted the fence and landed in the

back yard. He sprinted past the cluster of people that were busy ripping out chunks of something and stuffing it into their blood-stained mouths. A few heads looked up, but then returned to their grisly task.

Sophie took off after her son and stopped when she reached the back fence. Her son was now on the porch and kneeling at an open sliding glass door. When he turned, she saw that he was holding a small child in his arms. The child was crying and this now had more than just the casual attention of the group that had been gorging themselves on the body of the dog.

The group all began to get to their feet and turn in the direction of her son. Sophie ignored the fear coursing through her body and vaulted the cyclone fence in a graceful bound. She hit the ground running and was almost to her son when she saw a figure staggering out of the open back door of the house where her son had snatched the child.

"Mom, go!" Lawrence yelled as he slowed down just enough to shove aside a woman who was covered in blood and had a tuft of crimson fur hanging from the corner of her mouth.

Sophie was not about to abandon her son. She stood her ground until he arrived and then snatched the baby from him. "Get over the fence and I'll hand her to you."

Lawrence went over fast and spun to his mother with his arms outstretched. She thrust the bundled child back to her son and then went over in a hurry, this time just a little less gracefully as her pants leg caught and she flopped forward, dangling upside-down. From her current and awkward position, she could see an inverted view of the group of nightmares staggering and shambling her way.

She felt something tug at the leg that was hung up and then heard a rip. Falling, she was able to catch herself and roll to avoid any serious damage. By the time she managed to get to her feet, five horrifying caricatures of what had once been human beings were at the fence; all of them had their arms outstretched as they strained to get at the living beings just a few feet away.

52

Sophie took a moment to really inspect the assorted injuries on these people. It did not take her long to assess and determine that none of these individuals should be up and walking. One of them, a man who was completely naked, had a rip in his abdomen and strands of intestine were dangling from the wound. It was clear that they had been ripped in several places and were dripping the last of their vile contents in clumps and smears down the man's bare legs.

She also realized that she did not recognize a single one of these individuals. However, she did recognize the woman who had emerged from the house and was now making her way to join the rest of these abominations. She spun on her son and pushed him back towards Jamie's house.

"What on earth were you thinking, Lawrence Fredrick Martin!" Sophie continued to prod her son's chest with every syllable.

"Mom, I couldn't sit there and do nothing."

Sophie cocked her head and demanded an explanation. Her son explained that he had been simply watching out the back door when he spied the neighbor exit the house with the dog. Obviously she was taking the dog outside to do its business. She must not have had a clue what was going on. The dog started barking and Lawrence saw a group of individuals move up the side of the woman's house. The gate must not have been secure because they got in just as the woman rushed over to see what the dog was carrying on about.

"It happened so fast, Mom," Lawrence sobbed. "Two of them had her before she knew what happened. The dog lunged and tried to protect her but then the rest of the pack fell on the dog." He shuddered and wiped at his eyes before continuing. "The woman managed to get away, but she was all torn up and holding her side as she limped up onto the porch. She made it inside the house and shut the door, leaving the dog to be finished off."

The boy was quiet for a moment and then glanced down at the little girl in his arms that had miraculously fallen asleep after all the chaos. He went to the living room and laid the toddler on the couch and adjusted the blanket she'd been gripping so tightly through the whole ordeal.

"I heard a baby cry and I just couldn't stand here and do nothing," Lawrence finished. "I was afraid that..." Sophie saw her son's face change. He seemed hesitant to finish what he'd been about to say.

Putting an arm around his shoulders, Sophie hugged Lawrence and kissed him on the temple, leaving her face against the side of his. "I know, baby. I've seen them too."

***

Jonathan pulled into the driveway of the Senior Center. He hated the fact that his mother had decided to move into this place. It wasn't like her little house on Clay was that big.

As he got out of the car he paused again and looked at the bottoms of his shoes. Nothing. Getting down on his hands and knees, he looked underneath his car. Maybe he'd hit something, or perhaps a critter had crawled up inside his engine area and gotten itself killed. Now it was rotting. Satisfied there was nothing dangling from the underside of his car, he went around and popped the hood, yanking the little kickstand thing that kept it up so that he could get a closer look.

Still seeing nothing, he leaned down and gave a good sniff. He wasn't a mechanic, but it pretty much smelled like an engine should smell. He pulled the thin metal rod free and wedged it into its place and then let the hood drop with a loud clang.

A low moan from behind him caused Jonathan to spin around, the hair on his arms and the back of his neck already standing on end. He'd heard that sound before in Fumio's videos.

Three figures were coming his direction. He knew exactly what he was seeing, but that did not lessen the degree of fear that grabbed his bladder and gave it a good squeeze. The coppery taste of adrenaline soon followed and he reached in the open rear window of his car and grabbed the L-shaped lug wrench.

"No way," was all he could manage as the first of the trio actually stepped into a long beam of the rising sun and came into full and gruesome detail.

The woman was wearing the remnants of a nightgown that did little to cover her massive frame. She still had rollers in her hair and one foot was clad in a fuzzy slipper that looked like it might be glued in place by all the blood that had poured down her body from where her throat and right shoulder had been savaged. She had dingy brown hair and the bits that had come free of the curlers hung halfway down her back. Her face showed no emotion as she approached, but her hands were reaching and clutching at the air while her mouth opened and closed almost with hungry anticipation, causing her teeth to click together, but it was the eyes that had Jonathan transfixed.

He'd seen something in the eyes of the video that Fumio had sent, but it was something else altogether to see them in person. They were covered in a pus-yellow coating and the capillaries were shot with black that really stood out against the film.

"Hey," Jonathan called. The way they all stopped and then twitched and jerked around a bit to re-orient on him was a more than a little creepy.

Then the full force of the smell hit him. It was unlike anything he had ever experienced. Of course, he'd never been near a dead body except for his dad. And that had been at the funeral. That was the day he decided that he wanted to be cremated. It had been so odd looking inside the casket and seeing that body with all the makeup to try and make him not seem dead. He knew that his dad would have hated it. Even more, he would have told everybody to "quit their bellyaching and fussing and get back to doing something productive."

The woman staggered closer and the two men behind her sort of bumped against each other as they started towards where Jonathan stood beside his car with his tire iron in hand.

Suddenly he felt like an idiot. If this was really the start of a zombie apocalypse, how was he going to survive with nothing more than a little piece of metal? What he needed was a gun.

Suddenly, his nerve left him and he began to work his way around his car so that it was between him and the approaching...

"Zombies."

He almost felt stupid when he heard that word. He even looked around to see if perhaps it had come from somebody else. It just couldn't be possible. Zombies were not medically or scientifically able to exist. He and his friends had beaten that dead horse into the ground anytime they got together and saw one of the movies or played one of the video games.

Zombies simply could not be.

Yet...here they were. The woman staggering up the gentle slope of the entry drive to the Liberty Senior Center could not be living. Glancing at the two men; neither could they. One of them had a strange looking piece of himself jutting from a hole in his side. His clothes were torn up and he was even bloodier than the woman, and the other man was missing his nose, for crying out loud.

"Johnny Cakes?" a voice called from behind him.

Jonathan spun to see his mother standing in the doorway to the senior center in her purple and pink jogging suit that he'd bought her just this past Christmas. She was alone, and for that he was actually a bit thankful.

"Hurry up and come get in the car," he barked, his voice sounding harsher than he'd intended.

"Don't you use a tone with me, young man," Mildred Patterson shot back. "You might be grown up, but you will not speak to your mother in that manner. Do you understand?"

Jonathan spun on his mother and pointed to the car. "Get. In. Now."

As soon as she stepped off the porch of the senior center, it was clear that she could see the trio of approaching zombies. Only, it was not clear if she actually could see them for what they were.

"Jonathan...those people..." her face was screwed up with a look of total confusion and horror.

Now he knew that his mother was upset; she never called him Jonathan unless he was in trouble or she was very troubled. In fact, the last time that she had called him Jonathan was when she had called him to tell him that his father had died of a heart attack.

Giving the terrible trio an appraising glance, he guessed the time he had to be very little. It would be close. He dashed to his mother and scooped her wispy body up into his arms. He was briefly thankful that she was not the size of that female zombie that was now just a few steps away from the rear bumper of his car.

He reached his Toyota and gave the rear passenger side door a jerk. He hissed as he yanked hard on the handle only to have nothing happen. He almost never used the back seat, so the doors were almost always locked; which, considering how he almost always left the windows open, was sort of ridiculous.

He reached in and unlocked the door, pulled it open, and did his best to stuff his mom inside without hurting her. Ignoring her stammers, protests, and attempts at questions, he hurried around the front of his car and arrived at his door just a step ahead of the female zombie.

The lug wrench in his hand was basically forgotten. Instead, he lashed out with one foot and kicked the woman hard in her ample middle. She barely even staggered back a step. He was surprised, thinking that, as unsteady as she seemed on her feet, she should topple over easily enough.

Her hands reached for him and two fingers snagged the sleeve of his shirt. He brought one arm up defensively and batted the hand away and then jabbed outward, catching her in the shoulder. Once again his blow had basically no effect.

Jonathan pulled his door open and he now found himself forced to actually take a step closer to this foul monster in order to get inside his car. His right arm came up, and later, when he would replay this moment in his mind, it seemed as if the tire iron weighed about a hundred pounds.

He swung down hard, his blow connecting at the base of the woman's neck. She had not made a sound. Her hands were still reaching for him and now one of them had purchase on his sleeve down near his left wrist.

Jonathan jerked away and re-adjusted how he was holding the weapon in his hand. He had spun the sharp end used for prying off a hub cap so that it pointed away from him. With one massive thrust, he had driven that end up under the sagging jowls of this woman. The feeling had been strange and he swore he felt it as the tip plunged through the soft meat, burst through the mouth and then drove through the bone of the roof of the mouth and up into the brain pan.

It was as if somebody had hit the "off" switch. The woman collapsed in a heap, yanking the lethal weapon from Jonathan's hands as she did so. He made no effort to retrieve it and hopped into the car. He took off, making a hard left onto Old Norris Road and heading home to his little place on Cooper Street.

He looked in the rearview and saw his mother's expression. He slammed on the brakes and craned around to face her.

"Are you okay, Mom?" he asked with as much calmness in his tone as he could manage.

"That woman, Jonathan...you...you...you killed her." Tears streamed down his mother's cheeks and she was looking at him in a way that he'd never seen before.

Mildred Patterson was afraid of her son.

That look was like a slap to his face and stung inwardly a great deal more than any physical blow. Mildred Patterson was a small woman. Her son was easily two and a half of her if they were on a scale. Since he'd been thirteen, he had towered over the woman. Yet, she'd never hesitated to grab him by the ear and scold him if he got out of line. She had always known that he would never strike back at her. Not that she'd been a physical disciplinarian; she stopped using the switch when he'd turned twelve.

But right now, she was looking at her son and seeing a total stranger. She'd just witnessed him basically drive a piece of metal through a woman's head.

"Mom, you don't understand…" he began, and tried to reach back and put a comforting hand on his mother. She jerked away and let out a frightened shriek as if she feared that he might make her his next victim.

"Don't you touch me!" she yelped, Her hands went for the door and she forced it open and tripped over herself trying to get out so fast.

Jonathan put his car in park and jumped out as well. He came around the front of his car as his mother was scrambling to her feet. She threw her hands up defensively and began to wail.

"Please…somebody!"

Jonathan stopped and put his own hands up in the air. He thought it over for a second and then knelt on the ground, lacing his fingers behind his head.

"I won't hurt you, Mom." He unlaced his fingers and reached down slowly into his pocket with one hand. He produced his phone and slid it to his mother. "Call somebody. I won't move. But believe me when I tell you, I didn't murder anybody. It isn't what you think."

Very slowly, Mildred Patterson picked up the phone. Her eyes were wide and never left those of her son. She swiped at the phone and held it to her ear. A look of confusion came to her face. She pulled the phone away and stared at it, then tried again.

From his knees, Jonathan looked around at where they were. He felt his stomach drop. Just to his right was the cemetery.

"Oh crap," he whispered.

Dead: Snapshot—Liberty, South Carolina

4

Worse than Expected

Jamie spun after cutting down the last of the terrible figures that she'd faced off against and turned to see how the two men were doing. The chief was just taking down his last one as well. Her eyes found Stephen and she felt her stomach try to turn inside out.

The man was walking backwards. Even from this distance, she could see the glisten of tears on his cheeks. Looking at the small figure that he kept simply trying to shove away, she understood exactly what had reduced the man to tears.

The little girl could not be any older than four or five. Her tiny hands kept reaching out for the much larger man who apparently could not bring it on himself to finish her like he had the other zombies. A voice in her head told her that she needed to rush over and help him. However, her feet simply refused to obey that command. She remained rooted in place and could not bring herself to go to his rescue.

She felt the lump in her throat grow larger each time the child swiped at the large man. At some point he had obviously dropped or lost his weapons and was fending off the attempted attacks by doing nothing more than pushing the child back.

Chief Gilstrap must have witnessed it as well, because at last he rushed up from the side. His body blocked her view, but when he moved again and turned to face Mr. Deese, the child was no longer standing and was nothing more than a crumpled heap on the ground.

Slowly, Jamie's feet began to move forward. She approached the two men and then slowed to a stop when the details began to come into focus regarding the small child. That was not a sight she cared to see any closer than necessary.

"How is this happening?" Jamie broke their relative silence.

"I got no idea," Chief Gilstrap said with a heavy sigh as he removed his hat, wiped his face with his hands, and then slapped the hat back on. "Been hearing rumors, but it is sorta like Kentucky. You hear something, and then it is gone the next day and the person stops answering your queries. Had a chief over in Clemson shoot me an email last night about a nasty bit of business that happened at some big apartment complex near the college. The next day, it was like the man had vanished off the face of the earth. Sent him an email a few hours later and it came back saying the email address did not exist. I know for a fact that's a bunch of crap."

"That poor soldier mentioned something about this being worse than his chain-of-command was letting on and there was word that all of Japan and places over in that area going totally dark," Jamie offered.

"How could an entire country, much less that whole part of the world go dark and nobody hear about it?" Stephen scoffed.

"I'm just sharing what he told me."

"Yeah, well he was probably delirious. That is the biggest load of crap I've ever heard. Sounds like a bunch of that crazy internet talk."

Jamie locked eyes with Stephen Deese and saw that he couldn't maintain contact. She doubted he believed his own argument.

"Sorta like flesh-eating zombies walking around attacking people?" the chief said, obviously picking up on the other man's struggle to come to grips with what they had all just witnessed.

"I hate to say it, but this is exactly why the problem might be worse than we think. Nobody in their right mind is gonna believe it. And if the government is trying to keep it off the public's radar, then we might be much worse off than we realize."

"You think?" Jamie blurted, her hands gesturing to the bodies scattered on the ground around them.

The trio stood in silence for a moment, each obviously lost in their own thoughts as they took in the horror that lay as physical evidence before their very eyes. Jamie's gaze returned back to her house, but somehow, everything suddenly looked different. It was as if the world had grown darker. Her little town felt less safe, and extremely vulnerable.

The thought hit her like a punch to the gut.

Her town.

She was the mayor of Liberty. It was her duty and responsibility to see after the best interests of the citizens. She needed to act now and ensure that her tiny community was as safe as possible.

Her mind fast-forwarded through what little she knew of the movies. Just as quickly, she tossed all of what little she knew into a file in her head and promised to return to it later. Right now, she was only able to focus on one thing: everybody always died in those movies. It was on her to make sure that did not happen here.

"Gentlemen," she said, getting the attention of both men, "we need to get everybody in town together right away. This is not voluntary. Do what you need to, enlist anybody that you think will help, and get the word out immediately. I want everybody gathered…" She considered her choices and then came up with the most logical location that she could think that would be able to allow the entire town to gather in one place. "Tell them to be at the high school football stadium at 11 AM."

***

His eyes continued to flick back and forth between his mother and the cemetery. So far, there was no sign of any movement coming from the sprawling graveyard. Meanwhile, his mother had continued trying to get the phone to work. At last, she regarded him with a suspicious look.

"What have you done to the phone, Jonathan?" She thrust it towards him with accusation dripping from her words.

"I haven't done anything. What's wrong?"

"It won't work. I can't get it to call nine-one-one."

"Here, let me—" he began, but her squeal of fright and stumble backwards to get away from him froze Jonathan in place. He very carefully knelt back down and re-laced his hands behind his head. "Mom, I wish you'd listen to me."

"Listen to you?" Mildred Patterson snapped. "I don't even know who you are!"

Jonathan felt his stomach twist into knots as he watched tears trickle down his mother's face. Her disappointment and sorrow was clear. She was not seeing him; instead, she was seeing a cold-blooded killer. How was he going to convince her that there was something terrible happening and that he was just trying to save her?

Why couldn't a zombie show up now when he needed one? He was still mulling that over when his mother's expression changed. She cocked her head to one side and it struck him that she was listening to something. He couldn't believe that her hearing had been that much better than his and dismissed it to the fact that he'd been pre-occupied.

A car was coming. They were just a bit past the bend in Old Norris Road and that car would be coming around it from behind his mother. What he now feared was that it might actually hit his mother. She was just standing in the road, and it was clear that the oncoming vehicle was moving a bit faster than it should.

"Mom, hop in my car and pull it over…quick!"

Despite her advanced age, Mildred Patterson was no decrepit old lady. Her morning exercises had obviously kept her quite a bit more agile and spry than many people her age. She did as she was told, but her eyes still never left him and they narrowed a bit when he got up and moved off the road himself.

Did she expect him to just stay in the road and get run over? Better yet…is that what she wanted? All of these thoughts evaporated when he spied the vehicle rounding the corner. Despite everything, the last thing that Jonathan Patterson wanted to see at this exact moment was Chief Gilstrap's patrol car.

The vehicle slowed and came to a halt, the chief rolling down his window rather than actually getting out. The man stuck his head out of the window and Jonathan actually had to squint and rub his eyes to make sure he wasn't imagining things. There were dark flecks all over the man's face as well as a blackish smear on the right cheek that looked almost like it may be dried blood!

"Is there a problem here?" the chief asked, sounding absolutely exhausted.

"Umm…well…" Jonathan was not sure how to answer. In truth, yes, there was absolutely a problem here. However, the last person he wanted to reveal that to at this moment would be the Liberty Chief of Police.

"My son killed a woman!" Mildred Patterson stumbled forward, one arm outstretched and a finger pointing accusingly at her son.

The mood changed in the blink of an eye. Chief Gilstrap practically exploded from his car, gun drawn and pointed at Jonathan.

"On your stomach…NOW!" the man barked.

Jonathan did as he was told, a sick feeling growing in his gut. However, it was not just due to the fact that he would likely be booked and thrown in jail, it was what would happen in the weeks to come when this zombie problem grew worse and there was nobody to bring meals. He would die of starvation, locked in a tiny cell. Being bitten and turning into a zombie was suddenly gaining in appeal.

"Sir, I didn't kill anybody!" Jonathan protested as he felt a knee come down firmly in the middle of his back. The metallic clink of handcuffs followed, and he felt the cold metal tighten on first one wrist and then the other.

"Yes he did," Jonathan's mother insisted. "He did it right in front of me. He jammed a tire iron up through the poor woman's head!"

Jonathan was jerked onto his knees and spun around to face Chief Gilstrap. This close, it was clear that the flecks and the smear on the chief's face were, in fact, blood. Also, he could not help but let his eyes drift down to the man's hand where a near-perfect bite mark stood out on the skin. It had been wiped off, but blood still oozed from the wound and one rivulet was trickling down the man's thumb.

"Alright, ma'am," Chief Gilstrap said, the tone of his voice softening just a bit. He nudged Jonathan and locked eyes with him. "Did you kill a woman by driving a tire iron through her head?"

"She was already dead," Jonathan blurted.

Mildred Patterson stammered and appeared to be unable to string any coherent words together. The chief made certain that the woman was staying put and then turned his attention back to the Jonathan.

"What do you mean she was already dead?" he asked in a hushed whisper. The officer's eyes narrowed, but Jonathan did not think it was in anger or even disbelief.

"This is gonna sound stupid—" he started to explain, but the police chief cut him off with a mutter that Jonathan did not think he meant to blurt out loud.

"After tonight, you'd be surprised."

"The woman that I put down was torn up. She had most of her throat ripped open. And the two that were with her looked even worse. One of 'em had his guts hanging out. I know it sounds ridiculous—"

Again the chief cut him off. "Can you take me to them? Show me?"

Now it was Jonathan's turn to sound like he was confused. He had expected a number of possible reactions, but this was certainly not one of them.

"Umm...yeah, sure."

"Ma'am," the police chief turned to face the elderly woman who now looked as confused as she did horrified, "you can ride along with us, or you can take the car and return home."

Jonathan explained that he'd been picking up his mother at the senior center, so perhaps it might be better if she either returned to his house, or (and this was his preference) perhaps the chief could make her come along in the back so that she could see that her son wasn't a murderer.

"I don't have time for a lot of nonsense," the chief snapped as he spun and returned to his vehicle. "Ma'am, I need you to get in the car right now and come with me."

"I won't ride anywhere with that...that...monster!" Mildred crossed her arms across her chest and planted one foot for emphasis.

"Fine, stay here." With that, the police chief climbed into his patrol car.

Jonathan rushed over and stood at the front passenger door. He waited a moment and saw the chief glaring back at him like he was an idiot. He turned around and waved his cuffed hands as an explanation. A string of expletives erupted from the car and Jonathan heard the door open. As he waited to be for the cuffs to be removed, he saw his mother move meekly to the rear driver's side door and wait for the grumbling, cursing police chief to finish with her son and then come back to get in the car. He paused long enough to open the door for his mother and then close it again once she was inside.

After a very jerky and much-too-fast-for-comfort turn around, the police car was rocketing back up Old Norris Road towards the senior center. Jonathan was just starting to whisper a silent prayer that those other two zombies would be present so that he didn't end up being thrown in jail when the pair appeared directly in the middle of the road as the cruiser rounded the bend.

"Hang on!" was all Chief Gilstrap had a chance to shout before being drowned by the shriek of tires and the heavy and meaty thud of one of the walking corpses being slammed into head-on at over forty-miles-per-hour.

***

Stephen stood beside his wife Terri and watched the lady step up to the podium. The banner at the bottom of the screen read: Dr. Linda Sing, CDC spokesperson.

Stephen turned the television up just enough so that he could actually hear what this woman had to say. He noticed immediately the absence of any reporters blurting out questions. She was obviously not taking any.

"This ought to be a doozy," Terri sniffed as she leaned into her husband.

"I have been asked to address the issue of a peculiar illness that is apparently sweeping the country. While we are still in the preliminary stages of trying to figure this out, I want to make one thing clear." The woman leaned forward at the podium a bit and made it a point to almost glare into the camera. Her mirthless face looked as if she had perhaps not allowed a smile to creep across her lips in many years. The bright lights only washed out her features that much more, giving her a look that Stephen thought seemed very much like that of the zombies he'd just finished dealing with not more than ten minutes ago. "Those rumors of the dead coming back and attacking the living are beyond ludicrous. Ignoring the pure physiological impossibility, there is simply no way this can be considered with any seriousness."

"And that is how we are going to end up going the way of the unicorn and the dinosaur," he muttered as he muted the television. "I'm sorry, honey, I can't listen to this."

"I don't want to seem like I'm not supporting you, Stephen," Terri began, seeming to choose her words carefully, "but are you absolutely certain about this?"

"I know what I saw."

Stephen walked into the kitchen and poured a cup of coffee. He looked longingly at the plate of bacon and eggs sitting at the breakfast nook. Today was supposed to be his Friday. Terri always made him a hearty breakfast and spent a little time with him before she headed over to the elementary school where she was a third grade teacher.

Today would be different. He really wanted to sit down and eat, but the mayor had been very emphatic that they get everybody rounded up. He had been given a key to one of the patrol cars and was told which neighborhoods to take where he would be driving up and down the street announcing an emergency meeting at the high school. He'd also enlisted his wife's help. She was supposed to go in to work and have the school use its emergency call program to notify all parents with school-aged children.

They knew that a few people would slip through their fingers, but if they could get a majority of the town gathered, then they could rely on everybody else to get the word to those few who might miss what was going to be said this morning.

"And she wouldn't actually share the plan with you?" Terri was asking as Stephen filled his travel mug one more time and got ready to head back out.

"She wouldn't say a word, only mentioned that we were not going to go out like they did in those ridiculous stories."

Terri kissed her husband as he walked out the door and climbed into his truck. He waved to her as he backed out and gave a much closer look around just to be sure there was nothing out of the ordinary. Yes, he'd made certain that she had his entire arsenal laid out in their bedroom, the kitchen, and the living room, but that did not lessen his degree of apprehension about leaving her alone.

He turned on his stereo system and quickly tapped the CD back into the player when he recognized Dr. Linda Sing's voice.

That woman could talk as long as she liked about what nonsense it was to think that the dead were returning and attacking the living, but she obviously hadn't seen what he and the others had witnessed.

"One of them sumbitches bites you in the ass and you'll change your tune," he muttered as the twang of a rowdy country song filled his cab.

He reached the parking area where Chief Gilstrap had told him a car would be waiting. Sure enough, a police car sat parked in the lot next to city hall and the fire department. He pulled his truck into the space beside it and hopped out. Just as he locked his truck, a blaring siren caused him to jump. He'd gotten out of his truck with his shotgun in his hand and brought it to his shoulder almost out of instinct.

He tasted the adrenaline in the back of his throat and his stomach roiled, having only been filled with bitter coffee up to this point. The roll-doors on the fire department went up and one of the large red vehicles crept out, soon followed by the red Ford pickup that the fire chief often drove.

Both vehicles turned right onto Front Street and sped away from him, hanging another right on what looked like Hillcrest Street. The sirens began to fade and Stephen was just unlocking the police car when a thought struck him.

He jumped in the car, turned the key and took off out of the parking lot with tires burning rubber and sending up a cloud of acrid blue smoke. He reached Hillcrest and turned right just as he flipped the switches that activated the lights and siren of the vehicle. It wouldn't do for him to run over some poor pedestrian, and considering the hour, it could very easily be some kid on his way to school.

"That got dark fast," he muttered, scolding himself for allowing his mind to drift to the worst possible scenario so quickly. Still, it might not hurt to keep that part of his mind functioning if things shaped up like they looked to be.

He slowed as he pulled up to Liberty Elementary School.

Both emergency vehicles had pulled up in the drop-off lane and still had their lights flashing. Just as he pulled up behind the red pickup, he saw the last of the responding firemen duck inside the main entrance to the school.

He jumped out and considered his shotgun. In the end, he could not simply walk away and leave it behind. He tried to shove it under his coat but thought that might look even more suspicious.

Jogging up to the entrance, he paused for just a second when he heard a terrible scream come from behind him. He was already thinking of what to say to whomever it was that was blowing a gasket about his carrying a weapon into the school, but when he turned and the scream sounded again, he realized that it was across the street in the direction of the church.

He fought over what to do and decided that he would have to trust the firemen to not do anything foolish. His brain was already berating him before he'd gone two steps. Wasn't that the basic job description for firemen? Go someplace dangerous that nobody else would want to go and then risk your ass to save somebody else? For some reason, an image of a fireman climbing a stairwell against a tide of people trying to go down flashed in his head as he sprinted across the street and then ducked through some trees.

He would be approaching the church almost from the back. Just as he started up the little hill before reaching the small parking area in the rear of the church, he heard another scream. He put on a burst of speed and sprinted for the front of the quaint little brick church with its white steeple where the bells rang every Sunday to announce service.

As soon as he rounded the corner, he knew that he was too late. A small set of legs could be seen kicking in their final fits on the walkway that ran along the front of the church. A woman in a pair of jeans and a dark tee shirt was hunched over the small figure. The screams were now gurgles and weak whimpers; but that only allowed for the wet slurping and rending noises to be heard that much more clearly.

Walking up behind the female figure that had gotten down on all fours now and had its face buried in the midsection of a little boy that Stephen unfortunately recognized as Timmy Darcy, Ned and Stacy Darcy's boy, Stephen brought up his shotgun and leveled it at the back of the woman's head. He had a finger on the trigger when he remembered how the chief had said that it looked like these things reacted to sound. Reversing the gun, he raised the butt of it and brought it down hard on the back of the woman's head. A lot of folks did not realize that the front of the skull was designed to endure a heavy impact. The rear of the skull was the equivalent of an egg shell; sure, a bit thicker, but not anywhere near the strength of the front.

He brought it down twice more before it broke open. Shaking out his hands to rid them of the buzzing feeling, he grabbed the woman's body and jerked it off the Darcy boy. He was trying to figure out what to do when the eyes fluttered and opened. He looked into that filmed over gaze and tried to tell himself to end it quick. He raised his weapon to bring it down and once again faltered. This had been someone's child. Even worse, he knew the kid. He'd seen him at church, spoken with Ned in the store as this same child stood peeking out behind his dad's legs.

The child began to struggle to its feet and Stephen backed away. He warred within himself about what to do. The logical part of his mind screamed for him to put this thing down; it insisted that he was no longer looking at the Darcy child. The emotional part of his mind, a part he'd become adept at stuffing away during his time overseas but had worked hard to nurse back to health since his return, told him this was still just a child.

Across the street was the church's family center. There in the parking lot was a small trailer. He started backing away from the child and waited for it to follow. The zombie of Timmy Darcy was now on its feet. It cocked its head and regarded Stephen with its terrible gaze, but it made no move in his direction.

"Hey!" Stephen hissed. The zombie actually took a step back. "You've got to be kidding."

He snapped his fingers and still received no response. With a sigh, he brought up his weapon and steeled himself for the horrible task that he looked like he was going to be forced to act out. It was like a switch had been thrown. Without warning, the child lurched forward, hands coming for him and teeth gnashing.

He staggered back a few steps and angled himself towards the small trailer across the street. The entire time, he kept looking every direction for signs of anybody—living or dead.

Nothing; he wasn't sure if that was a blessing or a curse.

When he finally reached the trailer, he had to break open the locked doors.

"Now for the tricky part," Stephen said to the child as it stumbled closer.

He judged the child's movements and then dove in, grabbed the kid by the hair and slung him into the open trailer. He slammed the doors and pulled his belt off to secure them and prevent the child from escaping.

"Now what, genius?" he muttered.

As if in response, terrible screams came on the morning breeze from the elementary school.

***

Jamie stared at the screen of the television in disbelief. She knew Greenville well enough to recognize the downtown skyline such as it was. Plumes of smoke were rising from several locations in the background of the field reporter who looked to be stationed on the span of a bridge. She turned up the volume and crossed her arms as she listened.

"…as reports of unrest are coming from all over the city. Police and fire department resources are being stretched beyond capacity and the nine-one-one centers report that they are overwhelmed. From our position here on South Academy Street, we just watched a convoy of what appeared to be military vehicles roll past.

"There is still no word from Sky-chopper Four. As we reported earlier, they landed on the top deck of the parking lot across from Wellness Arena when they spied a woman trapped in her vehicle and surrounded by what appeared to be at least a dozen angry rioters.

"Wait...I am just now being told that reporter Cole Simmons is requesting to cut in. Cole?"

There was a flicker and then a new image came into view. This was at street level and Jamie immediately recognized the Greenville Health System and Sun Trust Bank building in the background. Smoke was pouring from several windows and sounds of shouting and screaming could be heard in the background.

"Thanks, Chet," the square-jawed man said as he looked into the camera with eyes that had just the slightest squint to them. "I am here on the corner of Spring and McBee just a few blocks away from where a crowd of the rioters has been reported. I can tell you that we have witnessed three separate auto accidents in just the past few minutes, and one woman just ran up to us bleeding from a terrible wound on her right arm. She said something about somebody biting her before running off.

"The mob should be coming into view shortly, and we hope to be able to share images with our viewers. I do want to repeat that, unless it is absolutely necessary, you should avoid downtown Greenville at all costs today." There was a shudder in the picture as the camera swung away from the reporter. Cole paused for a moment and then resumed his narrative.

"We have the first images of this mob, and as you can see, initial reports of this being some sort of racial issue are inaccurate as we see, people of all colors..." Cole Simmons' voice trailed off.

There was another moment of chaotic background noise and Jamie was certain that she heard the pop of a gun at least twice before the reporter resumed speaking.

"Brad, can you tighten up the picture on the leading edge of this group?" Cole's voice could be heard over the background noise.

The picture blurred for a moment and then came into horrifying focus. The leading edge of the oncoming mob instantly made Jamie think of those zombie movies again. There was a variety of injuries that no person could withstand and keep walking. A casual observer might dismiss this as some sort of flash mob hoax, but Jamie already knew better.

"Okay, can somebody in the studio please help sort out what we are seeing here?"

Jamie heard the annoyance in the reporter's voice. She had a feeling that he might be dismissing what he was witnessing with his own two eyes. After all, this was simply not something that anybody with one foot in reality could accept as fact...*until it came up and bit you on the ass*, a voice in her head mused.

"Cole, maybe you should pack up and get out of there," a female voice offered, obviously from the relative safety of the newsroom. "We are hearing reports all over town about people being attacked by violent mobs. The governor has just called for a press conference that is set to begin as soon as the president makes his address."

"C'mon, Brad," Cole's voice barked.

Jamie felt herself breathe a sigh of relief until the image of the reporter appeared and was now headed directly *towards* the oncoming group of what Jamie was certain had to be the walking dead. She felt a stinging sensation in her hands and looked down to see that her nails were digging into her palms.

"C'mon, you idiot," she breathed.

"Hey!" Cole could be heard shouting. "Can one of you..."

Jamie refocused on the television. The camera was a good fifteen or twenty feet behind the reporter who had closed about half the distance between himself and the crowd. She could hear heavy breathing and then a gagging noise.

"What in the world?" Now the reporter was staggering back a few steps. "Brad, are you smelling that?"

The reporter turned to face the camera. He had an arm up over his face in an obvious attempt to ward off the smell. Jamie's memory sent a sympathetic blast of that stench trickling down the back of her throat. She knew very well what the man would be smelling. There was nothing quite like it.

"Now run," she urged.

Her heart hammered as it dawned on her that the reporter now had his back to the approaching group of undead. He was still refusing to accept the evidence that had literally been right in front of him.

"I don't know what exactly might be going on, but let me reiterate the point that this is not something that appears to be based on some sort of racial division. The group of rioters seems to be a mix of all races, but for some inexplicable reason they have the look of one of those zombie-walk groups..." Cole's voice ceased reporting for a moment and then quickly resumed. "This is like that one group Kaley Chisholm reported on a few months ago that was raising money for local food banks. Only, apparently these people are not acting out of charity..." Cole turned back to face the oncoming group and his words died on his lips.

Jamie knew that it was too late. The first of the zombies was now within an arm's reach. Hands clutched at the man who now stood stock still, apparently rooted in place by fear as a pitiful squeak was almost drowned out by a chorus of moans.

The cameraman continued to shoot the scene, but it was also apparent that he was backing up. The reporter was now being dragged to the ground and the scream that came was enough to peg the audio and turn it into little more than a roaring sound that ended suddenly with an electronic shriek of feedback.

The image blurred again and then there was a moment when it looked as if the world was spiraling crazily. The cameraman had apparently tripped and fallen over backwards. The image of the reporter being savagely attacked was now replaced by a sideways view of the street and a nearby curb. A hand planted on the ground at the edge of the shot and then a pair of feet raced by in a blur.

There was another moment of just the skewed image of the street and then a studio shot that revealed three people standing behind a long news desk, staring to the left with varied expressions of horror etched across their faces. Somebody off camera must have gestured or done something to get the attention of the trio as they all three started and then began trying to compose themselves as they looked straight ahead at the camera.

At last, the woman on the left who Jamie actually recognized as being the traffic and weather person cleared her throat and began to speak. "Umm, I can't be certain as to what we just saw, but I believe this is far worse than we've been told. Do we still have the clip of that CDC doctor? Can somebody get that queued up, please?" The woman straightened and looked to her fellow news people and then continued to speak when it was clear that neither of them were going to do so. "I advise you to reconsider the words spoken by..." She squinted down at a stack of pages in front of her on the desk, rifled through them and then nodded in satisfaction. "Dr. Linda Sing of the CDC. Despite her denials and refusal to consider the possibilities, I think what we have seen just now flies in the face of her words. I advise—"

The screen flashed and then a picture of a sunny day in downtown Greenville with the station call letters, logo, and network affiliation popped up. The strains of a familiar tune being performed by an orchestra drifted from the television's speaker.

"Muzak?" Jamie laughed harshly. "The world is coming to an end and they are playing Muzak?"

Well, she was not about to let Liberty, South Carolina go down like that. This was her town. She had a plan, and if she could get everybody on board fast enough...they might just be able to ride this out until somebody got a handle on things. And, if they never did and this became the extinction event like in the movies, well then, they would not just survive...Liberty would thrive.

Dead: Snapshot—Liberty, South Carolina

5

The Meeting

Jonathan barely had enough time to put his arms up and grab the dashboard to brace for the impact. The body of the undead man folded over hard and slammed into the hood, rolled up and smashed against the windshield, and then flipped up and over the car.

Chief Gilstrap had turned reflexively but much too late. The car veered left and plunged off the road, nose-diving into the shallow ditch that ran alongside the road before coming to an abrupt stop with enough forward momentum that the rear end lifted a good three feet off the ground before coming down hard, blowing out the right rear tire in the process.

"Holy crap," Jonathan groaned and then hissed in pain as his brain became flooded with messages about his many injuries. He glanced down at his right wrist and saw it cocked over at an odd angle. His vision blurred and he used his left hand to wipe his eyes. It came away coated and slick with bright red blood.

"Are you..." Chief Gilstrap let the words die when he glanced over and got a look at Jonathan. He craned his neck to look in the back seat and paled.

That reaction made Jonathan forget his pain. He tried to turn, but couldn't, and went to work on his seatbelt which seemed to be stuck. At last he heard the click and wriggled free of it as he climbed onto his knees and looked in the back seat. His mother was leaning back, but the odd angle that her head sat on her shoulders gave away her condition.

"Mom," Jonathan cried.

The slap of a hand on his window made him jump and he spun back around in his seat, banging his fractured wrist in the center console of the police car. His vision swam as the pain returned with a renewed vengeance. Once it cleared, he could see the undead face of a man staring in at him. It brought a hand up and slapped at his window again in a futile attempt to get at the living being on the other side of the glass.

Torn between the grief of his mother's death and the anger at the undead creatures outside the police car that had caused this accident, Jonathan let loose with a howl of frustration. He reached down with his good hand to open his door and felt something grip his shoulder.

"Stay put, son," an authoritative voice spoke from behind him.

A piece of his brain reminded him that he was in the police chief's car, but he was currently incapable of rational thought. His mother was dead just a few feet away. Her last thoughts of her son had been that he was something terrible…a murderer. Tears began to well and drip from his eyes, mixing with the blood that ran freely from his busted open forehead.

The sound of a car door opening drifted into his jumbled thoughts. He turned to see the chief force his way out of the car. It looked like he tried to shut the door behind him, but was unable to do so. Jonathan could only watch as the man worked his way around the front of the car where a hint of steam now drifted up from the edges of the crumpled hood. He had a machete in his hand.

"Where did he get that?" Jonathan mumbled, unaware that his voice was a bit slurred.

He continued to watch as the chief jerked the zombie away from the passenger side and shoved it to the dirt. The angle of the car prevented him from seeing the zombie on the ground, but he was able to see the chief bring the machete up and then chop down hard. He jerked the weapon free and then moved down the vehicle. Glancing in the rearview mirror, Jonathan was able to make out a twisted and broken figure in the middle of the road several feet behind them. The chief walked to it with an odd calmness. The man stopped and seemed to study the twitching figure on the road for several seconds before raising the machete and binging it down once more, burying the heavy blade in the skull of the zombie.

Once again, the chief appeared to pause and study the corpse for a minute until he planted a boot on it and jerked his blade free. The man came back to the car and worked to pry the passenger side door open.

"Can you walk?"

Jonathan gave a weak nod and allowed the chief to help him climb out of the car. He started to turn and felt firm hands grip his shoulders.

"It's best you not look."

"But it's my mom," Jonathan insisted.

"I am so sorry," the chief apologized. "There is nothing you can do for her and we need to get moving before more of those things show up. Your car is just back the road a piece. If you give me the keys, I'll get us out of here."

"My mom has them," Jonathan managed around a throat that was growing tighter with each passing second.

The chief returned to the car and Jonathan stood there in the middle of the road. This wasn't anything like the video games or movies. He'd nearly died in a car crash. His mother had died and was now just a few feet away and they were going to leave her behind. A thought occurred to him.

"Why can't you call somebody on your radio?" Jonathan asked.

"You broke it with your left hand, and the antennae is lodged in the throat of that zombie we hit. And before you ask about phones, cell service is basically shot from what I have been able to see," the chief explained.

Zombie. Jonathan actually felt his eyes grow wide at the sound of that word. The police chief had used it like it was no big deal.

"You know what they are?" Jonathan asked meekly.

"I may not be the sharpest knife in the drawer, and I don't much enjoy watching those types of movies, but I haven't lived under a rock my whole life. I can't figure what else you would call 'em."

Jonathan felt a surge of relief. Then he felt nauseous. Then...he passed out.

***

Stephen had just started back for the school when a terrible thought gripped him. Terri was supposed to head to the school and help with notifying the town.

"Please don't be there...please don't be there," he chanted as he took off at a sprint back towards the elementary school.

He reached the back side of the church and paused. The fire truck and the red pickup were still as he'd last seen them. His police car was also right where he'd left it. There was no movement coming from the building. Deciding that noise was now second to survival, he cleared the safety on his shotgun and jacked a round into the chamber.

He was just across Hillcrest and jogging up the gentle hill between the road and the drop-off lane when he heard another scream. It was shrill and impossible to tell if it belonged to a man or woman. He fought the urge to charge in blindly; knowing that to do so might end up with his running into something he was not ready to handle. That would punch his ticket in a hurry.

"You can't be squeamish about this one, Stephen," he told himself as he approached the covered walkway that led to the entrance of the main entry hallway.

The door was still open and he paused just inside and listened carefully. A low moan could be heard to his left and up the first hall on the right. He hugged the wall opposite the hall he could hear noise coming from and moved slow, leaning forward enough to try and get a look. At last, he reached a point where he could see.

On the floor was one of the firemen. He'd taken off his jacket for some reason, and it was tossed to the side against the wall next to a pushcart with a large, plastic trashcan on it. There was a broom on the floor just a bit beyond the cart. Kneeling beside a woman in a skirt was a man in dark gray coveralls.

"Keeshawn," Stephen whispered, instantly recognizing the janitor.

Keeshawn Moore was a forty-seven-year-old African American man who'd been a janitor at the elementary school for over twenty years. He'd been born with severe autism. The one place he felt safe and comfortable had been the elementary school. He was often the first person to arrive and stayed until the last staff member left for the day. During the summer, a few of the teachers rotated and took turns coming to the campus and unlocking the door so that Keeshawn could sweep floors and wash windows whether they needed it or not.

As if he heard his name, the figure crouched on the floor raised its head and twitched around a few times until it found Stephen. Opening his mouth to moan, a piece of something fell out and landed on the linoleum floor with a splat.

As Stephen started down the hall, the body of the fireman began to twitch. Knowing that the sound would be thunderous in this long, empty hallway, Stephen considered trying to just crush the man's head, but when the body of the teacher on the floor began to twitch as well, he dismissed that idea and brought the shotgun to his shoulder.

"I'm so sorry," he whispered as he pulled the trigger.

The top part of Keeshawn Moore's head almost vaporized as the shotgun shell slammed into him at close range. A dark and chunky spray painted the wall behind the zombie as it staggered back and slid down with legs splayed out in front of the corpse with the body somehow coming to rest in a sitting position.

Stephen didn't have time to dwell on such things as he turned to the fireman. He winced as he saw yet another familiar face. He quickly banished the name from his mind and tried to force anonymity on the reanimated corpse with a big chunk ripped from the left side of the neck and a few large chunks torn savagely from the chest where the mangled Liberty Fire Department tee shirt now hung in tatters. The zombie staggered forward two steps and Stephen brought the shotgun up and fired into a face that was only a few inches from the barrel when he pulled the trigger.

He jacked another round and kicked the feet out from under the female teacher. Standing over her, he blinked away the tears that threatened, and pulled the trigger again. The boom was deafening and a dark slurry of brain, bone, and teeth sprayed in an obscene halo on the floor around the little bit that remained of the woman's head.

At last, it was simply too much. Stephen dropped to his knees and vomited. He heaved again and again until there was nothing left in his stomach. When he finally felt that he was done, he wiped his mouth with the sleeve of his shirt and headed for the exit.

His ears were still ringing as he emerged from the front door of the school. A familiar car pulled up and he saw a look of concern on Terri's face as she emerged, appraising him with eyes that knew him better than any other.

"That bad in there?" she said as the two met and embraced.

"Keeshawn." That one word seemed to hang in the air and add a chill to the world.

"Do I dare venture inside?" she finally asked.

"We need to do this and stem the losses before we are too far gone."

"How can it be this bad?" she asked, her face buried in his chest.

84

"People like that CDC woman telling everybody that what they are seeing is a lie. By the time somebody fesses up, I think it will be well past the point of no return." Stephen paused and surveyed their surroundings. He wasn't about to have one of those things creep up on him. "That Kentucky story was over a week ago, and Chief Gilstrap says that he heard something from one of his police buddies in Clemson. When he sent a reply asking for details, the email address came back as not existing and he hasn't heard from the guy since. If my memory serves, I think there was a story in the news about five weeks ago about some city in China being wiped out by a terrible plague. Their government refused international aid or something. This could have been building for weeks. The funny thing is that we have gotten so used to pop-up sicknesses and conspiracy theory loonies that we could have heard a dozen stories telling us there was something going on and we just ignored it."

"That's what I love about you, Stephen," Terri said with a soft chuckle as she pulled away from her husband.

"Oh? What's that?"

"You are just such a ray of human sunshine."

His wife grabbed a pair of handguns from the front seat and handed him his favorite .38. That particular gun had been his first gun. It had been given to him by his daddy for his tenth birthday and just felt like it fit perfect in his hand.

Armed and as ready as they could be, given the circumstances, the pair headed into the school to start notifying the citizens of Liberty about the big meeting. Less than ten seconds after they entered the building, the echo of a handgun being fired sent a handful of birds skyward from one of the many nearby trees.

***

Jamie and Chief Gilstrap stood next to each other in the middle of the high school football field. The stadium bleachers were filled on both sides, people milled about on the track as well as the field itself.

Two fire trucks were parked at either end and over two dozen men with rifles were perched on top of the press box as well as around the perimeter. Chief Gilstrap had been very selective in his choices and given specific instructions as to what to be on the lookout for. Jamie winced at how he had convinced these men of the danger they faced. Apparently Mr. Deese had managed to capture one of the zombies over by the elementary school. It had been little Timmy Darcy.

According to the very brief recounting of the incident that the chief had given, five of the men he'd initially picked had walked away after he put two rounds in the young boy's chest to illustrate his point. She had worked very hard making her mind wipe away the images of that scene that it tried so hard to construct and play.

She looked out at all the people gathered. Some had apparently seen the report from Greenville, but others were absolutely oblivious to what was going on in the world around them. The four large screens, which had been set up by some very enthusiastic members of the high school A/V group, were about to provide a harsh introduction. Even more impressive were the files on the computer of poor Jonathan Patterson.

The chief was eating a lot of self-recrimination about the death of that man's mother. Sophie had been the one to go out and pick up Mildred Patterson's body with a pair of newly deputized bodyguards. When she returned and took care of Jonathan's injuries, he had spoken of some videos that he'd received from a kid over in Japan that he played video games with on occasion.

She had watched them, but it was what was on the last video that might haunt her forever. Apparently Jonathan hadn't seen it yet, because it had caused the man to gasp and then turn away. She had looked over and seen the man clearly trying to fight back tears; then she just as quickly looked away, not wanting to embarrass him by having her witness him cry.

Unfortunately, that left her watching the video. The young boy on it was very clearly emaciated. His eyes were hollow and his lips were cracking to the point that red wisps of blood could be seen to leak from them when he spoke.

He was in a small apartment, and after showing some footage of the massive and catastrophic destruction of what she guessed to be Tokyo, the camera returned to the front door. A jumble of flimsy furniture had been stacked against that door, but the zombies had managed to claw through and create a gaping hole large enough for the occasional face of one of the undead to fill as they worked relentlessly at the barricade to get at the one living person inside.

In the final minutes, after a period where the camera had obviously been shut off to conserve its battery, the boy spoke one final time.

"Jonathan-san, they will be inside soon. I hope you have shared what I sent you, but I will never know. I am afraid there is nobody left alive here. I have not heard a scream in over three days. Mine may be the last one.

"I do not have time to send this. The power keeps going off and on, so I am hoping that somebody may find this and email it to you if power returns, otherwise this will be all for nothing. If they do not act soon, that will be impossible. The power has been off and on for the past two days. It just came back a short time ago, but I do not know if it will last. That is the only thing that gives me hope. Every time that it comes back on, that means to me that there must still be somebody out there trying to survive.

"I have kept a written journal, but my last pen went dry this morning. I had just enough time to write a note that now hangs on my wall above my computer." The image blurred, came to rest on a wrinkled piece of yellow legal paper with something scrawled on it in what must be Japanese, and then back to the boy's face. He flashed a weak smile.

A loud crash caused the boy to flinch and the camera jostled around to show that the door and barricade had finally given way to a horde of undead. The zombies pushed through, some trying to shove past or crawl over each other to get at the boy.

The camera fell to the floor and ended up facing a wall. In some ways, Jamie thought that might have been merciful; however, it also allowed for the imagination to go into overdrive and create its own imagery.

The sounds of whimpering and what, despite it being in another language, was obviously pleading and begging could be heard. There were moans and even some very peculiar sounds that were almost like that of a crying baby. Then came the first howl that turned into a scream of pain. From that point on, the screaming became worse and turned into something that could not be compared to anything that Jamie had ever heard in her life.

The sounds of wet slurping and greedy chewing were present and became even louder as the scream mercifully ended in a wet, gurgling sob. Then a spray of blood painted a section of the wall that had been visible during this last terrible part of the recording in a runny slash. For several seconds, the tape showed the blood as it dripped and ran, accompanied by the nightmarish sounds of zombies feeding.

Then, something apparently kicked the camera and it shut off. The next thing to happen was the surprise. A woman's face came on and filled the screen. She spoke in Japanese and the only recognizable word was "Jonathan-san." So far, nobody had been able to translate, but apparently this person was the one who sent the last email with this file as well as the goodbye email that Jonathan had received.

Jamie shook her head clear and once more turned her attention to the growing crowd. Despite Liberty's small size, when you gathered pretty much every man, woman, and child in one place, it was fairly impressive.

Chief Gilstrap gave her a nudge. "I think this is pretty much it. Go ahead, Mayor Burns."

Jamie stepped up to the microphone and tapped it experimentally. The sound boomed almost like thunder and she jumped back. After quickly composing herself, she stepped up once more.

Faces were all turning her direction. It was as if she could feel the energy from every pair of eyes; it was boring into her soul, causing her heart to flutter and her stomach to twist into knots. She pushed back the sudden urge to pee and then forced a smile onto her face.

"Ladies and gentlemen, thank you all for coming," she began. That sent a ripple through the crowd and then everybody hushed and now focused solely on her. "I don't know any good or decent way to say this, so please forgive me. I am going to be very blunt. Here it goes."

Jamie paused and tried to put together the right string of words to convey what she believed the town of Liberty was facing. She needed to prepare them for what they would see on that video, and she needed to keep everybody calm.

"For those of you who have already seen it on the news, there is something terrible happening. I will share the details with you in just a moment, but first, I wanted to let you know that this is worse than what we are being told on television." That sent another ripple through the crowd. "This morning, I saw with my own eyes…things…things that have no logical explanation. So, before I continue, I want you to watch on one of the screens that we have put up. You need to know that this is not some sort of joke. It is not fake. This is very real. You may want to prepare yourself…and those with small children, now is the time where you may want to go over to the soccer field. A screen has been set up there along with sound so that my address to you all will be shown there after this particular bit of unpleasant business is dealt with. "

Jamie stepped back and Chief Gilstrap got on his radio to help coordinate getting those with children who chose to leave the football stadium over to the soccer field. The fire department had brought in two more of its trucks to that location and a handful of the Liberty Volunteer Fire Department was ready to keep the kids occupied.

Once the first video started, Jamie tried to keep herself busy going over her notes and the things that she had prepared for the speech she would give. She had about an hour between all of the videos being shown and tried to block out the sound. She did okay until that first scream. It was just not like anything that she'd ever heard in her life. It carried not only the horror, but the excruciating agony that must come from being eaten alive.

The skin on her arms pebbled and a twisting feeling deep in her gut was enough to make her almost double over. It seemed to take forever, and a few times she looked up at the crowd almost expecting to find that everybody had left. There was a quiet that should not exist with this many people gathered in one place. There were a few times when she heard a person cry out, and more than a dozen times she heard somebody get sick. When the Greenville footage rolled, she heard even more gasps and cries of "Oh, my God!" coming from the crowd. Yet, through the entire presentation, not one soul left the Liberty High School stadium area.

When it was finally done, Jamie stepped back up to the microphone. All eyes were locked onto her. Many were red-rimmed or still in the act of shedding tears.

"Just before this meeting was called, there was an incident out on the highway. The military was already there and trying to deal with the situation. That tells me that this is not only worse than anybody in charge is saying, but also that it has come to South Carolina. We can't sit here and wait, that has never been the way of the people of this great state. Right or wrong, we have been leaders, not followers.

"I will be returning to city hall after this meeting to start making preparations to secure this town. My first priority is to all of you. Unfortunately, there is simply nothing in the books about how to prepare for what might actually be the zombie apocalypse.

"This might seem ridiculous, but I am asking for any of you

that might be..." Jamie paused, this was the part she had struggled with. She didn't want to alienate the very people that she needed most at this moment. "I am asking for those of you who may have been fans of this sort of thing to come forward. I believe that there are those of you here that are fans of zombie movies, novels, and comic books. Chances are, you have sat around with friends and discussed what you would do in this situation. Right now, I am not lying or over-exaggerating when I say that there are no bad ideas. We will have to come together, and this plan is not going to be conventional in the slightest."

She paused and looked up from her script and notes to see the reactions in the faces of her people. The expressions varied, but the one thing she did not see was a look of disbelief or even the slightest doubt. Despite how fantastic this scenario seemed, she had shown them that it was very real.

The A/V team had managed to come up with a copy of the news report out of Greenville where that one reporter had died. She hadn't asked how because she had tried to find it on the internet right after the station went off the air and come up with absolutely nothing—more proof in her mind that the government did know what was happening, at least to some extent, and were doing their best to hide it from the American people. Seeing this in someplace like Tokyo might be one thing, but to have seen that clip from just up the highway in Greenville was another matter entirely.

"I am going to ask all of you to return home and begin finding things that can be used as weapons. I can confirm that, just as in the movies, a head shot is the only way to put one of these things down. I can also tell you that it seems as if the bite is the way the infection spreads. Less than three hours ago, a spokesperson from the CDC denied that this was possible. You have seen for yourselves that this is very real. We are faced with the possibility of the entire world being wiped out by this. I do not intend for the citizens of Liberty to fall. We will come together and we will stand against this threat."

A single cheer set off an explosion of echoing cheers and a

wave of applause. Jamie waited for it to settle down before continuing.

"When you return home, besides weapons, I think that it is important that you gather all food and be prepared to ration. To prevent a run on the grocery store or any of the markets, I will be creating a team that will head to all locations in Liberty to get full inventories. Also, those of you with gardens, I am going to ask you to help your neighbors. The delivery trucks are probably not coming from this point on and so we need to plan as if we are totally cut off from the rest of the world…and that may actually be the case."

"Also, despite our holding this meeting in the stadium with a boost from the speakers you see mounted on the stands around you, we believe that sound might be something that attracts these things. That is why you see the armed presence around our perimeter. Also, we will have roving patrols and if you feel like you can be a help in that department, we could really use your help."

Once again Jamie paused. She hoped that this message was sinking in. She needed everybody to be on the same page. She'd already called the manager over at Ingles Markets. That conversation had been much easier than she had anticipated. Of course it helped that the manager had been watching the news in his office just before her call. He'd seen the situation in Greenville. He had already closed the doors and said he would ask for all of his employees to return immediately after the mayor's speech to help with writing down every single item in the store.

She had no idea how long the power grid would hold, but the window was probably a lot closer to being closed than she would like. They needed to do whatever they could to find a way to extend the life of perishables.

"I know all of you probably have questions, and I wish that I could take the time to address them all, but I think we need to start acting now. Every minute is precious, and we won't have nearly as long as we think before things go very badly. We need to come together and be a source of strength for each other. I am afraid that the trials ahead will push us beyond what we ever dreamed possible. No matter your beliefs, I will pray for us all, and ask for God to watch over us in what will very definitely be our greatest hours of need."

Another even more thunderous round of applause followed Jamie as she stepped away from the microphone. Chief Gilstrap was waiting for her and fell in by her side as they walked to the car. Mr. Deese and his wife stood beside it. The four climbed in, Jamie and the chief sitting in front.

She waited for the comments, questions, or perhaps criticism that she had convinced herself would follow. None came. The foursome drove to city hall in silence. Later, she would reflect on that drive and cherish those few moments of peace and quiet. It would be a long time before she had any of those sorts of moments again.

***

"I know what you said about no bad ideas, but that kid is barely fourteen years old," Chief Gilstrap argued.

Jamie sat back in her chair and regarded the man over steepled fingers that she rested against her bottom lip. They'd been at this all day. She was exhausted. If she looked anything close to how the chief looked, then she had to be an absolute fright. Just that thought made her brush her hands through her hair.

"He has some very good ideas," Jamie said as she stretched and cast a longing glance at her empty coffee cup. "Sure, a few of them are a bit silly, but he does make one very good point that all of the adults have missed up to this juncture." She arched an eyebrow at the chief and then spun her chair to look at the map of Liberty that was tacked up onto the wall.

Chief Gilstrap moved up and leaned against the edge of her desk as he studied the map as well. He traced his finger along a route and then pursed his lips.

"It's not a bad idea," Jamie insisted.

"Tell that to the people who have to leave their homes."

"It isn't going to happen overnight. But something tells me that the next time some of those things show up, folks are going to—" She didn't get to finish her sentence before the door flew open and a handful of heavily armed men entered.

"We have a bunch of them coming in from the woods just past the baseball field at the elementary school." The man who spoke had his left arm wrapped in a heavy bandage.

"What happened to your arm?" the chief asked, sounding much calmer than Jamie felt.

"Somebody…" The wounded man let that word hang in the air. One of the other men dropped his head; the others sort of took an involuntary step back as they distanced themselves from the apparent offender. "Somebody was a bit trigger happy."

"Mayor Burns, I think that you might need to issue a warning to the citizens about guns being a last resort," Chief Gilstrap said as he glared at the man who continued to stare at the floor. "Scared citizens and an enemy that pretty much looks like one of us…hell, used to be one of us…that is a lethal mix waiting for bad things to happen."

"And I guess that moves up the list of things we need to figure out," Jamie replied with a laugh that sounded a bit too sarcastic than she'd intended. "We are already unable to use our phones. They may come back, and there may still be periods where we get spotty service, but we obviously can't count on them. We need to be able to communicate with each other."

"Well, maybe one of those folks out in the lobby has the answer," Chief Gilstrap said as he started herding the group of men back out the door. "You are going to have to deal with this on your own for a while. I am going to head over to the elementary school and see to this new problem."

The door shut and Jamie fell back in her chair, sighing heavily. She'd only been out of her office a couple of times in the past ten hours; zombie apocalypse or not, a girl had to answer nature's call when it came.

"Howard, why did you have to go and die?" She looked over at the picture on the wall of the man who she had replaced. Getting out of her chair, she walked over to the photo and brushed it with her fingers. "I bet you would have a plan in motion and already be at home sitting down to dinner with the wife." She wiped the tears that welled up and flowed over the cusps of her eyes. "I don't think I can do this...I don't think I am the right one to lead these people through a zombie apocalypse."

"I bet you never thought those words would come out of your mouth," a friendly voice said from behind her.

Jamie turned to see Sophie standing just inside the door. Thankfully, she had shut it behind her after coming in.

"How much did you hear," Jamie sniffed, wiping away the last of the tears.

"Enough to know that you are just as scared as the rest of us." Sophie crossed the room and hugged Jamie. The two women stood that way for a moment. At last, Sophie broke the silence. "You are doing fine. You already have the entire town mobilizing."

"And apparently shooting each other." Jamie could not hold back a bitter laugh. "The zombies won't have to kill us, we'll take care of it for them."

"This town needs somebody to rely on. They need a leader that will keep them moving and doing everything they can to survive." Sophie took a step back and held Jamie at arm's length.

"Maybe the chief is better—"

"No!" Sophie snapped. "He is a great person, an excellent police officer. But this town needs somebody that can listen, plan, and then encourage others to act. I heard what that last boy proposed, he was talking about it before he came in to pitch it to you. I also heard the chief shutting it down before the poor boy was out your door. He isn't going to listen to anything off the wall, and I believe that it is just that sort of idea that will save us."

"You really think I can do this?" Jamie asked meekly, but

feeling a bit of encouragement flow into her and refresh the resolve she felt in regards to saving the town.

"I know you can."

"Thanks, Sophie." Jamie returned to her desk and took a seat, adjusting herself so that she was sitting up straight with her hands folded in front of her. "Go ahead and send in the next one."

"Right away, Mayor Burns."

6

From Bad to Worse

"Please, mama, help me, for the love of God!" Jared Crawford's voice went higher and higher as he begged for a mercy that would not come.

Chief Adam Gilstrap would have ended the man's suffering if he weren't up against the ropes himself at the moment—figuratively speaking of course. Ducking under the outstretched arms of the zombie in a soldier's uniform, he kicked out sideways and took at least a little bit of pleasure in the satisfying crack as the knee buckled inwards in a direction that it was most certainly never designed to go.

On the plus side, it dropped the zombie to the ground as its leg would no longer hold the weight of the body. On the negative, now the damned thing was crawling towards him and trying desperately to get its groping fingers on the chief's ankles. He swung the machete sideways and buried it in the side of the head of the female zombie that was just about to lean down and take a bite out of his forearm. Jerking free of her slacking grip, he stomped down on the hand that was about to grab his left ankle and then jerked his machete free of the woman's head as the corpse fell to the ground—all in a fluid series of motions.

He shoved the closest zombie to him into the trio that was right on its heels. That did not quite have the effect he'd hoped for and only the one that had been shoved and the scrawny looking girl-zombie almost directly behind it were knocked back enough to make a difference. Still, it was enough for him to move sideways past the fallen tree that had been between him and poor Jared Crawford.

The man was no longer screaming, and his legs were barely twitching when Chief Gilstrap approached from behind the five zombies that were all on the ground, ripping bits and pieces of the poor young man from his middle. One of the zombies that was actually facing in the chief's direction lifted its head to regard the approaching intruder. It apparently did not feel the need to stop shoving what looked like a long strand of misshapen sausages into its mouth and bite down. The brownish sludge that trickled down its chin as it chewed told the chief that those were likely Jared's intestines.

"So nasty," he breathed as he moved in behind the trio that had their back to him.

Using his belt knife, he drove the point of the blade upwards at the base of the skull, yanked free, and repeated the move as quickly as possible. He reached across and stuck that same knife into the open and emotionless left eye of the intestine muncher and then finished the fifth and final zombie in the same way.

Looking down, he saw the ruins of Jared Crawford's body. The young man's huge belly had been ripped open and blood was everywhere along with a variety of what remained of Jared's insides. Jared had been the fire house Santa for the past four years, stepping in on short notice and to honor his dad who had passed away suddenly from a heart attack just days before the Christmas holiday. All he'd had to do was get a can of that special paint for spraying his hair and beard silver. He'd been a good boy with an easy smile and a kind word for anybody he passed on the street.

Kneeling beside Jared, Chief Gilstrap drove the tip of his knife into the boyishly youthful face before one of those crystal blue eyes opened to reveal that horrible film and the black tracers. He looked up as footsteps approached and winced when he saw the third zombie child he'd encountered during this hellish melee.

The child had just stepped past a tree and spotted him. Once again the chief had a difficult time reconciling the behavior that he was witnessing. Unlike any regular zombie (a phrase that would strike him as funny if he had the chance to think about it), the children seemed to hesitate. Once, a little girl of perhaps nine or ten had actually tried to turn around and move away from him. There was something peculiar about the child version of the zombie, but for the life of him, he could not understand it. Just then, two more of the adult zombies stepped up beside the child and pushed past. As soon as they spotted him, he was out of time to observe. It was time to return to the gruesome business of killing.

He checked to his left and saw three more of his men locked in battle with at least a dozen more of the things, but it was now looking as if this might be the last of this little mob or herd or what-the-hell ever you called a large group of zombies. To the right, he saw a lone straggler. He considered letting it go until the larger group was dealt with and quickly vetoed that idea. If he lost track of it and it got into town, anybody hurt or killed by that thing would add to the weight already on his shoulders.

After one more glance to ensure that none of the other men were about to suffer Jared's fate, he stalked over to the zombie, machete at the ready. As he approached, something started to nag at him. Two steps later, he froze in his tracks.

He recognized this zombie. At least he was pretty certain that he recognized him. Moving around so that he could get in front of it, he got a better look that confirmed his suspicions.

"Son of a bitch," he breathed.

Now he was certain of this man's identity. He was staring at the zombie incarnation of Deputy Mark Reilly. He knew the man from just up the road in nearby Pickens. In fact, one of the first things he was planning on doing was trying to reach the Pickens Police Department and warn them.

And now…

"This is worse than we thought," a voice said from behind Chief Gilstrap as he was just about to end the zombie version of the Pickens deputy.

He turned to see his men coming through the woods. All of them were splattered with the blood and gore of the battle. He finished the grim task of putting down Deputy Reilly and was wiping off his blade when something about one of the men caught his eye.

"Jeff, can you step over here," the chief said, doing his best not to sound like he was about to explode from the frustration that was building exponentially with every new horrible discovery.

The man edged past the others looking both confused and concerned. As soon as he stepped into a beam of sun that was fighting to get through the canopy of trees overhead, Chief Adam Gilstrap winced as if he'd just been punched in the gut.

"Did you get bit by one of them things?" the chief asked, his eyes scanning the man for any sign of an injury. Unfortunately, the man was splattered with so much blood that it would be impossible to tell.

"No, sir," the man replied. He obviously picked up on the concern in the chief's voice because he began searching himself frantically.

"Just take it easy, son." Chief Gilstrap reached into his years of training and dialed in the voice he used when talking to an accident victim. "I just want you to be still. We'll get you back to town and get you cleaned up. Then we—"

"Jeff's one of them things!" Isaiah Newkirk practically screamed as he backed away from Jeff while tugging at the field machete that he had been using.

"Shut up, Isaiah!" the chief barked. "You hear any of them things trying to talk?" The young man dropped his head sheepishly and shook it.

"Why do you think I've been bit?" Jeff asked. He took a

100

step closer to the chief who moved a step back out of sheer reflex before he could catch himself.

"Your eyes, man!" Isaiah blurted. "They got them squiggly black lines in 'em just like them monsters."

"I said shut up, Isaiah!" Chief Gilstrap barked, spinning on the younger man.

He was immediately hit with a thought that gave his conscience a pang of guilt. In that instant, he'd wished it was this stupid, loudmouthed kid who was showing signs of being infected instead of a man like Jeff. His reasons were perhaps justifiable, but that did not make him feel any better about such thoughts.

Jeff Tucker was a family man with a wife and three kids. He was a regular fixture at various town events and an assistant coach for the Liberty Red Devils varsity football team. He was a leader for the men's group at his church and even volunteered during the holidays to deliver food and gift baskets to those who were having tough times.

Isaiah Newkirk was nineteen if the chief's memory served him. He wasn't a bad kid, and hadn't been in any real trouble that the chief could recall, but he would take one Jeff Tucker for every ten Isaiah Newkirks right about now.

"Let's just get back to town and have somebody take a look at you. It's probably nothing." Chief Adam Gilstrap swallowed the bitterness of that lie and felt his stomach churn. He thought he might be telling a lot of those sorts of lies in the next few days.

The men waded out of the woods and emerged on the back side of the elementary school. Looking up at the sky, Chief Gilstrap guessed it to be around dinner time. The shadows were getting long and a damp chill was settling in the air. Clouds rolling in from the east looked to be carrying a lot of rain. It was going to be a long night.

Like last night wasn't? a voice in his head mocked.

By the time they had reached the parking lot beside the school where they had all parked, he'd made another decision.

He altered his course and put a hand on Jeff Tucker's shoulder. "Why don't you ride with me? I want to take you to get looked at."

"Ah, man, can't it wait?" Jeff groaned. "Sheila and the kids ain't seen me since this morning. That town meeting probably has her scared out of her wits. Let me at least stop in for a minute and see them."

"I can't do it, Jeff." Reaching over and opening the back door of the cruiser, he gave a nod. "This is for the best. We can see a doctor and then I will take you home personally."

Jeff glanced down at the back door that was open and waiting. He looked back up at the chief with eyes that almost appeared to grow worse in the span of a few seconds. There was a hint of sadness that warred with the fear that had pushed through.

"You're a lousy liar, Adam. That's why we always invite you to card night." Without another word, Jeff ducked into the back of the police cruiser and pulled the door shut.

Chief Adam Gilstrap looked around. Liberty, South Carolina was a quiet town. Sure, there were dust ups and a few bad eggs, but for the most part, this was a good town full of good people. There had been lean times and plentiful; but what lay ahead was something so beyond belief that he wondered how these everyday men and women would fare. This would be a test that none of them had studied for, and he was certain there would be failures.

He looked down at the bandage on his hand. Since nobody had reacted, he was certain that his eyes had not changed. But if his hadn't and Jeff's had, what did that mean? How would they know if Jeff was infected? How would he know that he wasn't?

"Something tells me this is going to go from bad to worse in a real quick hurry."

The chief opened his door and climbed in the car. He turned the key and his radio went crazy. He turned it down so that he could hopefully get a better grasp on what the voice on the other

102

end was screaming.

"...just tell my wife that I love her, and that I'm sorry!" a voice said through what sounded like clenched teeth.

**

Clifton Martin pulled the phone from his ear and looked at it with a scowl. It had taken him almost an hour to get his call to go through. He knew that Sophie was going to be worried sick.

If she'd seen even a fraction of what he'd already witnessed, she would be absolutely terrified. But if she had gone down to the highway, then perhaps she knew more than he was giving her credit for. She was a smart woman, and despite the improbability of what was happening, she would not take long to connect the dots and figure things out for what they were.

When there's no more room in Hell, the dead will walk the earth. That classic movie line echoed in his head as Clifton "Cliff" Lawrence stuffed the phone belonging to his friend and fellow paramedic partner Terry Gibbs into his back pocket and took one more look around.

He was outside the emergency room entrance to Pickens Memorial Hospital. The sun was just coming up and he knew it was going to be a long day. He tipped the paper cup to his mouth and downed the last of the absolutely repugnant hospital vending machine coffee and grimaced.

A line of military trucks were filing into the parking area. Already a series of white tents were up and at least a dozen more were in various stages. The past several people to arrive at the emergency admittance area with bites or scratches had been sent over to the tents. That was not what was troubling Cliff. His eyes drifted over to the long, dark green tents with the big trailers in a row behind it.

In the past ten minutes while he'd been outside trying to get his call to go through, he'd seen at least twenty people carted into that long tent. They had the sheets all the way up in that universal sign for being dead, yet he kept seeing movement at the far end that looked like people being escorted to the trailers by men in full HAZMAT gear. The ones being escorted were being goaded along at the end of those types of poles that you see alligator wranglers use.

With a sigh, he headed into the hospital. It was almost like hitting a wall as the sounds of people crying and moaning and screaming came in a massive wave. The waiting room was absolute chaos. It was unlike anything that he'd ever witnessed in his life. This sort of thing might happen in the big cities, but in someplace rural like Pickens, South Carolina, that was just not the case.

A soldier in one of the doorways saw him enter and waved him over. "You need to stay inside from this point on, sir," the fresh-faced young man said.

"I told the captain that I needed to let my wife know I was okay. He gave me the go ahead to go outside and use the phone."

"Yes, sir," the soldier said curtly. "And now the new order is that all personnel are to remain indoors until further notice. There is a concern that this might be spread through airborne vectors."

Cliff knew a line of bull when he heard it. There was absolutely no indication that whatever was causing this bizarre illness could be spread in such a manner. Somebody was reaching, fabricating an excuse to keep them inside. That meant they were starting to get scared. *They damn well should be*, he thought as he simply gave the soldier his most polite smile and nod before edging past and entering the emergency room.

If the lobby was chaos, then this was perhaps a window cracked open to the pits of hell. There were doctors and nurses flitting about from one sectioned-off patient to the next. Many were splattered with blood and swapping out of their dirty gear and into fresh stuff with a speed of a super model backstage at a fashion show.

The orderlies were doing their best to keep the supplies of fresh gloves, scrubs, and other assorted necessities as well

104

stocked as possible, but it was a losing cause. Shouts for more gauze, gloves, alcohol and any other number of items echoed off the walls in a steady thunder. Interspersed under this madness were the sounds of heart monitors. Some were beeping, but others were sounding the "flatline" alarm.

People were dying faster than the soldiers could wheel them out. Almost on cue, two soldiers in protective gear hurried past with a gurney. The body was fully covered with a sheet. The pristine white linen was marred by a huge, dark red stain near the left shoulder.

"All I need now is Sarah Polley in a set of scrubs," Cliff whispered as he stopped at the first curtained patient area on his left and glanced at the chart sticking out of the fiberglass holder with the corresponding number. He scanned the assessment.

Patient reports being bitten by wife...

He grabbed the next one.

...injuries on left forearm consistent with human bite...

The next.

...three separate sets of teeth marks consistent with patient's account of having been bitten by three young women...

One after another they all told pretty much the same story. This was way too similar to the zombie movies that he'd seen over the years. People were being bitten by others and then becoming drastically ill, dying, sitting back up, and continuing the cycle. Add that to what he had seen with his own two eyes in the ambulance, and he was almost certain that he knew what was going on—despite how improbable or fantastic it might seem.

This had all the makings of the zombie apocalypse. So why in the hell was he still here in the hospital? Why wasn't he hauling ass for home to be with his wife and son? Did he think he was going to be the one person to come up with some magical answer and solve this fantastic problem, set the world right, and then become a global hero?

Heroes die way too often in these little horror stories, he thought as he took a more sharp-eyed look around the emergency room. And that brought up another thought: he always hated

105

when some father or parental type decided that it is more important that they try to help everybody else to the exclusion of his own family. He had always called bullshit on those moments.

"No dad is just going to bail on his wife or kid to go help a bunch of strangers because he wants to set a good example in the middle of the freaking apocalypse," he would argue.

And yet, here he was. In the emergency room of the hospital getting ready to wade in and hold clamps for people that were going to either bleed out or just up and die only to reanimate in a few minutes and attack anything around them that was still living.

He glanced at the door that led back to the waiting room. That was a bust. The soldier he'd had brief words with about being outside the hospital was standing there with his rifle slung over his shoulder and hands on his hips like he was something important.

Turning away from the curtain, he headed past the nurse's station and ducked around a corner that led to the x-ray and ultrasound area. He was amazed when he discovered gurneys lined up and down the right-hand wall. All of them had occupants with visible wounds in a variety of places.

"Hey, mister?" a scared voice called him from the second gurney that he passed. Looking down, he saw a girl who looked to be around ten years old.

Cliff stopped. The girl was strapped down to her gurney and had two very nasty bites on her left shoulder and right forearm that had been cleaned and bandaged. However, there was something else about her that grabbed his attention. The girl's eyes were shot full of black tracers that gave her a sinister appearance despite her being just a child.

He took a step towards the girl when a scream from back in the direction of the emergency room snapped his head around. A moment later, that scream was joined by others. The sounds of pain were nothing new to Cliff. His years as a paramedic had helped him become accustomed to such things but this was different. The person—*people*, he corrected himself as other such screams begin to join the first—doing the screaming were expressing a level of pain he'd never heard in all his time in the field.

He looked back down at the girl and staggered back a step. Her eyes had shut and she was now coated in a greasy looking sweat that had her blond hair stuck to her forehead. Her breathing was coming in short pants and the pallor of her skin was unhealthy and waxy.

"I have to get home," he stated out loud more to convince his own feet to start moving.

Stepping his speed up to a jog, Cliff Martin wove through the windowless maze of this section of the hospital and came to one of the other lobbies. He skidded to a stop when he saw a pair of military trucks parked right outside the series of doors that opened to an area that was curiously empty.

This was the general reception lobby of the hospital and would never be empty during normal weekday working hours. Of course it wasn't technically empty at the moment. He counted ten soldiers stationed in the open lobby. A pair of them were heading his way and he ducked back down the corridor he'd come down to reach this point.

Stopping at the stairwell, he gave the door a tug and sighed in relief when it opened. He stepped inside and started up. He was now on pretty unfamiliar ground. Sure, he'd come to this hospital countless times, but he certainly had not been wandering the corridors.

When he reached the second floor, he opened the door and stepped into a long hall that was lined with rooms on either side. He spied the nurse's station and felt his heart sink. Two soldiers were already there and one of them had looked up when he opened the door. There was no chance for him to get away without being seen.

"You aren't supposed to be up here," one of the men said, getting up from his seat behind the desk.

"I was—" he began, only to be cut off.

"Save it, pal. You and I both know that whatever was about to come out of your mouth was a big lie."

Cliff raised his hands when both soldiers brought up their rifles and aimed them in his direction. As they started toward him, he noticed that one of the men had an arm that was bandaged up. His heart came up to his throat when the man came close enough that Cliff could actually see the man's eyes clearly. They were just like the girl's downstairs.

"Were you bit?" Cliff asked trying to keep his voice as calm as possible.

"Barely broke the skin," the soldier scoffed.

"You may still be infected," Cliff pointed out. "How long ago, and are you feeling okay?"

"It was a couple of hours ago. Like I said, barely broke the skin. Damned thing got my hand as I was changing out magazines."

"So you have already been fighting with these people?" Cliff asked

"Stow that comment, private!" the other soldier barked before the private could answer. "This is still need-to-know material."

"Why would you think I am infected?" the private's voice showed just a hint of concern. His companion and apparent supervisor moved around in front of the agitated private, effectively turning his back on Cliff.

"I said stow it, Private Fenton!" The man put a finger under the other soldier's chin and started to say something else when he apparently noticed what Cliff had been pointing out. "Our orders...Jesus Christ! Okay, I need you to set down your weapon and hand me your radio."

"What? Why?" the private practically whined. He took a step back and started to shift his weapon.

There was a very loud report as the other soldier acted first and shot the private in the forehead. From his angle, the entire scene played out in a surreal slowness as he saw the flash from the muzzle, a sudden dark circle appearing just a bit off center of the private's forehead, and then an explosion of brain, bone, and blood as the bullet exited the back of the private's skull in an explosion of gore.

Cliff started back a few steps, but the remaining soldier spun on him with his weapon raised. "Don't you move an inch."

"Look, I don't want any trouble. I don't know anything, I didn't see anything, I—" Cliff babbled, his mouth suddenly dry and his need to urinate growing by the second.

"Shut up!" the soldier barked, jabbing his gun forward for emphasis. "And you could tell anybody you damn well please, but it wouldn't matter. We have standing orders to put down anybody we encounter that *might* be infected."

Cliff heard the emphasis on the word 'might' and felt his stomach tighten. If he wasn't careful, he would have a very unfortunate accident. Only, at the moment, that was way down on his list of things to be worried about. The barrel of the gun pointed at him seemed like the mouth of a cannon.

Do cannons have mouths? he wondered briefly. That thought filled his mind with the most peculiar images, and now he started to laugh. He was pretty sure that his sanity was cracking under the pressure and he was losing his mind.

The soldier cocked his head to the side as he regarded Clifton Martin. "You think this shit is funny?"

"Not at all," Cliff managed as he struggled to get his hysteria under control. "I think we are screwed seven ways to Sunday. My question to you is how long are you going to just follow orders blindly. You have to be seeing what is going on. Hell, you probably know better than me."

The soldier considered Cliff's words for a moment and then looked around like he expected somebody would suddenly burst onto the scene and catch him doing something he shouldn't. He lowered his weapon.

"You aren't a doctor." That was a statement, not a question. "You a medic or something?"

Cliff glanced down and realized that he had taken off his

jacket at some point. His light blue shirt and dark pants lacked any sort of patch. He'd been meaning to put them on his new shirts, but he'd been in a hurry when he left earlier this morning and had grabbed what was clean without realizing that he was technically out of uniform.

"I'm a paramedic from Liberty," Cliff said. "My partner and I had just transported a girl. She coded on the trip and then sat up. She got a bite out of my partner before we could restrain her. They took both of them as soon as we arrived."

"Then you won't ever see them again," the soldier said flatly. "Nobody has come out of quarantine in any of the locations that I have been in contact with over the past few days."

"Past few days?" Cliff shouted and then continued in a volume closer to normal after getting a grip on himself. "You mean this has been going on for a while and nobody is hearing anything about it? How the hell is that possible?"

"Since Kentucky, the orders have been for us to move fast and leave nothing behind. The plan is to make a statement when we get this under control."

"I don't think that is going to happen."

"You have no idea," the soldier said with a sadness that seemed like it was more of a thought that was mistakenly revealed out loud.

"It's that bad?" Cliff gasped.

"Worse…way worse. Word just came in few days ago that we have lost all contact with Japan."

"You mean like our embassy?"

"No." The soldier looked Cliff in the eyes and his lips pressed tight as if the words themselves were painful. "I mean the entire country."

"That's not possible."

Cliff had always been quick to dismiss conspiracy theory nuts. He'd actually started boycotting The History Channel when it started showing a series of UFO and ghost hunting programs. Maybe a channel like SyFy could get away with that sort of thing, but when he turned on The History Channel, he wanted...well...he wanted history. *Real* history.

"Oh, the façade doesn't have much longer before it shatters. You can only put your finger in so many holes before the dam gives way and the waters crash through. Rumor has it that a Special Forces team has been dispatched to Ohio to get the president's daughter."

Cliff realized that he had staggered back and ended up sitting in one of the chairs against the wall for people to use as they waited for prescriptions. His head popped up and he looked to the right, past the dead body sprawled on the floor in a pool of blood that almost looked black on the dark blue tile. The sign on the wall with the arrow almost grew before his eyes. If this was everything that he believed it could become, then...

"Are you going to shoot me?" Cliff got up and took a step towards the soldier.

The man seemed to consider it, and then he slung his rifle over his shoulder. "You got any ideas?"

"For starters, we need to get away from this hospital. I give it less than an hour before it becomes a place of nightmares."

"A bit dramatic, don'tcha think?"

"Considering what is happening and how exponentially fast it will grow? Nope. I think I am about as cool and calm as I can be."

"Okay, so how do you think you are going to get out of here?" The soldier walked to the big floor-to-ceiling windows that looked out onto the large parking lot below. "Looks to me like the place is pretty well secured."

"The tents!" Cliff finally blurted after thinking it over. He glanced over at the body on the floor. "If we put your friend there on a gurney and wheel him to the quarantine tents. You can be like my escort. Once we get there, I am sure we can slip out and duck into the woods."

"You're dreaming, pal. The tents are where the security is the highest."

Cliff considered that statement. He looked outside as well

111

and saw all the trucks that were parked around the outer edges of the parking lot. There had to be at least two hundred soldiers jogging back and forth or setting up what they probably considered a secure perimeter.

After a moment, an idea came. It was a terrible idea. It would be risky, but it was also perhaps his best chance to get out of this place alive. He wasn't sure that the soldier would go along with it, but Cliff was a realist. The movies might always offer some sort of way to sneak out, or perhaps the guy playing his part might be a master of martial arts and be able to karate chop his way out of this place. Clifton Martin was none of those things. And he couldn't outrun a bullet. He had no choice but to share his plan and hope that this soldier would come along. It was the only way he saw that would offer him even the slightest chance of seeing his wife Sophie and their son Lawrence again.

As he laid out his idea, Cliff saw reluctance and skepticism slowly turn to hope and enthusiasm. It was going to be risky, and the easiest part would be the first part. After that, it was going to be a roll of the dice.

"I never even asked your name," the soldier finally said as the two men opened the door to a small custodial store room full of cleaning supplies.

"Clifton Martin, but my friends call me Cliff, so I guess you can too," he tried to joke. The soldier considered the statement for a moment and then gave a shrug. "And you, how about your name."

"George Hoyle." The soldier glanced down at the insignia on his collar and then sighed. "Just got my promotion to sergeant, but I doubt that will be worth a damn in a few days."

"Under the circumstances, you may be more valuable than you believe."

"Says the guy with medical training," George snorted.

"If this goes as bad as it's looking, you better believe that order and everything that has held us together will decay and crumble. A man who knows how to think with a tactical mind is going to be pretty valuable if we have to start defending ourselves from raiders, looters…and worse."

"You make it sound like we're gonna end up living out some sorta *Road Warriors* scenario," George chuckled as he settled down on the floor with his back against the inward opening door.

"Actually, I think it will be worse than any movie could hope to portray. Hollywood had to worry about offending people and putting butts in the seats. I don't know if you've been paying attention to the news, but there are some sick bastards out there." Cliff couldn't help but shudder.

"I got news for ya, pal," George said with a grimace as he closed his eyes and did his best to ignore the screams that were now starting to grow in frequency and intensity. "They've always been out there. We just hear about them more because somebody decided that more folks would stay tuned in to the news if they knew a terrible story was coming up after a commercial break."

Cliff winced as another scream tore from somebody's throat as they begged for anybody to help. He reached over and switched off the light. Sitting down, he wondered if maybe he wasn't much better than some of those horrible people. Sure, he wasn't out there victimizing others, but he wasn't lifting a finger to help those who so obviously needed it.

***

"…here at World Wide News have just been given the following statement from the White House."

The person behind the desk had the haggard look of a man who'd been up for several hours and not seen a razor in a day or two. His button-up shirt was open at the collar and the tie had been pulled loose. He leaned forward as if he might be having trouble seeing the teleprompter.

"A state of martial law has been called for by the president and is now being approved by Congress. State officials will be given instructions as soon as the vote, which is expected to be approved with almost no opposition, is complete. Until then, residents are now urged to remain home unless you or a loved one has been injured by a person showing the most commonly reported signs of infection which we will keep up on the right hand side of the screen for reference. You are to bring them to the nearest local emergency room or mobile military medical unit. Several such locations have been set up and your local stations should have a list of these places. Do not attempt to care for the injured person by yourself. The later stages of infection are the most dangerous. This is the time when the person infected may lash out or attack friends and loved ones. It is also when the chance for infection is apparently greatest. The president still intends to address the nation this evening and give a statement on actions being taken and how best to avoid becoming infected."

The newsman sat back in his chair and rubbed at his eyes. A look of fear crossed his face as he glanced to one side for just a moment.

"Fine, I'm reading it, just relax," he muttered and then sat up straight again, doing his best to look professional, but the camera had zoomed in tight and a bead of sweat could be seen trickling down from his left temple.

"Due to such a high volume of calls, networks across the country have overloaded, and as you may have noticed, there is almost no cell or landline service. You are asked to refrain from using these services while repairs are being made and service is being restored.

"If you are in need of help, or if a member of your family has possibly been exposed to this infection and you are unable to reach one of the emergency shelters or medical centers, you are asked to hang a sheet in your front window. That will alert the patrols in your area of your need for assistance and they will render aid as soon as possible.

"Additionally, due to the high volume of individuals affected by this outbreak, area power companies are operating with skeleton crews in many cases, so you are asked to minimize your power consumption. These measures are temporary, but your cooperation will help as civil leaders strive to get things back to normal as soon as possible."

The reporter once again looked off camera. He leaned over as if trying to hear something and then pushed back from the desk and walked off camera leaving a wall of monitors behind him that normally played a variety of field clips, but now were strangely blank except for the test pattern. There was a pause as the cable news network's logo filled the screen and then the message was repeated where it would run on a loop for the next hour.

Dead: Snapshot—Liberty, South Carolina

7

Cliff

Cliff's head jerked back as he came awake with a start. It banged against the wall with a dull thud and he winced, his hand coming up to rub the spot.

"Welcome back," a voice whispered in the darkness.

It took him a minute to catch himself up, but slowly it all came back to Clifton Martin. He recalled the girl that had died in transit and then sat up and bit his partner Terry Gibbs, the apparent military takeover of the hospital and how Terry had been sent to a quarantine area, his decision to try and help in the chaotic emergency room and the much-too-late realization that it was an exercise in futility. Then he'd met Sergeant George Hoyle; a soldier who had not taken much convincing to abandon his post as the sounds of screams began to echo through the hospital.

That felt as if it had been so long ago. At one point, he remembered hearing screams coming from what sounded like right outside the door of the janitor's closet where they had hidden. He forced down the pangs of guilt over simply hiding out as the zombies overwhelmed the people in the hospital. But then he reminded himself that it was freaking zombies for crying out loud. He knew how this story was going to end and had decided to try and give himself a chance at getting back to his wife and son.

"You snore, by the way," George Hoyle quipped. "I had to reach over and plug your nose twice. I was afraid you would bring those things down on us."

"What time is it?" Cliff asked, his voice a bit scratchy. He needed water.

A tiny glow that seemed incredibly bright in the relative darkness flashed for a moment as George checked the watch on his wrist. "Almost eighteen hundred hours."

"You think it's safe for us to try and make our way out of here?" Cliff pushed himself up to his feet and stretched as much as he was able in the confined space.

"I haven't heard any screams or shooting in a few hours," George yawned as he made it to his feet as well. "There were a couple of them things pawing at our door a while ago, but they eventually went away. Which brings me to a point, you don't just go to sleep. You freaking die. I swear to God, a bomb could have gone off outside the door and I doubt that you would have budged."

"Remind me to tell you about the time I apparently slept through my mom and dad kicking in the front door because they were locked out and I slept through their banging on it, ringing the bell, yelling until they were hoarse."

"How big was your house?" George said with a chuckle.

"Not that big, but I was asleep on the living room floor about eight or so feet from the door, so it could have been a mansion, that doesn't really affect the outcome."

"More good information to have," George whispered as he opened the door just enough to let in a sliver of light. After he paused and was apparently happy that there was nothing that posed an immediate threat, he opened the door the rest of the way to reveal a lobby that now looked more like the killing floor of a slaughter house than a hospital waiting area.

There had been an unpleasant odor that, up to this point, Cliff had tried to dismiss as being perhaps something that one or both of them had gotten splattered with or stepped in from earlier, but when a wave of it rolled in through the open door causing both men to gag and cover their mouths and noses, he knew better. He'd been around his fair share of dead bodies. Heck, he'd even been on the scene of a lady that had apparently died and remained undiscovered for a few days until a friend made the awful discovery. None of that was anything like this. He could not recall anything in his life that could even remotely compare…except maybe the hint of it that he got when he was driving the ambulance to the hospital and his partner had called out that the girl in the back that coded was trying to sit up.

"Holy…" George's words died in his throat as two figures stumbled in from the hallway to their left. Both were wearing army uniforms.

"That is the way I came from. The ER is that way. Maybe we could—" Cliff's suggestion was cut off as three more came in from the right.

This group looked like one doctor and two patients. His eyes could not tear away from the doctor who looked as if perhaps he'd been leaning down close to one of the undead when it lunged and caught him. His entire nose was gone, leaving a hideous hole and a face that was a mask of blackening blood.

"Well, I didn't figure we'd get out of here easy," George finally said as he unslung his rifle and brought it up to his shoulder.

Cliff saw the action and reached over, slapping the weapon down. "You want to tell the world we are here?"

"They're dead," George snapped, jerking away angrily.

"Yeah, but if anybody managed to survive and is still in the area, they will hear us." Cliff paused and looked over at first the twosome, then the trio. "They're slow and uncoordinated. I don't think we want to head back towards the emergency room because that is where the biggest concentration of people was from what I saw. If we can move around behind the information desk and lure those three in a bit, we should be able to scoot out the other side and make it to the hallway with no problems."

George gave a shrug. "Fine, we can try, but what do you suggest we use as a weapon if we actually do have to take down any of these things?"

Cliff reached into the custodian's closet and pulled out a pair of push-brooms. He handed one to George who stepped back like he was being offered a venomous snake.

"What the hell do you want me to do with that?" the man exclaimed.

Cliff snapped his handle in two pieces over his knee after quickly unscrewing the head from the four foot long wooden shaft. He walked up to the closest zombie and drove the broken tip into its eye socket and jerked back as the thing crumpled to the floor in a heap.

Not waiting for the soldier, he moved to the pair that were relatively close together and repeated the gesture on each in quick succession. By the time he'd dropped all three, George was at his side.

"I don't understand how this is getting out of control so fast," Cliff remarked as the pair started down the long hallway, being careful at every intersection and open doorway. "These things are slow and pretty easy to take down."

They rounded a corner and he felt that last comment die on his tightening throat. Up ahead was a long, brightly lit hall that ended in another open waiting room of some sort. Wandering around in that room had to be at least forty of the walking dead; mixed in amongst them were several children between the ages of as young as three or four up to their early teens.

"The pediatric ward," Cliff groaned. "Maybe we should turn back and try the other way."

"I thought that you said the ER was a nightmare and likely with the heaviest possible population," George reminded.

Cliff could not force himself to move forward. He suddenly understood how this had perhaps grown so out of control in such a short span. The thought of driving his makeshift weapon into the face of some child was just not fathomable.

"Don't you go and check out on me now," George hissed, giving Cliff an elbow in the ribs for good measure. "What's on the other side of that area?"

Cliff thought about it for a moment. He brightened slightly. "There is another hallway, a nurse's lounge, and then the cafeteria which has doors opening to outside."

"Then that is where we need to go." The soldier looked at him and scowled. "Look, Cliff, them ain't real kids...not anymore they ain't. They are monsters just like the big versions." When it was clear that Cliff was still unsure, he added, "If it makes you feel any better, I'll take down any of the little ones who get close. You just take down the adults. Clear?"

Cliff felt his face grow warm with embarrassment, but he nodded. Deep down, he knew that those things staggering around up the hall were not living people; but that didn't make his heart ache any less. That had always been his biggest problem in the field. He hated when his calls involved a child. It was the stuff that gave him nightmares.

The pair started up the hall and were not halfway to the open area when one of *them* obviously noticed the two living beings coming towards it. It was a woman in olive drab fatigues, an empty holster at her hip. Cliff veered towards her and ignored the fact that she had most of her throat ripped out and her left arm savaged down to the bone almost all the way from her elbow to her wrist to the point where he could see the ulna and the radius amidst the tattered remains of muscle that hung in strands.

He ended her quickly and then his eyes spied something that made his pulse quicken with a little positive excitement. A large knife was still in its sheath at the woman's hip. He knelt down to grab it but had to stop when two more of the adult versions came his way.

"Loot later, we just need to get to the exit!" George barked.

"I wasn't looting," Cliff grunted as he jabbed his wooden weapon up under the chin of the closer of the two zombies. "I was...ouch!" Cliff yanked his right hand back, shaking it vigorously. When he'd stabbed the zombie, the piece of broom handle had gotten caught and turned his wrist fiercely as the body fell like somebody had just pulled the plug.

"Son of a—" George started to curse, but Cliff cut him off.

"I didn't get bit. I just got my wrist turned wrong when my poker got stuck in that damn zombie's head."

Cliff still had the one section of broom handle and adjusted his attack to be sure to avoid repeating the same mistake again. He jabbed and poked his way across the open lobby of the pediatric area, doing everything in his power to avoid looking at the zombie children. He was doing fine until he had reached the nurse's desk. That was when he literally tripped over a little girl that was hunched down almost on all fours. At first, he thought that he'd found perhaps the one sole surviving needle in this hellish haystack. Then his eyes saw the busted ribs jutting from the child's torso and the nasty rip in her belly. That brought the rest of her into focus and he did not see how he had ever thought, even for a moment, that this child could have been alive. She was covered in drying blood and her eyes had the look he now associated with the giveaway sign of the undead—besides the fact that they walked around with life-ending injuries, that is.

Then it struck him. This child did not attack. In fact, as he scooted away from her and tried to scramble to his feet, she simply remained hunched down. She watched him, her head twitching and cocking from one side to the other. Then she surprised him even more by scooting *away* from him.

Getting to his feet, he took off at a jog towards the hall that would eventually lead to the exit. They took two turns as his eyes kept watch for the signs and arrows that pointed to the cafeteria. At last it came into view and his heart felt like it fell through the floor.

The doors had been ripped off the hinges at some point. Inside, there were well over a hundred of the walking dead roaming about. Some were so badly damaged that they couldn't walk as they were missing one or even both legs. That was of little comfort.

"Son of a bitch!" George groaned again.

The two men turned and only made it to the first corner before they skidded to a stop once more. All the zombies they hadn't killed back in the lobby of the pediatric wing had fallen in behind them in pursuit. Also, it looked like they had picked up some company along the way. To Cliff's dismay, it seemed there were now twice as many child zombies as there were adult.

"Now what?" Cliff almost choked on a sob of frustration as he posed the rhetorical question.

"The hall is too constricting. We have a better chance trying to get through the cafeteria," George answered, not realizing that Cliff hadn't actually expected a response to what seemed to him to be a hopeless situation.

Cliff felt fear start to paralyze him, and he could not move as he stared at the approaching horde led by children including the little girl that he had tripped over. He wanted to run, but nothing his brain did could make his feet react. A sudden stinging pain to his cheek made him blink his eyes and shake his head clear.

"Don't you fucking quit on me, man!" George was in his face. "This was your plan, and we are going to get out of here, but you need to pull it together. Now c'mon."

George jerked his arm and they retraced their steps back towards the infested cafeteria. It actually looked worse the second time he saw it. Right in the doorway was a man who had been ripped in half by the looks of things. Actually, all that remained was his upper torso with the head and right arm still intact. There was an almost black trail streaming away from the abomination, and it ended at what remained of his lower half.

One zombie still sat on the floor munching on what Cliff was going to assume had to be the left arm. It was paying them no attention whatsoever as they approached, but that lone zombie was the minority. Despite their having moved quietly, several heads turned their direction when they reached the mangled entry doors.

"On three, we break left and right and run like mad," George breathed. "Staying close won't help us here. And maybe if we split up, it will confuse them or something." The soldier laughed, but it sounded forced. "If one of us goes down, the other has to keep running. The first one out hops into the first military truck he sees and gets the engine running. Wait as long as is safe, and then haul ass if the other one doesn't make it out."

"They leave the keys in the ignition on those things?" Cliff asked dubiously.

"Actually, none of them require keys. The last thing you want to worry about if you need to roll out in a hurry is finding the keys. They have a master switch. So jump in and get the baby running if you get out first."

Cliff nodded and looked at the best possible path for him. He was on the left and that meant he had the checkout counter. If he could make it there, then maybe he could run along the back side of the food shelves.

George patted him on the shoulder and then gave the countdown. Cliff took off at a fast jog. He did not feel safe going at an all-out sprint simply because the floor was a minefield of spilled food and pools of blood. If he slipped and fell, he might suffer more than just a sprained ankle or a bruised ego.

He reached the cashier's station and peeked behind it to make sure there wasn't one of those things on the floor. He breathed a sigh of relief and then scooted along down the narrow alley between the food counter and a wall with a series of windows where food was often passed through to re-supply things as the day wore on.

He could see the door and a new rush of adrenaline had him speed up a little bit more. He was a mere few steps away when he heard a yelp. He actually slammed into the door—he'd been moving too fast—but as he pushed it open, he glanced to his right. George was between a pair of tables and was kicking at something that apparently had him by the leg.

"Run dammit!" the soldier hollered as he brought one foot

up and stomped down hard on whatever had a grip on his leg.

Cliff looked outside and saw even more of the undead wandering the open lot. Several of the tents had come down and many were stained with blood. Two of the vehicles were now smoldering hulks, and the entire area looked like some of the scenes he remembered from the evening news when some city or town in the Middle East had been the location for some horrible firefight.

Unable to help himself as another scream came from the cafeteria, Cliff looked back. What he saw almost caused him to double over and be sick. One of the zombies had gotten behind George and bit down hard on the meaty part of where his shoulder connected to his neck. There was a spray of blood and he swore he could see the sinews of the man's flesh stretch and then tear away. Another pair of the creatures had him by the arm on the same side and were biting and tugging. The limb tore free and the soldier screamed in a way that hurt Cliff's heart it was so horrific.

The soldier made eye contact with him and Cliff saw the man's mouth move. "Run," he gurgled just before blood dribbled from both corners and then flowed down his chin.

Cliff backed out of the cafeteria and into the chilly open air of the evening. He had to shove away one of the closer zombies. This one had been a soldier. Cliff's eyes lit on the man's belt and saw another amazing looking knife. He would have preferred a gun, but it was likely that most of them had been dropped at some point. The problem being that that point was apparently not in this general vicinity. He took the zombie down in short order and jerked the knife free, not risking the time he would lose if he tried to remove the belt or the sheath

He spotted the closest truck but had to avoid that one. A soldier that had turned into a zombie was sitting in the cab. He could probably yank it out and hop in, but there were three other trucks not too far away and they all looked empty.

Taking off at a run, Cliff no longer felt the need to be cautious. The ground was relatively clear, and the blood stains on the asphalt were not likely to cause him to slip and fall. He ducked, dodged, and sidestepped every zombie along the way and finally reached the door of one of the large vehicles.

Yanking it open, Cliff climbed into the driver's seat and searched for the button to start the engine. He pulled the door shut as the powerful engine roared to life. Putting the big vehicle into gear, he started across the parking lot towards the exit.

He was veering around the zombies as much as possible, wincing when the bumper on one side or the other would clip one of the creatures that now all seemed to be converging on his location. He was just about to exit the lot and hang a right onto W G Acker Drive when a figure stumbled into the path of his truck.

Instinctively, Cliff slammed on the brakes. Up until now, he had been able to dismiss the zombies as anything human—with the exception of his problem with the child versions. They were just anonymous monsters that he had to get past in order to get home to his wife and son. Yes, the child versions had been a problem, but he still felt he'd been able to see the creatures mostly for what they truly were; until now.

Standing directly in front of him was the man who had been his partner in the field for the past four years. While there was an obvious transformation, and the face seemed to hang a bit slack on the skull, he still recognized Terry Gibbs.

"Oh, Terry," Cliff barely choked out his partner's name.

The man with whom he'd spent almost more time with than his own wife was standing there just staring at him with those horrible dead eyes. The bandages were now black and looked filthy. His mouth was a mask of darkness from where he had apparently attacked somebody.

Cliff considered what to do. If the situation were reversed, he hoped that Terry would do him the kindness of putting him down for good. That was exactly what he had to do now. He had to put the man down. It would not be like he was killing his former partner despite how this felt.

Cliff

That was not Terry Gibbs any longer. That was a monster wearing a distorted version of Terry's face. Cliff put the truck in park and glanced around to gauge how much time he had before things might get a little bit dicey. He decided that, if he hurried, he could do this one last thing for his former co-worker and friend.

Opening the door, the first thing that hit Cliff was that smell. With the walking dead all around, it was permeating the air. He did not think he would ever be able to get that stench out of his nostrils.

Gripping the knife he had just liberated, he approached the zombie that had handed him a cup of coffee this morning and complained that it was looking like it might be a long day. With each step, he felt his resolve waver. Yes, he needed to put his friend to rest; but was this still his friend in any way, shape, or form?

"Stop trying to chicken out," Cliff whispered to himself.

Zombie Terry was now making its slow, awkward way towards him. Looking around the parking lot, he could see so many other dark shadows milling about. This was well beyond being out of control.

It no longer mattered how this had happened. As far as he was concerned, it was now a point of simply accepting it and trying to survive.

He took the last few steps towards his target and brought the knife up. He initially intended to just stick it into one of those milky, tracer-riddled eyes. His hand started to shake, and he had to swat away dead hands that reached for him. His resolve was about to fade when one of those cold hands brushed the back of his warm, live ones.

That isn't Terry, a voice screamed inside his head. *Terry is dead, and that thing is an abomination to his memory.*

"Rest in peace, partner," Cliff said with a sob as he gripped the zombie by the shoulder and then drove his blade into the temple.

Terry fell to the ground, eyes still seeming to stare up at

127

him. Cliff knelt and brushed a hand down the man's face, closing those eyes forever.

"I'm sorry I can't take you back…give you a proper funeral. I don't think anybody will be getting one of those for a long time."

Cliff turned and started back for the truck. He winced at the bits of gore and viscera that clung to or dripped from the front bumper. He stepped around the door that he'd intentionally left opened and started to climb up into the cab.

Something clutched his ankle. To Cliff, it almost felt as if the world slowed down to slow-motion. One moment, he was climbing up, the next, he was tumbling backwards, his arms pinwheeling for balance. He landed flat on his back with a painful expulsion of air. His head bounced back with an agonizing crack that caused his vision to blur.

It took him a few seconds to get his bearings and realize that he was now sprawled on a parking lot with perhaps hundreds of the walking dead converging on him. He rolled over onto his side and saw the culprit; crawling from underneath the truck was one of those pathetic zombies that had lost its lower half.

A hand was reaching desperately for his leg and grabbed him as he struggled to overcome the pain and disorientation of his fall. He had to get to his feet and get inside the truck. Moving was not coming as easily as it should and, while he had not had all the wind knocked from him, he was still hurting badly.

Forcing himself up to a seated position, he was ready to stick his knife into the top of this zombie's head. He looked at his hand with amazement. It was empty. The zombie brought its head down to his right leg, hiding its ghoulish face as it bit down on his ankle.

Cliff tried to scream in pain but it was more of a weak mewling as he continued to struggle to suck oxygen into his lungs. He felt a white hot fire explode from that ankle as he watched the zombie's head lift when it tore away a strip of flesh. He tried to kick free, but his effort was feeble and he only managed to shove the scrambling corpse back a mere few inches. It went in for another bite as Cliff tried to wriggle free and this time got a chunk of his calf as a reward. He was on his belly now, and starting to regain some of his sense and ability to move. He made it to his elbows and lunged forward, pulling free from the creeping death that craved another bite of his flesh.

Trying to get to his feet, Cliff saw them converging from all over the parking lot, drawn perhaps by the sounds of his struggle, or maybe the smell of his blood. He had no idea which might be true, but he knew that if he didn't get into the cab of the truck, he would be torn apart. His screams would be like those he'd heard when the hospital fell, when the soldier had been pulled down in the cafeteria.

He managed to gain his footing, although he had to favor the injured right leg that dragged uselessly behind him now. He looked down at the half-corpse that was almost about to grab his foot once again. If it did, and it pulled him down, he knew that he would never make it back to his feet.

He hopped sideways and then past the outstretched arms and was now on the step that allowed him to climb up into the truck. Using all his strength, he heaved himself up and in, slamming the door behind him as he did so. He glanced out at the approaching mob and saw that he had just made it as dead hands slapped against the driver's side window.

The faces that looked in at him were all slack and emotionless except for their hideous eyes which seemed to convey an evil menacing. Other than that, they could be wax figures for all the feeling they showed. There was no anger, pity, or remorse. They simply wanted to get to him and feed.

He had to shift a bit to get his left foot to the accelerator since his right was practically useless. He put the truck into drive and started forward, dragging along the ones that had been able to get a handhold and shoving aside others. He finally broke free from the cluster that had managed to reach the truck and turned right, exiting the hospital and heading for Highway 178.

He reached up to adjust the rearview mirror and his foot

slipped off the gas pedal. The truck began to slow, but Cliff didn't notice. The eyes staring back at him were his...but not. He could see the dark squiggles already appearing.

"No," he whimpered. But he knew better.

He pushed on the accelerator again when he realized that the truck had come to a complete stop. The road ahead was dark with shadows and he turned on the headlights. He just needed to get home, but it wasn't long before he knew that he would never make it. His vision was blurring and his body felt like it was on fire.

He slowed and looked around realizing that he was the only person on the road. That seemed impossible, but looking ahead and behind, he could see no signs of approaching headlights coming from either direction. Glancing down, he spied the communications radio and switched it on. There was a hiss of static and then nothing. He had to force himself to focus as he searched for the frequency that he knew emergency vehicles in Liberty used.

"Hello?" he said as he keyed the mic.

Once again there was a hiss of static, and then nothing. He tapped his forehead a few times to try and regain his focus and then tried again. The frustration grew as silence remained the only reply. A figure staggered across the highway at the edge of his headlights but did not seem interested in him and continued on.

He knew he had only covered about five of the ten miles that would bring him into Liberty. Home. His head dropped and he forced his eyes back open. There was a foul taste in the back of his throat that was very similar to the stench he associated with the undead. It made him gag, but he swallowed hard and tried the radio once more.

"Who is on this frequency?" a voice finally answered.

"This is Clifton Martin. I'm a paramedic from Liberty just coming south on Highway 178 from Pickens Hospital. The military failed to secure the location. There were mass casualties.

The hospital has fallen, and I doubt there are any survivors…that includes the emergency and military personnel that were on hand." Cliff's thumb slid off the key and he leaned back in the driver's seat. A shiver rippled through his body and his teeth began to chatter.

"Cliff? This is Ivan Potter."

Cliff recognized the voice now. Ivan Potter was one of the members of the Liberty Police Department. He was Chief Gilstrap's right hand man and his scrawny stature had earned him the nickname "Barney Fife" when he put on his badge. Most people that knew Ivan also knew that appearance was where the similarities ended.

Three years as a state wrestling champ, Ivan could tie up men twice his size with a graceful effortlessness that earned him the respect of anybody who saw him in action. He was about six feet tall and maybe a hundred and sixty pounds right after eating Thanksgiving dinner. He had jet black hair that he kept short and parted down the left side. He had dark blue eyes and a nose that even he called a beak due to its size and shape. None of that mattered the slightest to his wife Hannah who was considered by most to be perhaps the prettiest woman in town.

"Ivan…you need to warn everybody. It's bad…very bad." Cliff gasped and felt a surge of heat ripple through his body, followed by a chill that had him shivering. He knew this was just about all the time he had left. "I know this might seem impossible…but the dead…" His hand lost its grip and he had to struggle not to drop the radio's mic. He knew that if it fell he would lack the strength to be able to pick it back up.

"Where are you, buddy?" Ivan asked calmly.

"On the highway. Took 178, but I just can't keep going. I can't see the road. I don't want to crash and hurt somebody else."

Cliff watched as a half dozen more of the terrible things crossed the road. One of them paused and turned his direction. Its mouth opened and Cliff imagined that it was moaning, but he couldn't really hear anything over the buzz. It took him a few more seconds to realize that the buzz was the voice on the radio. He knew that voice. It was familiar. Only, now he couldn't place it.

Another thought came as he stared blankly at the radio that now seemed to be shouting at him. The face of a woman filled his mind. She looked at him and smiled. A boy stepped up beside her and nestled under her arm. He knew that he should recognize them, but just as his own name had slipped from his memory, so did theirs.

It was like a surge of electricity jolting him awake. The names came and he knew who they were.

"I tried to make it home. I let people die just to give myself a chance. I failed. But I tried as hard as I could." Tears ran down Cliff's cheeks as he felt a new surge of fiery heat course through his veins. The terrible taste in the back of his throat now filled his mouth. "Please…just tell my wife that I love her, and that I'm sorry!"

More voices came and filled the cab with noise. He wanted to respond, but the strength seeped from his body and his hand finally lost its grip on the radio. Clifton Martin shut his eyes.

His breathing became short panting gasps. At last, he shuddered violently, all of his bodily functions firing off almost at once. A line of thick drool escaped the corner of his mouth; his eyes flew open one final time as he cried out.

Clifton Martin died. Ten minutes later, he opened his eyes.

***

Chief Gilstrap cursed and smacked the dashboard of his car. He would have to add Sophie Lawrence to the list of women he would be paying a visit to tonight to let them know that they were widows. As he pulled onto the road he wondered if maybe those who were dying now might not be making out with the best deal.

This was only going to get worse. As if to confirm his

thoughts, Jeff Tucker let a soft moan slip from his lips.

"Adam, I swear to God I wasn't bit," the man croaked. "But I don't know if I'm gonna make it. Don't let me turn into one of them things."

"I won't." He quickly got on his radio and called for Ivan to meet him in town.

Chief Gilstrap drove the short distance, his eyes scanning the streets as darkness fell and the lights began to come on. Eventually, he pulled up to the rear of the Baptist church across from the elementary school. Despite the relatively short trip, he had driven the entire way with one eye on his rearview mirror where he kept a watch on Jeff Tucker.

By the time that he reached the parking lot, the man had already slipped from consciousness and was covered in sweat. His body was being wracked by tremors and his teeth were clicking audibly.

He climbed out of the car just as another patrol car pulled up. Ivan emerged and shot a wary look in the back seat.

"You positive about this?" Ivan asked.

"No, but I am pretty damn sure." Chief Gilstrap opened the back door.

The two men reached in and pulled the unresponsive body of Jeff Tucker from the backseat. Together, they carried him to the door of the church. Pastor Johnson opened the door and ushered the men inside.

"The news has finally mentioned there being no communication coming out from most of Asia. Also, there are riots in London, Berlin, and even Moscow. This isn't just us. I guess that means it probably ain't terrorists," the pastor said in a rush.

"I still wouldn't count them bastards out," Ivan grumbled.

The three men made their way into the chapel. They laid the shivering body of Jeff Tucker down in the plastic tarp that the chief had told Ivan to request when he called the pastor.

"You should step out, pastor," the chief said as he knelt beside the visibly ill man.

He was actually surprised when the pastor only retreated as

far as the door. Looking up at Ivan, the chief saw that the man was standing with his head bowed, eyes shut, and lips moving in prayer. He doubted it would help, but he didn't think it could hurt.

It took another five minutes, but suddenly, the body of Jeff Tucker began to convulse, and then, surprising all three of the living occupants of the room, sat bolt upright. The man threw his head back and his mouth opened in a silent scream before collapsing with a long, rattling exhale.

"I made him a promise," Chief Gilstrap muttered more for himself than anything else. He removed his coat and put it over the head of the body. Drawing the knife that he now figured would probably be a constant companion from here on out, he placed the tip where he believed to be the location of Jeff's temple and then gave one solid thrust.

Securing the Town

"...reports out of Washington say that the president and a select group of government officials have left for Air Force One..."

***

"...attempts in Ohio to secure the daughter of the president have reportedly failed..."

***

"...rogue elements of the armed forces led by a Major Wanda Beers have broken away and have not been heard from in over three days..."

***

"...be the first to share this footage. If what we are seeing is true, then God have mercy on our souls."

There was a moment when the reporter simply stared ahead at the cameras, then the footage began to roll and filled the screen.

"Am I on?" the doctor asked whoever was operating the shaky, handheld video device.

"Yeah." It was one word, but the voice made it clear that whoever was holding the camera was agitated.

"Good. To whomever is watching, I am Dr. Linda Sing of the CDC. I am here to reverse my earlier statement that these people that are instigating attacks are not the dead come back. After detailed observation of a specimen that had no vitals and had been declared dead, I was witness to that individual sitting up and attacking another person.

"There can be no doubt that this person was dead only moments before. However, after the specimen was restrained, numerous things were done that a living person could not endure, much less remain conscious during. Additionally, I can confirm that massive brain trauma seems to be the only method of dispatching these…individuals—"

"They're fuckin' zombies, you stupid bitch!" somebody off-camera yelled.

Dr. Sing glanced to the left and pursed her lips before continuing. "Simple decapitation is not entirely sufficient. While the body will become inert, the head still seems to function and a bite that transmits the infection can still occur."

With that last statement, the doctor removed her glasses and leaned forward. It was not a necessary gesture. The dark traces in her eyes could be seen quite clearly.

"One of the telltale symptoms is the appearance of the darkening of the capillaries in the eye. If you are infected, I suggest you turn yourself over to the nearest FEMA center or military checkpoint. The only chance we have to contain this rests in your swift response—"

"That went out the window a long time ago while you fucking scientists sat on this information, you stupid bi—" another voice off camera hollered, but was cut off as the video ended abruptly.

The scene returned to the reporter at the news desk. He gave a nod to somebody off to his left and then sat up straight and looked directly into the camera.

"We here at the Global News Network apologize for the language heard in this clip, but felt that it was important to run the raw footage as we received it in order to hopefully convince those final holdouts who refuse to believe this to be what can now be termed…a zombie event.

***

"…and as day eleven since the confirmation by the CDC that this an actual zombie event comes to an end on the East Coast, we here at *World Wide News* want to express our sympathy to the friends and family of President Bransen.

"Washington has issued a statement that, due to the growing threat of large groups of what many are now commonly referring to as *zombies*, no effort can be made to salvage the crash site of Air Force One. They did confirm that recordings indicate an unnamed member of the Secret Service detail turned in flight. Before that individual could be subdued, the president was reportedly bitten by that agent on his left arm. Gunfire was heard during the last transmission. The location of the crash is being withheld for security reasons…"

***

Mayor Burns watched as the heavy machinery gouged large sections of earth from the ground and deposited it where it would become an interior berm that would act as another defense measure. You couldn't look anywhere and not see the citizens of Liberty sweating and toiling under the hot sun of what should be a beautiful spring day.

It had been an easier sell than she expected. Of course the deaths suffered early on had gone a long way to help illustrate her point. But it had been the arrival of that poor Ricky Porter that sealed the deal.

The boy had been ripped apart and barely recognizable; but enough people were able to identify him for it to resonate. He'd been walking through the field adjacent to the Liberty Church of God of Prophecy. Several people had been searching for the boy after Lawrence Martin got home and saw the open instant message dialogue he'd been having with his friend before taking off to the highway himself.

At first, only the crashed bicycle and a lot of blood had been found. Still, there were those who had refused to believe what they had seen with their own eyes on television and even in town as a few of the stragglers arrived those first few days. It took seeing one of their own stumbling along with his insides torn out and his face an absolute mess for it to strike home in everybody's hearts.

Now, the entire town was mobilizing to secure itself in the best way possible. It had been agreed that there was simply no way they could hope to seal off the entire area of Liberty. Instead, they had marked a sort of triangle that ran the length of Ruhamah Road from Highway 123 up to the train tracks which acted as the northern border all the way to Highway 178 and back down to Highway 123.

The sounds of several large semis snapped her back to what was going on around her. As the lead truck of a seven truck convoy came to a stop with it front bumper pressing against another big rig that had been parked earlier, the mayor made a note in her book and hurried over to greet the chief and his team.

"We found these up towards Easley. The highway is a mess that direction. Looks like folks trying to leave Greenville just decided they didn't care which lane they drove in as long as they could try to get away." Chief Gilstrap took off his gloves and stuffed them into his back pocket. The mayor handed him one of her pouches containing disinfecting wipes and he started cleaning his hands as he continued. "Looks like a butt load of them things came onto the road and started in on all the people stuck in their cars. The next trip up is gonna be nasty. We might want

138

to head over to the quarry and see if there are any trucks out there first."

"How much stuff do we have in the trailers on these rigs?" the mayor asked. She cast an anxious glance at the emblems and slogans plastered on the sides of some of the vehicles that were just now being opened by the teams assigned to unload anything brought in by the men and women venturing out.

"Well, one of them is a dairy truck which is damn near useless. The refrigeration was obviously shut off for the past few days. We pulled over and dumped the contents as soon as we got clear." Chief Gilstrap looked over his shoulder. "That Walmart truck is full of clothes. Most of it is for spring and summer, but the manifest has underwear and socks noted as well, so that will help. Other than that, the rest were busts. Produce and stuff that all went bad. That's actually what took us so long. We circled around to that area by the sewage treatment facility and dumped it all in that field across the highway. Figure it would do to start laying down some compost."

The mayor nodded her agreement. It wasn't a great haul like those first few when they'd brought in a truck full of canned goods, but they were making the most out of everything they did find.

"I figure another three weeks at least until we can get enough cars and trucks in place for the outer perimeter," Jamie said as she looked at the marks on her laminated map.

The plan was actually working. The fact that it came from a teenage boy had sat wrong with a few people for a while, but eventually folks started seeing the simple logic.

Building protective walls was certainly a must if they were going to stay safe against the undead. The trick was securing an area large enough for all the people of Liberty to occupy somewhat comfortably. Nobody liked the idea of abandoning their homes, but the reality was that there was no way to secure that much open territory.

The location they had selected would have to do. Folks were asked to open their homes and others began to turn the high school into living quarters. The main roads would be the first line of defense as vehicles were brought in and parked almost on top of each other. Wooden pallets and sand bags were then shoved and packed underneath to keep anything from making it through. The vehicles were going to be three or four deep if they could manage to locate and bring in that many abandoned cars and trucks.

Also, tomorrow, a team was headed out to try and locate trains. It would be preferable to use rail cars to barricade the train tracks. Plus, there was a lot of hope that perhaps some of those rail cars might still be full of useable goods.

Just inside that line of defense, heavy tractors and the like were being used to dig a trench several feet deep. The earth from that trench would then create a berm. Once that was done, then they could get to the task of actually building a proper wall/fence. Nobody expected this to be finished any time in the near future, but since it had become clear that there would be no help coming and the government was basically dissolved, the people of Liberty were going to do all they could to stand against this so-called zombie event.

"When do you and your team leave?" the chief asked after he took a long drink of water from the bottle he had in a pouch on his hip.

"Tomorrow," Jamie replied.

"Don't you figure that place has been emptied?"

"Maybe, but there may be some cargo trucks in the area that didn't make it to their final destination. The longer we wait, the more likely it is that anything and everything of use will already be scooped up."

The chief seemed to think it over for a few seconds, but finally added, "I still think going to that Superstore is no less dangerous and foolish than hitting a mall. This ain't the movies, kid."

Jamie smiled. Her title of mayor was pretty much a relic now. Sure, she was now part of the core group of people making decisions to try and help the town, but to say that she was the head honcho in charge? Not so much anymore.

"If you want the big rewards, you have to take the risks," Jamie parroted one of the chief's own phrases back at him. That had been his response when she asked why he felt it necessary to go practically to Greenville to locate the trucks they were bringing in to help create their defensive perimeter. He'd gone on to explain that the roads were probably going to yield a lot more of that sort of thing nearer the bigger cities. She hadn't been able to argue with his logic.

"But I still want to see if we can't push closer in to Clemson. The big box home improvement stores are probably packed full of the stuff we are going to need to get the produce farms up and running. We should at least be thankful that this is happening just heading in to spring. We will have a full season of planting and harvesting before winter comes," Jamie said, sounding overly optimistic even to her own ears.

"Yeah," the chief snorted, "I realize that the Titanic is sinking, but at least we have plenty of ice."

The pair headed over to the high school stadium where booths had been set up for people to sign in each day and fill the various work crews. That was one thing that had been decided upon quickly. Pretty much everybody able to walk was put to work. There was no job too small, and everybody was pitching in.

They stopped at the roving patrol sign-up booth and the chief grabbed the list of names. He had been put in charge of the town's security force.

"That reminds me." Jamie nodded to his list of names. "We will look for anyplace that might have ammunition. Sporting goods stores, the Walmart—"

"I keep tellin' ya that I am willing to bet that place has been emptied of anything useful." The chief rolled up the list of names and tucked it in his shirt pocket.

141

"Agree to disagree," Jamie said as she patted the man on the shoulder and headed over to grab the roster of those who would be joining her on this little journey.

***

"I realize this is your mission," Stephen Deese did his best not to sound annoyed as he squatted down in the tall grass beside Jamie Burns and brought his binoculars up to his eyes. "I just think you might be pushing the envelope a bit too much."

Jamie did not respond as she looked through her field glasses as well. The smoldering ruins of what had once been a Walmart Superstore sat in the distance, smoke still curling up from it as well as the other smaller stores that shared the large lot with the mammoth building.

The group of ten were just to the right of another building that had been a casualty of a fire: The Waffle House. Jamie had pulled their convoy over just as they came off the highway despite it being what Stephen considered an obvious waste of time. He could tell from a few miles out that there was not likely to be much waiting for them when they arrived.

"Then we press on closer to Clemson. The Lowe's is not far. Hopefully we will have better luck there." Jamie got up and stalked away.

It was obvious that she was more than just disappointed. She seemed to be angry. He would do as the chief had asked and keep an eye on the young lady. She was plenty smart when it came to running a town and implementing plans. He was not as confident in her ability out in what was fast becoming an apocalyptic wasteland.

Everybody piled in to the large trucks, Stephen driving the huge flatbed that they hoped to load to capacity with goods. As they drove, he saw zombies along the way; many would obviously take notice of the convoy and turn to follow.

Shortly after passing the Clemson City Limits sign, they exited the highway and turned right. The Lowe's stood at the head of a large entry drive. The parking lot was almost entirely vacant and the store was intact. Stephen glanced skyward and offered a quick thanks to whomever or whatever might be watching over them.

As they pulled into the lot, he spun the truck around and backed up to the large, home and garden gate. That seemed to be closest to what they were actually here for. Glancing around, he only saw a couple of lone zombies making their way for the new arrivals. He looked over at the young man in the passenger seat and considered if it might not be a better idea to handle it himself, but at last decided that he would be more helpful if he took part right away in the loading of things onto the truck.

"Go take down those stragglers," Stephen told the young man as he hopped out of the cab. He half expected the guy to gripe or complain, but it seemed that the zombie apocalypse was shaping people up in a quick hurry.

He watched the young man draw his spiked club and jog over towards the closest zombie. Satisfied that the job was in hand, he walked over to the other eight people standing around the locked metal gate to the massive, open garden area.

"What seems to be the problem?" Stephen asked as he joined everybody.

"Locked," one of the women groused.

Stepping past the small group of people, Stephen pulled a foot long metal bar from his hip and jammed it into the lock, after a few good jerks, the lock popped and the door swung open. He stepped aside and threw up his arm in a flourish. "The store is now open."

He saw sheepish looks being exchanged by several of the group—including the mayor. Despite people coming to grips with the fact that the dead were getting up and attacking the living, people were still having a problem overcoming certain social norms. The chief had made a joke after his first trip out

143

for trucks that he had never arrested anybody for grand theft auto, and now he was committing the crime several times a day.

"We are going to have to readjust our thinking on what constitutes good and bad," Ivan Potter had chimed in.

Slowly, the group headed in to the open aisles of the lawn and garden area. The first priority was seeds and fertilizer. He paused when two of the ladies stopped at a carousel displaying a huge variety of vegetable seed packets. They were picking through and putting the packs in the basket they had each snagged. Stephen stepped past them, grabbed the entire display and started carrying it to the truck.

Things started moving a lot faster after that.

It was only a moment or so later when the young man he'd sent to take down the stragglers came jogging back. "Hate to be the bringer of bad news, but I think some of those things followed the truck. I would guess around thirty or forty."

"Alright, everybody," Stephen called. "We got incoming. I need four people to come with me to take them down while the rest of you keep loading the truck." He felt his jaw clench a little when his eyes met those of Jamie Burns.

She was glaring at him, and he actually knew why and saw her side of it. This was her operation. She had planned it and made the list of people to come along. Here he was stepping in and calling the shots. The thing was, he just could not get past seeing her as a young lady fresh out of college with almost no life experience and a whole bunch of education that meant absolutely nothing in this new world that was unfolding before them.

"Hey, Burns, if you have a handle on things here, I will give you as much time as possible." Stephen mentally crossed his fingers and hoped that little offering was enough so that she felt like she was still running the show.

"Yeah...fine." The woman didn't even bother glancing back as she headed for the glass double-doors that opened to the actual store.

He wanted to suggest that she confine this run to what they could get out here in the open lawn and garden showplace, but he figured he's stepped on her ego enough today and pointed to the group that he would be bringing with him to take on the small pack of approaching zombies. Still, something was nagging at him about what she was doing. Yes, he'd been to this store a few dozen times and knew that there was a wall of gardening tools just inside that side entrance to the actual store that would probably come in handy. The thing was, most folks in Liberty had that sort of equipment lying around, or in their garages and sheds.

He and his group were halfway across the huge, open parking lot when the sounds of an alarm began to blare. He skidded to a stop and spun back to face the store. That had been what was bothering him. Sure, it wasn't like there would be any police dispatched to the scene; but in this new level of quiet that had fallen over a dead world…sound carried much farther.

"Screw it, ladies and gentlemen," Stephen shouted. "Everybody back to the vehicles. We are out of here."

"But we can still take these down and give the group enough time to fill up the trucks," the young man that he'd initially sent to deal with the two zombies called back.

"And perhaps get trapped by who knows how many more of those things that are now heading this way because of that alarm?" Stephen shook his head.

While not all of them seemed convinced that they needed to abandon this run, the group turned around and started back for the store. As they reached the open gate, Jamie and the others were all rushing out with pushcarts loaded with as much stuff as people could stack and still be able to move.

"I didn't think," Jamie said, her face crimson with embarrassment.

"None of us thought of that," Stephen replied, hoping that might smooth over her feelings from earlier.

It wasn't that he felt he needed to coddle her. It was just that, if they were going to have a chance at surviving this disaster, then everybody needed to work together and get along as well as possible. He knew that from his time overseas. He'd been with a squad that did not get along with each other, and it had damn near gotten all of them killed out in the field.

Everybody began tossing things up to the two people who had climbed up into the back of the flatbed. It was not long before they had everything loaded. Stephen looked at the pitiful haul they had managed to acquire and did his best to push aside his disappointment.

Still, they had at least come away with something, and up to this point, nobody had been hurt or killed. He had a feeling that was something they needed to be happy about. It was definitely going to get a lot harder from here on out.

The trucks rolled out of the parking lot, swerving and weaving to dodge the undead that had come in behind them. They hung a left on Issaqueena Trail and then north on Highway 123.

***

The four big Harley Davidson Ultra Classics roared out of the Cottages of Clemson development and turned right on Old Shirley Road. Curls of smoke were just starting to rise up from a handful of the residences at their collective backs. The foursome stopped at the intersection and one of the riders raised his hand, giving the signal for the others to kill their engines.

Pulling off his helmet, the one who signaled cocked his head to the side and listened. The other three did likewise and all turned to the left towards the sound. This man was the tallest of the gang, standing just over six foot three. His eyes sparkled with mischief and he always seemed to look like he was thinking of something humorous as a smile continuously played at the corners of his mouth.

"Somebody set off an alarm," the rider who had called for the stop snorted as he checked the pistols he had on each hip.

"That means walkers will be coming from every direction. I guess we bail on this little slice of heaven."

"Damn, Kevin, and we just started having fun," one of the riders grumbled.

"No worries, Trunk. We can—" the sounds of diesel engines up the road caused Kevin to stop talking. He eased his bike forward to get a better look at a small convoy rolled out onto the road in the distance and headed towards the highway. "See, Trunk?" Kevin turned to the man who had voiced his displeasure. A big grin split his face and his eyes crinkled with devious joy. "Looks like a new game just made itself available."

Mark "Trunk" Trees was by far the largest of the foursome. He looked like he spent a good deal of time in the gym before the zombies came. His arms were massive and veins ran like cords down his biceps as he unconsciously flexed his hands. His hair was a high and tight that would make any Marine proud. What little neck he had was hidden by massive shoulders that capped off his broad chest which he liked to show off; that was why he always opted for wearing an open leather vest with no shirt underneath.

"I hope it is more fun than the last one," another of the riders grumbled. He glanced over his shoulder from the gated community they were leaving. "Those college boys were a bunch of sissies. That last one started crying before we even hit him."

"Give the kid a break, Animal," Mark chuckled. "He had just watched three of his friends get pulled apart."

"Yeah, well that brings me to another point," Joe "Animal" Spencer said as he absently rubbed the leather saddlebag of his bike. "I get a leg next time. The arms come off too fast."

"No problem, Animal." Kevin nodded.

Joe "Animal" Spencer was tall and lanky. His arms and chest were covered with a variety of tattoos. His brown hair was shaved on the sides and the center was styled into a mohawk. He always wore a smile, but those who took a second to really look at the man's expression could tell that it did not reach his eyes.

The eyes gave the impression that true happiness had not touched his soul in a very long time.

Kevin glanced over to the fourth rider who had remained silent through the entire exchange. Bob Capka was not one for too many words. In fact, the last few people who had heard him speak had started to cry after he pulled away from where he had been whispering in their ears. Kevin had no idea what the man said, and if he ever gave it a second's thought, he would quickly tell himself that he didn't want to know.

Bob Capka was the shortest man of the foursome. His slight frame was deceptive and secreted under baggy clothing that hid a well-muscled frame. He had long curly hair that often hid his face when they were not on their bikes. Even before the zombies, Bob was never much of a talker. At least not out loud where a lot of people could hear him.

Kevin recalled their most recent stretch in the Greenville County Detention Center. One of the loudmouths in their pod simply could not keep his mouth shut in the day room where the television was mounted. Bob had gotten up from his seat and walked over to the kid that Kevin guessed to be in his late teens or early twenties. The kid had started to "nut up" when Bob approached. It was clear that he thought a fight was about to break out. But Bob had just stared at the kid, arms folded across his chest. Eventually, when the kid had run out of steam and began to get nervous, Bob had gestured for the kid to lean forward. It was like watching a damn hypnotist, Kevin remembered thinking. Bob had whispered in the kid's ear, and then just returned to his seat.

The kid had left the day room. Not a peep was heard the rest of the night. When it was time to cell in for count, that was when things got crazy. All of a sudden, the cops were running into the pod after the one doing count had called for assistance. The kid had hung himself. Since he'd been alone in his cell, there was nobody to officially blame and it was called a suicide. Kevin knew better.

Nobody in the pod said a word in the day room during television time for the rest of the duration that Kevin, Joe, Mark, and Bob were in the lock up. Kevin couldn't swear, but he thought he actually heard a few people sigh with relief when the four were done with their time.

"I say we follow those trucks," Kevin announced cheerfully. "I bet they are heading back to someplace with more people. Besides, I think Clemson is burned out. It took us four days to find that last little group that was trying to hide out. Hardly worth the time and effort."

"Sounds good to me," Mark said with a shrug.

"Beats doing nothin'," Joe chimed in.

Bob popped his bike into gear and started off in the direction that the trucks had gone. Kevin smiled and jammed his head back into his helmet. "I guess that's a yes from Bob."

The four bikes roared along until they neared the driveway that the trucks had exited. Dozens of zombies were stumbling out, obviously drawn by the departing trucks that had just left.

Bob had already stopped, shut down his bike, and climbed off. He was standing in front of a lone zombie. It would reach for him with slow, clumsy attempts and he would bat the arms down and push it away. This part always sort of creeped Kevin out.

For some reason, Bob always wanted to toy with the first zombie he was about to kill whenever they encountered a group. The way he tilted his head first one way and then the other was a lot like the zombies themselves; which made what he was doing even a bit more creepier.

Joe was second to arrive and got off his bike. He had a huge knife in one hand and a three foot long metal spike in the other. As he passed Bob, he jammed his spike into the zombie's temple.

"Jeez, Bob, just kill the damn things," Joe snorted as he stepped up to the next one and brought his knife up under its chin, driving it to the hilt and then jerking free in one swift motion.

Kevin held his breath for a moment and watched Bob. The man had turned and was watching Joe wade in and start taking down the leading zombies of this small mob. After a moment, Bob headed over to one of the walking dead, an elderly woman who was reaching with her gnarled hands as he stepped up to her with his aluminum baseball bat. With one swing, he snapped the knee inwards and sent the body to the ground. Moving methodically, he stood over the downed figure and then used the barrel end of his bat like a pile-driver and smashed it down once…twice…three times until the skull burst open like an over-ripe melon.

Kevin let out the breath that he had not been aware he was holding. Setting the stand for his bike, he hopped off and turned to look at his array of weapons. Besides the pistols he wore at his hips (and only used in an emergency since gunshots seemed to bring out zombies by the hundreds), he had three machetes, a very nice saber that he took off a zombie that had been dressed up as some Civil War re-enactor, two batons removed from a pair of zombie policemen that he had left dangling from a bridge by a length of cable around their ankles, and a briefcase full of assorted knives.

Cupping his chin with his right hand, he absently stroked his reddish-blond goatee as he considered his options. At last, he decided on the saber. It was just too nice not to get some serious use.

Clipping the scabbard to his heavy leather belt, he drew the weapon and slashed at the air a few times to warm up his arm. Lunging and dancing back and forth like any of the swordsmen he had ever seen on television or in the movies, punctuating each movement with a "Ho!" or a "Ha!"

"You gonna screw around all day, or are you gonna step in here and get to killin'?" Mark snapped as he grabbed a teenaged boy version of the undead by his hair and drove the knife in his hand deep into the side of its head.

"Oh…sorry," Kevin laughed.

150

He jogged over to the closest zombie and went into a whirling spin just as he got within range. His saber bit deep into the shoulder of the zombie. The man in the tattered business suit did not even seem to notice as he reached out for Kevin with grasping hands that brushed his heavy leather jacket.

"Crap," Kevin muttered as he brought up a booted foot and kicked the Business Suit Zombie away.

Taking a step back and gripping the weapon with both hands, he raised his arms and then brought them down hard with an overhead chop. The blade split the skull at enough of angle that the left third of the zombie's head came away, exposing the dark gore of its putrefying brain.

It took the four of them just about five minutes, but eventually the entire little mob was sprawled all over the entrance to the parking lot of a Lowe's. The alarm had continued to ring the entire time and now shadowy figures could be seen wading out of some nearby trees as well as coming from both directions along the two lane road that the signs called Issaqueena Trail.

"Mount up!" Kevin called.

"But there's more of them things coming," Joe complained.

"Dude, I don't think we'll be running out of zombies any time soon," Mark guffawed as he swung a leg over and brought his bike alive with a roar.

Bob walked past Joe, not even bothering to glance at the man as he wiped off his bat and slid it into its place before mounting his bike and starting the engine. Easing forward until he was next to Mark and Kevin, Bob paused to grab a band from his wrist and pull his hair back into a ponytail.

Joe looked around, his eyes almost seeming to give off a longing as he watched the approaching zombies. Kevin didn't think that the man had ever been quite the same after that one had grabbed him by the arm and bit down on his shoulder while they were looting that senior center.

Kevin also believed that the only thing that had saved Joe was the fact that the old man hadn't been wearing his teeth. The gums had nibbled ineffectively on Joe's denim shirt, leaving a gross stain of drool, but that had been the extent of the damage. Ever since that incident, Joe had been on some sort of mission where he gave the impression that he wanted to single-handedly rid the world of every zombie.

Twice the man had peeled away from the formation when he spied a small cluster of the walking dead. Kevin and the others had always gone after him and stepped in to help with the kill, but Kevin didn't think the man noticed...or cared. He was so solely focused on bringing destruction.

That had been demonstrated to the fullest one time in particular. Joe had pulled away and actually just dropped his bike on its side to go wade into a group of eleven walkers. Kevin had sighed and then turned his own bike to go render assistance. He parked and was just climbing off when a hand grabbed him. It was Mark. The big man shook his head.

"Just let him do his thing," Mark Trees had rumbled.

Kevin had pulled away and taken a step towards the melee, but then stopped and found himself waiting and watching. Joe had been like a very tall Tasmanian Devil as his arms whipped around in a flurry of head strikes and crippling shots that would take a zombie off its feet so that he could move in for a killing blow. When it was over, the man hadn't even acknowledged the trio who had stood by watching the ordeal. He had simply walked to his bike, pulled out a fresh batch of wipes and given himself a good cleanup.

As they drove down the highway now, distant specks on the horizon marked their quarry. The little convoy seemed to be driving the speed limit. Kevin's smile widened as they drew closer by the minute.

"Slow down!" Mark yelled, pulling up close to Kevin. "We might spook them. I don't care what the TV shows say, a motorcycle doesn't stand a snowball's chance in Hell against a truck."

Kevin nodded and let off the throttle. He hadn't survived that breakout from the jail's intake center, a shootout with a handful of state troopers, and a very large horde of the undead that had surrounded them in that diner (where they had crashed for the night that one time) just to become road kill for a bunch of scared little country mice that took off at the first sound of a useless burglar alarm and a small mob of zombies that numbered fewer than a hundred.

Yes, Kevin Staley thought as he smiled big despite the bug that had just flown into his teeth with a crunchy splat, *I have the whole zombie apocalypse in front of me, and I'm going to milk it for all the chaos I can manage.*

Dead: Snapshot—Liberty, South Carolina

9

"Where neighbors become friends."

Chief Gilstrap kept his lips pressed tight in order to keep himself from saying "I told you so." Jamie was pacing back and forth in the small counselor's office that had been converted into their new version of city hall. This room was plastered with maps of the area and showed the regularly updated progress of the outer defenses.

"...like he was in charge of the whole thing," Jamie ranted. She took another pull on the bottle that had been pulled from the drawer. "This was my operation. How would you like it if he just ran roughshod over you on one of your excursions out there?"

She seemed to consider the bottle in her hand. She held it out to the chief with a nod. He accepted it and allowed a small sip. He handed it back, expecting her to cap it and shove it back in the desk. What he hadn't anticipated was her taking a few more large gulps.

There was an uncomfortably long silence; and that is when the chief realized that she had actually posed that to him as a question. He spoke slow, making sure to pick and choose his words with care. He was of two minds on the subject. Part of him agreed that Stephen shouldn't volunteer for somebody else's op and then take charge, but he also needed to stress to Jamie that this was a new world and things changed on the fly.

People needed to be able to accept input in all situations if somebody might have a valid understanding of what needed to be done. He had recently learned that lesson when a boy young enough to be his grandson offered up what proved to be the most doable and reasonable defense plan for the city.

"I'll talk to him, but you need to be more open to outside input, Jamie."

The young lady threw her arms across her body and cocked her left hip as she leveled her stare on him. She seemed to waver a bit on her feet. She opened her mouth twice to retort, but then snapped it shut.

"You'll really talk to him, Chief?" she slurred just slightly.

Adam Gilstrap hadn't noticed until Ivan pointed it out that pretty much everybody in town had dropped the use of titles. Even the mayor was simply called by name even when she was operating in an official capacity, but nobody had gotten to the point where they called him Adam.

"Hell, you been chief here longer than some of these folks been alive," Ivan had laughed when the chief had asked the man why he thought that might be.

"As soon as I get the list of folks that are coming with me tomorrow. We are heading out first thing in the morning and I got a couple who keep putting their names on the list and…well…there's just no way I'd bring 'em out there with me. People's lives are on the line and I'm not going to reduce our chances of survival by bringing along idiots who think this is just some giant video game."

He opened the door and almost ran into Jonathan Patterson. The kid still looked like crap. His right wrist was in a cast and his forehead was practically one giant scab from where he'd busted it open in the crash.

"Hey, Chief," Jonathan said, his eyes immediately going to the floor. "Umm…there's some new folks just arrived."

"Okay?" He let that word drag out a bit to make it more of a question.

Why was he being told this? There was a group that was in charge of new arrivals. They would get their information and find out what sorts of skills these people might have that could be of use. So far, they had only gotten a trickle of folks from up around Pickens, and they were all mostly just relatives of folks here in Liberty, so they weren't exactly strangers.

"These guys came in on Harleys. There is something about them that is kinda creepy. You may want to come see for yourself."

"Look, Jonathan, folks have probably been going through hell out there trying to survive."

The first night after all the madness, Adam Gilstrap had done something he hadn't thought he would ever do. He had sat down and watched a handful of zombie movies. He'd had no idea there were so many, but he'd gotten a list of recommended titles from Sophie Martin's kid, Lawrence.

"I still think you should come see for yourself." Jonathan turned to go, his shoulders slumped and his head down.

"I'll give a look see, okay?" Chief Gilstrap did his best not to sound annoyed. He knew that Jonathan was still upset over losing his mom. He blamed himself for not telling people about the video files he'd gotten from that kid in Japan. The young man had the crazy notion that his telling somebody could have stopped this whole thing from happening.

"I can go if you want to go check your list," Jamie spoke up.

He saw the glance from Jonathan. Well, that was just another thing that people were going to have to get used to in the new world. While he was not what some might consider a "liberated" male, he was cognizant enough of the situation to know that men and women were going to have to shift back to Pioneer days where both sexes busted their asses and did what it took to keep everybody alive.

"Yeah, that would be a big help," Chief Gilstrap said as he left the room before the young man could say anything.

If Jonathan wanted to scowl, he could go right ahead; Jamie

was not in the mood for any crap right now. She would tear him a new one in short order if he dared question her ability to function in his stead. And with a little bit of a buzz, her tolerance might be down a few more notches than normal.

Walking outside, he could hear the sounds of approaching dusk almost as if he were camping. The world had grown so quiet so fast. He looked skyward and was not surprised to see the lack of any contrails. In fact, there hadn't been any since the day it was reported that Air Force One went down. He figured the wisdom was probably along the lines of, if it can happen on the president's plane, then it could certainly happen on a commercial aircraft.

That thought gave him a shiver. Now that he'd seen those things up close a few times, he had to imagine that the smell in such close quarters would be worse than any elevator fart. And how would somebody take one down at thirty thousand feet? Unless there happened to be an armed sky marshal, he figured that folks would be pretty well screwed.

Walking up to the row of sign-up booths he smiled and nodded appropriately at the greetings he received. He paused once to help Granny Criss into her scooter chair. As he did, he wondered how much longer they would have power. It was already spotty, and today it had gone out just before Jamie and her people returned and just come on a while ago.

Too bad for her it hadn't gone out while she was breaking in to that Lowe's store, he thought.

He picked up the list and sighed in relief when the two names he'd hoped would not be there were absent. Part of him felt bad, but he'd had issues with Reverend Jonah and his brother Chuck. The two seemed to constantly be on about how this was the "End Times" and people needed to stop building defenses against zombies and worry about defending their immortal soul.

Heading to his car, he had just opened the door when everything went considerably darker. He glanced up at the street lights and saw that they were all off.

"That's what I get for thinking," he said with a sigh as he climbed into his car and headed out to do his last drive around the perimeter for the day.

***

Jamie followed Jonathan. She hid her annoyance at the man since she undeniably saw the look he gave her at Chief Gilstrap's suggestion that she be the one to join him in checking out these new arrivals.

She considered the bit of a buzz she felt growing, but shoved it aside. She was more than fine to go see four new arrivals. The fact that Jonathan had come and not one single member of the actual team assigned that task told her that it was probably just him being over-dramamtic.

She walked outside and headed for the small north parking lot where they had determined that newcomers be brought back to when they arrived. That was when she had optimistically believed that they would become some sort of Mecca that people would flood to when the word got out that Liberty was shoring up a good section of town with the full intention of surviving this "zombie event" (as the media had coined it).

She was halfway there when the lights went out. Pausing, she reached inside her shirt and took out the small jogger's light. It was an orange disc that clipped on to her shirt and allowed her to see at least the area directly in front of her. She had a head-mounted light back in her cubicle in the dorm where she now lived, but this would do for now. It took her a few times to get the button to work, but she was fine. And besides, it wasn't like she had all that far to walk. Her new residence was literally a stone's throw away.

Jamie had given up her home to three families. She had wanted to show everybody that she was not going to ask the people of Liberty to make sacrifices that she was not willing to make her own self. That didn't mean she liked it; she missed her house and hoped that maybe someday she would see a time when she could reclaim it.

She hid a smirk when she heard Jonathan curse up ahead as he stubbed his foot and almost tripped over the small curb. Just as fast, she shoved her snarky thoughts away and tried to remind herself that Jonathan had been instrumental in helping show people just how bad this zombie event was on a global scale.

When she arrived at the intake area, she was almost glad it was a bit dark. The four men who stood waiting under the glare of a few hanging Coleman lanterns looked like a cross between a heavy metal band and a biker gang. The long-haired one in particular gave her the shivers. His eyes looked deader than any zombie's, and he didn't seem to notice that there was a crowd of people standing in a small semi-circle examining them like they were slides under a microscope.

Screwing up her courage a few notches and pasting her best smile onto her face, she dismissed the bad feelings as being influenced by a mix of Jonathan's paranoia and the whiskey. Making every effort to conceal her slight inebriation, she stepped into the light of the lanterns to greet the strangers. "My name is Jamie Burns." She extended a hand and thought she detected a hesitation in the heavily tattooed man closest to her.

"Joe," the man finally mumbled. "Joe Spencer."

"Kevin Staley," one of the men almost shouted as he stepped past the man who had given his name as Joe.

Jamie appraised this one and felt even sillier about her earlier concerns. This Kevin Staley person had the most charming smile. His hair looked like it was on fire in the glow of the lanterns and his teeth sparkled, adding perhaps just a bit more light to the scene. She liked this one right away and then fought off a blush as he reached out and took her hand.

"So great to meet you," the man said in a voice that sent a tingle up her arm and straight to her belly.

"Welcome to Liberty, where neighbors become friends," Jamie gushed, instantly scolding herself for being so corny as to

"Where neighbors become friends."

spout the town's slogan.

"Liberty…" Mark said the word like it didn't exactly fit in his mouth. "Never heard of it." He looked around, squinting with apparent scrutiny. "Kinda small as far as towns go."

"Says the guy from Smyrna," Kevin joked.

"Hey, we moved to Spartanburg when I was five," Mark shot back defensively.

"I don't think I got all your names," Jamie piped in, her voice cracking just a little as she did. She simply could not take her eyes off the one who had introduced himself as Kevin Staley.

"I'm Mark Trees," the broad chested member of the group who had made the small town quip said, reaching out to shake her hand with a grip that was just on the edge of becoming painful. "The quiet one is Bob…Bob Capka."

Jamie glanced over at Bob and barely suppressed a shiver that was entirely different from the type that Kevin induced. Maybe it was a trick of the lanterns, but she could not get over how dead his eyes looked. The problem was, once she'd made eye contact, she found that she couldn't tear her gaze away without considerable effort.

"We will need to get you guys in to see our medical staff." Jamie knew that she was stretching things a bit. Sophie Martin and two volunteers that were being trained on the fly could hardly be considered a proper medical staff; perhaps the dig at Liberty's small town status had hit her wrong.

"We're fine," Kevin assured her.

"Yes, but it is the protocol," Jamie insisted.

"Protocol," Joe snickered in a way that made the hairs on the back of Jamie's neck stand up, almost like how she would imagine a serpent to speak if it had the ability.

"I think we would know if there was something wrong with us," Mark growled. "We ain't stupid. We've been out in this crap long enough to know what can turn ya into one of them things."

"Guys," Kevin raised his hands in the air as he turned to

face the other three members of his group, "these fine people are showing us hospitality. It wouldn't be right for us to impose and ask them to break their protocols."

Jamie thought she saw a sneer try desperately to tug at the corners of the mouth of one named Bob. The barrel-chested man named Mark let a dismissive burst of air escape his lips, but he didn't argue.

Joe Spencer was a different story. "Maybe I'll just sleep outside your little perimeter. I ain't letting some stranger make me strip naked so they can look at my shit."

"We all seen ya naked, bro." Kevin smiled big and then gave a wink to Jamie that reignited her blush. "It ain't all that. How about we just let these people do what they feel they need to do. I think we will find that the rewards far outweigh such a minor inconvenience."

Jamie looked from one of the men's faces to the next. There seemed to be something passing between them that was not spoken. She shoved that thought away, certain that she was imagining things. She blamed it on the alluring effect of Kevin Staley's smile.

"If you gentlemen will follow me?" Jamie extended an arm towards the middle entrance on the front of the school building that sat by the north parking lot.

As she passed Jonathan, she saw a look that was part shock and part scowl etched on his face. She chose to ignore it and escorted the four men into Sophie's makeshift office.

***

Jonathan watched Jamie walk away. He suddenly felt like he was back in high school all over again. Despite being on the football team, he had never really felt like he fit in. He was husky (which most people simply just called fat) and a bit socially awkward. He doubted that Jamie even recalled they had been in the same graduating class. She'd even sat two seats in front of

162

him in AP English.

There was just something about those four guys that screamed the Tom Savini-led biker gang at the end of the original *Dawn of the Dead*. Hell, if that one guy had black hair instead of damn near being a ginger, he would fit the bill perfectly as Savini's taller brother. He even had a goofy smile on his face all the time like he had just thought of something funny and decided not to share it.

Part of him wanted to follow Jamie and the new arrivals to the intake office, but he had an idea forming in his mind and wanted to work out the details. With the power out, it was going to be a bit more difficult to pull off, but he saw this as a chance to draw from the power of his inner geek.

Besides video games, one of Jonathan's hobbies had been playing with electronics. He'd been the one to rig a motion activated camera at the Domino's store when the product inventory sheets started coming up with discrepancies. They'd caught the culprit the second day he set up the camera. That had actually been the thing that earned him his promotion to assistant manager and gave him his own shift to run.

After one more glance at Jamie and the newbies as they disappeared into the building, Jonathan headed for the gym where his cubicle waited. Of course, what he needed wasn't in the cubicle, he would need to venture outside the perimeter to his abandoned house, but the patrols were reporting that zombie encounters were rare, and even when they were discovered, it was in singles or just a few at most.

A small voice in his head told him that he was being an idiot. Wandering out all by his lonesome was bad enough. The fact that he only had the full use of one hand did not increase his chances. He quickly shut that voice up as he reached his cubicle and opened his footlocker. One good thing about this zombie apocalypse (he laughed whenever anybody used the media phrase "zombie event") was that it did not draw any attention if he walked past with a pair of pistols on his hips, a shotgun over his shoulder, knives strapped to his thighs and his prized replica of a Roman Centurion's sword.

He slipped through the gym and exited on the side that faced where the track and field events were held in the spring. Sticking in the shadows, he kept his flashlight shut off until he had cleared the school grounds and reached the clearing under the massive power line towers that bisected the countryside. Once he reached the woods, he flicked on his powerful headlamp and started making his way north.

Shortly after he reached Peachtree Street, Jonathan encountered his first zombie. The woman was naked and her blond hair looked silver in the moonlight. Her lower jaw appeared to almost be completely torn off. He briefly wondered how she might be able to bite in that condition and then quickly decided that he didn't care. A zombie was a zombie.

He let his shotgun slide off his shoulder and set it against a tree before drawing his sword. This was going to be the first time he used his Roman sword. A giddy tingle turned in his stomach and his mouth went dry as adrenaline flooded him.

He waited until the zombie was almost in striking range. She was now fully lit up by his headlamp. This gave him a better look at her terrible injury. He also saw several very small bite marks all down her legs. Pieces of flesh hung in strips in a few spots, but the wounds looked old. While they still seemed to ooze a little dark fluid, they had dried considerably. What hadn't changed was the terrible smell.

As soon as she took two more staggering and unsteady steps closer, Jonathan reared back and swung at the top of the zombie's head. The sword dug into the skull with a violent ferocity. Bits of bone and brain splattered up from the broken skull and the body collapsed in a heap. Wiping off his blade, he put it in its scabbard and then picked up his shotgun.

He was already regretting taking so much gear. It seemed like a great idea to be on that "better safe than sorry" train, as he left the safe zone, but things were starting to feel heavy. It was as if they were gaining weight with each passing minute.

164

He hadn't gone another ten feet when he heard the sounds of a low moan coming from his right. He turned and staggered back a step when three children emerged from the brush. It took him a moment to shake off the shock and get his mind to register that these were no longer kids.

They were monsters.

He started towards them and then paused. He had to have been imagining things. He took another step and gasped. Sure enough, the three children stepped back. One of them even moved behind the other two as if trying to put an obstacle in his path should he decide to attack.

For just a moment, Jonathan had a very difficult time seeing these three for what they truly were. His logical mind knew them to be the walking dead. Yet, they were acting as if they were afraid of him. Did this infection or virus or whatever the hell it was that made people into zombies react differently in children? Was there some part of their humanity still intact?

He'd heard a few stories about the children, but he had simply been too far into his own pain—both emotional and physical—to pay it any attention. He thought that Mr. Deese had mentioned something and even used one to show some of the others that this zombie stuff was real.

Kneeling, Jonathan reached out a hand towards the children. So far, this was not turning out much like any of his favorite zombie books or movies. A thought occurred to him. Perhaps the children were only partial zombies. Maybe for some unknown reason they didn't quite turn all the way. What else could account for them acting so different? They weren't attacking. That had to mean something. Perhaps he could redeem his huge blunder of not sharing those videos. If these children were special, perhaps they could be used to help the community somehow.

"Hey," he whispered, making his voice as calm and inviting as possible, "are you able to understand me?"

The trio continued to stay put. Their only reaction was the occasional shifting back and forth from one foot to the other. The one that had ducked back behind the others might have actually taken another step away.

"I won't hurt you," he called. This time, he made a "come here" gesture with his outstretched hand. As soon as he did, all three took another step back as if he had spooked them.

One of the children's head twitched, and its undead gaze went to his left and over his shoulder. Jonathan heard the twig snap in the nick of time and lunged to his right. The move was awkward, and getting up was not easy, but he made it to his knees as the zombie soldier staggered towards him with its arms outstretched.

He was in an awkward position and could not draw his sword and so had to resort to one of the knives strapped to his leg. Pulling it, two things happened almost simultaneously. The soldier zombie lunged, in what was more of a flop due to the zombie's lack of coordination, and the children suddenly began to come for him just like a regular zombie.

Catching the soldier by the chin, he shoved the head up and to the side so that he could drive his knife into the side of its head. He shoved the body away and rolled back just as the first child zombie tumbled forward and landed on his right leg.

Jonathan grabbed it by the hair and drove his blade down. His aim was just a bit off and he initially feared that he'd missed as the blade tip scraped a little to the side, gouging a chunk of hair and scalp, then it caught and pierced the head just above the right ear. The body went limp and the head was at such an angle that he could not free his weapon.

There was no way that he would be able to draw his other knife before both of the remaining child zombies were on him. Steeling himself for the pain that he knew was coming, Jonathan clenched his teeth. The two children both fell on him practically in unison.

***

Kevin dried his hands on the towel that had been handed to

him by some guy who he hadn't bothered to learn the name of when he'd entered a communal wash room. Mark and Joe were both finishing with getting cleaned up. Bob had vanished at some point and was nowhere to be found. He hoped the man didn't jump the gun. This place was a gold mine.

He'd noticed all the big rigs being pulled in and parked bumper-to-bumper as a sort of barricade. If he was inclined to settle down, this place would not be the worst choice. The problem rested in the fact that he had no desire to just settle in. He'd already seen enough to know that these people were putting in farmer's hours. He wasn't about to spend the zombie apocalypse busting his ass from sunrise to sunset every damn day.

He did notice that Jamie chick checking him out when they'd first met. If things went well, he might be able to get a little of that before he and the boys hit the road. He doubted it would take much convincing on his part considering how she was blushing like a school girl every time he looked at her. And he would *convince* her. Kevin Staley might be a lot of things: brawler, robber (he hated the label of "thief" because he felt it sounded sneaky and cowardly), and killer. One thing he wasn't was a rapist. None of his boys would do anything like that. They might kill a girl for saying no, but they wouldn't take pussy by force.

Walking out into what had once been the high school's main gymnasium, he saw rows of portable dividers that acted as four foot high walls for the residents of what amounted to a massive open dorm. That was the other thing that made him certain there was no way in hell he would be staying here for any longer than was absolutely necessary. They would find the supplies—hopefully this town had created some sort of central armory—grab what they wanted, and get the hell out of here.

"You got any ideas how we do this?" Mark sauntered up and rested against the wall, his huge arms folded across his massive chest. Somewhere, he'd found a toothpick and had it jutting from the corner of his mouth.

"We need to find out where they're storing shit," Kevin

167

said, after being certain that nobody was close enough to over-hear their conversation.

"Always making it harder than it needs to be," Mark chortled.

"And I suppose some sort of amazing idea managed to chisel its way into that giant square head of yours," Kevin said with unveiled sarcasm.

"Actually," Mark turned to Kevin with an arched eyebrow, "I think I know exactly how we do this fast and get gone before these hillbilly bumpkins know what hit 'em."

"I'm listening."

"These folks all abandoned their entire town. There are restaurants and I bet at least one grocery store just sitting there. We join up on one of the salvage teams or whatever they are calling them and head out. If we can all get on the same team and have the numbers, we just kill the locals on the team once we find someplace worth emptying. We load up and are out of here before these folks even realize we're gone."

Kevin thought it over. He caught sight of the back of Jamie's head as she ducked into a cubicle. This place was a gold mine, that much was for sure. He wanted to get loaded out to the max and be out of here before Joe or, God forbid, Bob, do something that put an end to this little vacation in an ugly way. That did not mean he felt they needed to leave in the next day or two. He wanted a little time to work on that Jamie girl. Who knew how long it would be before he had another chance at a bit of soft and squishy companionship.

"Sounds like a solid idea," Kevin finally agreed. "But let's hang here for a few days. No need to be in such a hurry. Besides, the longer we hang around…" He saw Mark open his mouth and hurried out the next bit. "Within reason, of course…the more detailed information we can come up with. Can you imagine if this place has gathered up ammunition and put it someplace central? Since I doubt they are worried too much about anything beyond the zombies, I would be willing to bet we only have to kill maybe one person."

"Where's the fun in that?" a voice whispered behind Kevin causing both him and Mark to jump.

"Jesus, Joe!" Kevin snapped.

"Nope...just regular Joe," the man replied with a devious smile. "And you may want to put those eyes back in your head, Kev."

"What are you talking about?"

"The way you are eye-humping that little blonde number...the welcome committee girl?" Joe leered at Kevin who returned the look with his best attempt at a scowl.

"Man, you gotta work on that," Mark snorted. "You look like you're constipated."

To emphasize his point, a young man in perhaps his twenties was emerging from the communal wash area. Mark leaned forward and gave the kid a fierce scowl. The guy almost tripped trying to swing wide of the muscular man.

Mark turned back to Kevin and Joe. "See? That's how you sport mean face. Maybe if you didn't smile so damn much. I bet your scowling muscles are flabbier than zombie tits."

The three men all headed for their individual cubicles. Kevin sat down on the cot that was going to be his bed. He lay down for a moment and tried to get comfortable. It wasn't bad; he'd slept on hard pans in county jail that were much less enjoyable. Still, he just could not bring himself to relax.

Finally, he sat up, peeked around and then rose up to peer over the wall of his cubicle. He staggered back when he came face-to-face with Mark.

"Dude, just go nail the broad and be done with it." For emphasis, the big man waggled his eyebrows.

Kevin knuckled the man lightly on the forehead. "Don't wait up."

Exiting his cubicle, he had to pull up and dodge a pair of kids who were maybe eight or nine as they raced past. One of them was screaming something about "I gotcha!" while the other called over his shoulder "No ya didn't!"

169

"Dead within a month," Kevin muttered and then headed in the direction he remembered Jamie being when he last saw her. It didn't take him long to locate her. She was having a conversation with the woman who had given him and the others their check-up. He thought her name was Sophie, but since he wasn't planning on staying very long, he decided that he didn't care.

He waited until there appeared to be a pause in the conversation before speaking up. "Hey, uh, Jamie...right?" He knew her name, but he wanted to come off as casual and non-threatening.

"Kevin." Jamie's face broke into a huge smile which she quickly forced down to merely happy and pleasant after a gentle elbow nudge from her friend. "Getting all settled in?"

"Yeah, pretty much. Look, I was talking with my guys and we really want to do our part to help. You folks have been so great. And bringing us a hot dinner while we were seeing the doc here was a real pleasant surprise."

"I'm not actually a doctor, Mr. Staley," the woman with the mocha colored skin said with a polite smile. "I was a nurse."

"Well you're about the closest thing to a doctor that I've seen in a while," Kevin said with an appreciative chuckle in his voice.

"Sorry it was just soup and sandwiches, but the kitchen is shut down for the night and that is usually what the men and women coming in from patrol get before hitting the sack. But I think breakfast is pancakes, so..." Jamie's voice trailed off and her cheeks turned a warm, rosy pink. It was obvious that she knew she was stammering and rambling. It was also very clear that she'd perhaps had a nice buzz going. This was almost too easy.

"I think I'm still a bit strung out from the road." Kevin winced inwardly at his cheesy line from an old song he loved. "You wouldn't mind showing me around, would you? Maybe point out which work teams will likely need the most help tomorrow so we can sign up and get to doing our part?"

Jamie shot a look at her friend and Kevin was almost certain that his chances were about to be shot down in flames when the woman gave a slight shake of the head. He practically held his breath until she looked up at him and gave a nod despite her friend's apparent disapproval.

"Sure, I am actually going to be working one of the sign-up booths tomorrow," she said as she pulled away from the nurse who was still trying to keep Jamie from leaving. "I was outside the perimeter today so I get to stay inside for the next few."

"Out hunting zombies?" Kevin flashed his best smile.

"No, nothing quite so bold or dangerous. Actually, I was out trying to find supplies. I had been hoping to hit that Walmart Super store, but the stupid thing was burned to the ground."

"Wow, that sucks."

"Jamie?" the nurse called after them as he opened the door leading outside.

"I'll be fine, Sophie," she called over her shoulder. "I'm sure Kevin here can handle anything that might stumble our way. Besides, we're just going right outside."

Kevin was glad he'd already been smiling or he might have ended up giving himself away. As he escorted her outside, his mind flashed back to the Walmart that Jamie had mentioned. He and the crew had torched that place. Actually, most of the fault had been Joe's. They had rolled in and gassed up, filled their extra emergency tanks, and then drove up to the big store front.

The doors had been busted and it was obvious that the place was a hive of walking dead. Mark had been disappointed. He'd really been looking forward to some clean underwear. They were discussing if there might be any possibility that they might be able to slip inside, but since none of them knew where the underwear aisle might be, they (meaning Mark and Kevin since the other two had remained silent on the matter) had decided to skip giving it a try.

No sooner had they made the decision when Joe had hopped off his bike with both of his five gallon gas cans. He'd actually dashed in through the busted door as he unscrewed the nozzles

171

on both containers.

Perhaps two minutes later he was walking out empty-handed. He paused just outside the main doors, produced a disposable lighter, grabbed a wadded up piece of paper from the nearby trash can, lit it, and threw it inside. There was a moment where nothing happened, and then a soft 'whump' was heard. A soft orange glow became visible. Moments later, a flaming zombie stumbled past the entry way visible to the four men who were now sitting on their bikes like they were parked at a drive-in movie theater.

"We checked out the Lowe's," Jamie paused and looked at the ground. "I screwed up and set off the alarm, so we didn't get nearly as much as we could have come away with."

"I guess it's not necessarily all a bad thing that you set off that alarm." Kevin returned his attention to Jamie and put an arm around the woman's shoulders to sort of test the water.

"What do you mean?" She looked up at him and he could tell that he was close to setting the hook and landing this fish.

"Well," he brushed her cheek gently with his hand and smiled down at her, "that alarm is how we sort of found you. We were not too far away when it sounded and so we headed over to see what was going on. We got there just as your trucks were hitting the highway."

Jamie did not look away from his gaze and Kevin decided to keep the eye contact. He was grateful that he'd gotten a chance to clean up a little while earlier. He noticed her lean in just a bit and so he lowered his head just enough. That proved to be the clincher. She closed the rest of that tiny space between them and allowed him to kiss her.

Now for the next step, Kevin thought after allowing the kiss to grow into something a bit heated.

"Umm, I don't think I can take you back to my cubicle. I mean, sure, there are those little dividers, but I doubt we would be fooling anybody."

Jamie pulled back and looked him in the eyes, and for just a

"Where neighbors become friends."

moment, he thought that he saw hesitation. He upped the wattage on his smile and then broke eye contact, staring at the ground, trying to play the shy role now.

"Sorry, I didn't mean to presume..." He let that statement trail off and shook his head.

A soft hand planted itself in the middle of his chest. He held his breath for that few seconds while he waited to see if she might push him back and end things. When her hand drifted up to his face and caressed his cheek, he had to fight to make sure that the smile he flashed was the right one. He didn't want her to see the wolf in sheep's clothing.

A few minutes later, she was leading him by the hand. As they ducked behind the stadium bleachers and stopped in some tall grass, he knew he'd won.

Dead: Snapshot—Liberty, South Carolina

10

Regrets and Death

With his left hand, Jonathan grabbed one child by the hair and tossed him sideways. Then, using the right hand, the one with his injured wrist, he grabbed the other child and shoved him away. Pain shot up his arm, but he ignored it as best he could. His mind was very cognizant of the fact that he was facing a life-or-death situation. His options were to endure a little pain now or become a zombie.

Using his elbows, he scooted back and brought a booted foot up just in time to kick away the child that had recovered the fastest and was now staggering for him with arms outstretched and mouth open wide. His boot caught the child in the chin and snapped its head back.

A new bolt of pain caused his vision to blur as he pushed himself up to his feet and staggered back a few steps to give himself some room. He pulled out his remaining knife and waved the zombie children in.

"Come on," he hissed. "You almost had me fooled, but now I'm on to your little tricks."

Both children came, but they were now simply just a pair of slow moving zombies and he ended them with almost no effort. As he yanked his knife free, he wiped the blade off on a piece of the tattered tee shirt the little boy had been wearing.

175

The sounds of twigs being snapped from all around him made Jonathan take off in a jog. He glanced down at the cast on his right wrist and frowned. He was going to have a hell of a time explaining that to Nurse Martin. He added that to the list of things he needed to take care of when he reached his house.

When it finally came into view, he breathed a sigh of relief. He made sure to look around before going inside. If any of those things were following him, he would have to take care of them, but the coast appeared to be clear and he slipped in the front door and breathed a huge sigh of relief.

Looking around, he suddenly felt like an intruder. It no longer felt as if this was his home. His eyes landed on a picture that almost appeared to glow in the shaft of light that shone through his living room window.

Walking over to it, he picked it up and looked at it through tear-blurred vision. It was a picture of him and his mother taken on a trip to Charleston a few years ago. He could see Fort Sumter in the background. He pulled the small knapsack from his back and opened it, placing the picture in with an almost religious reverence.

Moving down the nearly pitch black hall that led to his bedroom, Jonathan pulled out his flashlight with his left hand; somewhere along the way, he'd lost his headlamp. He was fairly confident that he would not need to battle any zombies for a little while, so he allowed himself to relax just a bit. When he opened the bedroom door, he scowled at the sour smell of stale beer and pizza. He wondered if this was how his place smelled to everybody who came to visit.

"No wonder you can't get laid," he groused.

Opening his closet door, he had to scramble back in a hurry and tripped over his feet as something large tumbled out at him. He let out a small grunt of pain as he reflexively used his free right hand to help break his fall. Shaking his head to clear it, he saw the dark shape at his feet and laughed bitterly. Standing up carefully, he kicked the vacuum cleaner aside.

176

How many times had he told himself that he was going to get around to cleaning up his closet so that the stupid vacuum cleaner attachment did not fall out every single time he opened the door? Add that to the list of things he'd always been meaning to get around to, but now he never would.

Kneeling, he pulled out a khaki camera bag and carried it to his bed. Tucking the flashlight under his chin, he reached over and opened the curtains to let in a little moonlight so that he might be able to see better.

Slipping the shotgun free, he set it on his bed and then began rummaging through his room for a few more things. He knew that there were plans for teams to start salvaging everything they could from the abandoned residences, but there were a few things he wanted for himself. Also, there were a handful of items he'd rather not have salvage teams finding. He pulled his box of "girlie" magazines from under his bed and stuffed them into the knapsack.

Heading into the bathroom, he grabbed a few more things and then trudged into the kitchen. In the cabinet above the refrigerator were a few items that he would turn over to Nurse Martin. He grabbed all the partially used prescription bottles and added them to the haul. Maybe if he gave her these, she wouldn't rip him a new one for ruining his cast and perhaps even reinjuring his wrist.

His last stop was the shelf in the small laundry room. He opened the cupboard mounted on the back wall and smiled. Two full bottles of Jack and a pint of peppermint schnapps. The last one he opened, taking a pull from the bottle.

Satisfied that he had all he'd come for—plus a few bonus items—Jonathan returned to his bedroom and grabbed his shotgun. He was just slinging it back over his shoulder when he heard what sounded like footsteps on his front porch.

Holding his breath, he heard the door knob rattle. The soft squeak of his front door's hinges came and now Jonathan was more than just a little scared. If it was a zombie, then they could open doors; that was a terrifying thought. If it wasn't zombies,

177

then somebody was nosing around town and breaking into homes.

"Jonathan Patterson...if you are in here, could you say something, please?" a familiar voice called.

"Mr. Deese?" Jonathan let out his breath and emerged from his bedroom. "What are you doing here? And how did you find me?"

"I'm out here because I was on patrol and heard a scuffle. I got there a few seconds too late, but it looks like you handled things well enough. I didn't want to yell and bring down more of those bastards, and you weren't too far ahead. I would have gotten to your house sooner if I hadn't run into a few of those damn zombies my own self."

Jonathan stepped all the way into the living room and saw Stephen Deese standing in his front doorway. He had a machete still clutched in his right hand and it dripping dark fluid on the carpet where a stain was slowly growing. For a moment, Jonathan was annoyed that the man would appear so thoughtless, and then he remembered that he was in the early stages of a zombie apocalypse and his stained carpet did not really register on any list of priorities.

"If you are trying to sneak about, you probably shouldn't wave around your flashlight while you rummage through your place." The man came the rest of the way in and shut the door behind him. "And that brings me to my question. What the Sam Hill are you doing outside of the safe zone in the middle of the night...by *yourself*?"

For a moment, Jonathan didn't know quite what to say. He was standing here with a knapsack slung over one shoulder and a second partially full pack on his back. He finally opted for the truth. He told Mr. Deese everything, including how he'd gotten a really bad feeling regarding the four men who had arrived on Harleys. He said that he could not explain it any clearer than to say they just gave him an uneasy sensation in his gut. He revealed his plan about setting up a few motion-activated cameras that would feed to an app on his cell phone once he found out where these men might be working.

The older man seemed to think things over for a few minutes and Jonathan became increasingly anxious as he waited. At last the man clapped his hands and leveled his gaze at Jonathan.

"I guess it is getting hard to just dismiss things and say it is stuff of fiction considering the fact that we currently find ourselves living in a lousy B-movie." Jonathan breathed a sigh of relief, but the man held up a finger and his voice became stern. "That doesn't mean I necessarily buy into what you're sellin', kid. If you end up being wrong, I don't know nothin' and I don't wanna hear my name falling out of your mouth. Now, let's get back home before anything bad happens."

The pair returned in relative silence and Jonathan actually found himself a bit annoyed that no zombies happened upon him now that he had some help. As soon as they were back inside the perimeter, they separated and he headed over to the booths where people signed up for work details. What he saw only made him more certain than ever that he was on to something.

"Why would we just trust these clowns on a detail headed over to the market?" he scoffed quietly.

That was a blessing and a curse. The good thing was that Domino's, his former place of employment, was in that little complex where the market was located. If he was going to set up his equipment, then this was the best setting possible. He still had his store keys and would have no problem slipping into the empty pizza store. The bad thing was that Mr. Deese had specifically told him to get to his cubicle and not do anything else stupid tonight.

He briefly considered his options. It wasn't a perfect plan, but he doubted there really was such a thing. Before he did anything else, he needed to go see the nurse. In fact, if it went like he expected, then it might actually help him pull off his little scheme.

***

Jamie sat at the sign-up table and found her mind constantly replaying the events of two nights ago. She had regretted it less than five minutes after it was over. This was not like her. She had never just had sex with some random stranger. Hell, she could count her lovers on three fingers.

Four, she reminded herself. How had she tossed all her morals out the window so easily? She kept trying to tell herself that it was the madness of the past several days mixed with the booze. It had destroyed her defenses and left her emotions bare so that everything was going at hyper speed. That might explain how sensitive she'd gotten over Mr. Deese and the way he'd stepped in and taken charge of her mission.

After all, it wasn't her mission. It was for Liberty. It was for everybody living inside their little community.

You need to get your head together, she scolded herself. *You have a responsibility to this town and this is not a time for you to be acting like some stupid schoolgirl. Howard Merchant saw something in you. Isn't it about time you start behaving like the person he knew you to be?*

She would talk to Kevin tonight when he got back from the run he'd signed up for. She would explain that they needed to take a step back and slow things down. He seemed like such a sweet guy. She just knew that he would understand. If not, then that would be his loss.

"We have a problem," Sophie's voice broke into Jamie's reverie. She jerked her head up to see her friend standing with a piece of paper in her hands. Mr. Deese was beside her looking more than a little annoyed.

"It seems that Jonathan Patterson has decided to leave." Sophie shoved the crumpled piece of paper at her.

"What are you talking about?" Jamie took what appeared to be a note from her friend and read it. She looked up with an expression of confusion. "I don't understand."

"This is partially my fault." Mr. Deese stepped forward. "I caught him outside the perimeter. He had slipped out and went to his house in the middle of the night. He had a couple of packs loaded up, but I didn't think anything of it after I gave him a bit of a lecture and escorted him back here."

"That's when he came to see me in the middle of the night because he had ruined his cast. I told him I wasn't going to just get up and go to the infirmary because he couldn't follow simple instructions. I checked it to make sure he hadn't done too much damage and then I wrapped it tight with an Ace bandage and told him to see me later. When he didn't show up yesterday, I figured he was just sulking. I didn't think anything of it." Sophie sounded more than a little distraught, and it was clear that she was in the process of heaping as much blame as possible onto her own shoulders.

"When I didn't see him around yesterday, and then again today, I made a trip out to his place and found that note tacked to his front door," Mr. Deese assumed the narrative. "After making sure he wasn't just hiding out in his house, I asked around, but there is no sign of him."

"Well," Jamie scrunched up her nose as she considered the situation, "it's not like we have a rule saying that folks have to stay here. I feel bad for him, but he is an adult. If he wanted to leave, then he is obviously free to do so."

"You don't think we should look around for him? He damn near got himself killed that night he slipped out," Mr. Deese pressed, sounding like he might be trying to take a little of the blame Sophie was trying to assume.

"I think it's unfortunate, but anybody can leave anytime they want. And it might seem sad...even a little cruel, but we can't spare resources to go looking for a grown man who might be having a bit of a tantrum."

Jamie got up and turned over her seat to her shift replacement. There were still at least a couple hundred people roaming the booths set up on the football field. She joined the pair and steered them away from everybody.

"Look, I understand that you might be upset about this, but I'm honestly surprised more people haven't left." The pair stared at her with open amazement and a hint of confusion. "We make everybody work a six-day week from sunrise to after sunset. Many of our citizens have friends and family that they have no idea as to their condition. People are starting to get a little frayed. We are probably going to lose a few more, but let's not start putting ideas in people's heads. I know what I saw on that little drive to the Lowe's the other day. We may be the anomaly in this apocalyptic equation. All I saw were burning buildings, zombies, and death. Nothing out there that I witnessed gave me any hope that this might be somehow temporary."

Mr. Deese gave her a curious look and then shrugged his shoulders. "If that's how ya feel." And with that peculiar comment, he simply turned and walked away.

Jamie waited until he was out of earshot and then grabbed Sophie by the arm and led her just a bit further from the remaining individuals that were scrambling at the last minute to get their name on tomorrow's work detail lists.

"I did something stupid," she blurted.

"Slept with that Kevin guy, didn't you." It wasn't a question. Sophie had her best "stern mother" face on and her arms folded across her body.

Jamie dropped her head and mumbled that she had. She waited, certain that she was about to get a very angry lecture. All she got was silence and she was beginning to believe that might be even worse.

"Girl, I guess everybody is entitled to a little selfishness as long as it doesn't hurt anybody else."

"You aren't mad or disappointed?" Jamie's head came up slowly. Sophie was smiling.

"Did you give me a ration when I got knocked up and married right after graduation?"

"No, but you and Cliff were a couple that had been together basically forever. Everybody knew you two were going to get married."

"Someday, sure. But I had to turn down a full basketball scholarship. Instead of becoming a doctor like I dreamed, I became a nurse."

"You say that like it's a bad thing. You are an amazing nurse."

"But I would have made an amazing doctor," Sophie said wistfully.

"Still, I don't see how that can be equated to this. I barely know the guy. In fact, I had to dredge my brain to remember his last name." Jamie paused and fought back the tears that threatened to spill from her eyes. "I'm not that kind of girl."

"I know that." Sophie put an arm around Jamie. The two stood huddled together for a few moments. "So maybe you take a few steps back. If this guy is as nice as you think…he'll understand."

There was a sudden flurry of what she now recognized as small arms fire. It sounded distant, but with several teams outside the perimeter the past few days, she dismissed it as anything to be concerned about as she and Sophie headed across the field towards the main school building. The two women had their arms slung over each other like soldiers coming off the battlefield, each of them offering commiserating squeezes as they shared tears and let some of the pressure inside find a release.

Jamie had just wiped her eyes and was composing herself when a voice called out from the tower on top of the stadium press box using one of the police bullhorns. "We have trucks incoming, but there is something wrong."

Running over to the steps that climbed up to the press box with Sophie on her heels, she thought that she was prepared for the worst. Her mind was already weaving an image of the trucks from the quarry coming up the road in a convoy with a few hundred thousand zombies on their tail.

Scrambling up the ladder mounted on the back wall of the press box, she went through the trap door and then climbed up to the tower's lookout platform. She spied the convoy approaching from the north as it rumbled down Ruhamah Road. She could not see anything that might cause alarm.

"Take a look with these," the person on duty said as he handed over a set of binoculars.

Jamie brought them up to her eyes and then gasped. She pulled them down and rubbed her eyes as if that might change what she saw. Looking again, she confirmed her initial assessment. Still, something was wrong. This could not be happening.

The eight massive earthmovers and dump trucks were in a line. The only thing wrong with that was that there should be twelve; but that had nothing to do with Jamie's reaction. Strapped to the grills of each of the four lead trucks was a single figure. She could not take her eyes off the man lashed to the front of second truck.

It was Kevin Staley.

***

Kevin pushed the big loading bay cart down the aisle and started pulling off every can, stacking them in a plastic crate. As soon as he filled one, he set it neatly and then moved the next one into position. He could not help but hum and sing softly as he worked; the song *Master of Puppets* providing the soundtrack to his task.

He could not believe that these backwater idiots could be so gullible. They had put him and the other three on a twelve person detail to the local grocery store. They were supposed to empty out the entire place and load everything that was still good into the open bays of three big delivery trucks that had been put on loan from that ridiculous barricade they were trying to create.

At the moment, his only concern was that they would have to find new Harleys. He'd become rather fond of his bike and did not like leaving it behind. Also, they would still have to head back towards the town.

The good news was that they would be on the very outskirts of the safe zone. Apparently the morons in charge had decided to use some vinyl door and window manufacturing building as the armory. The building was just inside the northern border of what they were trying to secure. A massive amount of ammunition was being stashed in a smaller detached building in the very back. They would actually be able to drive right up to it.

The bad news was that the main building was being converted into dorms just like the high school. There was a lot of activity at this place. Also, apparently they had decided to put a guard on duty. Of course, the person was more of an inventory clerk who was responsible for signing in any ammo being dropped off to add to their stockpile. By the time that person realized what was going on, they would be spraying blood from a slit throat.

They would load as much as they could in as short of a time as possible, and then roll out. People would still be wiping the tears from their eyes by the time he and the fellas were a hundred miles away. Today was going to be busy; but it was also going to be one very long adrenaline rush.

As he reached the end of the aisle, he paused to take a drink of water. Glancing in both directions, he spotted Bob emerging from his aisle. The man gave him a nod and then pushed his big trolley out the front doors. This was the last load. It was time for the fun to begin.

He pushed his own cart out, following a woman who looked like she belonged behind the counter at the local library more than she did out here where the zombies had started to take note of their presence. Four of the members of the team had been put outside to deal with the walkers that were converging on the huge open parking lot of this little strip mall with its grocery store, pizza joint, haircut place, nail salon, and fitness center. That was up from just one when they had first gotten here yesterday, two first thing this morning, and now up to the four that were currently running around, jabbing their long spears into the heads of every zombie that came their way.

Joe had volunteered this morning which, while not really the plan, came as no surprise considering his hard-on for killing zombies. As Kevin exited the store with his last load, he saw Joe dancing past one of the members of the team to take down a zombie that would have most likely gotten its hand on the older man.

He shoulda just let the zombie do some of the dirty work, Kevin thought as he pushed up to the open doors of the trailer that looked to be over three-quarters of the way full. Bob had already walked away from his cart, oblivious to the dirty looks and scowls of the two men that he'd left to do all the grunt work of loading the haul up into the truck. Until this last load, he and everybody else had stayed with his or her cart and helped hand the content up into the trailers. Kevin watched as Bob vanished back inside the store.

He did not envy whomever it was that Bob Capka met next. Of course, that first person might have the luxury of a quick death. The rest might not fare so well.

A scream brought Kevin out from behind the back of the truck where he was in the middle of handing his crates up to the large, librarian-looking woman inside. He'd been wondering at that exact moment if this woman would have been pretty in a few months after the zombie apocalypse forced her to cut down on the snack foods.

A smile split Kevin's face when he discovered the source of the scream. Joe had run the man he'd just saved clean through with his spear and was guiding his struggling victim towards a throng of seven or eight zombies. He continued to watch as the man was grabbed by the first walker to get close enough and then jerked free of the spear and dragged to the ground where he was pounced on by the others.

Joe wasn't foolish enough to think his actions had gone un-noticed and spun just as the other two people who had been charged with keeping the lot secure came rushing for him with their spears raised. They were screaming for him to get on the

186

ground as they closed from almost halfway across the huge asphalt wasteland that was strewn with corpses from the past two
days of killing.

It almost reminded Kevin of the scene from *Raiders of the
Lost Ark*. The rule had been made very clear that guns were a
last resort. With the undead not posing what was considered a
serious threat or coming in large enough numbers to merit concern, nobody had seen fit to carry one.

Well, Kevin thought, *almost no one.*

Joe drew a semi-automatic .45 caliber from where he'd kept
it tucked against his spine and under his loose denim shirt. The
first shot hit the woman that had been charging, catching her solidly in the right thigh. She buckled and fell hard, bouncing off
the concrete with an audible smack. Joe was actually kinder to
the man. Two shots to the chest dropped him.

By then, the people in the back of the truck were emerging
to see what was going on.

Kevin turned and stepped into the first one. It had been the
pudgy woman with the pretty face. He already had his big KA-
BAR in hand and drove it up and into her flabby belly. She
gasped and blood spewed from her open mouth as he gave it an
extra twist before pulling it free.

The man who was right on her heels ended up stumbling
backwards as he caught on rather quickly as to what was happening. He landed on his side, fumbling for the blade he was
carrying on his own belt.

"Ah-ah-ah," Kevin taunted, wagging a finger at the man as
he stepped over and stood over his body.

Reaching down, he grabbed the man by the hair and drove
his still dripping blade into a mouth that was open and poised to
scream. There was a gagging gurgle and the guy flailed while
death came with painful slowness. Kevin left the KA-BAR jutting from the man's mouth as he snatched the blade that had
been intended for him from the ground. His victim's hand
clutched open and shut impotently as Kevin looked down on the
man's final death throes.

187

"I'll have my knife back," he sneered as he placed his boot on the man's forehead and yanked his KA-BAR free while shifting his newest acquisition to his left hand.

A scream from within the store made him hurry his pace as he returned inside. Just as he entered the open front doors, he winced out of reflex. A body hurled past on his right and slammed into one of the thick plate windows, sending a spider web of cracks racing across its surface.

"Dammit, Trunk!" Kevin snapped. "How about giving a call of heads-up."

"Sorry," Mark apologized as he stalked over to the stunned figure sprawled on the floor where she'd slid after being thrown. Leaning down, he stomped into her chest once and then grabbed her head with both hands and jerked hard to the right until there was an audible crack. Looking up, he wiped his forehead with the back of his hand. "Snapping necks is harder than it looks in them Stallone movies."

"Where's Bob?" Kevin asked, his eyes scanning the interior of the store.

"Saw him back in the pharmacy with that brother and sister." Mark pointed to the rear of the store.

Kevin nodded and headed towards the back. "Get Joe and have the trucks ready to roll. I'll get Bob."

He picked up a lantern that was sitting on the floor. They had placed several throughout the store and had them lit even during the day since it was deceptively dark not too far past the checkout lanes. He had come down the far left of the store and turned the corner when he heard a peculiar sound.

Raising the lantern, he saw a figure hanging from what looked like an extension cord. The cord was secured to an overhead pipe in the ceiling and now swung back and forth as the figure at the end kicked and struggled. He continued forward, but had slowed considerably. By the time he was close enough to make out the details, the body had ceased its struggle and simply dangled limply.

188

Bob was standing behind the sister of the pair. He was resting his chin on her shoulder and his lips were moving, but Kevin could not make out what was being said. The sister was staring in open shock and horror up at her brother and, by this point, Kevin seriously doubted that she heard anything that Bob was saying either.

"Time to go, Bob," Kevin called.

The man looked up through the long hair dangling in his eyes. That was the only indication that he had heard anything. For just a moment, Kevin felt fear try to creep into his belly as he looked into Bob's dark gaze.

There was a flash of something metal and then Bob stepped from behind the twenty-something woman who was still so transfixed on the image of her brother hanging from the ceiling that she did not react. Blood sprayed from her throat in time with her beating heart, and at last she realized her fate. Staggering back, the woman dropped to her knees, hands trying in desperate futility to staunch the flow of blood.

Despite the voice in his head that screamed in warning, Kevin turned his back to the scene, which included Bob, and started for the front of the store. He stepped out into the late afternoon sun and sucked in a breath of clean air.

"Okay, boys, let's swing by that little armory they got going, grab what we can as fast as possible, and then hit the road." Kevin climbed into a truck and flinched as Bob chose to join him.

The three large trucks pulled out of the parking lot and hung a right on Main Street, following it around the dog leg as they cruised towards their ultimate destination.

***

Chief Gilstrap climbed up into the big dump truck. This one would be parked someplace where he could get to it if there ever came a need. It was a tank minus a gun turret and would probably be able to mow through a pretty massive horde of the undead

189

if it ever came to that.

He was coming up on the market where he thought he might check in and offer some help if the salvage team was still working on getting everything loaded up. He was just passing a body shop on the right when he saw the big eighteen-wheelers pulling out of the market's parking lot.

"Looks like we might have almost everybody home for dinner," the chief said with a smile.

Having the store emptied out was a huge event. This would give them a clear idea of how much food they would have as they got the gardens up. Between hunting, fishing, and farming, they would hopefully be able to sustain themselves. Of course, he hadn't eliminated the possibility of sending out teams to forage and scavenge abroad. There was no sense in letting things go to waste.

He was coming up on the market when a figure that was definitely not a zombie darted out in the road ahead and began waving his arms around like a maniac. He put on the brakes and was surprised to see Jonathan Patterson standing in the middle of the road. There was a look on his face that put Chief Gilstrap on high alert.

As he climbed out of the massive dump truck, his head was on a swivel as he looked everywhere at once while still keeping Patterson in his field of vision. Something was definitely wrong.

"They killed 'em!" the young man blurted, pointing back towards the market parking lot. "Killed all of 'em and they are leaving with the food!"

"Wait," Chief Gilstrap barked, silencing the man. "Who killed who and who is leaving with the food?"

"Those bikers that arrived a few days ago. I tried to warn you guys, but nobody wanted to believe me."

"What the blazes are you going on about?" The chief was close enough now that he could get a whiff. Nope, no signs that the kid was drunk.

Jonathan Patterson shoved a cell phone at the chief. "It's

here. Not everything, but enough. Just look!"

"Phones haven't been working for days, young man," the chief ignored the device being thrust at him.

"Sure, but my battery powered cameras are working just fine. I had the feeds tethered to my phone and it is all on film. Just look, for crying out loud."

Chief Gilstrap was tired. He had no idea what this kid was babbling about, but if looking at some grainy video would shut him up, then it would be a small price to pay to return home, wipe himself down with a warm, wet towel, and then sleep for about twenty hours. Of course he doubted that he would get anything close to that amount of sleep, but a man had to have dreams.

He took the cell phone and tapped the sideways triangle that would start the video rolling. The first thing he noticed was that the footage was far from grainy. In fact, the picture was clearer than what he saw on his own home television.

He watched as a few of the store's salvage team were moving around to deal with approaching zombies. Then he saw one of them walk over and thrust his spear through the chest of one of the other team members. The picture zoomed in and he instantly recognized the victim…and the killer. The problem was that he knew the victim's first and last name. He had played softball with him in the park during Fourth of July picnics.

The killer's name escaped him. All he knew was that it was one of those four men who had just arrived on motorcycles—one of the four men that Jonathan Patterson had tried to warn him about. He only watched a few more seconds of the video. He didn't need to see anymore.

"They just headed for town in the trucks with all the supplies," Jonathan said in a rush.

Why would they head towards *town?* Chief Gilstrap thought. Surely it could not be simply to get their motorcycles. They could break in to any shop in the country now and take the bike of their choosing. Then it hit him. He knew exactly why they would be headed towards town. At this precise moment, Chief

Adam Gilstrap felt like an idiot. He had allowed strangers to come into his town. He had not said a word against them just signing on for one of the most important salvage operations of the town's lives.

In short; he had acted like a rookie...or worse.

Turning to face the rest of his team that had joined him on this truck acquisition, he took off his hat and wrung it in his hands as he spoke.

"I don't have a lot of time to explain, but we have four very bad men about to swoop in and probably take at least half of our ammunition. This is not a game, and I will warn you that if you come with me, you may have to shoot and kill a living human being. That is not a thing that you should take lightly. If you come, be prepared for the worst, and if you choose to sit this one out, there will be no man or woman who thinks less of you."

Chief Gilstrap climbed up into the truck and was not surprised to see Jonathan climb into the passenger's side. What did surprise him a little was to see all of the trucks in his convoy follow him as he turned left on Maplecroft Street instead of Peachtree Street.

As the trucks neared the entrance to the vinyl door and window manufacturing facility, the sound of a single gunshot was able to be heard over the roar of the massive engine of the dump truck.

"Dammit," Chief Gilstrap cursed.

11

Casualties

Kevin brought the lead truck to a stop at the end of the long entry drive that led to the farthest rear end of the door and window facility. He turned so that they were facing out to aid in their departure; not that he expected anything to go wrong. Bob was already climbing out before they came to a complete stop. Kevin set the brake as the other two members of his gang jogged up. They had parked out on the street just before the right turn onto South Norman Street.

He had not bothered to concern himself with setting the safety on his handgun as he approached the large, detached storage shed where the ammo had been gathered. He still could not believe their luck. These people were still so stuck in civilization and the way things were that they could not see the reality. This was a new world akin to the days of warlords and kings.

Kevin Staley would be both. He would secure his place with a ruthless selfishness. He and his three friends would create an empire from the ruins and sit atop it like lords. They would have people throwing themselves under the umbrella of their rule willingly. For that to happen, they needed some necessities. This haul would set them up perfectly.

He sort of wished that Jamie chick would have come along, but he hadn't even considered asking. She was entrenched in that small town mindset. She'd even quoted some silly sentiment about Liberty being "where neighbors become friends" or some such nonsense. He had not even tried to make her an offer. She would have probably run off and told that relic of a cop that really seemed to be running the show.

Unfortunately for the people of this town, the cop wasn't really on the ball. He was just as slow in realizing that the world had not begun a slow decline into chaos; it was already here in full effect. Not that Kevin was complaining. It had made their job that much easier.

In a way, he might be doing these folks a favor. After this little disaster, maybe they would learn their lesson and become more capable of survival. Either that or they would all starve and die before the end of the first winter. It made no difference either way as far as Kevin and the others were concerned.

Kevin was about ten feet from the side door that opened to the storage area where the ammunition was kept when a young man emerged from a single door beside where a pair of cars were parked. That single door actually went into the main part of the complex.

"What do we have here, fella?" the man asked as he took off his ball cap and wiped his forehead.

"Actually just here to pick up some stuff," Kevin replied casually.

"Excuse me?" The man pulled up and regarded first Kevin and then Bob who had altered his course from the location of the ammunition and was now headed towards him. "What would you be picking up?"

"Ammunition of course," Kevin replied with a laugh. That had been just enough to get the man to look his way and take his eyes off of Bob who was now only a few strides from him.

As soon as the man's head turned that fraction, Bob had a knife in his hand. He jumped up onto the small landing just as the man was turning his attention back. The knife flashed and then plunged into the unwitting fool's throat. Bob pulled it out, guided the man to the ground, and then started back for Kevin.

By then, Joe and Mark had crossed the rest of the distance and reached the entrance to the ammunition's storage room just as Kevin opened the door. Kevin stepped inside and gave a pleasant nod to the lone woman who was standing in front of a stack of crates that went to the ceiling. She had a clipboard in her hand and was busily jotting down something.

"Can I help you?" she asked without even a drop of concern in her voice.

Kevin was glad that they had not only gotten cleaned up, but they had also been given a fresh change of clothes. He was actually wearing a Liberty High School football jersey. The black did an excellent job of hiding the blood.

"Here to help you with the inventory," Kevin lied.

"Kinda late for that," the woman snorted. "Figures help would show up after I got most of it done."

"Oh," Kevin could not suppress the mirth in his voice, "we aren't here to count."

Just then, Bob entered behind him. The woman's expression changed instantly. Kevin turned and saw a slash of bright red blood that had sprayed the once-white tee shirt that Bob had donned. He turned back to the woman, stepping aside to allow his friend to do what he did best.

Grabbing the first box, Kevin actually winced. Bob was astride the flailing woman, hands locked around her throat as he allowed her to slowly wilt to the ground under his grip. Joe and Mark hurried in and did not need to be told what to do. That was just another thing that Kevin believed put his group of four ahead of an entire town: nobody needed to be told what to do. He supposed that having sign-up sheets and that sort of thing might be fine for some folks, but it simply wasn't his cup of tea.

They found a pallet jack and started loading it. A moment or two later, Bob fell in and began to help. They had the first load out and were piling it into the back of the open cargo bay when the sounds of approaching vehicles could be heard.

Kevin recalled something about that cop leading a group out

to bring in more trucks for that silly barricade and considered shrugging it off. He had climbed up into the bay and sent Bob and Joe back to get the next load. Mark was just shoving another crate in when something about the approaching engines got Kevin's attention: they were slowing.

"Dammit all to hell," he swore, causing Mark to look up at him.

"Problems?" the large man rumbled.

"I think we're about to have company. Go grab the others...I think we are gonna have to maybe fight our way out of this."

"What?" Mark turned back towards the road as a convoy of various large vehicles slowed where he and Joe had parked their rigs. "Aww, man."

"I said go get the others, Trunk!" Kevin snapped. "Let me do the talking."

Mark dropped the crate he'd been holding and took off at a jog for the storage shed. Kevin hurried to the cab of the truck and grabbed his binoculars. Standing on the step of the driver's side, he brought the glasses to his eyes.

"Fuck me runnin'," he cursed.

He saw a few people climb out of some sort of earth mover and a cement mixer. After a small meeting at the dump truck in the lead, they jogged over and climbed into the cabs of the rigs carrying their supplies. He saw the chief lean out the driver's side window of the big dump truck in front and signal practically right at him.

"That answers that," Kevin sighed.

Joe, Mark, and Bob emerged from the doorway. Mark and Joe both cast concerned glances back towards the road where the convoy was now moving again. It did not go far and Kevin felt his stomach churn just a bit more. They were parking across the exit. There would be no way out now.

"New plan, boys." Kevin climbed out of the cab and drew his pistol. "Time to split up. Trunk, you come with me. Bob and

196

Joe, you guys cut through those woods." He pointed to the right. "Make your way out of their little perimeter and get to the highway. There should be plenty of old beater trucks in that shitty little town that can be hotwired. Meet up at that BI-LO in Easley. We can re-group and figure out what to do from there."

The two men nodded and took off at a jog for the trees. Mark stayed silent until they vanished over the edge of the pavement and into the tall grass. "Why are we going back towards Greenville? That place is a—" he began, but Kevin cut him off.

"A death trap? Yeah, we aren't going that way. I think maybe we would be better off if we ditched those two and took off on our own." The big man seemed confused and his eyes darkened a little. "Problem, Trunk?"

"We've been like brothers for a long time, Kev," Mark replied.

"We can discuss this later." Kevin gave the other man a shove. "Time to run."

The pair ducked back around the building and headed south. They were in the trees just as the sounds of massive diesel engines rumbling to a stop were heard.

Kevin ducked under some branches and began to weave through the dense growth. He could hear Mark already wheezing behind him.

The guy has a massive chest and huge arms, but he can't run worth a damn, Kevin thought with a hint of annoyance.

They had not gone far when he spotted a clearing up ahead. Through the trees he was able to make out the shapes of gigantic power line towers. He thought that he might have a better idea about where they were now. Unfortunately, if they turned to the right, they would come out right by the school in just a short distance. The other way was the same direction he'd sent Bob and Joe.

He was weighing out his options when a voice shouted from his left, "Stop where you are and put your hands in the air."

"How many times have I heard that command?" Kevin muttered.

***

Chief Gilstrap was pretty sure he was angrier at himself than anybody else. He'd been about as irresponsible as he could have possibly managed. In his opinion, he had acted just like the bumpkin, backwoods cop those four men had assumed him to be. He'd been a regular country mouse since this whole nightmare began.

Despite all he'd seen, despite the little he'd learned from a handful of movies, he had just not taken this seriously. Maybe he kept hoping that the government would get a handle on things. Sure, power was out, media outlets had spewed warnings in the last days, but he refused to believe that the world was going to be wiped out by zombies. That was just not possible.

Now his community was paying the price for his negligence. He had allowed absolute strangers to just waltz in and join perhaps the singular most important mission that the community was undertaking—the gathering of food. Sure, he hadn't sent them alone, but he had allowed *all* of them to go out together.

"Those are our trucks!" Jonathan blurted, pointing at two big rigs sitting just before the intersection with South Norman Street.

The chief pulled over and grabbed his portable radio. "Ivan, you on?"

"Right here, chief," a voice replied almost instantly.

"I think we have a problem." He related what Jonathan had told him as well as a short version of what he'd seen on that horrible recording of the massacre at the market. "I'm at the door and window factory. It looks like they drove one truck right to the fucking ammo storage. I don't have eyes on anybody yet, but I am going to move in. I need you to come in from the south if they try to make a run through the woods. I know this is going to

198

go down fast, so grab who you can and get moving. I am going to send part of my detail to grab the two rigs these assholes left beside the road. I'll send them north on Norman and have them circle back to Peachtree. That should cover their most likely route of escape."

"I'm already on the move, chief," Ivan replied. "I have a few men headed for Highway 123 just in case."

Adam leaned out his window and gave the word for every-body to get going. One of his team called out, "Where you gonna be?"

Looking over to the big truck that was pointed out obviously to expedite their departure, he thought he saw movement from back by the ammunition storage. "I am going to block the exit and then a few of us are going to go in on foot and take these animals down."

A moment later, he was climbing out of the dump truck. When he drew his pistol, it dawned on him that he had never once found the need to pull out his gun for a call during his en-tire career in Liberty. He had laughed at the shows on television where cops seemed to have their weapons out of their holster more than in. His wife had told him that he should consider it a blessing. Truthfully, he did. He saw nothing exciting or reward-ing about taking another human life. It was possible that he might be about to take four in a very short while.

He had five of his team with him. He'd told Jonathan to stay in the truck, keep it running, and lay on the horn if he saw any-thing. He'd been happy when the young man had not made a fuss or insisted on coming along. Besides having the same doubts he had regarding the four men and one woman following him as he hugged the wall of the long building, Jonathan was wearing a cast on his right arm; that made him pretty much use-less in a fight.

He moved to the end of the building and peeked around the corner. The semi was still running, the back still open, but there were no signs of anybody moving around. Edging a bit further out to get a better look, his eyes lit upon a body sprawled on the ramp that led from one of the doors that opened to the main building. He noticed the large pool of dark fluid spread out in a lopsided halo around the corpse.

It was Isaiah Newkirk. He would deal with his guilty conscience later. The kid's face still had an expression of surprise and pain etched into it. He held up a hand to signal everybody to stand fast. Having been out in this insane zombie infested countryside with these people for a while, he was confident that they knew what his gesture meant. He didn't have time to check as he ducked low and dashed for the storage building.

He edged around the corner and then hurried down the length. Rounding this corner would put him right by the entrance. Pistol at the ready, he stayed low to minimize his chances of being shot—people shooting at adult-sized targets automatically tended to fire high. Holding his breath, he risked a look and saw the open door. Still on alert, his body a spring being tightened almost to the point of snapping, he made it to the door. Looking inside, he saw legs sticking out from beside a stack of crates.

He listened for a few more heartbeats and was only able to hear his own blood pounding in his ears. He ventured inside, but it only took him a few seconds to ascertain that the place was empty except for the dead body on the floor. He didn't have the luxury to do anything other than glance and confirm that Gretchen Criss, Granny Criss' daughter, was dead. Her eyes were dull and staring up at the ceiling without seeing anything.

He rushed out and waved his team forward as he moved to the next corner of the main building and took a look. If these four tried to slip around the building and back up to the road, Jonathan would've spotted them by now and laid on the horn.

Knowing that Ivan would be coming up from the south, that left east. Motioning to his team, due east was the direction that Adam Gilstrap took off in. He stayed cautious, but also knew that he needed to move with urgency and purpose. That was the only way that he was going to have any chance at catching these murderous bastards if they had opted to try and escape to the east back towards the heart of town.

They were just emerging where Tillman and Clemson intersected when the sound of an engine turning over snapped his head to the left. He took off at a sprint, the sounds of heavy footfalls behind him letting him know that his team was right on his heels. About two-thirds of the way up Clemson, there was the boom of a shotgun and a scream. Seconds later, an old blue Ford pickup was just backing up onto the road. Adam Gilstrap stopped cold and brought his pistol up. He only had a second or two to make his decision.

He sighted on the head that he saw through the back window and was about to shoot when a fire truck appeared at that end of the street, effectively blocking the exit. The truck veered suddenly and tried to cut through the yard of the house at the end of the road. It clipped a tree as a second big red response vehicle arrived. The pickup slammed into the first fire truck with a metallic crunch. A plume of steam signaled the death of the pickup, but both doors flew open indicating the passengers were apparently fine.

The one with the long hair had just managed to get a few steps when somebody that had been riding in the back of the fire engine flew through the air and tackled him. The other one fared even worse. Two large men decked out in the protective gear of the roving patrols which included a lot of modified football equipment slammed into him like he was a lineman's sled.

Looking around, the chief searched for the other two. Already, some of the people who had been housed in the residences in this small neighborhood were coming out onto the porch to see what all the racket was about.

"Sumbitches tried to steal my pickup!" an angry voice shouted. "Didn't have the decency to ask, just hotwired the damn thing and was taking off."

Chief Gilstrap walked up to see Craig Whalen standing where there used to be a gate. Now, all that remained was a bunch of twisted metal. He was cradling a big double-barrel shotgun that still had bluish smoke drifting from the business end.

"How about you go give the fellas some help securing those two," the chief suggested. The look he saw on Craig's face told him that those two would be getting exactly the sort of treatment he hoped for. Turning back up the street to the growing number of citizens, he called out, "Anybody see two other fellas sneaking around? One of 'em is a beefy sort, the other is tall, has reddish hair and a goatee."

The looks on the faces he could see told him that the other pair hadn't been spotted. He cursed under his breath and almost as if in response, his radio crackled.

"Got eyes on 'em, chief!" Ivan reported, more than just a hint of excitement in his voice. "They took off when I told them to surrender. They went back into the woods and are on the run towards Southern Vinyl."

"Taking them alive is not, I repeat *not* a priority."

The chief turned to the onlookers who all had varied expressions of confusion on their faces. This needed to be remedied. People were still trying to live life as if things were mostly okay. The level of denial was on a massive scale, and part of it was because maybe only a small percentage of the citizens had actually seen an animate zombie up close and for real. That was going to have to change if there was going to be any chance for the people of Liberty to have at least some shot at survival.

"I need a vehicle," he called. He felt his annoyance grow as they all seemed to be looking to each other for a volunteer. "NOW dammit!"

That did it. A young man started for him, digging in his pocket as he hurried over pointing to the driveway he'd just come from. "It's the red Chevy, chief."

Taking the keys with a quick nod and a thanks, he hurried over and jumped in the driver's seat. Bo Summers hopped into the passenger seat. Bo Summers was perhaps as large as the big man from the foursome, but not in a gym-created way. Bo was what the chief considered country-boy big. Even this early in spring, he was already sporting a farmer's tan. His hands were massive slabs of callous from bucking hay and other backbreaking farm work. He'd been on every mission so far that the chief had helmed and had not complained or griped even once.

"What's going on, chief?" Bo asked as they did a quick turn around and headed for Maplecroft which would take them to Ruhamah and back to where they had left the big trucks destined for the slowly expanding barricade.

"You mean besides the zombie apocalypse?" The chief gripped the steering wheel tight as he took the left turn in a wide skidding slide.

"You really think this is it?" Bo asked in a voice that sounded very much unlike the tough guy he had known for over four decades.

"I think it is worse than we can imagine. I think that we might be fighting a losing battle…but I also think we will do whatever we need to do until we can't do anything else."

"And what about these four pieces of garbage? How did that happen?"

The chief swallowed the bitterness in the back of his throat. "My fault. I guess I didn't want to believe folks would go rotten so fast."

"You're a damn cop, Adam. How the hell can you not think there are bad people who will take advantage of this?" The huge man threw his arms up gesturing to the countryside they were driving past.

"We ain't seen this sort of thing here in Liberty, at least not on this level. Not saying we are all angels, but it's not like we have murders and rapes happening every day." Chief Gilstrap sighed. "But you're right…I dropped the ball on this one."

"Dropped the ball?"

"Can we do this later?" the chief said as he brought the car to a stop beside the dump truck. Jonathan was leaning out the window with a confused look on his face.

"What is going on?" The man opened the door and managed

to climb out using the three rung ladder to help get down.

"We have two of them over on Clemson. Ivan said he spotted the other pair coming out of the woods, but they turned around and might be headed back this way." The chief stepped out into the middle of the road and shielded his eyes from the setting sun as he scanned the tree line for signs of anything.

He saw the flash…but did not have a chance to react. He felt like a fist punched him in the center of the chest. Staggering back, he tried to get a breath, but nothing seemed to be happening. A coppery taste filled his mouth and he felt something trickle down his chin. A burning sensation flooded his pain receptors as he choked on a mouthful of blood while still gasping in futility for a breath that showed no inclination of making its way into his lungs.

He could hear a buzzing sound. Looking up, he saw Bo standing over him with a rifle in his hands. It looked like he was screaming something. Adam Gilstrap tried to hear what the man was yelling, but it could not make its way past that buzz and ringing in his ears. Maybe if he just closed his eyes for a moment and focused on catching his breath; besides…he was suddenly more tired than he could ever remember being in his life.

***

Jonathan winced at the sound of a gunshot from way too close. He felt something warm splatter his face. Reaching up, he wiped with his left hand and staggered back when it came away bloody. A second later, he realized that he hadn't felt a thing. If he was dying now, then maybe it wasn't such a bad thing. There was no pain.

The chief crumpled to the ground beside him and was flat on his back, staring up at the sky with a pained look on his face. After blinking his eyes, Jonathan saw the dark stain on the chief's shirt. It was growing before his eyes, and then there was the blood leaking from the corners of the chief's mouth.

The sound of a rifle seemed to explode right next to his head. Ducking, Jonathan glanced over to see big Bo Summers with a .30-06 pressed to his shoulder. He fired a second time and started yelling something about staying on the ground or the next one was gonna be in the face.

When did I hit the ground? he thought as he realized he was now flat on his belly, and right next to the chief who was making a strange, wet wheezing sound that reminded him of sucking through a straw when the drink glass was basically empty.

He heard the sounds of shouting and rolled over to see a group of men advancing on two of those bikers. Both were on the ground with one clutching his leg and the other curled up in the fetal position. There was a lot of hollering about "Don't move!" and "My leg!" but to Jonathan it was just noise. He was looking over at the chief who was almost as pale as a zombie. The only reason that Jonathan knew the chief wasn't one of those things was because he was just pale. There were no hints of blue or gray discoloration, and his eyes were not filmed over and shot through with those black tracers.

"The chief's been shot," Jonathan said, his voice barely a whisper. He looked around and realized that nobody had heard him. "Hey, get some help over here!" Jonathan made it to his knees and crawled over to the chief. "The chief has been shot!"

Looking over his shoulder, he saw that everybody was busy throwing those two bikers onto their stomachs and checking them for weapons. A hand brushed his face and Jonathan actually let out a little scream. Looking down, he saw the chief's lips were moving, but he couldn't hear.

He leaned down so that he could, his ear almost touching the chief's lips. "Say that again, chief. What can I do?" Try as he might, Jonathan could not dredge up one single thing from any of the first aid classes that he had attended during high school health class or the mandatory ones he'd been forced to go to when he became part of the Domino's management team.

"Tell her…lock it down. Keep our people safe." There was

a slight gasp, and then a long, slow exhale.

Jonathan popped up and looked down at the man who had been the Liberty, South Carolina Chief of Police for what seemed like forever. The man was still staring straight up, but his eyes were not seeing anything.

And they were changing

A feeling of rage overwhelmed him, and before he realized it, he was on his feet and stomping towards the two bodies lying face down on the side of the road. The closer he got, the faster he moved. The men restraining the bikers had their backs to him and so nobody even noticed until he shoved past two of the men kneeling on the back of the one with the reddish hair.

With everything he had, Jonathan kicked the man. His booted foot found ribs and there was a satisfying crack.

Somebody grabbed him after the third kick. Jonathan thrashed and squirmed, trying to get in another solid boot to the ribs of the bastard lying on the ground. The biker named Kevin looked up at him, a slight trickle of blood now seeping from the corner of his mouth, but nothing like what he'd seen coming from the chief. He was staring into the man's eyes, all his rage threatening to explode in his chest.

The man made eye contact with Jonathan…and then he smiled.

12

"Thank you."

"I say we drag them out of town and feed them to some of those monsters!" somebody shouted from the gathered throng that looked to be pretty much anybody not currently on watch or patrol.

Jamie stood on the small stage and looked around the packed high school football stadium. The faces looking back at her were a mixture of fear, hurt, and—most of all—rage. She was having a difficult time not letting herself spiral down those same paths.

At first, she had been shocked when the trucks pulled in with the four men lashed to the grills. Two of them, Kevin Staley and Mark Trees, were bleeding from apparent bullet wounds. Joe Spencer, the slender man with all the tattoos had a busted nose, black eyes, and a gash where his teeth had come through the flesh right below his bottom lip.

Then there was Bob Capka. He was a bit scraped up, but showed no signs of having been injured physically in any other way. He was also the only one of the four who had not said a word. In fact, she hadn't heard him speak one time since his arrival. And now, with the four men chained up in the boiler room of the high school with armed guards watching them twenty-four hours a day, he still had not said a single word.

207

She was about to ask why these men were tied to the trucks when Ivan, Bo Summers, and Jonathan all piled out of the second truck in the convoy. They didn't say a word to anybody as they went to the rear of the giant dump truck. Ivan made eye contact with Jamie and had motioned her over. She and Sophie rushed to where the man stood, and as she got close, she saw tears in the man's eyes. She had no idea what could cause a man like Ivan Potter to cry, and in that instant, she wasn't entirely sure that she wanted to know.

She had not even realized that she had not seen the chief until the back of the dump truck was opened to reveal what was inside the dump bed. Her hands had flown to her mouth, but it only managed to partially stifle the scream. Standing in the open bay was Chief Adam Gilstrap. Only…it wasn't him anymore; not really.

This obscene caricature of the Liberty Chief of Police had a dark stain that had spread to almost the entire right side of his shirt. The eyes staring back at her were filmed over and shot full of black tracers. His skin was a bluish-gray and hung loosely on his face, giving him a pathetic look that further removed whatever this thing was from the man he'd been; the man that Jamie Burns remembered.

She had turned to Ivan, but was unable to ask the question. Perhaps she simply did not want the answer. Yet, it didn't take a college degree to know what the general report would include.

"They did it," Jonathan whispered.

He stepped up beside Jamie and handed her his cell phone. She looked down and saw a video that was ready to be played. As she watched the footage, she felt an icy chill run up and down her spine. Her blood felt like it froze in her veins.

As she watched the video, Ivan had lured the thing that used to be the chief to the rear of the dump truck's bed. The thing had actually stepped off the lip and landed on the ground with a terrible snap of bone, then began to struggle to its feet. Ivan and Bo had thrown a coat over its head and then cuffed it and led it to a

"Thank you."

nearby groundskeeper's equipment shed.

"What are you doing?" she had asked when they came back.

"Not a damn thing until we talk to Sarah," Ivan had said solemnly.

"I'll do it," Jamie offered.

"You sure?" Ivan asked with a hint of doubt in his tone.

"This is my responsibility. I would like for you to see to the dispersal of this crowd. This is something I have to do." She had turned to Bo Summers. "I want you to secure the prisoners in the basement of the high school. Put a pair of guards on them. They are not to be left unsupervised for even a moment."

She recalled being a little surprised when there was not even a hint of questioning as she barked orders. She turned to Sophie after that and told her that all she wanted her to do was ensure that the prisoners did not bleed out. They would stand trial for their actions.

That had been the statement that caused a few people to start voicing protests. She had spun on the cluster of people gathered and leveled her angry glare at them all. "I don't want to hear it, people. We will do this right."

Before another word could be said, she had turned and walked away. Her eyes spied the police cruiser and she decided that would do fine. She was just getting behind the wheel when the passenger door opened and Jonathan Patterson jumped in beside her.

"I will deal with you later," she said. "I don't have time right now."

"Deal with me?" he sounded perplexed.

"The note? You were supposedly leaving Liberty, and then you just happen to be in place to record that footage."

"I will explain everything while you drive over to the chief's house," the man had said.

He related his plan and how he figured the only way he could ease his suspicions was to watch these guys for a while. He honestly had not expected anything like what happened. If he'd figured for a moment that the four men were capable of

209

such violence, he would have probably not possessed the nerve. At the most, he just figured they would steal a bunch of supplies or something like that.

He gave his account of what had taken place when the chief got shot, but there was something else he seemed to be struggling with. Jamie waited, but she did not need to be distracted when she walked up to the chief's house to inform his wife about what happened to her husband.

"Just spit out whatever it is, Jonathan," she finally said, sounding a bit harsher than she wanted, but right now she just did not have the patience.

"The chief's last words…they were for you. At least I'm pretty sure they were."

Jamie pulled the car up in front of the chief's house. She shut off the engine and turned to face the man beside her.

"He said to tell you to…to lock the town down and keep the people safe."

Jamie considered the words for a moment. Part of her was stunned. If she had been honest with herself at any point up until that moment, she truly believed that the chief had not held her in any esteem. He certainly hadn't shown her anything resembling the respect that she felt she deserved. Then a little phrase that her dad had often said rang in the back of her mind.

Respect is earned, not given.

Up to this point, had she done anything to merit that respect? She had been tentative and petulant to the point of ridiculous. Sure, there was nothing in the mayor's handbook (God, how she wished such a thing actually existed) about how to lead your community through the zombie apocalypse.

Since returning to Liberty after college, she had been the picture of what she believed a proper government official should be. But she had been following text book examples, saying all the right things. Had it all been just an act? When she'd been handed the office of mayor, she had been stunned. Yet, she knew all of the administrative things that needed to be done. What she

210

"Thank you."

did not know was how to deal with scenarios that weren't in the book.

Climbing out of the car, she had told Jonathan to stay put. This was something that she needed to do on her own. And so she had walked up to the door and knocked. When Sarah Gilstrap opened the door, her expression changed in an instant and Jamie was amazed at how the woman had known before she'd even spoken the words. She hadn't known the details, but she knew the ultimate result and the reason for the visit.

Jamie decided right then that she was going to give the woman as much information as she had. Surely the wife needed to be aware. Then another idea struck her.

"We will be trying the four men for murder. Would you care to be present?"

The woman had nodded. The two shared a few tears and then Jamie asked the second part of her question.

"We need to…put him to rest. Do you want to be present for that?"

After a long pause, the woman wiped her eyes. "I'll do it."

A half hour later, Jamie was standing by the grounds keeping shed. Ivan had gone inside with the chief's wife. A moment later, they both emerged. Two days after that, the trial had been called to order. In less than ten minutes it had been postponed until the next day.

Word had spread fast and when Jamie arrived at the high school she was stunned to discover a line several people wide that wrapped all the way around the building. She decided that if everybody in town wanted to be present, then she would accommodate them.

A platform was hurriedly constructed in the center of the football field. The next day, she called the court to order.

"We want our lawyer!" Kevin Staley had called as he was led in shackles to the chair where he was cuffed and firmly secured.

"You will be acting in your own defense," Jamie replied, nodding to Bo Summers who quickly shoved a ball gag in the

211

man's mouth. "But you will speak when it is your turn, and not a moment before."

With that, the trial began. One by one, all those who had been part of the chief's team were brought forward to give their accounts. The last person called had been Jonathan Patterson. Unfortunately, there was no power, so his video could not be shared, but Jamie had already come up with a solution. She selected twelve people from those in attendance and had them come up to view the footage of the massacre in the market parking lot.

Once Jonathan's video was watched, she said that the prosecution was resting its case. She had Bo and Ivan bring Joe Spencer forward first. She asked him if he had anything to say in his defense. After a string of threats and profanity, she simply nodded and the man was restrained and returned to his chair. Next she had them bring Bob Capka.

"Do you have anything to say in your defense?" she asked.

The man flicked his head just enough to get the hair out of his eyes. He leveled his empty stare at her, but he did not say a word. Fighting the urge to look away, Jamie held his gaze as she told Bo and Ivan to return the man to his chair. She finally let out her breath once his back was to her and he was being led back to his seat beside the others.

Mark Trees was next. She posed the same question to him as she had the other two.

"You people are all on borrowed time," Mark scoffed. "You think we're the only ones out there looking out for ourselves?"

"Looking after yourselves?" Jamie shot back. "We opened our town to you and gave you a safe place to live."

"Safe?" Mark laughed. "Maybe you haven't been paying attention, but there ain't no place safe no more."

"What gives you the right to just come and take what is ours? Kill our people?" Jamie stood up and approached the man. "You're nothing. You came here with the intention of preying on those you thought were weaker than you."

"Thank you."

"You are weak." Mark looked up at Jamie with a sneer on his face. "You and these people trying to make some sort of wall using cars and trucks...that you are stealing by the way. You really think that will save you? You think we are the worst things out there?"

"No," Jamie said before the man could continue. "You are just the worst thing we have met so far. But your sort won't be causing us problems like this ever again."

She motioned to Bo and turned her back on the man to return to her podium. She had saved Kevin Staley for last. Part of her dreaded hearing this man speak. She had been fooled worse than any of the other people in town. She had no doubt that he would say things in an attempt to embarrass her. What she would not do is try to lie and cover up the truth; that was probably a big reason the world was in the state it currently found itself.

Steeling herself for the worst, she gave a nod to Ivan. The newly appointed chief of police walked over to the last man and led him to the front of the stage. There was no struggle, and even with a ball gag in his mouth, Jamie could see the man at least attempting a smile. Once the gag was removed, Ivan took a single step back and stood at parade rest just behind and to the left of Kevin.

"Mr. Staley—" Jamie began.

"Oh c'mon, sugar tits, you of all the people here can call me Kevin." The man gave a salacious wink just before Chief Potter punched him in the back of the head. Kevin made a slight grunt, but by the time he lifted his head again, he had a smile plastered on his face again.

"Let's try this once more," Jamie said firmly, although she could tell that her cheeks were probably red enough for people in the back row of the bleachers to see. "Why would you and your friends come here and do what you have done?"

"Not bothering with the word allegedly, huh?" Kevin sniped.

"You know," Jamie came from behind her podium, "that

213

was always something that bothered me about the old system. You could have a person on video committing terrible acts. Their face could be seen clear as day, yet they were somehow allowed to plead not guilty."

"Guilty until proven innocent then," Kevin said with a shrug.

"Are you actually claiming innocence?"

"I don't even know what the charges are," Kevin shot back. "Nobody has done so much as read off counts or anything. If it's rape, I don't recall you ever saying the word no, but then again…it would just be your word against mine so I doubt I'd get any love from the jury." Kevin made an over-exaggerated look to the left and then the right. "Oh…wait. There ain't no jury. I guess you are the judge and jury on this little show."

"Do you want charges?" Jamie asked as she took a few steps closer to the man. "How about murder? Theft? Will those do?"

"So you and your little raiding party have receipts for those groceries?" Kevin shot back.

"The people of Liberty were bringing all the stock from the grocery store inside our safe zone for the use of all its citizens," Jamie answered calmly, not allowing herself to be baited by the man who continued to look up at her with that same smile plastered across his face.

"So that's a big no. And then there are all the cars and trucks you people are heisting to make your silly little wall."

"The vehicles we are commandeering were abandoned."

"So when you take shit that ain't yours, its commandeering, but when me and my boys take stuff…well, then it's theft? Seems to me there is a big double standard going on here."

"We have operated within the limits of securing what is ours and only taking that which has been abandoned."

"You can paint it any color you like, but your people are stealing shit just like you accuse us of doing. Correct me if I am wrong, but that Lowe's you guys hit wasn't part of this town. Y'all are thieves and bad guys just like you claim me and my

"Thank you."

boys are. The difference is that you think you can just claim you are doing it for your town and that makes it okay. Stealing for three or three thousand is still stealing."

"Fine, let's drop the theft charges and just talk about the murder." Jamie shot a smile at Kevin as she locked eyes with him.

"They shot first," Kevin said with a shrug.

"That is a lie and we have you and your men on video as they assaulted and killed the team at Ingles Market." Jamie forced herself to remain calm. She did not want to come off as smug, but she knew she had the upper hand.

"You have any idea what happened *inside* that market?" Kevin growled. "Your people attacked us. We were just defending ourselves. I bet your video don't show any of that, does it?"

Jamie opened her mouth, but then she paused. *No*, she thought, *there is no footage of what happened inside the store.* She shook those thoughts away and took another step towards the man. She was now close enough that she could have reached out and touched him if she chose to.

"You're lying," she said simply. "You and your people came here with the expressed intent of taking our supplies. You killed people in the process. On the charges of murder, how do you plead?"

"Does it matter?" Kevin's voice still sounded flippant, but she thought that she detected just a hint of nervousness. Also, she was certain that bead of sweat trickling down from his temple had nothing to do with the heat. It was sunny, but far from being hot.

"I will ask you again," Jamie replied, a sense of calm sinking into her as she prepared for what was next. "On the charges of murder, how do you plead?"

"Am I speaking for just me, or are you making me speak for them?" Kevin titled his head to indicate his three companions.

"How do *you* plead?"

"Innocent. Guilty by insanity?" The man laughed. It started as a chuckle and morphed into all out laughter, but there was a

215

sinister quality to it.

"You might be insane," Jamie agreed. "But that does not give you the right or the excuse to commit the horrific, callous, and evil acts that you and your friends have committed here."

"Am I evil?" Another burst of sinister laughter exploded from his lips. "Yes I fucking am."

"That's enough," Jamie said, nodding to Ivan.

The man actually looked relieved as he strapped the ball gag back into place. Jamie waited until the man was returned to the bench seat with his companions. Once he was secure, she stepped forward to address the crowd. Up to this point, only those closest to the stage had actually heard the events taking place. The steady hum of conversation throughout the proceedings indicated that things were being passed along to those unable to hear.

Now she picked up the bullhorn. As soon as she did, a hush fell over the audience. She could practically feel the weight of the citizens of Liberty as they all seemed to lean forward as one entity.

"Ladies and gentlemen, we have four men who are accused of murder. Just a few months ago, they would have gone through a lengthy process where every loophole and twist of words might have been employed to set them free. The facts are that we have video evidence that show three of the four men in the actual act of killing the members of the salvage team they were sent with."

Jamie waited a moment and surveyed the faces of the crowd. She saw their anger, and on a few faces, she saw the pain of loss. Her eyes paused on those of Sarah Gilstrap. The woman was a blank slate, her face expressionless. Sophie had mentioned prescribing something for some of the people who had lost friends or loved ones. She briefly wondered what they would do in a few months when the small supply of pills and ointments they currently possessed were all gone.

"While the one individual was not actually seen committing

"Thank you."

any of the murders, there were bodies found inside the store that might be attributed to him. That would not have been considered a strong argument before the events that have befallen our world, I think they are good enough now.

"We cannot deny that we are living in a different time that may call for a new way of doing things. Today is one of those moments. I am going to put it to all of you as a collective, and I ask for a show of hands." Jamie paused when Kevin made a snorting sound. She glanced over to see his eyes dancing with glee as he shook his head in obvious amusement. "All who cast a vote for guilty, please raise your hand."

She had not thought it might be an issue, so she was not concerned with actually counting. The fact that it looked like every person present had a hand in the air made things so much easier. Still, she would complete the process.

"Put your hands down now, please." She paused a few seconds. "Now, for those wishing to cast a vote for these men being not guilty?"

She swept the crowd twice, but she did not see a single hand in the air. She hoped that they would never have a trial held in this manner again, and the Old World remnant of her mind was throwing out words like coercion, intimidation, and mob justice. She slammed the door on that part of her mind and nodded.

"And what should the penalty be?" She actually regretted the words as soon as they left her mouth as voices began to scream a variety of possible deaths.

"I say we drag them out of town and feed them to some of those monsters!"

"Burn 'em!"

"Firing squad!"

The suggestions were varied, and a few were even a bit gruesome in their creativity. At last, she held up her hands. Much slower than when these proceedings had begun, the crowd eventually became quiet enough so that she could speak.

"We will hang these men tomorrow. I will ask a few of you with carpentry experience to please meet with Chief Potter afterwards to make the preparations. The gallows will be built here and those who wish to attend are welcome to do so. I would ask that children not be brought to this event."

With that, she set the bullhorn down on the small stand beside her podium and walked over to Ivan Potter. He was in conversation with Bo Summers and Jonathan Patterson when she reached him. The three men turned to her, their talking ceasing immediately.

"Take the prisoners back to where we were holding them," Jamie said.

"Any other instructions?" Ivan asked. "Do we keep them shackled or increase their guard. Do we do what it takes to ensure they don't kill themselves?"

"Absolutely," Jamie said after only a few seconds of thought.

"And last meals?" Bo piped up.

"No," Jamie answered even faster than she had regarding the question about making sure they didn't commit suicide. "We are not wasting any more resources on those four."

"Damn," Jonathan breathed, quickly blushing as if he just realized that he'd spoken that out loud.

"And I want the gallows to be equipped to drop them all at once."

***

Bo Summers hammered in the last nail. Stepping up onto the actual platform, he jumped up and down. The first time was a bit tentative, but then he really gave it all he had.

"I think we can find you a bouncy house, Bo," Ivan called up.

Bo pursed his lips for a moment and then shrugged. "Let me check my bucket list. I think jumping up and down in a bouncy house during the zombie apocalypse is number eighty-three."

Ivan shook his head and climbed the stairs. Bo turned his at-

"Thank you."

tention to the four nooses that were hanging from the big cross beam. They looked nothing like the ones you saw in the movies. It was just a strand of hemp rope with a slipknot. A thirty pound sand bag was at each trap door to expedite snapping the necks of the four men. It would be tied to each man's ankles. When the lever was pulled, the doors would open and the bag would drop.

"The end," Bo whispered.

"What's that?" Ivan asked.

The man glanced over at the new chief and shrugged. "Nothing…just thinking out loud."

The sun had risen at his back. Already there was a small crowd gathering.

"Welcome to the Dark Ages." Bo walked over to the lever. This was the last test. He gestured to Ivan. "Hook those sand bags to the nooses.

Chief Potter clipped each one as he'd been asked and then stepped clear. Bo looked up and saw that, in just that short amount of time, the crowd had practically doubled in size and more were filing in. He waited for another moment and then gripped the lever with both hands. He pressed his lips tight and pulled.

Four sand bags fell through the open trap doors and then bounced a little before gently swinging back and forth several feet above the ground. When he looked up, he noticed a few of the onlookers having a change of heart, turning around and heading against the crowds for the exits.

"Hard times ahead," Bo whispered.

A few seconds later, there was a ripple of noise from up towards the school's main building. Shielding his eyes, Bo could see the six man detail and Jamie Burns leading the four prisoners down the path towards where the gallows had been built.

A few bottles and rocks hurled through the air. One struck the largest man of the group. Bo thought his name might be Mark. He decided that, besides not really knowing for sure, he didn't care. These people had come into the town of Liberty and done terrible things.

219

From the platform of the gallows, he could look out over the entire crowd. There were a few roped off aisles—one of which the condemned foursome were being led down—allowing some of the folks normally on roving security to patrol the throng. Bo glanced over at Ivan and saw that the man was frowning.

"Problem?" Bo sidled up to the newly appointed police chief; although he doubted the title meant much anymore.

"I would hate for one of them bastards to die from a head wound before we get them up here," the man replied.

"Well then, tell the folks to knock it the hell off."

Bo turned and walked away. It seemed like a simple enough solution to him. He watched Ivan scoop up the bullhorn and switch it on.

"Ladies and gentlemen," the chief called. For a moment, there seemed to be no reaction from the crowd as the catcalls and angry shouts continued to be hurled along with a few assorted projectiles. "HEY!" Ivan shouted, eliciting feedback from the bullhorn.

Bo smiled as he saw so many people jump in unison. Walking over to the stairs, he opened the gate to allow the approaching group to come up and join him on the platform. The foursome were all shackled and had their hands cuffed behind their backs. Additionally, there was a heavy chain connecting them to each other. Each man still had a gag of some sort in his mouth except for the one with the long hair hanging down in his face. Bo guessed that one didn't need a gag since he did not seem inclined to speak.

"Folks, these men have been sentenced to death for the murder of several of our citizens. We will not bring ourselves down to their level by acting like uncivilized animals," Ivan announced to the people gathered for the execution.

Bo unclipped the belly-chain on the first of the prisoners from the group—the one covered with tattoos all over his arms and chest—and led him to the farthest noose from the stairs. The man started to resist as the noose was slipped over his neck, but

220

"Thank you."

as soon as Bo cinched it a bit, the man froze like a deer in the headlights.

The next man was the muscular one. As Bo led him to his noose, he saw sweat beading on his forehead and running down his temples. This one was a little more difficult to get the noose on, and a pair of the escorts had to come up and help.

Next was the one with the long hair. Bo had barely gotten his belly chain off when the man just started to stroll over to his noose. He even ducked his head through it and then stood casually like he was waiting for a bus.

Last was the one with the reddish hair and the goatee. Similar to the one with the long hair, this one made no effort to resist and actually ducked his head through the noose for Bo.

After the escorts departed the platform, Jamie Burns came up and motioned to Ivan for the bullhorn. He handed it to her and the woman stepped to the very front of the platform.

"We will give these men a chance to speak their final words." She turned to the four, dropping the bullhorn so that what she said was heard only by them and maybe a few of the closer onlookers. "If you just start spewing a bunch of threats or profanity, I will just nod to Mr. Summers behind you and he will pull the lever. Are we clear?"

The men all nodded. Jamie went to the tattooed man. She whispered something that Bo couldn't hear, but the man nodded and Jamie indicated for the person standing behind him to remove his gag.

The man cleared his throat. When Jamie offered him the bullhorn, he shook his head and mumbled something once the device was away from his mouth.

"A priest or a pastor?" the man coughed.

Jamie turned to the group that had acted as escort and motioned with her hand. Pastor Johnson slipped through the group and climbed the stairs. Bo could tell that the man was uncomfortable coming up on a gallows.

"Can you pray with me?" the man asked once the pastor reached him.

Bo stepped back out of earshot. A man's business with God was nothing he felt he should be eavesdropping in on. It was something personal and private, and while he believed that these four were brutal killers and deserved the fate in store, he also believed they deserved a shred of privacy if they wanted to try and throw a Hail Mary in God's direction and hope that the Big Guy caught it. At last the pair were finished and Jamie nodded for the pastor to step back over by the stairs and wait if he was needed again.

Next was the big guy. Jamie repeated her question to him about if he had any last words he wanted to offer. The man tried to yell something. Even with the gag in place, Bo recognized the words "Fuck you!" when he heard them.

Next came the long-haired fella. This one had Bo curious. He wasn't wearing a gag and didn't seem the least bit concerned about what was about to happen. His skin was dry, not a bead or droplet of sweat could be seen.

Jamie paused in front of him and made the same offer she had given the other two. The man cocked his head and seemed to consider her. For several seconds, the two were locked in some sort of stare down. Finally, Jamie stepped back. The man smiled and then his gaze just drifted away from her.

The last man was waiting with a smile that peeked around his ball gag. Bo fought the urge to walk up and smash the man in the back of the head. Jamie actually seemed to handle his lascivious looks much better.

"And you, Mr. Staley, anything to say? Keep in mind, all I do is nod and Mr. Summers over there pulls the lever."

There was a pause, and then the man gave a single nod. Jamie reached up and unbuckled the gag, letting it fall to the ground. She stepped back and shrugged at the man who, Bo believed, realized for the first time just what his situation entailed.

"You people are all doomed." Kevin Staley glanced briefly over at Jamie to see if she might be getting ready to nod. Her face remained stoic as she seemed content to let him speak.

"Thank you."

"We've been out there, and if you think we are the worst that humanity has to throw at you, then your bubble is gonna burst in a very painful way. We were simply doing what we felt needed to be done to ensure *our* survival. We found your little town by following a group of *your* citizens, led by that woman." Kevin tilted his head towards Jamie. "They were out looting on the out-skirts of Clemson. So before you pass judgment on us, you might want to look in the mirror." Kevin paused and locked eyes with Jamie as soon as she turned his way. "What depths will you people go to in order to see to your own survival? I have a feel-ing we will be considered saints when we sit next to you. And when you reach that defining moment, remember the fate that you decided should be ours."

Jamie waited for a moment to be sure that he was finished. He pursed his lips and made a kissing gesture in her direction.

"The ladies and gentlemen of Liberty, South Carolina find Joe Spencer, Mark Trees, Bob Capka, and Kevin Staley guilty of murder and sentence you to hang by the neck until dead." Jamie turned her back on the crowd and faced the four condemned men. "May God have mercy on your souls."

Bo gripped the lever. Just before Jamie nodded, all four men reacted. The man with the tattoos bowed his heads as if in pray-er. The muscular fella screamed one final curse into his gag, and the man who had given the speech stood tall and started to laugh. All of those reactions were what Bo considered to be pretty normal considering the circumstances.

It was the reaction of the man who had not spoken a word, the man named Bob Capka, that was the response he would pon-der and sometimes wake from a nightmare when it replayed in his sleep. Bo was almost certain that he was the only one who heard the man as he broke his silence. The words were spoken so softly, that sometimes he tried to convince himself that he had not heard anything, but Bo Summers knew that was a lie. Those final words would haunt Bo for the rest of his life and actually give him chills whenever he heard another person speak them.

Just as he pulled the lever, he heard Bob Capka whisper,

"Thank you."

13

As Time Goes By

Sophie sat in the small office. Her son had volunteered to help unload the food trucks. That left her alone with the little girl that he had saved. As had been her norm since that day, the girl sat silently on a chair. The dolls, coloring books, and stuffed animals all remained untouched. The girl stared at the floor and still hadn't spoken a word.

The problem was that Sophie could not remember her name. Glancing at her watch, she saw that it was close enough to be considered lunch time. She pushed away from the desk and went to the small cupboard. Three boxes of crackers and some peanut butter were all that she had. She'd only kept that just in case her blood sugar got a little off kilter; which it did whenever she spent twenty-four hours straight in her office.

"Want to walk over to the school for lunch?" Sophie said in her sweetest voice which took considerable effort considering how tired she was at the moment. "I think they are serving up spaghetti today."

It was no surprise when the girl just continued to sit in total silence and stare at the floor. Grabbing her belt with the required self-defense weapon—she carried a nondescript machete with a worn wooden handle—she strapped it on and then reached down for the girl's hand.

"I hate ba-sketti," the girl mumbled.

Sophie took a step back and regarded the girl like she might if the words had come from the chair that the girl was now vacating. She'd asked Lawrence every single day if the girl had spoken to him and he had assured her that she hadn't.

"Trust me, Mom, if she speaks, you'll be the first person I tell," he usually answered. The last few times he had simply rolled his eyes and left the room.

"Honey, can you tell me your name?"

The little girl looked up at her and slowly shook her head. "Mama says I'm not a-supposed to talk to strangers."

Sophie rubbed her eyes with her index finger and thumb as she suppressed her frustration. An idea popped into her head and she knelt down. "I bet you are allowed to talk to doctors and policemen, aren't you?" The girl seemed to think it over for a moment before nodding tentatively. "Well I am Dr. Sophie." While not exactly true, she was the closest thing the town had to a doctor at the moment, so her little white lie came out easily enough.

"Megan," the girl whispered after a slight hesitation. "My name is Megan Jones."

"Well, Megan Jones, since you don't like spaghetti, what would you like for lunch?"

Again the girl was silent. Sophie started to think that perhaps she had shut down again when, at last, the girl looked up at her with a hopeful gleam in her eyes. "I like peanut butter."

"Well then you happen to be in luck."

Sophie unbuckled her belt and hung it on the hook beside her desk as she went back to her small cupboard and produced a box of Saltines and a jar of creamy peanut butter. She cleared away a space on her desk and set down the food. Opening her bottom drawer, she produced two foil pouches of orange drink. For the next twenty minutes, Sophie listened as Megan decided to make up for several days of not speaking.

***

Bo scrubbed his face and stared in the tiny mirror beside his wash basin. He could still taste the sourness of having been sick at some point last night. His eyes shot a wistful glance at the bottle of Johnny Walker Red that sat on the floor beside his bed. It was now minus just over three-quarters of its contents. Last night, it had been full and still in the box.

He noticed that somebody had done him the favor of placing a bucket beside his bed. He had no idea who, but he thanked the anonymous person as he grabbed the sloshing red pail and headed for the closest exit so that he could dump it someplace outside. His mind began to play disjointed bits and pieces of the evening as he made his way through the fairly crowded gymnasium-turned-dorm.

The nightmare had come again even through his drunken haze. This was one of those times where that man had turned right to him and spoken those two words.

All his life, Bo had been seen as one of the 'good old boys' of the town. He was usually one of the first to step forward when somebody needed a little help around their property. On weekends, he had volunteered at the Senior Center, and for the past several years, he had been one of the most successful youth football coaches in the county. That had led to him being asked to assist at the high school.

Nobody ever asked why Bo Summers had not married. Nor had anybody ever questioned his fairly regular trips to Greenville. Bo was not somebody that most folks cared to question. It wasn't that he was mean; far from it. He was better known for his huge heart. He just had a terrific knack for deflecting questions anytime folks got personal.

Nobody was more surprised than Bo to discover that he was gay. He'd chalked it up in his early years as simply being shy around the ladies. He had stifled that voice in his head that tried to clarify his attraction towards men.

Then he'd met Oliver Tandy, a physical therapist at Pickens

227

Memorial Hospital. Oliver had been the one to awaken parts of him that he had tried for years to keep shut away. The problem was, a man like Bo just did not broadcast his orientation in a small town like Liberty. Sure, some folks would be able to see past the label; but too many would not.

The zombie problem in Liberty had caused Bo to be able to forget everything for the first several days, but now that things were starting to level out—at least as much as he figured they would in a zombie apocalypse—thoughts of Oliver had seeped into Bo's mind.

Oliver had long, curly hair much like that Bob Capka fella. Perhaps that was why he occasionally saw Oliver's face on that body just before it dropped through the trap door.

He had missed the sign-up for Jamie Burns' expedition heading up to Pickens Memorial Hospital. Now he was actually considering something very stupid. Despite his ability to take care of himself, Bo Summers was not so foolish as to believe that was sufficient to keep him alive out in the hellscape that was their new reality. If the walking dead didn't get you, then there were raiders and just plain old accidents.

The days of antibiotics being readily available were about to go away. They were set to enter a period where a simple cut could become infected and kill a person.

When he gave it serious thought, he did not actually expect to find Oliver alive. He'd heard the stories of what had happened at the hospital from a few of the survivors who had made it down to Liberty. The place was a nightmare and said to be crawling with zombies. If Oliver was in the hospital when the military presence failed, he was as good as dead.

The thing was, he needed to at least check. If he didn't and the day arrived when Oliver came walking up to one of the roving patrols, he would never forgive himself...and it was likely that Oliver wouldn't either. If he could get up to Pickens and check Oliver's apartment, which was literally within eyesight of the hospital, then he could at least find something close to peace

228

of mind.

Of course, if he found Oliver and the man happened to be alive, then he would have an entirely new situation to deal with. That would be small potatoes compared to everything else going on and probably make coming out easier than it would have ever been before the zombies showed up.

Bo laughed at the thought and jumped when a voice called his name from across the parking lot. Looking around, he spied Sarah Gilstrap headed his direction. She had just moved into the dorms yesterday allowing a third family to move into the house that she and the chief had called home for so long.

Obviously she'd gotten an early start to whatever she had going on today since she was not only already up and about, but dressed in full protective gear. He briefly wondered what sector she would be patrolling as he waited for her to cross over to him. Just before she arrived, he quickly set the pail on the ground and scooted it away with one booted foot.

"Did you hear?" Sarah asked as she picked up her pace to meet Bo.

"I doubt it," he said, wincing at the sound of his own voice.

"They need two new volunteers for Jamie's trip to Pickens." The woman gave a knowing smile to Bo, her eyebrows raised slightly.

"Since when?"

"Since they have decided that you can catch this zombie crap by getting blood in an open cut."

Bo thought it over for a moment and then an idea struck him. "Okay, so why are you so excited…and why are you telling me?"

"Wow…you really were drunk last night," Sarah said with far too much cheer in her voice for Bo's liking.

A cold feeling started in his stomach and began to spread through his body as he assumed her reason. What had he said? And who had been present?

"Sweetie, relax. Nobody cares. There are slightly more pressing issues right now. Besides, there has been a lot of speculation for the past several years. I can't believe that you felt you needed to keep that a secret." Sarah stepped up and gave the big man a hug. She quickly drew back. "Oh…but you need to clean up a bit. You smell awful."

"I will right after I go make sure that I am on the list. I missed it and was actually starting to consider making the trip alone."

"We know," another voice said from behind Bo, causing the big man to jump.

Ivan Potter walked up and gave Bo a friendly punch in the shoulder. It was the same way he'd greeted Bo for years. Bo was having trouble hiding his amazement.

"And no need to worry," Sarah spoke up. "I already signed you and me on to the team. You need to hurry up. We're leaving in a little bit."

Bo stood there watching as Sarah and Ivan headed across the parking lot. After being rid of his bucket he stopped at one of the outdoor clean-up stations. This was a new development just being put in place. A large basin was kept full of water. That basin was hung over a fire that was kept stoked by some of the grade and high school kids. (Everybody had to pull their weight these days…even the youngsters.) You scooped out a bucket of warm water and hung it in a curtained off area where you took a very economical shower.

Just as he finished, he thought he heard a low rumble approaching from the west. That must be the team sent to get the train to help secure the northern part of their safe zone. Today was shaping up to be a nice one. He was already feeling the weight of a decades-long secret sliding from his shoulders.

"Who said a zombie apocalypse was a bad thing," Bo mused as he started putting on his gear for the trip north.

***

Jamie climbed up onto the top of the massive earth-moving

vehicle. Her eyes could not help but drift back to the stain on the road as she'd made the climb. This was where Chief Gilstrap had lost his life. She prayed that a rain would come soon and perhaps wash some of it away.

"Here it comes," Ivan Potter was standing beside her and pointing to the west.

Shielding her eyes from the glare of the afternoon, she could see the shimmer of something moving their direction. It was not long before the low rumble could be heard as well.

The day after the hanging, a team of ten had been sent west. A train had been discovered by one of the foraging teams and it was decided that now was as good a time as any to go fetch it. This train would be halted on the tracks to help create their northern "wall" between South Norman and Peachtree Streets. Once the train was stopped, they would disable it and then tear up the tracks for a good distance in both directions.

They had lucked upon one train that would easily span the entire length. An added benefit was that there did not seem to be any tanker cars that might eventually spill their toxic payloads. Most of the cars were empty except for a few that were loaded with automobiles that would be unloaded and added to the barricade that was starting to slow down in its creation. The teams bringing in vehicles had to range farther out and only a handful of people were volunteering for those missions.

This particular team had been gone for eleven days. There were those that had started to wonder if perhaps they'd fallen prey to zombies or a band of raiders like Kevin and his group. Last night, a red flare and then a blue flare had been spotted to the west. That was the signal that meant the team was approaching and would arrive the next day.

A low moan caused Jamie to look away from the train. A single zombie was wading through the tall grass. Two people broke away from where the growing crowd was waiting at the railroad crossing and made short work of it.

Jamie had been thankful that, at least up until this point in things, they had only encountered a handful of zombies here and there. Some of the teams going out lately were reporting seeing groups numbering in the hundreds and even the thousands. That had her nervous about her own upcoming mission towards Pickens.

She and twenty others were going to be taking the three eighteen-wheelers that had brought the shipment from Ingles Market along with two more that had been brought in from the highway. They would be driving to Pickens. The hope was that things had cleared out enough so that they might be able to salvage medical supplies from the hospital as well as hopefully some more food.

At last, the train rolled past and eventually came to a stop. Jamie and several people from town came up to the lead engine where a woman emerged from the car, her left arm bandaged and her eyes showing the obvious signs of infection. She was dripping with sweat and her skin was already looking waxy.

"So…many…" the woman heaved before collapsing to her knees. She looked up at Jamie and a grimace of pain creased her face. "Not sure if we could make it back."

Jamie rushed to the woman, but Ivan caught her around the waist. He held her back as two other people that were in Sophie's newest group of students slapped on Latex gloves and approached the downed woman cautiously.

As they did, one of the cargo doors opened with a loud clang. Everybody holding a weapon spun almost in perfect unison with weapons leveled. Two men emerged, hands up and calling out for everybody not to shoot.

After a quick debrief, Jamie had a lot to consider before embarking on her own mission. Of the ten people sent out on this run to fetch the train, only three had returned, and only two survived. Those two shared a horrific tale about the degree of destruction and ruin that had befallen almost every single place they passed through.

They shared stories of entire residential neighborhoods burned to the ground. The cities in every direction were overrun

232

by thousands of the walking dead. Some of the herds were said to number in the tens of thousands and left a trail of destruction in their wake that rivaled any tornado, hurricane, or even tsunami.

"They just have so much mass behind them that they push cars aside. Fences fold down like paper and even some small buildings have eventually broken under the pressure," one of the men recounted as he allowed the medical person doing the inspection of his body to check everywhere for any sign of a bite or scratch.

But it was what the other man shared that clicked home for so many of those who heard. It forced Jamie to require her team to change the equipment they had to carry.

"Larry Mane didn't get bit. The best we could figure as we checked him out was that he must've gotten some of the zombie blood in a nasty cut on his right hand that he had suffered breaking a window the day before. He had zombie blood all over that arm and hand. He didn't get a single scratch. That is one thing everybody agrees on. Only, within two hours of the fight, his eyes had changed and he started acting sick. Just before sunrise, he let out a long exhale and was gone. We all had a good guess as to what was going to happen next, but nobody wanted to spike Larry unless he actually sat up."

Ivan had listened to the rest of the report regarding what happened to the others, but Jamie needed to make sure that she and her team were as prepared as possible. After meeting with Sophie and being astounded that the little girl that Lawrence had saved was not only doing better, but now had turned into quite the chatter box, she decided that they needed to take contamination precautions.

Her team all picked out goggles or face shields. Some also chose to wear respirators or masks that protected their mouths. Two members with open sores were eliminated from the team as a precaution.

As she finished packing her own backpack, a knock came at the opening to her cubicle. She turned to see Bo Summers and

Sarah Gilstrap standing there with packs in their hands.

"We are the new volunteers," Bo said in his usual relaxed manner.

"I decided that I needed to get more actively involved," Sarah said simply.

Jamie was very happy to see Bo, but she felt sort of odd when it came to Sarah. There was just something about how her eyes did not seem to be able to hold contact.

Oh well, she thought, *I can't worry about that right now. As long as she doesn't do anything to endanger the mission, I can't really turn her away.*

Jamie rummaged through a notebook on her fold-up desk and plucked a pair of pages. She gave them a quick double check to ensure that they were what she wanted and then handed Bo and Sarah each a single page.

"Our top priority when we reach Pickens is to hit the hospital as well as the pharmacies marked on the bottom of the page. This is the priority list of the medical supplies that we need according to Sophie," Jamie explained as she gave her own equipment a final inspection. "You will also notice that we have listed two locations as fall back spots should you get separated. Both of those spots are secure and have a cache of supplies."

The pair nodded and then fell in behind Jamie as she left her cubicle and headed to the main entrance to the school where the team was instructed to muster. She arrived as a few of the members were sharing tearful farewells with friends or family.

With both her parents gone, this was the first time that she truly felt alone. She had not realized until this very moment that she'd become so focused on her school, then a career, that she had let almost all her personal relationships wither and die. Sure, people might know who she was, but nobody really *knew* her anymore.

***

234

Jonathan flexed his good hand. He'd been very good about doing all the physical therapy exercises that Sophie had assigned him. Having been through his share of injuries from his years in football and other sports, he knew the value of rehabbing.

"My town went to the zombie apocalypse and all I got was this fractured wrist," he snorted.

Kneeling beside the marker that had been placed in honor of his mother, Jonathan hoped that she'd been right and that there was such a thing as Heaven. If so, then hopefully she now understood his actions at the end of her life. If that was the case, then perhaps she would understand what it was he was about to do.

He and seven others had been sent towards Easley. There was report of a band of raiders in the area that were not simply out snatching up supplies. It had been decided (in a town hall sort of meeting right after that hanging) that the citizens of Liberty would not engage folks who were outside their town's boundaries. Also, if they encountered groups abroad that laid claim to a specific area, they would withdraw peacefully.

When Jamie returned, there was going to be a vote about whether or not they would officially close their gates to any and all outsiders. Jonathan—as had all seven other members of his detail—had cast a vote in a sealed envelope that was handed to Chief Potter.

Things were changing so fast that Jonathan hardly recognized his town anymore. He hadn't been surprised when somebody had spray painted over the old town motto that was on the side of the abandoned city hall building.

"*Where neighbors become friends*" had been changed to "*Where strangers will be shot on sight.*" He thought that it showed a certain lack of creativity, but that did seem to be the direction that the town was headed.

It wasn't as if they were being hit by an influx of survivors seeking sanctuary, but he doubted that any newcomers would be welcomed for the foreseeable future.

"You ready, big man?" a voice spoke from behind him.

Jonathan turned to see all the members of his scouting force gathered at the entrance to his cubicle. All the spiked bats, machetes, spears, and assorted bows gave the team a foreboding appearance. His brain quickly reconciled the reality of what stood there waiting for him.

A grocery store clerk, a math teacher, a bartender, a construction worker, a grade school cafeteria worker, a fast food counter person, a fireman, and him...a pizza place assistant manager.

Worst Village People tribute band ever, he thought. *Not a single soldier or Special Forces commando in the mix*, he mused.

This was the group headed out to see if they could locate any potential targets that merited a larger team being sent to retrieve supplies. Also, they would all be piling into a pickup truck. When they returned, they were supposed to each be driving a vehicle that could be jammed into the growing barricade.

"Yep," Jonathan gave himself a quick pat down to ensure that he had his all gear and then joined the team.

They headed east on Highway 123 until the still smoldering ruins of the outskirts of Easley came into full view. Jonathan shook his head in disbelief. Certainly he expected a degree of senseless vandalism; even the lawlessness like that gang of four made sense in a weird way. What he did not understand was why people would just destroy everything. It was like humanity wanted to be done and over with.

They passed a massive development on the right that looked like it had once been all upscale housing. Now, the only thing that remained were skeletal shells of blackened wood and stone.

They came upon the Pendleton Street exit and saw a row of bodies crucified beside the highway. There were large signs hanging around the necks of many of the squirming undead with accusations of heathen, unclean, blasphemer, and unholy.

"Glad we have dodged that bullet so far," Jonathan breathed as they drove slowly along the edge of the emergency lane.

"I wouldn't count your chickens," Alex Singleton quipped. "There have been rumors of a small group starting to meet. They apparently are discussing whether or not they wish to remain with...and this is a bit of paraphrasing, so forgive me if I am not spot on with the accuracy, but something about the "deniers of God" or something like that."

"Let me guess," Jonathan groaned. "Reverend Jonah Simms and his brother Chuck."

"Nailed it," Alex replied as he slowed the truck. "And it looks like we are on foot from here."

A roadblock had been built to span the entirety of the highway just as they emerged from a particularly thick cloud of smoke that acted like a curtain across the road just past the overpass prior to their intended exit. Jonathan knew that a few groups had ventured this way before, and nobody had said anything about this roadblock; so that meant this was something recent. Part of him was happy that there might be others who were surviving. That part was engulfed by fear when a bunch of gunshots sounded and a series of bullet holes marched across the windshield.

A round slammed into Alex Singleton's chest and then another hit him in the head, blowing his brains across the rear of the pickup's cab in a hideous design of bone, brain, and blood. He felt something tug at his shirt and reflexively ducked down.

There was an eruption of screams from the back of the pickup and another burst of gunfire that slammed into the engine block with deadly efficiency. He felt the vehicle slow and then it shuddered violently as it continued its forward momentum a bit further. The sound of the tires being shot out came and then the truck slowly ground to a halt.

"Hands in the air!" a voice shouted from somewhere close.

"We didn't—" somebody answered from the back only to be cut off by another burst of gunfire that ended with a yelp and the sound of something falling just on the other side of the cab.

Jonathan considered his options. He briefly deliberated on the option of playing dead, but these days, that might still earn him a bullet to the head. He was still mulling over the possibilities when the passenger door was opened with a scream of protesting metal.

"And what do we have here?" a voice said almost in his ear.

***

Ivan looked around what used to be just a counselor's office at Liberty High School. He recalled a few trips to this as one as well as the principal's office when he'd been a student here. Looking around, it dawned on him that this was the very room where he had spoken to Chief Gilstrap about what it would take for him to become a member of the police force.

Getting up, he headed out to the hallway and made his way outside. As he did, a few people greeted him with words or a wave. He returned them, using people's names when they popped into his mind.

The sun was just starting to set. Jamie's group had only been gone for a few hours. They wanted to get close, but not venture into Pickens until they observed for at least one full day. With the world in the state it was in, it would be a simple matter to hear any gunshots and determine at least the general direction. Also, the night allowed them to scan for possible campfires.

As he strolled toward the old door and window factory where he currently resided, it was almost difficult to tell that this was basically the zombie apocalypse. He could hear birds singing and the chirp and hum of bugs. Nothing gave away the fact that the world had spiraled into a massive extinction event.

It took him a few seconds to realize that he was hearing something out of the ordinary. Once it dawned on him, he froze and began to search the sky. With the world so quiet, he thought that it should be much easier to discern the direction the sound was coming from, but it seemed to be echoing off of everything as it grew louder.

He had trees on both sides and took off at a run to reach the clearing ahead where Farmers Hill Road intersected on the right. Just as he reached his destination, there was a thundering boom. He looked up in time to see a pair of fighter jets fly past at incredible speed. It looked as if they were barely skimming the tree tops as they sped west.

It took him a moment to realize that he was waving his arms like a madman. "Like they would have seen you," he berated himself.

Still, he stayed put for several minutes as he waited and hoped that just maybe they might bank around and head back in his direction. He had finally resumed walking again when he heard a distant booming explosion. It had come from the west.

He turned his body until he thought that he was in the general direction of the sound. It was getting dark, but in the waning light, he could see a plume of smoke rising skyward. For just a moment he felt a tinge of panic. The Oconee Nuclear Station was to the west, but he was pretty sure that it was just slightly north of Liberty. This cloud was definitely to the southwest.

He was about to continue on his way when he thought he heard somebody scream. The sound was coming from up Farmer's Hill Road. That was outside the boundaries of the safe zone. As far as he knew, there weren't any patrols in this area.

Drawing his Beretta 96 A1, he climbed over the cars to his left and headed up the road. He moved over to the side of the road and stayed low, using the tall grass for cover. With darkness coming fast, he also had plenty of shadow to utilize. After taking a moment, he was able to hear what sounded like voices. He actually rubbed his ears to be sure that he wasn't imagining things.

The scream had ended abruptly, but now he thought that he heard singing. He veered off to follow a heavily rutted dirt road that led off from the main paved one. It headed up into some trees where, as darkness crept across the countryside, he was able to make out a slight glow.

"Something isn't right here," Ivan whispered as he crouched down in some scrub brush.

He was able to look across a small clearing to a copse of trees where a group of people appeared to be gathered around a fire. He felt his blood chill as he recognized one of the voices at the same time the actual fire came into view.

Reverend Jonah Simms was standing just to the right of a large burning cross. On the other side was the hulking figure of his brother Chuck. What looked like a crudely built altar was just in front of the two and a figure was lashed to it. Judging by all the thrashing about, it was not voluntary. Gathered around were several people wearing hooded sweatshirts or caps pulled down so that it was virtually impossible to tell who they were.

Ivan considered his options. He did a quick head count and was distressed to discover that there were over fifty people gathered around. That was too many people for him to handle on his own. He would need to return to the safe zone and recruit a team to deal with this. The only problem existed in the fact that he would be consigning whomever was tied to that altar to whatever terrible fate the Simms brothers had in store.

"…have brought this terrible judgment upon humanity with all the sin and profanity that they have allowed into this world with their loose morals and evil ways." Jonah Simms lifted his arms into the air and the glint of light off of metal shone brightly for a second. "In Revelations chapter twenty-two, verse fifteen, it is written and The Word says, *Outside are the dogs, those who practice magic arts, the sexually immoral, the murderers, the idolaters and everyone who loves and practices falsehood.* These were the times we lived in, and it is that thing abhorrent to God that has brought down the End Times. We must now step forward and show our righteous and angry God that we have not strayed…that we do not wish to remain with the sinners, and desire that he bring us home so that we may worship at his feet."

There was a chorus of "Amen!" and "Praise God!" from those gathered. Ivan had to fight everything in his mind and body not to rush in and stop what he knew was about to happen. That person on the altar was going to be murdered and he could do nothing about it.

"When the sun next rises, it will do so on our town having been cleansed of the unrighteous. We will be like the Angel of Death that God sent down to Egypt. We will move this night and smite all the sinners who have led us to this path. Then, we will open the gates and let the demons of Hell come and claim what is theirs as we commit ourselves to our God and beg that he bring us home."

Ivan slipped back the way he came. It gnawed at him all the way as he ran back to the high school. If he was correct in his assumption, these lunatics were about to come in and murder the people of Liberty. The problem was that he had not been able to clearly make out anybody other than the Simms brothers.

He was about to enlist citizens of Liberty to kill their own. If he was very lucky, then the entire congregation of those following Reverend Simms was present at that little meeting.

Just as he reached Ruhamah Road and cleared the vehicle barricade, he heard another scream from back the way he'd come. It was muffled, but it still reached his ears and plunged into his soul much like he imagined the dagger plunging into that poor victim's heart.

What was it about the zealot types that made them feel they were the only ones with the answers...the only ones who followed God? He had been a church-going man all his life and felt that he'd certainly had his flaws, but mostly he was a good person.

These zombies weren't a punishment from God. They were probably the result of something that humanity had done. Bio-weapon, GMO crap, or maybe a nasty strain of the flu that came as a result of how it mutated over the years. Who knew? But more importantly...who cared?

If they were going to have any chance of survival, then the people of Liberty needed to band together, not separate themselves based on some crazy idea that God had decided to pass some mystical judgment on mankind.

The solar powered lights that marked the main entrance to

the gymnasium appeared up ahead. Ivan had a plan. He didn't like it, but he didn't see any other option. He saw little chance that this night ended without a serious amount of bloodshed.

14

Deliver Us from Evil

Sophie had just tucked Megan in when a commotion caused both her and the little girl to start. She recognized the voice of Ivan Potter, but she could not make out what he was saying.

"Okay, sweetie, you stay put. I'll be back in just a moment."

Sophie noticed it right away. A change came over the little girl. Her features went blank and her gaze became unfocused. It was almost as if somebody had hit a switch that shut the girl off.

"Megan?" Sophie whispered.

The girl didn't react. She stared straight up just as she had in nights prior. The sounds of more voices joining the commotion brought Sophie's head up.

"They are coming with the intention of killing us in our sleep!" Ivan shouted.

People were near the main doors to the gym, gathering around the chief and firing off a dozen questions at once. Sophie glanced down at the little girl one more time. She gave her a kiss on the forehead and then went to investigate what all the fuss was about.

"The only ones I saw clearly were the Simms brothers," Ivan said louder as people began demanding to know exactly who he was talking about. "They were talking about sacrificing the blood of the innocent to show God that they were worthy.

243

After that, they were coming here with the intention of killing as many as they could." He paused and his face seemed to brighten and then cloud over just as fast with a realization.

A sick feeling had begun to form in Sophie's stomach. She shoved through the gathered crowd. There were some who sounded afraid, but others were actually dismissing the chief's claims.

"This morning they brought in Joshua's sixteen-year-old daughter. They said that she was having some female issues. They were demanding to know if she was pregnant. It only took a very brief check-up to put that to rest." Sophie hated sharing intimate and personal secrets, but she felt this was important considering the circumstances. "The girl is a virgin...I assured them that there was no way that she could be pregnant."

"We need to—" Ivan began, but the sound of a nearby explosion cut him off. Seconds later, the wail of a siren filled the night air with sound.

"Oh, my God," Sophie gasped. "They're going to bring every zombie for miles around right here to us."

As if to confirm her fear and add credence to Ivan's accusations, a flurry of gunshots erupted. Ivan climbed up onto somebody's desk so that he could be seen by the gathered crowd.

"Like it or not, there are those who believe this to be some sort of biblical event, and that it is up to them to prove they are worthy of God or life in Heaven. This is not the time to try and reason with people like this. They pose a threat to our survival and I see no other way to deal with this than to eliminate them." The chief looked around the room and his eyes briefly paused when they met Sophie's.

"Are you saying that we are going to have to kill our own?" a voice shouted above the din of worried conversation.

Another volley of weapons being fired came from outside. The chief did not say a word; he simply drew his pistol and climbed down. Sophie watched him head for the door. She pushed through to catch him and grabbed his arm just as he was opening the door that led outside.

"Did you see Lawrence when you were out there?" she asked in a whisper.

"Why would I have seen Lawrence?" the chief replied to her question with one of his own.

"He and Chastity Simms have been sort of seeing each other on the side," Sophie said, glancing around like she might be afraid of others overhearing. "That was part of the reason that I was so thorough with her check-up. I'm just worried that..." Her voice choked off as she attempted to swallow the lump in her throat.

Ivan Potter understood instantly why she might be concerned for the well-being of her son. Joshua Simms made no secret of his dislike for anybody who was not Caucasian. It wasn't like he walked around spouting racist drivel, but anybody who listened to him talk either in his tiny pulpit or in one of the local taverns was aware of his separatist ideology.

One of his common retorts when he was accused of being a racist was, "I ain't sayin' the coloreds need to be shipped back to their country of origin...I'm simply statin' that the mixin' of their type with ours goes against God. Ever hear of the tower of Babel?"

"I'm coming with you," Sophie stated, patting the pistol on her own hip for emphasis.

"I can't let you do that." Ivan shook his head.

"You can't *let* me?" Sophie barked.

"You are too important...too valuable to this community." Ivan placed a hand on her shoulder, keeping her from stepping through the door. "I will look for Lawrence. I promise."

Sophie tried to protest as several other people began to flow past, heading out to confront people who had been neighbors...maybe even friends. Now they were the enemy.

"Please bring him home," Sophie said as she stepped back to allow still more of Liberty's citizens to rush out into the night.

When the door shut, she looked around and was surprised to

see less than half the people living in the gymnasium had actually joined in the defense. More had stayed behind and were making a point of not holding eye contact with her or any of their fellow citizens.

As she returned to her cubicle to wait for the chief to bring back her son, she wondered if she would have been as anxious to rush out and commit murder in the name of self-defense. Could she actually take the life of a living person who was looking her in the eyes?

As she sat down in the chair beside Megan's bed, her lips began to move as she bowed her head and recited the only prayer she could remember.

"Our Father who art in Heaven..."

***

Ivan stood in the parking lot. By his best guess, less than a quarter of those being housed inside the school gymnasium had come out to help. That still gave him a huge numbers advantage, but this was troubling. Too many people were shrinking back and hoping that others would pick up their slack.

Turning to the first person he saw, he called out, "Take three people with you and get over to the door and window factory. Gather as many people as will come. Time is of the essence."

The woman gave a curt nod and slung her rifle over her shoulder. She seemed to have no problem finding three people to join her and they quickly hurried off into the darkness towards the other main housing area. He swiftly repeated the process and sent another team to the residential neighborhood. Most of the houses had at least four families living under the roof.

Moving to take the lead, he held up his hands to try and get everybody's attention. "They are up the road here. I am guessing they blew a hole in the barricade by Farmers Hill Road. That is right by where I saw them gathered. None of our patrols is up that direction, so if you encounter anything coming this way, shoot it on sight."

He quickly dispatched four people with hunting rifles to the roof of the house across the street and outside the barricade. Everybody else was sent to positions up and down the barrier. Most climbed up onto some of the big trucks or busses that helped make up the wall of automobiles.

It did not take long for shadows to start appearing from the north. From his perch atop a trailer of a big rig, he saw that they were moving down both sides of the blockade. That part had him confused until he watched a pair scurry over to a car and open the hatch where the gas nozzle would go. A flash and then a flame could be seen. They were using the cars as bombs. The shadows rushed forward and prepared to repeat the process when one of the snipers on the roof apparently had a good shot. The single report of a rifle was followed by three more in quick succession.

Two bodies fell to the ground, but the people moving down the inside of the barricade took off in a run. They were just about to the road that turned into the school when something flammable arced into the air and landed in the midst of the largest portion of the group. There was a concussive 'WHUMP' and a bright flash that made Ivan cover his eyes. That had not been one of the cars blowing up; that was a bomb. And it had come from his people. He could only think of one person in all of Liberty who might have already made an improvised explosive device and he was suddenly glad that the man was on his side.

Sections of grass were now ablaze, and in the flickering light of those fires, Ivan spied three individuals walking through the downed bodies, many writhing on the ground in agony as flames devoured them. Single shots were being fired at pointblank range, ending the thrashing about with a final sharp report.

He rushed up to find Stephen Deese, his wife, and another man doing the grisly job of executioner. All three had bandanas around their faces, adding a spookily anonymous quality to their appearances as they killed.

"Any sign of Jonah or his brother?" Ivan asked over the sound of the siren wailing to the north.

Stephen fired a single shot into the head of a woman who was looking up at him with a snarl of rage on her face and blood trickling from the corners of her mouth. He looked up at Ivan and gave a curt shake of his head.

"Well, they are the ones behind this," Ivan said. "And if we don't take them down tonight, we will likely have to deal with them again in the future."

Stephen turned to his wife. "You two got this?"

"Yep," Terri Deese looked around and gave a nod. "I think we only have a dozen or so left."

The man leaned in and kissed his wife on the cheek and then turned back to Ivan. "You got any idea where they might be?"

"I know where I saw them last."

"Best get moving then," Stephen growled. "I think the sooner we pluck this nasty weed, the less likely we have more sproutin' up in the future."

"You sound like you knew about this," Ivan panted as the two jogged up Ruhamah Road towards the continuous and annoying wail of a siren.

"I didn't know who it would be, but I can't say I'm surprised." Stephen paused and grabbed Ivan by the shoulder.

Coming their way were a dozen or so of the undead. They were just within the glow of Stephen's head-mounted spotlight.

"Yeah, the Simms brothers blew a hole in our perimeter up ahead…almost forgot about that part," Ivan muttered with a scowl.

The two men put a bit of space between each other and approached the zombies. With well-placed swings of their machetes, the undead were taken down with minimal effort.

"We need to find that siren and shut it off first," Stephen now had to really shout to be heard above the din.

They veered towards the sound and discovered what was basically a red child's toy bullhorn with a fire truck sticker on it.

That toy was switched on and sitting beside an actual bullhorn that was acting as the amplifier and broadcaster. Stephen raised a booted foot and stomped on the toy before reaching down and switching off the actual bullhorn.

"Points for creativity." Stephen was looking down on the busted plastic toy when Ivan stepped up beside him.

"Whatever," Ivan said with a shrug. "They were up Farmers Hill."

Stephen pulled the small knapsack from his back and produced four cylinders. He handed a pair of them to Ivan.

"What are these?" Ivan turned the cylinders over in his hands.

"Be careful," Stephen gripped the chief by the wrist.

He moved one of the devices so that it could be easily seen using his headlamp. There was a small covered recess and what looked like a tiny toggle switch set in it was revealed when Stephen thumbed the cover aside.

"Flick this switch and you have ten seconds to get rid of the device," Stephen explained.

"Those were your explosives," Ivan said with appreciation.

"Funny, I was just headed over to the school when the siren started. It didn't take a rocket scientist to figure it out once you and a bunch of people came bursting out of the gym with weapons drawn. It made it easier when one of the lunatics fired at you guys."

"Wow, we actually caught a stroke of luck on the right side," Ivan laughed as the pair walked through the smoldering ruins of where a section of the parked cars had been blown. "We should set a detail to emptying these babies of all their fluids. Otherwise we are open to somebody else doing the exact same thing. Don't know why that thought never occurred to me before."

"I think we are all on a steep learning curve," Stephen whispered, his pace slowing.

Ivan slowed to match the man and began searching for whatever had caused him to suddenly change his pace. Just ahead he thought that he saw something move across the road.

Stephen pointed and then signaled with one finger to each side. He pointed to himself and the right, then to Ivan and indicated left. Ivan nodded, tucked the two devices into the pouch at his hip, and headed into the tall grass.

He had only gone a short distance when he heard the sounds of heavy breathing just ahead and to the left of his position. Creeping forward even slower, he considered pulling out one of Stephen's explosives, but thought better of it. They were already outside the barricade and who knew how many zombies that siren had brought their direction before it had been stomped into bits and silenced?

"...have you turned your back on your servant?" a voice whimpered. "Has Satan truly won? Has he taken this world for his own to do as he pleases like he did with Job?" There was a wet cough and then a soft groan of pain.

Ivan hurried forward with his pistol at the ready. He smelled him before he saw him. Chuck Simms was on his back looking straight up. His hands were clutching his belly. The man seemed to sense his presence, but he did not move.

"Go ahead, finish me and send me to my Father. You all deserve this hell," Chuck Simms spat through teeth clenched in pain.

"You people give Christians a bad name," Ivan retorted.

"You can call yourself a Christian all you like, but the Great Deceiver will be coming for you as he begins his thousand year reign. And then our Heavenly Father will emerge from the heavens and reclaim this world in the name of His Holy Father."

"What book did you read?' Ivan scoffed.

"Just you wait and see," Chuck Simms cautioned. "Satan and his minions are here, and they are coming for you. Why else would none of our faithful have yet to fall to them? I've been bitten, but I still live. I am saved, chosen by God."

A low moan came from the darkness further up Farmers Hill Road. Ivan grabbed the flashlight hanging from his belt and clicked it on. He scanned up ahead and saw several figures stumbling towards where he stood over Chuck Simms.

"I'll leave you here then to take it up with them." Ivan nodded to the approaching zombies.

He flashed his light down on the man's sweaty face and saw absolute fanatical conviction. A yelp and a meaty thud to the right told him that Stephen had probably found Jonah. He swung his flashlight over and Stephen Deese gave him a wave as he began to head over, wiping off the blade of his machete as he did so.

"Satan's minions will have nothing to do with me, but you...you will all perish in agony."

Ivan turned and met Stephen part way. The two men started up the road in silence. They were just cutting through the jagged hole in the barricade when a scream shattered the relative quiet of the night. It started like any regular scream, but it morphed into a maniacal laughter that made the hairs on both men's necks stand on end until it came to a sudden and merciful end.

"You left him alive for the zombies?" Stephen asked, sounding incredulous.

"He said they couldn't hurt him...something about how he had been bitten but that God saved him."

Stephen stopped suddenly. "The chief was bit."

"Umm...no. The chief was shot."

"Before that," Stephen corrected. "When we went out to the highway. One of those things got him on the hand, but he never showed any signs...until he finally died from being shot."

"That seems like something we should tell Sophie. I bet it will make more sense to her. Especially with people dying who haven't been bitten and all that. Seems to me that this is like the AIDS or Hep C," Ivan speculated.

"You go on ahead, I will stay here and keep watch on this breech. Send me some support as soon as possible. We need to seal this spot as quick as we can."

"Will do." Ivan started away and then paused. He turned to Stephen, a sheepish expression on his face. "You think I shoulda put Chuck down instead of leaving him for them things?"

"I don't know what to think about much of anything anymore," Stephen replied, not bothering to look back at the chief.

***

Jamie peered out the window. She could see several of the walking dead roaming the streets outside. From the second floor of the townhouse, they could actually see the hospital. Just looking at it gave her shivers.

It was the stuff of nightmares. So many bodies littered the ground, and the stench of death was so thick in the air that it coated your mouth and nose no matter if you were wearing a mask or respirator. Even with the gauze pads coated in Vick's VapoRub stuffed up your nose, you could still smell the rotten sickly sweetness.

She moved away from the window and went to the stairs. Her eyes fell on Bo Summers. The man was still sitting on the floor beside the front door. He'd been silent to the point of brooding ever since they'd busted in to this place, taken down that one zombie, and then dragged it outside.

To compound the odd feeling she was getting, Sarah Gilstrap was seated right beside the big man and absently stroking his arm. Every so often she would pat him and lean in to whisper something. She certainly hoped these two hadn't suddenly snapped. This was not the time or the place.

The rest of the team was scattered around the townhouse. Some were sprawled on the floor, others the couch. Two people had flopped down on the bed and were snoring softly. She slid down and took a seat at the top of the stairs, her mind drifting like the dust motes flitting past her eyes in the sliver of moonlight that shone through the window.

Was this how things were going to be from now on? Was life going to be reduced to these moments venturing into a dead world for supplies? Would all of them make it back?

This was so much scarier than any movie. To see people walking around with massive wounds, parts missing, or bits of them hanging out from gaping holes in their bodies was truly awful.

The drive up to Pickens had been close to disastrous as well as heart wrenching. They had been travelling up Highway 178 and happened upon a multiple car accident. It looked like the people inside had suffered terrible fates as most were still strapped into their cars but had endured attacks that left many with chunks of their faces, shoulders, throats, and upper body torn away.

Then they had encountered a lone military truck sitting on the road just a few miles outside of Pickens. They were not intending on stopping. After all, it was just a single truck with what looked like just the driver-turned-zombie in the cab. As they were edging around the vehicle, Jamie could not help but stop when she glanced over and recognized the man. It was Clifton Martin staring back at her with dead eyes. She saw his hands come up and paw impotently at the smeared driver's side window. He tried to gnaw at the glass as well, and his efforts only increased when she got out of her truck and walked over to the military transport.

"Oh, Cliff," she had gasped.

In the end, she put him down. She knew that was what Sophie would have wanted. Of all the zombies she had killed so far, this had been the most difficult. There was something to be said about staring into the face of somebody that you once knew just before driving a short, metal-tipped spear into their eye socket. She just wished that she'd had time to do more for the body than simply have it lifted back into the cab of the truck.

The next bit of horror had come when they passed the burnt ruins of the Pickens County Sheriff's office. Apparently some of the bad guys that Kevin Staley mentioned had come here in large numbers. It looked like heavy explosives had been used as bits of the main building were littering the highway. Several of the cars in the lot had been blown up and bodies were strung up from anything high enough to keep their feet from touching the ground. Many were in sheriff's uniforms and had obviously been strung up alive and left to squirm so that the undead could get to them. Some were missing legs and other had been ripped in half. There were even a few strands of rope swinging in the breeze that had been snapped. A variety of profane graffiti had been spray painted on the signage leading to the area as well as gigantic letters on the actual asphalt of the parking lot that read: "Fuck the Police!"

Despite what Kevin had said, she wanted to refuse to believe that humanity could spiral into such depravity so rapidly. People were essentially good at heart...right? What she was witnessing with her own two eyes led her to believe otherwise.

When she returned, she was going to be holding a vote. Up until now, she had thought maybe she might be going too far in her desire to live up to Chief Gilstrap's final words. Yet, now she felt maybe she was not doing enough. The vote to seal Liberty off from the rest of the world had really been a knee-jerk reaction; or at least that what she had believed until now.

"Hey, Jamie?" a voice whispered, snapping her out of her morose thoughts. She looked up to see Michelle Bennett standing over her. "There is light just to our right over by the elementary school. It looks like a lantern. It hasn't moved for a while, but it absolutely was not there fifteen minutes ago."

"Keep an eye on it." Jamie rubbed her eyes and stifled a yawn.

"You don't want anybody to go check it out?"

"Why?"

That response seemed to confuse Michelle. The woman opened her mouth twice before finally speaking. "What if it is somebody who needs help?"

Jamie knew that what she was about to say might not come across as proper with some. Still, if she was going to follow through with her plan to seal Liberty, then she needed to start acting like the leader that those who had entrusted her with this position thought her to be.

"We are not here for anybody but the people of Liberty. We have a list of priority items to try to acquire. Our only directive involving others is that we will back off if somebody has laid claim to an area. We are out to salvage and scavenge, not start a war...and we aren't here on a rescue mission."

She waited for the backlash and was surprised when the woman simply nodded her head. "Okay, then I will make sure we keep an eye on that light and inform you if it looks like somebody is trying to wave us off or anything like that."

Jamie leaned against the rail and let herself relax just a little. By morning, the lookouts had reported nothing other than that single lantern. It winked out just a few hours before sunrise and no sounds or other indications of survivors manifested the rest of the night.

"Okay." Jamie stood at the front door, her entire team assembled around her awaiting instructions. "I want to divide the team in half."

She had given it a lot of thought as she drifted in and out of her catnaps. She had decided to have Bo take one group and she would lead the other. They would enter from opposite ends of the hospital. Bo's group would be tasked to the emergency room area. Her group would be hitting the main prescription pharmacy. Since they would likely encounter a lot of undead, time was of the essence. Both groups were going to move in fast and have ten minutes to grab all they could.

"Hopefully you have all familiarized yourselves with the list, but with as many zombies as we have, I think it is just best to grab anything you can. Bandages, alcohol, iodine, basically anything you can stuff into your satchels. I know that Sophie went through a lot of trouble to prioritize that list, but I don't think anybody realized how awful the hospital would be." Jamie looked around as she spoke and saw grim determination staring back at her.

"Do we meet back here?" Bo asked. "Or would you rather we made for one of the fallback locations."

"If we can meet here, try this spot first. Who knows…maybe we will do this in waves. Nothing says we can't go back in. Sort of like disturbing a hornets' nest," Jamie answered. "We get things riled up, but once it calms down, maybe we can make a second and even third attempt."

That seemed to satisfy everybody and after some handshakes and claps on the back, both teams headed out into the morning sun. They moved together down Monroe Street, and then separated at the highway with Jamie leading her team up to W G Acker Drive and Bo taking his group straight across the open field and up the small hill. They would be coming in from the south and Jamie from the north.

As she and her team hurried down the long, winding drive, they passed rotting corpses and smoldering military vehicles. It seemed impossible that so much carnage could exist in such a small area. If it was this bad here, then the major cities had to be beyond comprehension.

Fortunately, there did not seem to be much activity along the way. They followed the road as it curved around the side of the hospital and came to a rear entrance. Jamie signaled for the team to halt. They would be crossing a parking lot with what looked like the tattered remains of several large tents.

This was the end of their clear run. Several zombies could be seen milling about. A few pawed at cars that contained more of their number, most likely entombed forever. She turned to the group.

"Okay, this is not going to be pretty. We make for that entrance." She pointed to a set of double doors that had been blown off their hinges. "Once inside, everybody stay close. If it moves, take it down. I don't want us to leave anything behind that could present a problem when we make our exit. Most likely we will be in an even bigger hurry on the way out."

Looking around, she saw lips tightly pressed and eyes sharp and focused. These people knew what was in store and were prepared to do what needed to be done. And while that was

256

great, she was noticing a lot of the people in town sitting back and seeming to be happy with allowing others to do all the hard stuff; just another thing to add to her list of issues to take care of when they got back.

As she got up and started towards the hospital in a low crouch, she had a realization that put a smile on her face. She had thought in terms of *when* she returned to Liberty…not if.

***

Bo took the lead as they approached the Pickens Garden apartment complex. Oliver's two story townhouse was at the far end looking out over Monroe Street. The hospital was just beyond that, across the highway.

He'd been glad when Jamie accepted his idea of using that location for their observation point without any questions. As soon as they had parked in the lot, he had wasted no time getting out in front. He wanted to be the lead on this in either case when it came to Oliver. If he was alive, then he wanted to be the first face Oliver saw; and if he was dead, then it would be him that put the man to rest for good.

He reached the door and pulled the bandana from his face. It would suck to break in and have Oliver shoot him thinking that he was a looter. Of course, with the Halogen head lamp he was wearing, he would likely blind the man for a few seconds and be able to call out.

He opened the door and was greeted by a figure standing in the middle of the living room. A wave of that all-too-familiar stink came at him full force and made his stomach seize just a bit. The figure in the living room turned to face him, head tilted to one side. There was a dark stain on one arm that had strips of the applied bandage dangling from it.

"I'm sorry you were alone at the end," Bo whispered, and then stepped forward and drove his blade into the temple of the thing that was no longer his beloved friend and companion.

Sarah was right behind him and patted him gently on the

shoulder as the two entered the townhouse and made sure that there were no other zombies. Once they finished, Bo had to just sit down on the floor and hide his head in his hands. Not only did he want to avoid any questioning glances, but he could not watch as Oliver's things were rifled through as the team searched for anything useful. He knew it was a necessity, but he didn't have to like it and he didn't have to participate.

He felt Sarah sit beside him at some point, but he was so emotionally numb that he barely paid any attention to whatever soothing words she was whispering to him. His mind tried to reconcile the fact that he had come here knowing the most likely outcome. He also told himself that at least he had closure. None of that provided him any real solace.

At last Jamie rounded everybody up and split the team in half with him and Sarah sent to try and gather supplies from the emergency room area. He knew that would probably be the area with the heaviest concentration, but he did not say anything. Jamie was actually doing a really good job leading this team and he did not want to seem like he was trying to undermine her leadership. Besides, he really wanted to get in a few good licks against these walking bags of filth. He may never know which zombie ended his Oliver, but every zombie he met from here on out was the potential culprit in his eyes.

As they left Oliver's home, Bo took one final look. He doubted that he would ever see this place again after this mission. He briefly considered taking one of the pictures from the wall or something else that might remind him of Oliver, but in the end, he decided against it; at least for now. He needed to be focused on the mission.

They made their way down Monroe Street and then the two groups split up. He led the way as they jogged across the sloping lawn that led to the front emergency room entrance. They could see the gaping hole where a series of doors used to exist. Beyond that, the way actually looked surprisingly clear.

Taking a deep breath, Bo motioned for his team to charge.

As they crossed the open paved lot, some of the team veered off to take down a zombie in order to keep their retreat as clear as possible. When they entered the emergency room, the team came to a stop. The area looked like somebody had taken black paint and flung buckets of it at the walls, floor, and even the ceiling. Bodies were missing heads where shotgun blasts at pointblank range had taken them away, leaving jagged stumps and a splatter of gore in sinister parody of a halo where the body lay sprawled out or slumped against a wall.

The bodies were soldiers, doctors, nurses and patients. Some were missing limbs...or worse. Snapping his fingers to get everybody's focus back on him, Bo pointed to the door that led back to the actual emergency room where patients had been treated. Once inside, they would empty carts and bust open lockers. Sophie had provided a hand drawn map indicating where some of the desired items would be stored.

A collection of bobbing lights hurried through the waiting room and reached the door that was their destination. By now, a few of the team had stopped, bending at the waist to be sick. Whether from a combination of the sights or the smells, Bo had no clue; he waited patiently for each person who was forced to stop.

Once everybody gave him the thumbs-up sign, he gripped the handle and pushed in the door to the room. Faces turned in their direction, all of them slack and emotionless. Tracer-ridden eyes appeared in the beams of light, but there was no point of red, or green light reflected back. These were all members of the walking dead. Their gazes gave no sort of reflection. For some reason, that struck Bo and gave him a chill. It wasn't as if he did not already know what these were, but the added effect of their dead eyes not reacting to light simply increased the level of this already surreal experience to one that caused him to shudder.

"Move fast and stay in pairs," Bo hissed. There was no sense in being silent, the zombies knew they were present and were even now staggering towards members of his team. He felt Sarah press up against him and he patted her shoulder.

A zombie lurched in front of them and Bo drove his knife into its temple. He quickly kicked it away and strode to the next, repeating his move. As he veered for a cluster of three, he called softly over his shoulder to Sarah, "Start filling those bags. I have your back."

He did not even look to see if she obeyed or gave any sort of acknowledgement. It was time to visit some revenge on the undead. Sure, he knew they had no concept of his fury, but each kill brought him a degree of comfort. He was just pulling his blade from the top of the skull of a female soldier zombie when a hand clasped his left ankle, sending him sprawling on his face.

"Bo!" he heard Sarah yell.

15

Supplies and Fortifications

Ivan Potter moved among the bodies that had been dragged to a small section of grass just beyond some trees on the north side of the high school. While it was no secret what had taken place the night before, he did not see a reason to have everybody subjected to looking at the dead bodies of those who had been part of the Simms brothers' little cult.

That word rang around inside his mind for a second and he shoved it aside. Ask him a month ago about a cult popping up in Liberty, South Carolina and he would have busted a gut laughing. Now, he was looking down at a woman that had served him pie in one of the town's small restaurants. Kneeling beside the body, he brushed his hands down her face to shut her eyes.

"I think we have all of 'em," Stephen Deese said as he and another man laid down a body a few feet away.

"Can you believe they sacrificed their daughter to the devil?" one man whispered to another as they left the area and headed back to the school.

The word on this was going to be spread to everybody by nightfall. If folks got carried away or even more frightened, they might have a witch hunt on their hands.

Ivan stood and turned to Stephen. "Get the entire town here within the hour. I want to try and get this situation under control as much as possible."

"Probably a good idea, I've already heard people whispering about who else might have been secret members of this little society." Stephen wiped his forehead with a towel he had hanging from his back pocket and then headed towards the gymnasium.

Ivan moved down the line, trying to look at these people as the folks he'd passed on the streets or in the grocery store aisle, but for some reason, they all seemed different now. If such seemingly good people could go bad so fast, and in such a radical way, what did that say about those on the fringe? Even worse, what about some of those sick bastards that he knew to be out there?

Those bikers might have been a very small tip of a very large and ugly iceberg. Just twelve hours ago, he had been having doubts about Jamie Burns and her plan to seal off Liberty from outsiders. If he could not trust the men and women of this town, glancing down at his mailman he suppressed a shiver, then he sure as hell could not trust an outsider.

He paused at the body of Chastity Simms. Of all the bodies laid out here, this was the only one he considered a victim. He simply could not understand the mentality involved in such a thing. To believe that murdering your own child would bring God's favor?

"She told me she was scared that her dad was going to do something crazy," a voice whispered from behind him.

Ivan turned to see Lawrence standing a few feet away, tears running down his cheeks. He was holding a handful of wilted wildflowers in one hand; they were dangling at his side as if he had forgotten them.

"She couldn't have guessed it would be this," Ivan said. He walked over to the distraught young man and put an arm around his shoulder. "And I don't think anybody could have guessed anything so crazy would have happened here. These were our friends and neighbors. It all feels so impossible."

"Sort of like a zombie apocalypse?" the boy sniffed.

"Good point," Ivan conceded.

Lawrence laid the bouquet beside the body and then followed Ivan back to the school where two teams were getting ready to start work on shoring up the defenses around the train. Logs were going to be rolled under the cars to keep zombies from being able to go underneath, and strands of barbed wire would be strung between them. Also, platforms were being constructed and would eventually be mounted on each end of the train as well as a spot in the center.

Sophie was standing in the entry doors her hands shielding her eyes as she scanned the throng of people going about their business. A terrible feeling punched the newly appointed chief in the gut and he turned to Lawrence and grabbed his arms.

"Tell me you have seen your mother since last night when all this crap happened!" he exclaimed.

"Uhh...well..." the boy stammered and sputtered. "Actually..." He let that word draw out for way too long.

"Dammit, kid," Ivan growled, grabbing Lawrence by the elbow and steering him towards his mother.

A minute later, he was easing away from one of the biggest ass chewing sessions that he'd been witness to since the day that he'd vomited on Sister Mary Beverly's shoes at the church picnic during his sixth grade year. It wasn't so much the throwing up that had gotten him in trouble. It had been the fact that he and three other boys had slipped away from the party and gone to Lionel Wilson's house and raided his parents' liquor cabinet. He'd never even been able to smell Southern Comfort again without his stomach tightening up. Plus, he always felt a residual burning on his butt. He was pretty sure his mother had whipped his ass at a felony level.

As he was heading over to see if he could help one of the train details, he could not help but chuckle. Just a month ago, Sophie Martin would be receiving a visit from social services at the least. Right now, people were just walking past like nothing in the world was happening.

***

Jonathan stared into the gun leveled at his head. The fear he felt was at war with what he was seeing. Sure, the woman holding the gun was a big woman. In fact, he thought they might be pretty close to the same weight class if they were wrestling. Her face was ruddy and she looked like perhaps she had been in more fights than he'd ever taken part. Still, he was having trouble reconciling that a woman was holding him at gunpoint as four others climbed over his truck and stripped the rest of the people that had been with him on this run of all their belongings. They were even taking folks' shoes and socks.

At least they were leaving the underwear, he thought morosely.

"Something funny, fat boy?" the woman holding the gun snarled.

Jonathan's eyes returned to the woman holding him prisoner. He shook his head. "Not a thing. I was just thinking that I was grateful you folks weren't stripping my friends of their drawers."

He had no explanation, but a feeling of indescribable calm was settling over him. He was pretty sure that he was going to die any moment and that there really was nothing he could do about it. With all options off the table, it was as if his brain had simply come to terms with fate and shut off the fear.

"Trust me, if we see something in our size, we take that too," the woman shot back.

"We didn't come here looking for trouble," Jonathan said, his eyes no longer focused on the gun. He looked into the eyes of the woman that he figured would be his executioner.

"That's funny," the woman said with a mirthless laugh. "Every group of raiders and rapists that we have encountered always say that once we have the drop on them. Yet, when they catch and kill one of our people, or they set fire to our shelter, steal our food…well then…"

"We were just out scouting for supplies ourselves," Jonathan replied. "We even had orders to pull back if we encountered a group that had a claim on an area. We sorta figure there are enough places to search that we don't need to encroach on others."

"And just where is this benevolent community that you supposedly hail from?"

Jonathan thought it over. He shot a glance back to the bed of the pickup as one of the women of this group plucked rings from the fingers of one of the dead bodies. He could only see the hand, so he could not tell who was currently being pillaged, but seeing such disrespect for his friends steeled his resolve.

"You really think I would tell you?" Jonathan finally answered.

The woman cocked the hammer on her pistol and pressed it against his forehead. "Yes...I do."

"You're gonna kill me anyway, so why should I do anything to help you vultures?"

That earned him a smack in the cheek with the butt of the gun. He felt the hot pain of split skin followed by a trickle of blood running down the side of his face. His right eye started to blur and his vision dimmed just a bit for a few seconds. But he refused to acknowledge the blow by reacting or even wiping the blood away.

"That doesn't mean I have to kill you quick." The woman leaned forward, her sour breath adding to the already unpleasant situation for Jonathan.

"And you are saying that these so-called raiders and rapists are the bad guys? I mean, I get it. There are some bad people doing bad things and taking advantage of this situation, but what makes this anything close to right?" He sort of looked around to indicate the scene of carnage surrounding them.

"The days of right and wrong are over. It is simply about survival now."

"That's a pretty narrow view."

"The days are past when you give people the benefit of the

265

doubt, young man." The woman eased back out of the cab of the truck and motioned Jonathan to follow. "So is television therapy, tabloid shows passing themselves off as news, and participation trophies."

Jonathan edged his way out of the truck and almost fell, his vision on the right side now virtually non-existent. The woman with the gun made no effort to prevent his fall and actually stepped back as he landed gracelessly in the trampled grass of the roadside.

"What does any of that have to do with anything?"

"Exactly," the woman answered cryptically.

Great, he thought as he saw two dozen women moving around the wreckage, *I get to die at the hands of a lunatic.*

"Now, get on your knees and lace your fingers behind your head," the woman ordered.

Jonathan did as he was instructed. He saw the bodies of his companions being dragged from the vehicle and tossed unceremoniously into the weeds and brush that grew alongside the highway. Part of him wanted to jump to his feet and just go out swinging as he watched two women swing the body of Alex Singleton by his wrists and ankles back and forth twice. On the third swing, they let go and the body flew a few feet and landed with a meaty slap on top of the growing pile of his stripped down team members.

"You gonna give us something useful, or do we have to do this the hard and ugly way?" the woman asked.

She looked Jonathan in the eyes as she spoke. What he saw was a total emptiness. This woman did not care about him one way or the other. This wasn't a ploy or a bluff. She was going to kill him eventually. His only option was whether his last moments were filled with horrible agony, or he simply took a quick bullet to the head. He weighed his options and came to the conclusion that it was very likely that she would get her answers one way or the other.

"Liberty," he sighed. "Our group is from over in Liberty."

The world went dark in the blink of an eye.

***

They jogged past the sign that read "PHARMACY" with an arrow pointing down a long hallway. Jamie stepped over a corpse sprawled on the floor and motioned for the team to follow. She slowed at each spot along the hallway where an intersection occurred.

It was unnerving to say the least the way noises echoed in this massive building-turned-tomb. The sounds of moans could be heard along with those horrific baby cries. That was still the hardest thing to hear in Jamie's opinion. In her mind, she knew that there could very well be that one time when a baby might actually be the source of that sound, but the baby cry had become such a cautionary tale that people were becoming numb to the noise.

At two separate intersections she was rewarded by stepping into a zombie that had come to a stop and was simply standing there waiting. They reminded her of spiders in that sense, and this was their web. Much like the spider, as soon as they sensed her presence, they moved in for the kill, but fortunately they were very slow and awkward. She usually managed to drive her spiked staff into its head before it even managed to take a full step.

They finally reached a set of service windows where people would hand over their prescription slips and then sit in the big lobby at their back and await for the medication to be bottled and ready for them to take home.

She motioned for two members of her team to take down the few zombies roaming around the chairs and assorted plants and magazine racks. She and the other three hurried to the customer service windows where they already had their first stroke of luck. The metal roll-down doors had not been lowered and locked by whomever it was that had last been working in the pharmacy.

Jamie pulled the knife that Ivan had given her. The tip of the handle had a nifty little knob that supposedly shattered even emergency glass. She did as he'd instructed and rapped it against the bottom right corner of the window. Sure enough, it went white with cracks. She used her gloved fist and shoved in, sending a cascade of tiny cubes of glass.

"Cool," she breathed.

Turning with a smile, she climbed up and in. Looking around, it seemed that the last person working here had obviously had at least some idea of what was happening. There were a lot of emptied pill lockers. Still, there were several things on the list that were plentiful. Also, there were little bags on a set of shelves with unclaimed prescriptions just waiting.

After a quick assessment, it was clear that they would basically be able to empty this room out if they stuffed all their packs full and had some of those out in the lobby hand in theirs. In no time, they had the little room emptied of anything useful.

One at a time, she and the others climbed out. They were right by a set of doors that led outside. The only trouble with that came in the form of the fifty or so zombies all gathered around, pawing at the glass. There was even one that had gotten stuck in the revolving door. Its arm had somehow been wedged in between the jamb and the revolving door itself. By the looks of things, it would not be stuck in there much longer. The limb looked twisted and deformed to the point of snapping in two with just a few more yanks.

"Back the way we came," Jamie announced.

She remained just as cautious on the return trip. Being careless at this point was just stupid. They only had one corner left, and a surge of hope had filled her. She should have known better.

For whatever reason that drives a zombie to do what they do, they rounded that last corner to the lobby by the exit to discover it thick with the undead. There had been the sounds of moans and all that since they entered the building; the emptiness

268

had made being able to judge the nearness of the sound almost impossible.

"Okay, we head back the way we just came," Jamie announced. "There is a second passage that leads to a service corridor. Sophie said that there is a metal door, and we will have to pry it open. It's gonna be noisy, which is why it was only for emergency use, but it is there or we risk the exit back at the pharmacy lobby area."

She led them back, glancing at the piece of paper that Sophie had given her. She had to keep looking up to see the little plaques mounted on the walls to confirm that she was going the right direction. At last they rounded a corner that led only about twenty feet and ended in a solid metal door.

She had two members of the team rush to the door with the pry bars and start attacking the latch. It only took about thirty seconds, but between the noise and seeing the pursuing zombies round the corner just a short distance away, it felt to Jamie like it took forever.

Jamie had her back to the pair opening the door as she watched the approaching horde. The frightened scream from behind her and in the direction of the door caused her to jump and spin, turning her back to a wall of walking death that was drawing frighteningly near. She turned just in time to see both her team being enveloped by a writhing wall of undead arms.

One of them looked right at her, eyes wide with fear, but she was certain that she saw reproach and accusation as well. If it were not for the fact that the individual was shrieking in agony and a zombie leaned in and tore a chunk from his cheek while another ripped away a piece of the side of his neck, she was positive that the person would be cursing her name.

The other had been pulled to the floor and three of the undead were ripping at clothing as they sought the soft flesh of the belly. This one was kicking and flailing, but could not be seen except for those thrashing legs that jutted from the pack of zombies that had dragged him down.

"Run!" Jamie yelled. "We take our chances at the doors exiting the pharmacy."

She bolted, hearing the footfalls of the others falling in behind. They retraced their steps and emerged in the lobby. Already, at least ten zombies had filtered in from the different hallways that opened up from this large, open room.

An idea struck Jamie as her team came to a stop. All of them were casting furtive looks over their shoulders back the way they'd come as if they expected the zombies to suddenly gain the ability to run and appear hot on their tails instead of the good ways back they should all be.

She gave the undead outside an appraising look and noticed how they were all riled up at the re-arrival of her and her group. The others in the room were all re-orienting on them and beginning their awkward stumbles and shambles in the new direction towards fresh meat.

"Michelle, you and the others go to the far end of the windows," Jamie instructed.

"What about them?" the woman managed, visibly frightened as well as winded as she gestured to the zombies that had come back like the tide.

"Kill them obviously." With that, Jamie edged back closer to the shadows and moved in the opposite direction she'd sent her people. "I want you to start tapping on the window. Make some noise and draw them to you. I am going to break the window at the far end once it is relatively clear. As soon as I do, make a run for it."

She kept checking back and forth between her people and their progress attracting the zombies gathered outside and then taking looks each direction at the main hallways. A few lone stragglers arrived first from the hallway across the lobby from her but closest to where her team was making noise. When the group that had been following them rounded the far corner, she knew they had run out of time. It was going to have to be good enough.

Moments later, there was a loud crack and the sound of a

massive window cascading down in a glass rainstorm. Jamie and her team emerged and dashed to the tree-lined road that would take them back to the townhouse. They had just reached Monroe Street when a series of screams came from back towards the hospital.

***

Bo looked down to see a teenaged boy zombie trying to gnaw on his steel-toed boot. With his free leg, he kicked hard and smashed it in the face, crushing its nose, but doing little other damage; certainly not enough to get the zombie to let go. He jerked away and managed to get to his feet before it could grab him again. He stabbed down on the back of the head of this one and felt the tip of his machete scrape on the tiled floor.

More of the team seemed to be involved in fighting zombies than in grabbing supplies and Bo was thinking that this trip might not be worth what they came away with if something didn't change soon. Another zombie, this one a female in dark and heavily stained scrubs, staggered out from behind a hanging divider. This one had a syringe still hanging from one arm just below a very tightly cinched piece of rubber tubing.

Bo did not have the time to ponder the scenario that would lead to such a situation. He simply stepped in and drove his blade up and under the jaw. Jerking back, the zombie fell and he moved for the next one after checking on Sarah. She had popped a wall locker open and was busy scooping the contents into her open pack.

Good for her, Bo thought. *She isn't wasting time reading labels. Let Sophie sort this shit out when we get it back home.*

The raid was now in full swing as half the group fought off zombies while the other half tried to grab as much as they could and stuff it into their packs. There was almost no conversation with the exception of the occasional "Look out!" or "There's one!"

Bo had just taken one down and turned to find the next. He

271

looked around and saw the others who had been doing battle looking around with the same looks of confusion on their faces. There did not seem to be another zombie around. At least there were none in the actual emergency treatment area.

"Okay, folks," Bo called. All heads turned to him and he flashed a smile. "Grab what else you can stuff into the packs and—"

A distant shriek cut him off. Everybody winced and seemed to hold his or her breath. When it mercifully stopped, there was silence except for the sounds of heavy breathing as the group slowly exhaled almost in unison and sucked in the next huge breath.

"Okay, that sounded like maybe one or two people," Bo said a bit quieter than before. "Not saying that is a good thing, but…" He fumbled for what to say and finally threw his hands up in the air. "You all know what I mean. Now grab what you can and let's get the hell out of this place."

They did not need to be told twice. There were a couple of last minute snatches and grabs as people took the last few things available to them and then assembled at the door.

"Okay, we have no idea what we drew to us with all this noise," Bo lectured. "I want you all to be ready for a fight. The objective is to get outside as fast as you can. I know that we had a thing about taking down everything we saw on the way in, but now it is about getting out alive. That means you keep moving forward no matter what happens. If one of us falls, you can't go back for them. They either make it out or they don't."

"What if the way is blocked?" somebody spoke up.

The sounds of moans and hands pawing at the door to the treatment area of the emergency room seemed almost thunderous in the few seconds before Bo answered. "We don't have a choice. I don't know about any of you, but I have no idea where those three doors lead to." He pointed to the various other exits for emphasis. "It could take us deeper into the hospital and this is not a place that I want to get lost in."

That seemed to settle it for everybody. They all took a few seconds to cinch their backpacks tighter, check their weapons, and their protective gear.

Bo counted down and then pulled the door open. In the time since they had come in, cleaned it out, and then moved into the actual emergency room to gather supplies (and kill the zombies that had lingered since the hospital fell), the waiting room had become overrun with the undead.

Somebody let out a startled cry, but Bo simply gritted his teeth and stepped through the doorway and chopped hard, bringing his machete down on the crown of a man in a filthy HAZMAT suit. The zombies had apparently done the hard work, ripping away the hood when this poor soul had been attacked.

He felt something latch onto his left leg as he took a few steps forward to meet the oncoming wall of undeath. Glancing down, he saw a child of maybe six or seven emerging from under an end table that had probably held an array of old, dog-eared magazines once upon a time. Without hesitation he brought his gloved fist down on the top of the zombie child's head. It sprawled flat and he stomped hard on its back as he put down the next zombie to stagger forward. As soon as he pulled his blade free, he stabbed down. He did not need to look to confirm his kill; the sudden cease in movement under his boot told him all that he needed to know.

"Run for the exit!" Bo bellowed.

He heard a gasp from his left and glanced over to see Sarah Gilstrap just standing face to face with a female zombie. It was wearing a Pickens County Sheriff's uniform.

"Oh, Jenny," Sarah choked out as she pushed the zombie away as it reached for her.

Bo noticed that she was not making any move to end the creature and he turned back to take the thing down, breaking his own rule. He was pretty sure that Jenny had been Adam's sister. He grabbed it from behind and by the shoulder, spinning it away from Sarah so that she would not see the thing's face. With one swift move, he drove his weapon into its right eye socket and then pushed it away and into another pair of zombies that were closing in. He started to resume his exit when he realized that Sarah wasn't moving. She was staring down at the body of the zombie that he'd just killed.

"Let's go!" Bo snapped. Still the woman did not respond or even act as if she'd heard him. He slapped her hard across the cheek.

"I just can't," the woman whispered.

"Oh no you don't!" Bo snarled. He grabbed the woman by the arm and jerked her forward and then slung her past him in the direction of the exit.

Sarah stumbled and collided with two other members of the team. All three fell to the ground in a heap. Bo cursed and grabbed the first person he came to by the back of the neck, yanking him to his feet. He reached for the next as something clutched at his backpack, pulling him sideways, causing him to trip over one of his fallen comrades.

Landing on his stomach, Bo felt whatever had grabbed him fall on top of him, effectively pinning him to the floor.

He could feel dead hands pawing at him and trying to get at his flesh through the pack and the heavy leather jacket that he wore. Heaving back with one elbow, he felt it connect solidly to the thing on his back, but it had almost no effect as the zombie continued to maul him.

Another of the undead fell on his legs and he felt his knee twist painfully. Looking straight ahead, his eyes met Sarah's. She had her head turned as she held a zombie inches from her face as it snapped and gnashed its teeth.

A surge of strength seemed to fill all of Bo's extremities and he pushed up and made it to his hands and knees. His machete was a few feet away, but his KA-BAR was still on his belt and he whipped it out. Reaching around, he grabbed a handful of hair and jerked the zombie forward so that he could stick it with his blade. Another of the undead fell on him, knocking him sideways.

274

With a snarl, Bo rolled and ended up on his side. A zombie was just leaning down to take a bite out of his arm and he jerked away in the nick of time. A scream sounded from behind him, but he could not tell if it was Sarah. The scream was shrill and quickly reached a pitch that hurt his ears.

Another zombie lumbered towards him, this one looked like it might outweigh him by a good fifty pounds. It had a nasty rip across its taut belly and something black and jelly-like was slapping against the gray skin, covering the bellybutton. One arm had been gnawed down to the bone from just below the elbow and apparently all the way to the wrist.

There was a hiss and a thud just as the creature reached him and was staring down with its dead eyes. Bo knew that this thing landing on him would be his death sentence. But just as it looked like it was going to flop on top of him, that sound came and the tip of a crossbow bolt was jutting from its open mouth. The zombie tottered and then crumpled to the ground, landing hard just to his left; in between him and the last place he'd seen Sarah.

A hand reached out of the shadows and Bo took it. He got to his feet and found Sarah Gilstrap looking at him, tears streaming down her cheeks.

"I'm not ready to die…to give up," she whispered.

"Then move your ass and let's get out of here." Bo turned her towards the exit and gave her a nudge. He glanced down to see one of his team members on his back. His dead eyes were staring straight up and three zombies were crouched around his unmoving figure. They were still ripping out bloody handfuls of his insides and stuffing it into their mouths.

More zombies were coming from every direction. If he took even those few steps to end that scene to kill the zombies and stick that poor unfortunate to keep him from joining the ranks of the undead, he might not make it out of the lobby.

Stepping through the decimated portal, Bo walked out into the sunlight and instantly felt the warmth on his skin. It was as if his body needed to absorb as much of the sunlight as possible.

275

Looking at the rest of his team, he realized that they had lost four people. He'd been so focused on what was happening to him, he'd obviously missed other members being taken down.

"I sure hope to hell that this was worth it," Bo mumbled as he started across the parking lot towards the grassy slope and Oliver's apartment.

When they arrived and found Jamie's team already there and waiting anxiously, Bo felt himself relax just a little. After a very brief conversation, the group voted unanimously to return home right away. All of them had seen enough of the inside of the hospital to last a lifetime. Within minutes they all found vehicles to commandeer.

As they neared the town, they were stunned to discover what had taken place in their absence. Their vehicles were quickly put to use to fill the holes that had been made by the Simms brothers and their followers.

Jamie waited until the crowds dispersed and then pulled Ivan and Stephen Deese aside to discuss tomorrow's town meeting and vote on closing their borders. They had wandered up to the train car barricade and she was still discussing the possible fallout of such an idea with Ivan and Mr. Deese when the sounds of engines approaching from the north came just seconds after somebody shouted, "We got an incoming caravan!"

16

Going Tribal

The big truck rumbled to a stop as Jamie, Ivan, and Stephen made it up on top of the large green cargo car. Across the tracks and parked in a line were a dozen vehicles stretching back up South Norman Street. There was a long moment where nothing happened.

The front windows of the trucks had heavy screens, boards, and even sheets of metal covering them. There was a slit to see out, but that made it impossible to really look inside. At last, the driver's side door of the second truck opened and a very large woman emerged. She was wearing what looked like police riot gear including a helmet with a tinted face shield, and had an impressive looking rifle slung across the front of her body.

"Is there a Jamie Burns here?" the woman shouted.

Jamie glanced over at Ivan who shrugged. Stepping forward, she answered, "I'm Jamie Burns. Who are you and why are you looking for me?"

"We have something that belongs to you."

The woman leaned back inside the truck for a few seconds and then stood back up. A moment later, the passenger door opened and two more women emerged and then hauled out a limp form. They let whoever it was drop unceremoniously to the ground at their feet.

"This man was caught with a group of your people. They were trying to come in and steal what is ours. This man says that they were sent by a Jamie Burns to scavenge supplies."

"We made it very clear to any of our teams out searching that they were absolutely not to take from another settlement or engage in hostile actions against others." Jamie moved closer to the edge of the car shaking off Ivan's hand from her elbow.

The large woman turned to the other two, covering her mouth with her hand and saying something that was impossible to hear from this distance. Jamie tried to get a better look at the person on the ground but still could not make out who it was.

The large woman finally walked to the front of the truck and took a spot standing over the downed body. "I want to make things perfectly clear," the woman hollered. "If you come into Easley, you will be considered thieves and raiders."

"All of Easley?" Jamie called back. "I mean, can we drive through towards Greenville on a specific road?"

The woman paused for a moment and consulted with the two that were standing just a few feet away. As they spoke, Jamie caught a glint of something in the trees to the right of this woman.

She turned to Ivan. "We will not ambush these people. That is not who we are. As long as we are communicating, consider it a banner of truce."

"We don't send out teams of one," Ivan replied coolly. "Ask her where the rest of our people are."

Jamie turned back and was about to ask where the rest of the people who had been with the one on the ground were when the woman answered.

"You can use Highway 93 and rejoin 123 on the other side of Easley."

"I think we can agree to that," Jamie called back.

"Good, now, tell your people to back off," the woman opened her jacket and produced a metal cylinder with a wire that ran back into a vest that looked to be rigged with several blocks of some sort of explosive.

"What people?" Jamie hoped that the woman simply meant those who were gathered on top of the train cars.

"If you want to test me, just be aware that I am very confident that I am wearing enough high explosives to take you and everybody within about fifty yards with me." The woman moved the hand holding what was apparently the trigger switch for emphasis.

"Then perhaps you can tell me where the rest of that person's team might be." Jamie was not sure if the woman might be bluffing. She did not necessarily want to press the issue, but revealing an explosive and threatening to basically become a suicide bomber that would also kill all of her own people just seemed a bit desperate.

"They are all dead," the woman answered without hesitation. "We spared one—"

Several of the Liberty people who had been onlookers up until this point suddenly began drawing weapons and shouting threats. Jamie was about to yell for everybody to settle down when a single gunshot sounded.

The large woman staggered and fell to her knees. A dark bloom appeared on her chest. She looked up at Jamie a terrible grin on her face. She held up the cylinder and made a show of her thumb coming off the button.

For a heartbeat, nothing happened. Jamie was just letting out her breath when a bright flash, a concussive blast, and a ball of fire erupted, engulfing the woman, and a large area around her. The body on the ground and the two women that had been standing with the large woman also disappeared in that massive ball of fire. The blast was enough to knock Jamie back and hit her with a gigantic wave of heat, but after a quick check she saw that she wasn't smoldering.

Getting to her feet, she looked around and saw others doing the same. Ivan was nowhere to be seen and she spun when she heard his moans. She scurried to the edge of the train car and saw him on the ground. He was cradling one arm that was bent awkwardly and his right leg was bent back at a terrible angle. There were three others on the ground also moaning in pain.

The eruption of gunfire caused her to fall flat on her belly. Looking back to the convoy of cars and trucks, she saw several of them backing away. In the back of a few of the pickups, figures were crouched and spraying lead from their automatic weapons.

Gunfire was returned from the trees as the people that had been moving to flank this group took very carefully aimed shots. On two separate occasions, a body in the back of one of the trucks spun and fell out and onto the ground.

The last truck eventually vanished around the bend. Jamie climbed down to Ivan and knelt by his side. "Don't move." Looking up at the first person she saw, she yelled, "Go get Sophie. Tell her we have injured here and need her to bring all her people."

She looked Ivan over and tried to hide her worry as well as force down the nausea. The arm and leg were both bent in such a grotesque manner that it was almost impossible to look at and not feel her gorge rise. She didn't know about the leg, but the arm that was busted had bone sticking through the skin. This was very bad.

A man walked up to Jamie. It took her a moment to recognize him. It was Phillip, the guy who had managed the Domino's Pizza.

"Jonathan is dead," the man muttered and then trudged away, his gaze seeming to see nothing as he kept tripping and stumbling over every little thing his feet contacted.

A feeling of guilt tried to assert itself, but Jamie forced it away. If these people had already killed the others who had been with Jonathan Patterson, then it is unlikely they intended to ever let the man go.

At last, Sophie and half a dozen trainees arrived. Sophie went from one injured person to the next as she prioritized them according to severity of injury. When she reached Ivan, her lips pressed tight and she did not meet Jamie's eyes.

"Jamie, we will take him from here," Sophie said and then whispered something to one of her helpers.

"Don't jerk me around, Sophie," Jamie snapped. She got to her feet after easing Ivan's head from her lap.

Sophie grabbed her by the arm and pulled her away from the man as one of her students knelt and produced a syringe. Jamie watched as the man jabbed it into Ivan's upper thigh and then turned back to the woman who had her arms crossed over her body and her lips pressed so tightly that they were turning white at the edges.

"He isn't going to make it, Jamie," the woman whispered.

Jamie jerked away. "What the hell are you talking about?" She ignored the heads that all turned her direction. "It's a busted arm and a busted leg. How is that—?"

"Nobody has the ability to give him the treatment that he needs. Both of those injuries need surgery. We don't have the resources, and if we attempt it and fail, that is a lot of medication gone that we can't afford to lose."

"What are you talking about?"

"At the least, that arm need to be pinned together. I don't have any idea how to do that. It isn't just a simple break." Sophie took a breath and forced herself to speak quieter. "He is a high candidate for infection. And the pain he would endure…there is just nothing that I can do."

"But what about all the stuff we brought back from the hospital?" Jamie pressed.

"Just his injuries alone would put an incredible dent in our supplies. I'm sorry, Jamie. The best we can do is send him off peacefully."

It took a few seconds for the meaning of those last words to sink in. Sophie had just started away and so Jamie had to lunge after her, grab her arm, and spin her around.

"Don't you dare!"

"It's already done, Jamie. There was enough morphine in that syringe to send him to a peaceful and pain free death."

Jamie turned and looked down at Ivan. The man's eyes were shut, but the wince of pain that had etched his face just a few moments ago was already gone. He really looked like he was just drifting off to a sleep.

She wanted to scream. She wanted to demand that something be done, but her rational mind was already telling her to let him go. She walked back to the man and knelt beside him. Taking his hand, she decided that he at least deserved to not be alone in his final minutes.

She prayed softly as she waited. It was only a few moments later when she felt the man take one final breath, and then let go with a long, slow exhale. She reached down and checked the carotid for his pulse just to be sure and then got to her feet.

She was still trying to decide what to do when a young girl, in her early teens at the most, jogged up to her. The girl had a busted lip and one eye was swollen almost shut. It took her a few seconds to realize why the girl would be present—the junior high kids were all part of the detail that put up the barbed wire and helped roll the logs in place to seal up the trains so that zombies could not get through.

"One of them is alive," the girl reported. "Mr. Deese says you should come."

***

Stephen moved back when the massive woman revealed that she was wired with explosives. That had been something he did not understand before the zombie apocalypse. What in the world could make a person think there was any upside to blowing yourself up as a form of attack. You would never know if you had been successful or not.

He noticed both Ivan and Jamie actually move *closer*. The gunshot caused him to flinch and duck down. He looked up to see the woman drop to her knees...and then the explosion came. He was suddenly flat on his back staring up at the cloudless sky.

His ears rang for a moment and it took him a few seconds to get to his feet. When he looked around, he saw that most of the damage had actually been done to the convoy that the big woman had been a part of. Still, there were plenty of folks on his side that looked to be injured.

The gunfight erupted and he desperately wanted to use one of his own explosives, but he did not feel confident that he would not take out some of his own people in the resulting blast. Drawing his Beretta, he returned fire as the survivors of the convoy made an uncoordinated retreat.

Once the last vehicle vanished around the corner, he scanned the scene. Movement in the wreckage of one of the smoldering trucks on Norman Street got his attention. There looked to be plenty of people tending to the wounded, so he took off at a jog for this potential survivor.

He reached a small Toyota pickup and saw the passenger trying to free herself from the shoulder harness. She had to be in shock which would explain why she could not understand how the piece of metal that was pinning her to the seat was her actual problem.

Stephen moved over to her side of the truck and grabbed the door. He had to give it a few yanks to get it open, but at last it came free with a terrible groan of metal. The woman's head lolled over to him, and for just a moment he thought that she might be one of the undead. Her eyes were bloodshot, but they were red.

"That blast really fucked you up," he quipped as he pulled his knife and cut away her seat belt.

He gave the scene a close inspection. After a moment, he decided that he could not think of any way to get her out other than to yank that piece of metal free.

"This is gonna hurt," he cautioned just as he grabbed the end of the piece of metal and pulled it out as fast as he could.

The woman groaned and her eyes rolled back in her head as she slipped from consciousness. Removing his glove, he checked her pulse before continuing. *No sense in dragging a zombie out of the truck*, he reasoned.

He pulled her free and inspected her as much as he dared and then produced a piece of clothesline from a pouch on his belt. Once he had her wrists tied, he stood up and waved over one of the kids that appeared to be standing around unsure of what to do or how to help.

"Hey, kid, go tell Chief Potter and Mayor Burns that I got us a prisoner," he called.

"Where are they?" the girl asked, looking around as if she expected the pair to be hovering above her head.

"They were on the green train car over there." Stephen pointed. "Maybe start in that general area."

The girl wandered away looking confused. Not for the first time, Stephen wondered if maybe the next generation had a shot at survival. Of course he'd had those thoughts *before* the zombie apocalypse; he gave them even less chance now.

At last he spotted Jamie headed his way. She looked like somebody had just shot her puppy.

"Chief Potter didn't make it," she said in response to his questioning expression.

"Damn," he muttered. "We can't keep taking hits like that."

"He appears to be the only casualty so far."

"And what about you? You look a little beat up. You okay?"

He had given the young lady a quick up and down inspection. Her face was smudged with dirt and blood. She had a pretty nasty lump on the side of her face and a cut over one eye.

"Fine," she brushed aside the concern. "So you found one of them alive?" She walked over to the girl on the ground and stared down at her. "Jesus…were they all women?"

"I think so."

"So what do we do with her?" Jamie crossed her arms over her body and appeared to be studying the woman intently.

"She has information." Stephen looked Jamie in the eyes, hoping that he was conveying his meaning without having to say anything.

There was a very long moment of silence. Jamie walked around the body, lips pursed and hands clasped behind her back. At last she stopped.

"Do what needs to be done, Mr. Deese. But I think it best if you maybe take her to that house around the corner and outside of the safe zone. I have a feeling there might be those who would disapprove."

Stephen cocked his head. He had honestly expected her to be one of those who might not approve of coercive methods of interrogation.

"I will see what I can find out. Where will you be?"

Jamie thought it over for a moment. "I have to go see Hannah Potter. After that I will be at the high school."

Stephen watched her walk away. Reaching down, he scooped the woman up and threw her over his shoulder. As he walked, he found himself whistling the song *Little Red Riding Hood*.

He reached the house just around the corner from the train tracks and set the body down to deal with a pair of elderly zombies coming his way from across the street before opening the door to the house. He walked through the place to make sure that it was empty and then went outside and grabbed the woman.

He pulled out a chair from the kitchen table and heaved the limp figure into it. Grabbing the nearby coffee pot, he yanked the electric cord from it and tied one ankle in place. Going over to a nearby lamp, he repeated the process.

Comfortable that she would not be able to run off if she woke, he searched the closets and returned with a set of sheets. He cut them into a few strips and finished securing the woman. Walking over to the refrigerator, he held his breath and opened it. Despite his precautions, he could taste the foulness of the rotten contents in the back of his throat as he pulled out a pitcher that looked like it might have been iced tea once upon a time.

He turned just in time to see a zombie wandering past outside. An idea came to mind and he quickly ripped a few more strips off the tattered sheet.

It took much longer than when he'd secured the living woman, but eventually he had the zombie tied to a chair as well. This one looked like he had been the stereotypical college frat boy with his Emo haircut and Fallout Boy tee shirt.

Grabbing the pitcher of rancid tea from the table, he walked over to the woman and threw it in her face. The woman jerked awake, her sputters and coughs muffled by the gag. Stephen had stepped back and now stood glaring down at the woman.

"I want to lay down the rules here for you just so that there is no misunderstanding." Stephen moved over beside the zombie. It rolled its head his direction and bit down impotently on the gag in its mouth. "I am going to ask you a series of questions. Any time I don't get an answer or feel that you are being dishonest, I will undo one of the straps holding Mr. Bitey here in place. By my count, that gives you seven chances. That is counting the gag which I will now untie just to demonstrate my sincerity."

Moving behind the zombie, Stephen untied the piece of cloth and moved away. As he did so, he watched the woman's expression. The reaction was exactly what he had hoped for. He saw the fear very clearly etched on her features. She was far more afraid of that zombie than he thought she might ever be of him.

"First question is a simple one. Your leader claimed that you guys were from over towards Easley…is that true." He received a very slight nod. The woman only shot him a quick glance, but then her eyes returned to the zombie.

"Here is an odd question, and really more of a curiosity than anything important. Just remember, if I think you are lying, I undo one of the strips keeping this fella secure." Stephen walked around to the woman, making sure to keep wide of the zombie that was now making strange gurgles and low growls as it gnashed its teeth in frustration at not being able to reach him. "Does your little band consist solely of women?"

This made his captive's head pop up suddenly. Her eyes

went wide and he saw something else flash across her face.

"Easy," he said, throwing his hands up, "it's nothing so sinister, I assure you."

She made a show of glancing down at her bonds. She looked back up at him with an arched eyebrow.

"You're still dressed," he offered. "I'm just curious."

The woman said something that was garbled by the wash cloth stuffed into her mouth and kept secure by one of his linen strips. He reached over and tugged at the knot. He let her spit the rag out since he was in no mood to be bitten—zombie or not.

"Yes," the woman said and then paused as if considering what to say next. "We were all just returning from a women's retreat. Our bus arrived at the church late at night. We'd heard the warning and the announcements about the possibility of martial law being declared. Our driver would not take us home and said that he just wanted to get us off his bus and go find his family. He left us in that parking lot." Again the woman paused, but this time it was to swallow the lump in her throat.

"A bunch of them just came out of the dark. Three of us were taken down before we could break into the church. Once we got the door secured, we discovered that our phones were basically useless. We also found out that we were trapped. By morning, there were at least a hundred of those awful things outside banging on the doors and walls trying to get in."

He'd heard enough of that story for now. Raising his hand, he stopped her from saying anything else. "How many?"

The woman stared at him. She frowned and her head dropped. "I don't know."

Stephen yanked one of the strips free that held the zombie's torso secured to the chair. The zombie immediately renewed its efforts to get at him and the woman tied across from it.

"I mean it!" the woman exclaimed. "I don't know how many of us made it after Candice blew herself up like a moron."

Stephen suppressed a smile. At least he and this woman were on the same page about one thing.

"How likely is it that your friends come back for more?"

Stephen locked eyes with the woman. This was one of the important questions.

"You haven't been out there much, have you?" the woman replied. "We get hit almost daily. You are just the latest. The thing is, y'all seemed like a much more organized threat than the usual groups of raiders. We needed to know what we were up against."

"Why would you need to be up against us? Jesus, you say that you ladies were coming back from a retreat! I have to suppose that you are all regular church-goin' ladies...unless your story was just a cover." Stephen glanced over at the zombie that was still biting at the air in a futile attempt to latch onto him. The woman must've seen his look and began to almost babble.

"No cover story. We just had no choice but to get tough in a hurry. After what that one man did to Penelope..." the woman gushed, but her voice cracked and faded at the end. "It's like we landed in the middle of Sodom and Gomorrah. The worst sorts seem to be much more abundant than...well...than regular types."

"So you strap bombs to yourselves and kill on sight?" Stephen shot back.

"We just got invaded earlier that morning. We honestly thought that it was more of those folks come back for more."

Stephen considered the woman for a moment. Looking into her eyes, he came to the conclusion that she was either being honest, or she was pathological. Either way, he was losing steam when it came to doing anything to this woman in retaliation for what had happened by the train tracks.

"If I let you go, what happens next?" Stephen knelt in front of the woman and put his hands on the arms of her chair. "Do we need to be watching for a bunch of your friends to show up with bombs strapped to your bodies? Is there going to be a war? If there is, I want to warn you...we aren't just some ladies auxiliary group holed up in a church or whatever. We are a town of people determined to survive this zombie apocalypse by any

288

means necessary." He paused for a moment and considered his words. "Jamie was not kidding when she said that we have given our scavenging teams very strict and direct orders not to cross into territory if somebody is there laying claim to it. I think I can even follow up and make sure that our people hold to that boundary your leader—"

"Candice wasn't our leader. She was just the biggest one of us and so we had her doing all the talking," the woman cut Stephen off.

"Whatever." Stephen gave a dismissive wave of his hand. "What I am saying is that we would have no trouble staying out of your area. There are plenty of places for us to search for supplies."

The woman regarded him silently for several seconds. "You really got your entire town secure against this?" She made a nod towards the zombie across from her in the chair.

"The town? No. The people...pretty much. We pulled back into an area that we felt we could hold easier. At least for now. Once we get this first area fully secure and feel confident that we are through the worst of it, we will push back out and probably annex more and more of the town."

A voice in his head told him to ease up on giving away secrets. Whether this woman was being totally truthful or not did not mean that information did not have a way of being leaked or spread.

"We don't want any trouble," the woman said.

"You coulda fooled me with that business back by the tracks," Stephen replied sardonically. "You show up, throw the only survivor of our scavenge team on the ground and then go all jihadist."

"To be fair," the woman's head snapped up and her expression changed to one of anger, "your people took a shot first. You had snipers in the damn trees or some such crap. So don't stand here and act like you and your people are the victims in this."

Stephen shrugged. "Okay, but we can go back and forth over who is the most wrong all day. What it comes down to is that I want to know why I should let you go. You haven't really revealed anything. Every word out of your mouth could be a cover story."

"We are holed up at New Image Church by the elementary school," the woman blurted. "Before this disaster, there were thirty-seven of us. We range in age from nineteen to sixty-five. Anything else?"

Stephen pulled his knife from his belt. As soon as he did, the woman began to scream. Out of reflex, he lashed out, his fist smashing into her jaw. Her head dropped and she went limp.

"I was just going to cut you loose," he hissed to the unconscious figure. A low moan from outside was his answer. He rushed to the front room window and looked outside. "Double dammit!" he swore.

He glanced at the zombie tied to the chair and decided not to take any chances. He jammed his knife into its temple and then headed out to the front yard to greet the five more zombies that had arrived.

The first one would remove the last doubt from anybody who might still be on the fence about the whole zombie thing. It had no left arm. There was a nasty stump where the arm had been ripped away at the shoulder socket. The throat was so badly ripped that the head sat on its side, almost resting on that mangled shoulder. The chest had been torn apart and there were rib bones jutting out like an inverse pin cushion.

Once he put the last zombie down, he returned to the house. The woman was still out cold. Looking around, his eyes spotted a hatch in the ceiling down the hall that led to the bedrooms and bathroom. He went to it and was thankful when a ladder folded down after he opened it.

It took some work and he felt something tighten in his back as he hoisted her up and into the attic, but he felt better about it that just leaving the woman untied on the ground floor where something could stumble in and get her.

As he walked back towards the train tracks, he seriously

hoped that he had not made a terrible mistake.

Dead: Snapshot—Liberty, South Carolina

17

The Vote and a Slice of Normal

Jamie stood at the podium. She hated the fact that she needed to speak into a bullhorn, but this was something that the entire
community needed to hear first hand. There was no way she
would trust this to people spreading it like a post-apocalyptic
version of the grade school game, Postman.

"Ladies and gentlemen of Liberty, I come before you today
with a matter of a very serious nature." She looked out at the
faces and tried to judge the response she was about to receive.
Beside her, Stephen Deese and Bo Summers stood at parade rest
like a military honor guard. Taking a deep breath, she resumed
her speech. "As many of you are now aware, we have come under attack by an outside group. They executed one of our teams
of scavengers and then came here and detonated an explosive
that took the life of Chief Ivan Potter."

Once again, Jamie paused. She wanted that to sink in. She
had always enjoyed watching those trial shows and imagined
what it must be like to stand in front of a jury and tell them the
story that gets them to pass the desired verdict.

Her concern rested in the people who still seemed to refuse
to accept the reality of what was happening around them. She
noticed that anytime teams were called to leave the safe zone, it
usually consisted of the same people over and over. There was a

large percentage of the population that had yet to really see what was out there. There were even those who had yet to see an actual zombie.

"Recently, we even came under attack by some of our own people. This group believed that killing all of us would get them to Heaven. Jonah Simms sacrificed his own daughter as an offering before leading an attack on his fellow citizens of Liberty. Many of you were present for the carrying out of the execution of four men who not only murdered several of our people, but also attempted to steal our main source of food as well as much of our guns and ammo."

Again she paused. Scanning the faces, she was surprised to still see so much passive indifference. These people, her people, they truly seemed to be unaware of how dire the world situation had become in such a short time. Looking over at Stephen Deese and Bo Summers, she gave a slight nod.

The two men went down the back steps that lead up to the combination platform and gallows. A moment later, they came back up the stairs. Each of them had a long pole like the sort that animal control officers used when wrangling a dangerous dog or cat.

The zombie that was led up onto the stage had been a man in his middle age. His brown hair was matted and filthy; his face was smeared and crusted with dried blood. His right arm had been savaged and was missing below the elbow. His nose was also missing with only a dark and terrifying crater remaining.

"This is what is out there. This is not just some flu or virus. This is a horror story come to life." Jamie drew the knife at her hip and looked over to Bo who gave a slight nod.

She moved in close and plunged the blade into the middle of the zombie's chest. It lunged, the one good arm swiping at her and the stump acting as if it still had its hand attached as it waved impotently. Jamie left the knife in its chest and then walked back to the front of the stage.

Again she scanned the crowd. The faces that she could see

were a mixture of reactions. She saw knowing nods from those who had accepted this new world. She was surprised at how many people seemed to be absolutely stunned; many looked overwhelmed and could not look on the zombie for more than a few seconds without looking away.

"This is not a game, people. This is really happening and we may be one of the last holdouts of humanity. Teams that have ventured as far east as Greenville report that the city is in flames. To the west, Clemson is a wasteland. I am sure that the situation is the same no matter where you go. We are not the norm...we are an exception."

She hated this next part, but with all the activity of the past few days, this one incident would not add that many more zombies to the numbers starting to gather along their borders. Pulling out a small .22 caliber pistol she returned to the zombie and took a spot just a few feet away.

"These are not people," she held the bullhorn to her mouth and called. Then, taking careful aim and again making certain that Bo and Mr. Deese were ready, she fired a bullet into its chest. "See? Nothing."

She fired five more rounds into the thing. The zombie barely twitched, and it made no indication that it was even aware it had been shot. Again Jamie walked to the front of the stage and raised the bullhorn. "Call them zombies if it makes you feel better. I don't care. But the reality is that these things are driven to attack the living. If you are bitten, you become one...just like the stories."

She chose not to add the part about there being a possibility that some people might be immune. Holstering the pistol, she walked over to Bo and put out her hand. The man checked with Stephen to ensure he had his pole gripped tightly as the zombie thrashed and struggled to get at the nearby living beings that remained just out of reach. Stephen nodded and Bo set his pole down. As fast as possible, he unslung the shotgun he had over his shoulder. He handed the shotgun to Jamie and then picked up his pole once more.

"Now, some of you might still refuse to believe what you are seeing. You may believe that this person is simply sick and too delirious to register what has been done." Jamie brought up the shotgun and again checked with both men. They nodded and leaned back just slightly as if those extra few inches might help.

After moving to just a foot or so away, Jamie pumped the action of the shotgun and then aimed at the midsection. She briefly noted that either Stephen or Bo had removed her knife and then she pulled the trigger. The blast was massive and the butt of the weapon kicked hard into her shoulder. When the blue gray smoke cleared, there was an enormous, ugly fist-sized hole blown through the undead man.

Jamie again moved to the front of the stage, set down the shotgun and retrieved the bullhorn. "As I said, this is not a joke, a hoax, or even something that I believe the world will be able to recover from. Some of you have resisted taking an active part in helping to ensure our safety and chance for survival. To that end, I am going to institute a complete census. After that is finished, I will enlist some of you to help me create teams. Every team will rotate through the various duties that we need to have performed. They include scavenging, patrols of our perimeter, and disposing of the zombies that gather at our barricade."

She saw some of the people looking hesitant and others downright terrified. She had laid down the fear. Now it was time to offer comfort and pitch her final edict.

"You need to know that all of us are afraid. Look around. You are not alone, but we will come together and we will secure this safe zone. We will create a defense force that every man and woman will serve in some capacity. You have to be aware by now that the zombies are only a small part of the problem. The living have actually inflicted more harm on our community than the zombies. I realize that what I am about to propose will seem cold and heartless, but after speaking with many of you, I believe it is the right choice. It will give us the best chance at not just survival, but at having a life. I need you all to understand that there will be hardships ahead that will be unlike anything we could have ever imagined just a few short weeks ago." She took a deep breath and glanced back at Bo and Stephen who both gave her a nod. "That is why I am officially calling for a vote to seal off our community. We need to be able to take care of ourselves before we can offer aid to others. Also, it is clear that there are people out there who will take advantage of us if we are not extremely vigilant. I do not believe we have the energy to spare to keep one eye on strangers who may or may not wish us harm. This should not be permanent, but I do believe that it offers us the best chance at survival in the long run."

Jamie stopped talking and once more scanned the crowd. She did see a few heads shaking, but most people still appeared to be a bit overwhelmed. She would have to thank Bo later for the advice about showing them the zombie and demonstrating their inhumanity.

"I want to put it to you all. After all, we are still citizens of Liberty, South Carolina. I believe that we can maintain a democracy where all of you are part of the process. So, let's see if we can do this with a show of hands. If you agree to seal our town from outsiders, please raise your hands."

It was a slow process, and the people were not nearly as unified about this as they had been during the vote for a verdict of the four bikers. When she asked for a vote of those opposed, she felt her heart sink. It was simply too close to call. She could not make this decision without having the majority of support from the people.

"Okay. I can see that we will need to have a more formal vote."

Now it was her turn to be thankful to Stephen. He had warned her that the people still might not be able to let go of the old ways. It was simply not a normal thing to be okay with excluding people who may be in need of help.

"We have tables set up in front of the high school. When you sign your name to the census, please take one of the cards on the table and cast your vote for or against. There will be large boxes by the entrance to the school for you to drop your ballot. We will ask for people from both sides to help with the counting. I hope to announce the results in the next few days." She scanned the crowd and pointed to a group of three that she recalled having voted against the proposal. "I would like for you three...and..." she scanned the crowd and pointed out three who she remembered voting in favor, "...the three of you to please come up here."

Once the six were on the stage, she continued after nodding for Stephen and Bo to remove and dispose of the zombie. "These people will be counting the ballots. I will be pairing them up according to how they voted so that a person for and one against will count together and verify the vote. As I said, I want this to be as transparent as possible. We need to be a community that stands together, and the only way that will happen is if we work hand-in-hand and side-by-side for the same common goal. Survival."

The town meeting was ended and people began to file out and head to the tables where they would fill out the town's roster and cast their vote. There was a subdued sobriety that she could almost feel as a physical presence. This was the last step away from the world they all knew just a short while ago. She was still struggling with this new reality after days of being up to her neck in it. She did not envy those last holdouts who had tried to ignore and wish away the situation.

As the last few people trickled out, Jamie turned to Bo. "Well, do you think the vote will go our way?"

The man considered her for a moment and then stepped close after looking around to see if anybody might be listening. "We have a few people in the crowd preaching the word for your side."

Jamie opened her mouth to protest. She had just said that she would make sure that there was transparency. She was of the mind that people in the upper levels of government had sat on something very important and allowed the zombie apocalypse to come on in full swing. Still, she was only trying to give the people the best chance at survival. She could not undo what had been done, but she was responsible for seeing that the people of Liberty had a shot at making a life for themselves in this post-apocalyptic world. If that meant swaying people's opinions, well, that wasn't actually dishonest. It wasn't like she was manipulating the vote.

"Keep me posted on how things appear to be going," Jamie said.

She headed down and took her place in line to sign the census and cast her vote. She wanted to make sure that she was seen as being on the same level as everybody else. No special treatment…no head of the line privileges.

***

It had been close. Bo moved down along the wall of cars and trucks inspecting for any areas that might allow the undead to slip through as he considered the past few weeks.

The vote had passed by a very narrow margin. Less than forty votes separated the two sides. Since then, they had turned away five groups and a few dozen singles and couples that had arrived. It was funny, but now that there had been a vote and this was an issue, they were suddenly seeing an influx of survivors.

There had been more in the past two days than in all the days combined. They were coming from every direction. The last group that arrived had come all the way from Columbia. They said that the capital was demolished and that fighting had broken out in the streets between rival gangs, police, and people just taking advantage of the chaos. Over half the city was nothing but smoldering ruins and zombies were seen in at least two herds numbering in the tens of thousands just south of the city.

Jamie had been hospitable and polite. She had even allowed them to trade some goods with some of the citizens of Liberty, but when they were told that they could not stay, things got a bit heated. In the end, the sixty or so people walked away when they found themselves facing over a hundred armed members of the Liberty militia.

The Liberty militia, Bo mused.

The day after the vote was finalized Jamie had made him the commander of the newly formed armed forces of Liberty, South Carolina, dubbed the 'Fighting Tigers' and currently numbering over three hundred men and women between the ages of fifteen and fifty. It had been a pleasant surprise when the call was put out for volunteers and so many people had stepped forward.

Stephen had been named the new chief of police at the suggestion of Sarah Gilstrap. He had joked privately that he wasn't very excited about the post considering that it appeared to be cursed. Bo had toasted him and handed him the bottle of Jack that the two men had shared the day they were both sworn into their respective offices.

That was another thing that he had to give Jamie credit for. She was trying to give people ceremonies and things that felt formal and familiar. Maybe it was working because the two teams that had left this morning consisted of over half of their numbers that would be making their first trip outside of the safe zone.

"Commander!" a voice called.

Bo turned to discover a young man shifting from one foot to the other in obvious discomfort. "What is it?"

"I gotta pee really bad, and I still got two hours on watch." The boy was speaking with his mouth covered by his hands in an effort not to broadcast his predicament to everybody within a hundred yards.

"So go," Bo replied.

"Where?"

"Son, please tell me that you haven't lived your whole life without taking a whizz in the outdoors."

"Well...no...but..." He tilted his head to the left.

Bo turned to see the reason for the young man's distress. A short distance away, sitting cross-legged on the roof of an old

Greyhound bus was a girl with long blond hair. Currently she was scanning the distant trees with her binoculars.

Bo pinched the bridge of his nose with his fingers in an attempt to stave off the headache that wanted to bloom behind his eyes. Considering the living quarters and what they faced ahead in the next few months, modesty was going to have to be a thing of the past like so many other hang-ups that people refused to let go of.

"Just find a bush, son," he snarled as he walked away.

The next several days were more of the same as he turned his group of everyday people into at least moderately competent guards. Twice they were forced to increase their watch personnel after being attacked by raiders. Because of those incidents, the people of Liberty began to take the security posts much more seriously. Even those who were initially against closing the borders to outsiders changed their tune for the most part after one expedition outside the confines of their secured perimeter. They returned with tales of another settlement that had apparently been infiltrated and then attacked from within.

Another pleasant surprise for Bo was that there did not seem to be a lot of talk at all about his personal life. Those who knew either hadn't said anything, or people simply decided that they didn't care. He only wished that Oliver had been alive to see this day. He also regretted the fact that, in all the hustle and hurry to get away from the hospital, he had come away without anything from Oliver's house.

Now that he was the so-called commander of the Liberty militia, he was allowed to patrol the zone or stand watch. What he wasn't allowed to do—at least for the time being—was venture outside on the supply or scouting expeditions. Of course, he didn't really have too much time to be upset. So far, they had located nine settlements or areas that other survivors had secured and declared as their own. Also, they had even opened limited interactions with the women in Easley who now made occasional trips to Liberty to trade goods.

As Bo settled into his routine, he occasionally found himself amused at how the books and movies had portrayed the zombie apocalypse. He could not recall many instances where almost an entire town managed to survive.

As the seasons began to shift from spring to summer, the gardens were showing promise. Several of the supply runs had yielded all sorts of farming equipment. Most of what they found was converted into manual operation as fuel was starting to reach the point where it was no longer useable.

There had been a meeting about getting a solar grid set up, but that was probably going to have to wait until next year as the people who had volunteered to take charge of that operation now had to read up on the process. Stockpiles of wood were already being laid aside for the coming winter as that would likely be the main source of heat for everybody. He had a brief thought about the people in the colder climates. Did zombies freeze?

All in all, Bo felt that just maybe things were going to be okay. The only thing he could not do anything about were those terrible nightmares.

***

Stephen nodded to Bo and the man pulled the lever. There was a loud clap and then the sound of a rope going taut as the body dropped through the trap door. This was the fifth hanging in as many weeks. It was a bad sign that folks were becoming desperate.

This last couple had been turned away just two days earlier. Obviously they had chosen to risk their lives and sneak inside the perimeter in an attempt to steal some supplies.

Also, there was talk of another large band of raiders in the area. If what they had heard was true, this group had wiped out a dozen small groups of survivors. Worse still, they were supposedly packing military hardware and numbered over a hundred.

While they were likely no match for the people of Liberty, they could inflict some serious damage. Bo had already called off any further excursions outside the safe zone by any teams until this potential threat could be either dismissed or eliminated.

The latter option had been the focus of last night's meeting. He, Sophie, Sarah, Bo, Jamie, and Pastor Johnson now made up the town's council and had met for almost four hours. They had a map of the area with every known outpost, settlement or camp marked. They also had flagged pins that noted reports of raiders.

"We need to start keeping tabs on a few of those larger zombie herds," the pastor had insisted.

It had been agreed. The last thing they discussed had been the hanging of the two thieves. That was when the pastor excused himself. He had made it clear that he would not sit in on those discussions. The vote had been unanimous.

"I am not sure that having the bodies taken outside the safe zone and put on display with their crime on a placard around their necks is doing any good," Sarah spoke up after the vote.

"We keep doing it…at least for now," Jamie insisted. "Who knows how many folks we would be dealing with otherwise? We are only seeing those that are very desperate. I say we keep it up."

The meeting had been adjourned, and the next day, the couple had been led to the gallows. The crowds were becoming noticeably smaller now. The spectacle of the public hangings had lost their newness. Stephen wondered if that was a good thing or a bad thing. Were the people simply accepting things as they were? What did this say about their community?

"Sparse crowd," Bo muttered as he stepped up beside Stephen.

"Yeah, I was noticing that myself."

"You have your team assembled to get these bodies out to the highway?"

"Yep."

Stephen gave a wave and motioned Lawrence over. The young man was the captain of an eight person detail that would transport the bodies out to Highway 123. The bodies would be hung from the overpass at the 178 junction with signs declaring them as thieves.

Before long, the bodies had been loaded into a horse-drawn cart. Stephen watched the team leave through the gate and then headed over to the old door and window factory. His wife Terri should just about be done teaching her classes for the day.

As he walked up to the building, he spotted Sophie coming out. Little Megan was holding her hand and talking at a million miles an hour. It made him feel good to see the little girl recovering nicely. She still had moments where she would shut down, and it was a process to learn the things that would trigger her. Already, Sophie had learned never to say that she would be right back. Those words acted like a switch for little Megan. The guess was that those were probably the last words the girl's mother said before she went to her death at the hands and teeth of the zombies.

"Lawrence is probably going to be a little late for dinner," Stephen said to Sophie by way of greeting. "We had some difficulties. One of our...umm..." He glanced down at Megan who stared up at him with her big, brown eyes. "Well, let's just say that there was a lack of cooperation. So Lawrence got a late start with the transport team."

"That's okay," Sophie said with a shrug. "I think this one deserves a trip to the playground. She got a perfect score on all her knots today."

"I tied the square knot five times and Jack kept making a granny knot," Megan twittered, her smile showing where she had lost a tooth recently.

"Wow, looks like you will be joining one of my teams before long," Stephen joked.

"I don't get to go to archery class for two years," the girl giggled.

"Well you just keep doing well. Time will pass before you know it and I think you would make a great member of the militia...maybe even the commander someday."

"Oooo, Mama Sophie, can I be a commander?" the little girl

squealed, hands clasped under her chin.

"Maybe, but you have to keep doing your homework…and your chores."

She had added that last bit sort of hastily, and Stephen had to hide a grin when Megan deflated just a bit. It became even more difficult when the youngster turned to him with a quizzical look. He pasted on his most stern expression and gave a single nod. He looked up and saw Sophie mouth the words "thank you" as she took the girl's hand again and started off in the direction of the playground.

"How goes the day, Commander?" Terri Deese joked as she walked up to her husband and joined him.

"Hopefully not as lousy as yours," he sighed.

Together, the couple walked hand in hand back towards the high school. The slight bulge in Terri's middle was just starting to show. Part of him was excited by the possibility; however, a bigger part of him was scared to death. He shoved those fears aside for the moment and told himself that he would take it one day at a time and enjoy every moment with his wife. It was a luxury that many could not partake.

***

Sophie handed Jamie the small piece of plastic. The woman looked at it and then tossed it in the garbage.

"Maybe we should do another?" Jamie almost sobbed as she plopped down in the chair and hid her face in her hands.

"Hon, we could do another dozen. You're pregnant."

"Son of a…" She let the sentiment die on her lips as the door opened and Megan walked in with a cup in her hands.

"I brought you some water." The girl set the cup down and then looked back and forth between the two women. "Did Jamie get a shot?" the girl whispered loudly.

That made both women laugh. "No, I didn't get a shot, sweetie." Jamie scooped up Megan in her arms and gave the girl a kiss on the cheek before setting her back down.

Together, all three exited the little exam room and walked out into the hallway. The high school was its usual bustle of activity as people went about their daily routine.

"You need to head over to school," Sophie said to Megan as a group of children walked past in the direction of the factory.

The little girl gave Sophie a hug and took about five steps before spinning around and running up to Jamie and giving her a hug as well before skipping away to join the other children.

Once the girl was gone and Jamie looked around to ensure that there would not be any ears within hearing distance of her whisper, she said, "Let's keep this quiet for now."

Sophie understood her friend's reasons. Granted, it wasn't her fault that she'd gotten pregnant. She was willing to bet that only a fraction of the people would even put it together that the child had to belong to that biker, Kevin Staley. Sadly, the apocalypse had not put an end to wild rumors and gossip. It would be out there soon enough.

"Doctor-patient confidentiality," Sophie said, locking her lips with her fingers and tossing away the imaginary key.

The two headed around the school towards what had once been the baseball field. In its place, long rows stretched out, each with signs labeling them: corn, squash, beans, tomatoes. They had about thirty different varieties of fruits and vegetables growing here. Just through some trees were the beginnings of an orchard. Beyond that was the livestock area. Things were starting to shape up nicely. If all went as planned and they had the solar grid in place next year, they might become the zombie apocalypse version of a superpower. There were already plans on the table to set up the next settlement centering on the elementary school and the nearby neighborhoods.

Things were actually moving faster than any of them had imagined. The loss of her husband was still something Sophie hadn't dealt with, and she was actually worried that the normality that was settling in would force her to do so very soon.

"One thing at a time," Sophie whispered.

306

The Vote and a Slice of Normal

18

Tough Choices and Dark Clouds

"We have a situation," Bo said.

Jamie looked up from her desk where she had been studying the latest inventory reports. She sighed and ran her fingers through her hair. It was her last day before her turn for a shower. She could feel the oiliness of her hair leave a residue on her fingers and scowled in disgust.

"Please, because what I need now is *another* situation." She closed the ledger and rubbed her tired eyes.

"Actually, this one is at our gates."

"Another survivor or group that wants in?" Jamie stood up and strapped her weapons onto her hips. "And let me guess, they demanded to talk to whoever is in charge because their situation is special."

"Not exactly," Bo replied cryptically.

"I really don't have time for this."

"I get that, but I think you need to see to this one personally. The sentry on watch said she can't make the call."

"There is no call to make!" Jamie exploded, her tensions coming to a boil. Even by her best estimations, this was going to be a very lean winter. They were going to be lucky to feed their own people, much less outsiders.

"Okay, then," Bo replied, his voice continuing to hold almost no emotion.

Together they walked out of the school. Under Sophie's orders, Jamie could not ride one of the horses and so they had to trudge through the mud and soggy ground from the past few days of late afternoon thunder storms that had jacked the humidity up to nearly unbearable levels.

By the time they reached the section of the barricade, both Jamie and Bo were drenched with perspiration. Jamie felt like she could scrape her body off with a squeegee and come away with a Dixie cup full of moisture from her skin.

She climbed the ladder after Bo and heaved herself up onto the platform where a very nervous young lady was waiting. She stepped aside so that Jamie could look down at whoever had shown up at their walls.

In an instant, she knew why the girl on watch had struggled with enforcing the edict. The woman below looked like she might fall over if so much as a slight breeze came along. Her eyes were sunken and the tattered rags she wore did not conceal how gaunt her frame was from lack of food. Her dark hair was clumped and plastered to her head, making Jamie instantly feel guilty about her own hygienic musings of just a few moments ago.

Worse than the visage of this horribly malnourished woman were the two children who clutched at each of her hands. While not nearly as emaciated as the young woman, it was obvious that they were on the verge of collapse due to starvation.

Her heart felt like it would break and she suddenly had no saliva in her mouth. This was going to give her nightmares later.

Her mind quickly reminded her of what she knew to be the facts of the town's food inventory as well as the best case projections from the garden. The people currently living inside the safe zone of her town were most likely going to suffer some casualties when fall and winter came.

The increased activity of the lawless gangs that roamed the countryside made it difficult to send out teams smaller than fifty. The problem with that was that they had also been forced to send those teams out with the most minimal of supplies. The logic was simple: the teams would forage to supply themselves as they went, and if they found a sizable cache of goods to take, then they could bring back what they did not consume. It was not a perfect system. But the reality was that, after one team of twenty left with a full week's worth of rations and then never returned, the decision was made that they could no longer justify sending out food since there was no guarantee that any would be brought back for the community.

"Please," the woman croaked after a long silence, "if you won't let me in, then take my babies."

Jamie wanted to be sick. The reality was that the woman would be more welcome than her two children. One looked to be three or four. The other perhaps six. In both cases, they were truthfully little more than a drain on supplies with no return. Besides what it would take to nurse them back to anything close to healthy, they would use resources and provide nothing for the community.

"I'm sorry," Jamie forced herself to speak. "We just can't allow anybody to come inside."

"Can you spare a little food at least?" the woman pleaded. "It's been so long…" Almost on cue, the children began to wail at the mention of the word food.

"I'm sorry," was all that Jamie could say in response. She turned to walk away.

"You can't leave us out here…the zombies…and they aren't even the worst thing," the woman croaked. "You don't know what I've seen."

"You would be surprised." Jamie whispered.

"We're not leaving!" the woman wailed. "I will stand here and scream until every zombie for a hundred miles is pawing at your walls."

"If she doesn't leave, shoot her," Jamie said, turning to go.

"No." Jamie was just stepping down the ladder when a very soft voice spoke.

"Excuse me?" she asked, climbing back up.

"I won't do it." The sentry grew bolder with each word and her voice grew louder as she gained confidence.

"It wasn't a request," Jamie snapped." Maybe you forgot about the standing orders. We will not be allowing anybody inside."

"Then you kill her." The sentry shoved her crossbow at Jamie.

"Perhaps you would like to join her," Jamie said between clenched teeth. "I just finished the inventory, and we are going to be very tight on supplies. Tossing you out reduces the consumption by one more mouth."

"Jamie," Bo cautioned.

"No, we are not in any shape to take in others, and I don't think some of the people truly understand that. It isn't that I would not love to help. You don't think my heart is breaking for this woman and her children? But we are facing our first winter in a few months and risk losing some of us due to hunger." Jamie paused and then turned to the sentry. "It is to the point where I don't believe that I will make it to term with the baby I am carrying. I don't like it, but I have come to accept that reality."

The sentry stared back at Jamie. The woman didn't speak, but her eyes flitted between her belly which still showed no indication of the life growing inside her and then down to the children standing at their barricade.

"I can't do it," she said plainly.

Jamie felt her anger fade. She mentally stepped back and looked at the situation and what she was asking. At last, she reached out her hand. There was no need for an explanation. The sentry unslung her crossbow and handed it to Jamie.

"Now, I am going to ask you to go." Jamie turned her focus back to the woman below who had grown silent while she observed the situation unfold over her head. "I am sorry about your problem, and I truly wish that there was something I could do to help. The reality is that there is not. You have three people to feed. I have almost three thousand. I imagine we will be starving and the day will come when I look back and envy you."

"Envy me?" the woman barked. "I am out here in this hell with two babies, no food, and you dare to say that you envy me!"

Once more, the children began to wail. The noise was loud and grating. In the bushes across the clearing that they were still actually in the process of knocking back to increase visibility, a rustling came. A moment later, three zombies emerged. The woman saw Jamie's gaze shift and she turned around to see the horrible creatures stagger out and orient on her and the children.

"I can take them out, but you and the children need to run," Jamie called down.

The woman spun back to face her, her expression one of absolute bitter fury and hate. "If you can so easily sentence us to death, then maybe you should be forced to watch. I'm not leaving. Either give us something or I will stand here and scream until I bring every zombie down on you and your people."

"I can't," Jamie said with a sigh.

The zombies were drawing closer and now there was more movement from the left and the right of their position. Bo brought his crossbow up and took down the closest zombie as it drew to within about twenty yards of the woman and her children.

"We can't run anymore!" the woman cried. "Don't you understand, you heartless bitch?"

"I understand that I have a responsibility to the people here. I am sorry. You have no idea—"

"NO!" the woman shrieked. "You don't get to apologize and try to make yourself feel better."

The zombies continued to draw even closer, and Bo was lining up another shot. Jamie turned to him and put her hand on his arm. When he looked at her, she saw the tears starting to brim and she cursed herself for not crying as well. She knew that they could probably kill zombies for the next several minutes, but it was not going to do anything more than delay the inevitable. Maybe if the woman saw that there really was no other choice, perhaps she would run.

Liar, the voice in her head spat. She knew that voice was being honest. This woman was not capable of running anymore. It was visibly apparent that she had reached the end.

Jamie forced herself to consider their suffering and how it was now her responsibility to end it. She was the one who had called for this edict. She was also the one who was very aware of their own grim situation when it came to their supplies.

Currently there were eleven women pregnant that she was aware of, and it was Sophie's opinion that they would be lucky if half of them carried to term based on Jamie's food assessment. That meant the child inside her currently had about a fifty percent chance of being born.

"You need to run," Jamie pleaded again.

The woman looked up at her with eyes that had gone almost as flat and empty as those of the zombie. She opened her mouth and screamed. This caused the children beside her to wail even louder as they looked with horror from their mother to the approaching and growing horde of walking dead. There were now over twenty that had emerged from the brush and oriented on the trio.

"Jamie," Bo whispered, trying to pull his arm free and raise his crossbow as the nearest walking dead was now only a few stumbling steps away from being able to reach out and grab one of the three.

"No," Jamie insisted and forced his arm down.

"You're insane," the sentry breathed and retreated to the ladder that would take her down and allow her to run back to the school.

"I am trying to keep us alive," Jamie insisted. She spun on the woman and glared down at her. "If you are so outraged, then perhaps you would like to trade places with her."

The sentry pushed away from the ladder and turned, running back towards the school. The sound of Bo's crossbow being fired caused her to spin back to the situation at hand.

"I told you no," she snapped as another zombie fell to the ground. "How many more can you take down? Ten? Twelve? Then what?"

"Can you really do this?" Bo shot back, stepping close to her and glaring down with a face that was growing purple with bottled anger.

"I don't have a choice."

"Yes you do. We can find a way."

"And where do we draw the line? Do we let people in based on cute? Is it just women with children, or any woman? What about a group of teenagers? Where do we cut it off?"

Bo stared at her; his mouth opened twice and then snapped shut. Jamie reached out and placed her hand on his arm but he jerked away. Just then, the woman shrieked; but this was not a scream just for screaming's sake. This was the scream that anybody who had heard before knew it for what it was.

Jamie turned as the woman struggled feebly while a zombie latched on to her shoulder and ripped away a chunk of meat. The children both just continued to stand as if frozen to the spot. One had its mouth open in a scream that was being drowned out by that of the woman. The other looked to have simply shut down and was standing there with an open mouth that emitted no sound.

Jamie brought the crossbow to her shoulder and sighted in on the back of the woman's head. She took a deep breath, held it, and then fired. The bolt went into the top of the woman's skull and silenced her scream.

She reloaded as fast as she could, but did not have it done fast enough as another zombie fell in the screaming child, dragging it to the ground. The zombie covered the child and made it impossible for her to get a shot off in order to end the suffering. She swung to the child that still stood in shocked silence. Tears finally filled her eyes and blurred her vision as she tightened her finger on the trigger.

"I'm sorry," she whispered, and then squeezed.

The child toppled, dying in silence. Bo stepped up beside her and fired down into the back of the head of the zombie that was crouched over the mewling child. It collapsed, effectively pinning the little one underneath. Jamie had her crossbow reloaded and looked down to see the child's arm struggling to get free from under the body. At last, a head poked out. She fired and a relative silence fell. The only sounds now were those of the moans and groans of the approaching undead.

She had no idea how long they stood there as the zombies continued to come, attracted by the sounds and now simply moving in the last direction they'd been drawn.

She was still staring down at the dead body of the silent child when there was a distant rumble from the west. It continued to grow, and then she felt the ground shift from a tremor.

"Earthquake?" she asked, turning to Bo in confusion.

The man was staring towards the direction of the setting sun. His eyes were wide and a look of amazement was warring with one of fear. She moved a bit and saw a large cloud rising into the sky.

"What..." her voice trailed off as the direction caused a bell to ring in her head.

"Oconee Nuclear Power Station," Bo said softly.

Together they watched the cloud grow larger and start to flatten out at the top. It was positively massive and just the sight of it sent a feeling of dread into Jamie's gut. Could it be that all they'd done, all they'd fought to secure was for naught? This was no simple fire, and there was little use in denying where this had to be coming from. Jamie spun around and threw up as her body simply refused to find any way to process what she was seeing.

"Do we run?" she finally asked after wiping her mouth.

"Where?" Bo continued to stare west at the dark and still growing harbinger of doom.

Looking around, Jamie saw that many of the zombies had turned around and were now plodding off in the direction of the distant blast. She had a fleeting moment of hope until she re-membered that Greenville sat to their east. That probably meant that all those zombies were now trudging right for them. She stared down at the corpse of the woman with the crossbow bolt jutting from the back of her head.

"You got off easy," she whispered.

Dip your toes into a world that is perhaps more frightening than any zombie apocalypse…

Enjoy a sneak peek at—

UnCivil War: A Modern Day Race War in the United States
(Available now!)

Prologue

"We, the jury, find the defendant, Samuel James Anderson...not guilty of Manslaughter in the first degree," the young foreman read from the index card in his slightly trembling left hand.

A moment of silence hung in the courtroom; then, like an avalanche on a snowy mountainside, the sound built to a tremendous roar. On one side, officers of the Seattle Police Department cheered and slapped each other on the backs. There were smiles all around. On the other, members of the African-American community glared, scowled, and cried out their protests at the injustice. Another one of their own had been shot and killed by a police officer...who would apparently get away scot-free.

"Murderer!" an elderly woman screamed as she fell into the aisle on her knees. "You killed my baby boy!"

Jerry Burns scanned the crowd, his eyes taking in as much detail as possible. As he exited the courtroom and headed down the mostly empty hall of the courthouse's second floor, a buzz was already building in the hundreds who had not been able to secure a seat inside for the announcement of the verdict. He could actually feel the anger mounting around him. This was not going to be a pretty scene.

Seven months earlier, Officer Samuel James Anderson—Sammy to his friends—and his partner Adam Redding responded to a bank robbery in progress at the King Street branch of

318

Pacific Savings and Loan. When they arrived, the suspect could be seen through the large front window brandishing a shotgun. Officer Anderson ignored protocol when the suspect seized a visibly pregnant woman and used her as a human shield while he moved to the door.

"You mother fuckers come closer and I spray this bitch's head all over the sidewalk," the young man yelled.

"Let's talk this over!"

That is what the court transcripts claim Officer Anderson said in response. In truth, nothing was actually said by either officer. They shared a glance and Officer Redding got to his feet with his hands in the air. As soon as the suspect's attention turned, Officer Anderson rose from behind the bumper of the squad car and fired. His bullet struck the suspect just above the right temple.

The preliminary investigation was already finished and hadn't even garnered a mention in the Seattle Times. It wasn't until an anonymous witness told a reporter that she had video from her cell phone that clearly showed no attempt was made to negotiate with the bank robbery suspect. Within two days, every local news station in Seattle was playing and replaying that footage.

During the trial, the defense attorney for Officer Anderson made a big deal about the poor audio quality and instead had the jury focus on the dollar figure paid to the shooter of that video by the media. The PR firm hired to represent the Seattle Police made it a point to trot out every non-white member of the force to "prove" that racism was not a problem in the city. Officer Anderson was regularly seen on the news returning from calls where he rescued kittens from trees and helped blue-haired, elderly ladies carry their groceries to their homes (that he just happened to be cruising past when the need arose).

Meanwhile, the criminal record of Lionel Wells was traced all the way back to his childhood where he entered the system at age nine after being caught shoplifting a pack of bubble gum from a Kwik Mart. The "habitual criminal behavior" of the late Lionel Wells included three traffic tickets and a fourth degree Domestic Violence arrest.

Jerry ducked into the men's room and whipped out his phone. He'd purposely sat beside the door to the courtroom so he could slip out as soon as the verdict was read. He was going to get the story out first this time. After being scooped by Action News Radio during the mayoral race when the incumbent was caught leaving a gay bar arm in arm with a garishly dressed transgender male who looked nothing at all like his wife, Jerry was going to beat everybody to the punch—including Action News Radio.

"This is Shelly," an agitated-sounding voice answered on the second ring.

"Not guilty," Jerry said. There was a moment of silence where he was almost unsure whether anybody was still on the other end of the line.

"*Not* guilty on the Anderson story," Shelly yelled without bothering to cover the mouthpiece.

"There's more," Jerry added after shaking his head to clear the ringing.

"There always is with you, isn't there?"

"This has nothing to do with us." Jerry felt a headache, the kind that only Shelly could give him, begin to throb in his temples. "The folks in the courtroom are really agitated."

"Did you think otherwise? After all, the police aren't high on the African-American community's list of favorite people as of late. Hell...as of ever."

"No," Jerry insisted, "this is something bigger."

"So get the story." Shelly was obviously done with this conversation. "*That* is what we pay you for."

Just as he thumbed his screen to end the call, a loud crash sounded from outside. He quickly went to video mode on his phone in case there was something good that he could sell to one of the local networks, and opened the door. Almost as if on cue, a body slid past on the polished granite floor; not just any body, this was a uniformed police officer!

The next thing that struck Jerry was the wall of sound. The yelling, screaming, crying, and cursing were tremendous. Moving out of the doorway for a better look, he saw what could only be described as a free-for-all melee. He brought up his phone and started capturing video; this was going to rake in a fortune. The judge had demanded that all news teams keep their camera crews out in front of the courthouse building.

As his hand held the phone up to record the fight, his eyes scanned for anybody else who might be doing the same thing. He felt a surge of actual giddiness when he couldn't find a single soul "rolling tape" on this scene. However, his reporter's eyes were beginning to register something else: except for a few uniformed officers of varying shades of mocha wading in to help their comrades, this fight was clearly divided on a racial line.

Jerry's eyes caught a sudden flurry of movement just to his right and he turned as three young gangbanger types—in their mid-teens at the most—wrestled an officer to the ground. One of the youngsters had pulled the police-issue handgun free from its holster. Jerry instantly brought his phone around just in time to catch the youth firing three shots into the chest of the downed policeman.

There was a split-second where the melee froze; it was like a Hollywood special effect. That was the moment it could have stopped. That was the moment Jerry would always think of when he wondered if things could have gone differently. What happened next was a furious escalation of the fighting. Packs of African-American men and boys mobbed the heavily outnumbered Seattle Police Department. It didn't help that most of those in attendance were in civilian clothes or dress uniforms without even a set of handcuffs.

Jerry ducked back into the bathroom after he'd gotten what he deemed a sufficient amount of footage. Besides, after the shooting of the downed policeman, the rest of the footage was filler and fodder. He segmented the video with expert ease and sent the files to his personal email. None of this would matter if his phone was destroyed and the footage lost.

As he leaned against the door and took a moment to catch his breath, he began to notice an angry buzzing sound. With more caution than he was usually known for, Jerry took slow steps to the barred window. It only opened about three inches. *Probably to keep some of the folks who come out on the losing end in the courtrooms from taking that last leap,* Jerry surmised. Outside was chaos. It seemed that the fighting inside was simply the warm-up. Pockets of angry African-Americans—men, women, and even children—had been swept up in the fury he'd witnessed in that hallway.

"This is why I left L.A.," Jerry grumbled as he tapped the screen on his phone to call the station.

Chapter 1

"...as reports continue to flood in about the possibility of riots flaring up outside the Seattle Public Courthouse in response to the 'Not Guilty' verdict of Officer Sam 'Sammy' Anderson—"

Click.

"...as many as seven injured according to unofficial sources—"

Click.

"...even rumors of shots fired—"

Click.

Shelly Casteel set down the remote after switching the television off. It had been over three hours since KTKK had cut into the midday call-in talk show with a 'Breaking News' report from Jerry Burns, live at the courthouse. Of course, by now, nobody except for commuters stuck in traffic on the freeway were listening to their radios anymore. Once those first videos hit the air, it was all about the graphic footage.

Still, she had an ace up her sleeve. Unfortunately, it came wrapped in the package that was Jerry Burns; field reporter, direct link to the mayor...and ex-lover. Her phone rang and she saw Jerry's newest Facebook profile picture show up on her screen. Jerry was grinning smugly at the camera phone he was obviously holding while leaning precariously out a window. Below, you could see the mob of people outside of the courthouse.

"When are you going to get here?" Shelly demanded as she answered on the second ring.

"Shells," Jerry laughed; he knew how she hated when he called her that, "I may be a while. There is no sign this is going to die down, and I ain't leaving this bathroom until it does. Have you seen what is going on? My lily-white ass would be pummeled if I go out there now."

"The director from the network will be here in ten minutes." Shelly pinched the bridge of her nose with two fingers. He'd *promised* to deliver exclusive footage that would blow everything else away.

"This is why you need to go to my computer and get my email."

"Why didn't you tell me this an hour ago?"

"I figured I'd be there in time and, quite frankly, I wanted to bask in the glory."

"So how do I get in?"

"The password is 'Sh3llB1tch'. The 'E' is a three and the 'I' is a one," Jerry explained.

"Cute." *Why did she always hook up with such assholes?* Shelly asked herself. "And you say that you won't sell for less than fifty?"

"Trust me, when you see what is there, you'll understand."

"You know how Brent is with money."

"Bastard makes us pay for our own booze at the Christmas party…yeah…I know how Brent is," Jerry grumbled. "I also know that he would mortgage his house and prostitute his teenage daughter if he thought it would garner him an 'in' with the national folks."

"I just want you to—" A loud crash from Jerry's end cut her off.

"Shit!" was all she heard before the line went dead.

The dolt probably tripped over himself getting to the mirror to check his hair. He'd call back soon enough. She had a meeting to prepare for and needed to get to a mirror herself now that she thought of it.

She flipped open the closet in her office and turned the light on above the mirror. Her hair was an absolute mess. How many times had she run her hands through it in agitated frustration today? She ran a brush through her thick brunette tresses and did an emergency triage on her lipstick. As always, her eyes looked great. They were her best weapon and she used the hazel orbs every chance she got.

"Shelly?" A knock made her jump. Fortunately, her closet door was between her and the entry to her office. She quickly fixed her smile and stepped out to greet her visitor.

"Brent," she used that breathy voice honed during her years as an air personality on the radio station she now managed, "how nice of you to stop in."

"You said you have some footage that will bury everybody else."

Typical Brent; all business. She just hoped that Jerry wasn't over-selling himself on this like he had his abilities as a lover.

***

The door to the bathroom flew open causing Jerry to drop his phone. Two angry-looking, young, African-American men barged in. One of them had blood dripping from his hands and rushed to the sink.

"Told you ya shouldn't of hit that pig in the mouth, you already—" the uninjured one was saying.

Both men froze when they noticed Jerry. There was a moment of silent tension as they each stared at Jerry who was bent over partway in the act of picking up his phone.

"Hi, guys," Jerry finally said while trying to keep the tremor out of his voice.

"You gotta be mutha fuckin' kidding," the bleeding man said.

"Thought all the white folks was cleared out of this place and hiding in their living rooms," the other sneered.

"And I thought all the fun was over for today," the bleeder said through a wince as he suddenly seemed to remember his hand.

"I don't want any trouble," Jerry said, immediately regretting how he sounded so incredibly weak.

"None of y'all white folks do when we standin' right in front of ya," the bleeder said as he thrust his hand under a faucet. "But when we's gone, then you all gots plenty to say."

"You pro'ly one of them folks run his mouth when the camera is on you asking if that cop shoulda got off," the other added, taking a step towards Jerry.

"Actually," the gears began spinning in Jerry's head, quickly displacing the fear, "I'm a reporter for KTKK radio. Maybe you two would like me to interview you; let you get your side of the story out for people to hear."

"How you gonna do that?" the bleeder asked, looking skeptical. Still, there was something in his eyes that Jerry recognized instantly. He'd been out in the field enough to see when somebody wanted to take a chip off of their fifteen minutes of fame.

"I can ask you questions," he waved his phone, "and record the interview on this. When I get back to the station, I clean it up and it goes on the air."

"Whatcha think, Cleon?" the bleeder asked as he wrapped his hand in paper towels.

"I think you bumped your head, Tyree." Cleon shook his head and continued to glare at Jerry.

"Gentlemen, you could be the voice against injustice," Jerry urged. "Millions will hear you, and it could be those words that change the course of events for a city. You could be famous."

Jerry let the word hang in the air for a moment before pressing a few touch screens on his phone. He was absolutely recording. However, he had also called Shelly. He just hoped she answered and paid attention so she would know what to do.

***

Brian Hillis followed the two men down the wooded trail. They occasionally whispered amongst themselves, but at no point did they so much as glance back at him. Brian did his best to pick landmarks that would stick in his memory. Right now he knew that he was about five miles outside of Salmon, Idaho. The road—if a pair of ruts that led into the woods could be called such a thing—was just past a roadside tavern called Whitey's. Fitting considering the main clientele were members of a local white supremacist militia group.

Brian had spent the last eight months infiltrating this group. It was rumored that they had big plans: assassinate the president. They were part of a wave of discontent blaming the new administration for everything from the economy, to the lack of tourism in New Hampshire. There were a lot of groups out there that made brash claims around a few beers and a bottle of whiskey. The problem with this group was that they had apparently made a practice run on the governor of the state of neighboring Washington.

It had been a very efficient operation. They had covered their tracks so well that it was really only a fluke that led the boys at Langley to this particular gang. A video camera in a pawn shop across the street from where the governor made his last fund-raising speech caught two men leaving the scene amidst the chaos. After some enhancement, one face was identified: Bill Hayes.

Bill Hayes had been a member of an elite Marine task force and served with distinction in Afghanistan, Iraq, and Libya. His field of expertise was the elimination of high-priority political targets. His work had made national news more than a half dozen times, only, he was never credited. The deaths were usually attributed to some local group that the United States wanted to see gain prominence. That almost always meant that they had somebody that the American government could put in power that would "work towards a new democratic beginning."

"You guys taking me to Canada?" Brian asked after another hour of walking. He was slightly amused at their assumption that walking him in circles and criss-crossing the same area for this long would disorient him. If he was correct, and he was confident that he was, then they weren't more than two miles away from where they'd parked the truck.

"Just a bit farther," the fat one with the forked beard, Jessie Klemm according to the files he'd studied before going undercover, replied.

Jessie was a book you didn't want to judge by its cover. He looked like a typical rednecked moron; he was anything but. Jessie had earned his Expert Marksmen status with the Navy SEALS. He'd eventually been dismissed from service for assaulting his lieutenant. According to reports, he shattered the man's jaw and cheek with one punch. His only words of defense to the inquiry and court-martial had been, "No nigger is gonna tell me what to do."

"You gots someplace to be?" the skinny one missing his top and bottom front teeth snorted. That would be Will Tomkins. His book was more like a pamphlet. High school drop-out and juvenile delinquent with a lifetime of petty crime on his record, Will was a flunky and nothing more.

"Nope," Brian made sure he sounded as bored as possible, "but if I wanted a tour, I'd have called the chamber of commerce and asked for one."

"You sassin' me?" Will stopped and spun around.

That's the problem with flunkies, Brian thought, *they're always trying to prove they belong.* "Does it show?" Brian stopped walking.

He knew well enough that groups like this had certain codes of 'honor' they lived by. One of the biggest ones was a bizarre sense of what they classified as respect. What it basically amounted to was being the bigger bully. If somebody gave you any crap, you busted them in the mouth or they passed you in the organization's status.

"We ain't got time for this," Jessie grumbled.

"But he—"

"Then take it up later," Jessie cast a glance over his shoulder at Brian and smirked. "This is gonna be done today one way or the other."

Brian kept his eyes locked on Will, but he didn't like the sounds of things. There was something in Jessie's voice that portended something very ominous.

They resumed walking. About ten minutes later, Brian spied a clearing. They had finally stopped walking in circles. This was a new area that they hadn't already tromped through a dozen times. A moment later, they were walking through a small complex of cabins. It was obvious that nobody was here...or at least anybody that wanted to be seen.

They stopped at what looked like an old-fashioned well. It was about three feet high and circular. It even had a little wooden roof over it and a spool of rope with a bucket dangling just above the open hole. However, there was also a nylon cord that vanished into this well. It was tied to a stake that was driven into the ground.

Jessie put on a pair of gloves and began hauling on the cord. His arms bulged at the effort. Whatever was at the other end of that line wasn't light. It still took Brian a moment to realize what it was when the payload finally came in to view.

The body fell to the ground with an unceremonious thud. Will stepped close and nudged it with his booted foot. It stirred and made weak coughing sounds. Brian tried to conceal everything he felt. Will might be a clueless idiot, but Jessie was another story entirely.

"So?" Brian looked Jessie in the eyes. "You keep a nigger in the well...big deal."

"Time for you to join the organization, Chet," Jessie said, producing a .22 pistol.

Chet Atkins; that had been the name he chose as his cover. As a boy who grew up in Chicago, that sounded about as backwoods as he could imagine. Chet just felt like a good old boy's name.

"Okay." Brian glanced at the body that was beginning to stir and make strangled pleas to be let go. "So what do you want me to do? Shoot the guy?" He was glad he hadn't decided to add a laugh at the end of that question. Jessie wasn't smiling.

"If you're with us, then this is no big deal."

"Of course," Will piped up, he'd produced a six-shot revolver and was spinning it on his finger by the trigger guard, "you back out now and we have to go through the exit interview." He laughed way too loudly at his own joke, no doubt thinking that he was being witty.

"So I pop this guy, and then what?"

"We go meet up with Bill and the rest. There is a meeting tonight," Jessie said, thrusting the small handgun at Brian.

Brian took the weapon and stepped up to the man sprawled at his feet. He was told to "infiltrate at all costs" when he was given this assignment. He knew that this would be buried by the department when he revealed it during the debrief. And it wasn't like this group was being infiltrated to be taken in; there would be an order to eliminate with "extreme prejudice" at some point. That's how the department stayed out of the news. After Waco, there had been an organizational shift in how extremists were dealt with in order to avoid media backlash. The department had learned that, even if you are dealing with nutcases that are willing to torch themselves and their followers, the government would be the scapegoat.

Brian took the weapon and stepped up to the man. He quickly discerned that this was some poor, homeless wino. All the telltale signs of chronic alcohol abuse were present. There would be nobody looking for this guy. That didn't make him feel any better about what he was supposed to do. He hoped desperately that, when he pulled the trigger, it would fire a blank or something. Somehow, he didn't think that was likely. This group really hated people of color. Not just blacks, they were known to be involved in actions against illegal immigrants. Well, Brian didn't think these guys cared if they were legal or not, just as long as they were Mexican.

"Please—" the man rasped.

Brian pulled the trigger. There was a soft pop. At first he thought he might've been wrong. Maybe it was only blanks. Then, the small hole in the man's forehead began to ooze blood. The man rocked back and fell on his butt. He sat, legs splayed out in front of him for a few seconds. His hands came up to his face and pulled away. The man looked up at Brian, his mouth opening and closing like a fish out of water.

A loud boom sounded, making Brian jump. He spun to see Will blowing across the barrel of his revolver in dramatic fashion.

"Can't stand to see 'em suffer." Will shrugged. "Just like putting down any sick animal."

"What the fuck is wrong with you!" Brian strode over to Will in three quick steps and slapped the big .357 out of the man's hand. While he was upset at what he had just basically been forced to do, he had no way to get it out of his system; Will had provided the perfect diversion. "I was standing right there, you stupid bastard!"

"It was an easy shot!" Will defended himself weakly. "My four-year-old kid coulda made that shot without comin' anywhere close to you."

"Then maybe *he* should be here!"

"Enough!" Jessie barked. "Will, hand me your gun."

"But—" the man tried to protest.

"Chet did what he needed to do in order to be accepted. You didn't have any right poaching his kill." Jessie walked up to the much smaller man and held out one big hand.

Will handed over the revolver, his eyes downcast like a scolded dog. Jessie stuffed it in to one pocket and turned his attention back to Brian. "You just cost me twenty bucks."

"Huh?"

"I bet that you were a fed," Jessie said with a shrug.

"And what made you think that?"

"First it was just an impression, but then you seemed to be too tailor-made for our organization."

"I don't follow." Brian did his best to look confused. Yes, he was going to have to be *very* careful around Jessie.

"You have a few things on your criminal record, nothing major, but all involving incidents with niggers or spics, not so much else as a speeding ticket. It was just a bit suspicious. And you know what they say…if something is too good to be true."

"And now?" Brian asked, careful to watch the bigger man's eyes.

"Now you're in…and I'll still be watchin' ya."

There was a long silence. Will continued to sulk from his reprimand and, therefore, had nothing to offer. Brian was suddenly certain that he was going to have to kill this former SEAL. He just hoped it wasn't going to be a hand-to-hand situation. He was confident in his martial arts skills, but he was equally certain that this man was better.

"So," Jessie finally broke the uncomfortable silence, "let's go meet the boss and see what has his panties so bunched up."

***

Sacramento, California—Russell "Trix" Clay sat at the recording studio's massive mixing console. The girl on the other side was proving that there wasn't a voice in existence that Auto-Tune couldn't fix. She kept looking out at him through the glass between each verse and giving him a "thumbs-up" gesture with the accompanying look that begged for approval. On cue, she finished another verse and flashed him the look and the gesture. Russell plastered on his biggest grin and popped his own thumbs up in return.

He had to admit, this was so much easier than porn. He'd spent most of the 80s making cheap video tapes and pimping.

Now, he could make a demo for some no-talent girl who thought she was the next Madonna or Janet Jackson, get a few weeks of having his dick sucked, and then move on to the next potential "star".

The blond in the studio was simply the latest in a string. She was eighteen, or at least claimed to be, and had the five hundred bucks for the price of the "Rising Star" package. That was another thing...the bitches were paying *him* to suck his dick. Of course, they thought they were paying for studio time and a promotional package; and he always gave them a CD of their session when he was finished with them and ready to move on to the next one.

The generic sample track faded out and the girl pulled off her headphones. Russell flipped the switch to open the intercom. "That was great, Sheila."

"You're supposed to call me "Sheba Street" when I'm in the studio, remember?" The girl had an even worse talking voice than she did a singing voice if that were possible. "You said that if it helped me get into the vibe, you would refer to me by my new stage name in the studio."

"Sorry, Sheba." Russell made at least a minimal attempt to sound like he meant it. That was okay, tonight he was gonna take it out on her ass...literally. "So maybe you should run through the song again, but this time try to put some anger in the hook."

"You think I need to sound more gangsta?"

God, Russell thought, *nobody said that word anymore, did they?* Well, nobody but suburban white kids who thought that saying it made them one. Most of these kids would actually shit themselves if they came face-to-face with a real Hard-timer.

Just then, the door to the studio opened. It was his so-called business partner, Tremont Epps. Tremont played the role of record label executive when it was Russell's turn to be the studio producer. They switched roles every month or so depending on how long they wanted to bang the new prospect; and that of course depended on which "Star" package the girl bought.

"Trixie," the man came in and flopped down into the other leather seat, "I been calling your cell all day."

"Yeah, well you know I turn it off when I'm in here, Tre," Russell pronounced it like "tree" because he knew it pissed Tremont off. He wanted it pronounced "tray".

"Man, you ain't been seein' what's going down in Seattle."

"They finally get an expansion team to replace the Sonics?"

"No, man, they's riotin'," Tremont said with a big smile that showed of his gold front tooth.

"The fuck you mean? You mean *rioting* as in a bunch of stupid white folks wearing bandanas on their faces and spray painting that stupid anarchy symbol on the fronts of banks, or you talking South Central?"

"I don't think they got enough bruthas up north to pull the real deal, but they got it bangin' up there." Tremont fished out his phone and his fingers flew as he navigated the screens until he found what he was looking for. "Check this shit out." He handed the phone to Russell.

The footage was shaky, and it took Russell a minute to realize what he was seeing. The video finished and then restarted on a loop. This time, Russell paid closer attention. Sure enough, there it was again. To the left in the picture, a uniformed police officer went to the floor under a pile of young brothers. There was a muffled 'pop' and one of the youngsters was looking at the gun in his hand like he'd never seen it before. There was an instant where all those around him stood there shocked, then they all started pounding the shooter on the back and cheering. Russell looked even closer and saw the small dark pool forming on the polished floor.

"Little man shot a cop?" Russell handed the phone back. "Where did you get the video?"

"It's on every channel right now," Tremont replied. "But I wouldn't have come for just that." He flipped through a few

334

more screens and handed the phone back to Russell. The footage was almost all the same in that it was mobs of black men and women on the streets. They were standing their ground against tear gas canisters and rubber bullets. Windows were being smashed, cars tipped or lit on fire, and a lot of yelling and screaming.

Russell watched a few clips before handing the phone back to Tremont. He sat there silently for a moment until an annoying buzz snapped his attention back. He looked up to see Sheila glaring at him with a hand on one hip. As soon as his eyes met hers, she pressed the intercom buzzer again.

"I thought I was gonna do the hook thingy again sounding angry," the girl snapped in a poor impersonation of an angry black woman that just came off sounding uneducated and spoiled.

"Just talking with a guy from the recording label," Russell said out of habit.

"He's from the label?" the girl shrieked, proving that her voice *could* in fact get more annoying.

"Yes."

"Oh. Em. Gee. I'm sorry…I'll wait. You two talk or whatever you need to do…did he hear my demo? Is he gonna—"

Russell clicked off the intercom and turned back to Tremont. "We're set up for a riot here."

"But the riot is *there*," Tremont said, tapping the screen of his phone. "And I bet you they ain't got nothing in the way of riot preparation like South Central and the LAPD. We might have to drive a few hours, but it's still about the message, right?"

Russell sat quietly again. They'd had this planned out for over two decades. In that time, probably half their numbers had filtered out. All that were left were the hardcore believers. There would be some logistics to work out, but Tremont had a point. They'd planned to go heads-up with a police force that was trained in riot response. Seattle might have some crude plans in place, but nothing to deal with what he had in mind.

"Get me street maps. Google should have the pictures we need," Russell finally said. "Call the whole group, tell them I want everybody packed and at my house in six hours. If anybody has family in Seattle, we need to know."

"Actually," Tremont looked a bit sheepish, "I already called everybody. We can be ready to roll in an hour. I told ya I've been trying to call you all day."

Russell felt a bit of that old anger surge. It must've shown in his eyes because Tremont scooted back in his chair.

"I wasn't going over you, brother." Tremont raised his hands in defense. "It's just that you ain't been taking any interest in the cause much lately. You been busy—"

"Nailing stupid white girls," Russell finished the thought. "No, you're right, Tremont. I guess I got lazy. It's just so easy to do when you start running a game that keeps you in cash and pussy."

"You still want to wait 'til tonight?" Tremont asked. "I can call the brothers and tell 'em."

"No, Tremont." Russell shook his head. "It is time we live by our creed."

"The time is now," both men recited together.

Chapter 2

Benny Richards pulled on his goggles and tugged the drawstrings for his hooded sweatshirt tight. He tapped his pocket to ensure all his "gear" was ready. Taking one last look at the television, he felt his heart race a bit. They were rioting downtown. He never missed a riot if he could help it. He might even see about upgrading to a better flat screen while he was out.

Leaving his studio apartment, his phone buzzed. It was work. Like he was gonna come in to the copier shop today. Besides, if what he'd seen on television was correct, the copy store was likely to get some of the riot overflow. The windows were as good as broke. In fact, he smiled behind his bandana; maybe he would throw the first brick.

Taking the stairs three at a time, he bounded down the four flights and out onto the street. Up the hill, he could see the smoke. He'd been in so many protests that he thought he might actually be getting immune to tear gas. He started up the hill at a fast walk. Running would only draw attention, and he wanted to get to the action *before* he had to deal with the police.

As he neared, he could hear the soothing buzz of an angry crowd. He paused for a minute and scratched his head. For a moment he'd forgotten what this one was about. *That's right*, he thought, *some black kid got shot robbing a bank or something.* He briefly considered the possibility that he might not be wanted at this little demonstration, but quickly dismissed it. People who are pissed love anybody willing to take their side, or in Benny's case, at least acting like they are. Benny just wanted to break stuff. He could care less about the cause as long as there was some breaking and burning going on.

He thumbed his iPod for some good thrash metal and resumed his fast walk to the scene of the mayhem. Just as he crested the hill, a group of ten or so black guys came into view.

"Fuck the Seattle Police!" Benny yelled. He pulled the brick from his pocket—he always brought his first 'throwing' brick—and chucked it at the largest window in sight.

The group stopped and seemed to have a quick meeting of the minds. *Cool,* Benny thought, *I can clique up with some brothers. Better to run with a pack, plus, if the cops show, I won't be as likely of a target.*

The group started walking his way and Benny thumbed down the volume on his iPod. "S'up, fellas?" They continued walking his direction, but there was something in their faces that caused Benny to pause. They looked…pissed. At him!

Without warning, the group broke into a sprint. Benny stood stock still. His legs refused to listen to the voice in his head that screamed for him to run. *So this is what a deer in the headlights feels like,* his inner-voice scoffed.

The group hit him in a bum's rush that sent Benny sprawling. He'd been in a few mosh pits. There was a cardinal rule; if you ever lost your footing, the first thing you do is cover your head. That didn't help for long. As the kicks continued and things inside him broke or ruptured, Benny's arms couldn't stay wrapped around his head any longer. As he lost consciousness, his last thoughts were, *What did I ever do to these guys?*

***

"…currently traffic is at a standstill on I-5 as protesters have started throwing firebombs at passing motorists. Chief of Police Michael Rhodes says that his men are working to restore order, but advises all citizens to stay clear of the City Center area as well as the stadium complex…"

***

Grady Moses sat on the bench and took out his handkerchief. At eighty-seven, all this walking was getting a bit tiring. He watched a group of young brothers and sisters trot past.

"Stay solid, Oh-Gee!" one of them shouted.

Stupid kids, he thought as they disappeared around a corner. Today's generation didn't know diddly-squat about proper rioting. Hardly any buildings were burning, and he'd passed at least a dozen shops without a single busted window. Now Watts...that was a proper riot. These kids are just running around willy-nilly without really *doing* anything.

Grady spied a golf ball-sized rock in the gutter and climbed wearily to his feet. It took him a few seconds of strained effort to bend that far over to pick it up, but eventually he held the stone in his hand. Looking around, he saw one of those overpriced coffee shops that sit on every corner in the city. White folks loved paying too much for a cup of coffee.

Clutching his cane in his off hand, Grady crossed the street to the coffee house. Inside, he could see a few customers. They were all face down in their laptop computers or hammering away madly at their newfangled computer phones. Not one of them noticed as he raised his arm, cocked it back, and hurled the rock at the giant window. Of course, seconds later, every head in the place—after coming up from wherever they ducked when the glass shattered and crashed—was staring out the window. All they saw was an old man hobbling away on his cane.

"Damn kids musta run past," one of the customers finally said with a weak laugh. "At least they didn't hurt that poor little old man over there."

***

Jerry sat down on the counter where the row of sinks lined the wall. The two young men had finally said all they could think of and left. He had to admit, one of them was actually quite well-spoken.

Wow, he thought, *are you that much of a closet racist?* He admitted to himself that he fully expected the two men to ramble on about a bunch of "white man always keepin' a brutha down" crap. Tyree actually made some very strong points about how the entire police system was designed to protect its own from within,

"…and not just against the African-American community," he'd said. "Like that retarded boy that got Tazed, cuffed, and beat down…that was a white boy. Only, none of the cops got in trouble…they was cops. *That* was their defense."

Jerry pushed a few buttons and sent the audio file to his email. He would call Shelly in a bit and tell her about it, but first, he needed to get out of this place. He'd talked his way out of one beating, but he doubted his luck would hold. After the two had left, he quickly brought up the local newsfeed. The situation was escalating, and now it looked like it would be a couple of days at least before things settled down.

Cautiously, he opened the bathroom door. The floor was a shambles, but appeared to be empty. He hurried across to the courtroom. It would be good to have a few shots of the aftermath. The door was mostly off its hinges, which was impressive given the size of the door and the sturdiness of the hinges.

Jerry was unprepared for what he saw when he peeked inside. There were two dead bodies in the aisle. One was wearing the tattered remnants of a policeman's dress blue uniform. There was an ugly dent on the side of his head and a trickle of blood had dried on that ear. A few feet away, a husky young Hispanic girl was sprawled partway in between the benches of the third and fourth row. Jerry recognized her as the stenographer.

A faint rustling sound caused him to stop in his tracks. It was coming from the docket area. He looked for anything that he could use as a weapon to defend himself and found nothing,

"Hello?" Jerry called out. His voice sounded way louder than he was comfortable with. "Who's there?"

He considered backing out and beating a hasty exit, then he heard the soft moan. Advancing cautiously, he followed the sound to the judge's bench. Behind it, a halo of blood pooling around his head, lay sprawled the judge who had presided over the Anderson trial.

Jerry rushed over, looking for something to use to stop the bleeding from the nasty gash on the judge's forehead. Finding nothing, he tugged at the robe. It wasn't very absorbent, but he was able to wad a section of it up and press it on the wound.

"My chamber," the man rasped, "my pills are in my chamber."

"Pills?" Jerry asked, confused. Pills weren't going to do any good in stopping the bleeding.

"My heart..." the judge coughed, and his face scrunched up from the apparent pain.

"Why don't I call—" Jerry stopped in mid-sentence. Call? Who would he call? He'd seen outside, and the rioting was all around the courthouse. It was unlikely that emergency crews could get to them. And even if they could, it wouldn't be any time soon.

"Okay, sir," Jerry climbed back to his feet, "you stay here and I'll be right back." Did he really just tell the judge bleeding out from a head wound and possibly suffering a heart attack to stay put?

He went to the door behind the judge's bench and tried the knob. It opened and he wondered briefly if judges ever locked their door when court was in session. Was there a need? *God*, he thought, *where the hell is my brain going? There is a riot taking place, and I am having possibly the most convoluted inner-monolog in history. I need to get my mind back on track.*

He was relieved to find the bottle of heart medication sitting out in the open on the desk. He'd only just realized that he hadn't bothered to ask where it might be. Hurrying back, he caught the acrid stench of a bowel movement. Jerry dropped the bottle of pills and flopped down in the judge's enormous chair. *Correct that*, he thought, *the* late *judge's chair.*

***

Brian followed Jessie into the smoky tavern. There were already a couple dozen men standing around in groups talking loudly in Southern accents—which Brian considered peculiar since they were in Idaho—that were laden with plenty of expletives and an abundance of the "N" word.

"I see our boy passed his initiation," one of the men just inside the door said to Jessie as they entered. "Guess you can pay up when we get back."

"Get back?" Jessie stopped, turning to the man who Brian was almost certain was called "Slimmy".

"That's what this meetin' is all about," Slimmy said with a grin. "Buncha uppity niggers is putting Seattle to the torch. Word is, we aim to cruise on over and see about doin' some crowd dispersal. Everybody knows that coon they got for a governor ain't gonna let nobody do nothin' to stop things. Hell, he'll probably invite the rioters to the mansion for dinner."

"So we gonna drive to Seattle and bust some heads?" These were the first words Will had spoken since being reprimanded by Jessie. He sounded way too excited.

"Seems to be the rumor," Slimmy said with a nod and a wink.

Great, Brian thought, *how the hell am I going to contact the office and set up a time to bust these yahoos if I am on the road to Seattle?* He didn't see a time in the near future where he would be able to get to the locker he kept at the bus station where he kept his cell phone. The one he carried was a simple

342

burner phone. He cursed how lazy he'd become when it came to memorizing phone numbers.

"Well it looks like we'll have one more set of knuckles in the mix," Jessie slapped Brian on the back, if not a little too hard to actually be friendly.

"So he popped that piece of shit?" somebody called out.

"You won't be seein' him beggin' outside the liquor store no more," Will snorted.

"You'd think them beggin' ass welfare monkeys would get the clue when their friends keep turning up missing," Slimmy wheezed and lit another cigarette to replace the one he stubbed out as he spoke.

"Ain't none of 'em got a lick of sense," Jessie agreed. "I can't believe there are still any left in this town. They're like roaches. Kill a hundred and two hundred more will come crawling out from under the garbage can."

"Can I get everybody to take a seat," a voice rose above the din.

Brian turned to see the group's leader, Bill Hayes, as he stepped up onto the small stage at the back of the bar. The man looked just like the picture in his file. His reddish-blond hair was a wavy mop on his head. His broad chest and arms bulged with muscle that could easily be seen under the black tee shirt. The long scar down the right side of his face where, according to his military file, a North Korean assassin had managed to get in one swipe with his blade before Bill Hayes caught him in a choke hold and snapped the man's neck, showed up a bright white in the bank of lights over the stage. He actually was reported to have stitched his flayed face in the bathroom of the hotel room where the attempted assassination took place.

"I don't know how many of you have been watching the news." Bill's voice didn't boom, it simply carried throughout the room at a volume that everybody could easily hear. "It seems that another piece of shit criminal that got shot while breaking the law has caused a member of the Seattle Police Department to go on trial. When the jury reached a just and proper verdict of "Not Guilty," the niggers got mad and started trashing the court-room. Things got out of hand, and now they are rioting in the streets, demanding justice."

A murmur went up through the room. Bill seemed content to let that continue for a while before raising his hands to settle the crowd. Brian was only a little surprised at how quickly silence fell on the smoky room. It was obvious that Bill was very much in control.

"Tonight we will load the 'Scenario Alpha' packs into the RVs and head west. We should arrive just before sunrise. As of yet, the National Guard is not on the scene. We will utilize police scanners to pinpoint the law enforcement activity and strike where they are not.

"I want all team leaders to meet me in the office for individual assignments." Bill scanned the room for a few seconds before continuing, "And I want to welcome Chet Atkins to our family. He just returned from pledging with Jessie and Will. Welcome, Chet." With that, the man stepped down and made his way to a single door situated between the bar and the stage.

"Guess I joined at just the right time," Brian said to Jessie.

"We'll see." Jessie shrugged and headed to the same door Bill had gone through. Brian decided that it wouldn't do any harm to have a drink. Besides, he was still a little shaky from the day's earlier activities. A hand caught his shoulder and he turned to find Will's glowering face.

"We ain't done with our beef," the man hissed and walked away before Brian could respond.

Brian shrugged off the comment and headed towards a much needed drink. He did his best not to recoil in disgust as the words of congratulations and exuberant back slaps followed him to the bar. The only good thing to come out of it was the fact that he didn't have to buy either beer, or the shot of bourbon.

***

"...and with nightfall, law enforcement spokesmen repeat that there is now a curfew in effect for all of King and Pierce counties. It is requested that all residents remain indoors while efforts continue to bring this situation under control. One source expressed optimism that things would be returned to normal within the next seventy-two hours. In other news, city council-men will meet with the mayor on Sunday to address the city budget deficit..."

***

Russell stared out the window as the scenery whizzed by. Other than the few towns they'd passed through, the entire state of Oregon had seemed like nothing but forests and farms. Why anybody would want to live in such a podunk state was any-body's guess. They'd crossed over into Washington over an hour ago, and as far as he could tell, it wasn't much different. *No wonder these states have such lousy sports teams*, he mused.

"We got about an hour before we get there," Tremont said from the driver's seat. "I been listening to the radio, and they are putting a curfew in effect."

"We gonna get there before dark?" Russell asked, shaking himself to clear his head.

"It'll be close," Tremont replied, "but we should make it. My only concern is if they have any sort of roadblocks in place—"

"We already discussed that," Russell cut the other man off. "If it comes to it, we will do what we have to do. What differ-ence does it make when we kill the first cop? You getting cold feet now that the shit is about to go down?"

"No," Tremont snapped, "I just don't want to bring heat on us until we get into the city and make that first strike. I know what you said, but I think it makes a difference if we roll in under the radar. You know as well as I do that the moment we kill a cop, the game changes."

"You want to try and talk our way past a roadblock with what we got in this car or any of the others? You think a carload of niggas cruising into the heart of a riot ain't getting pulled over and searched?"

"No, but—"

"Ain't no more 'buts' to be had. We gonna do what needs doin' before they get a chance to stop us," Russell said with finality and turned to look back out the window.

They drove in silence for the next forty minutes. Slowly, fields and forests began to give way to housing developments and industry. A large body of water to their left came in to view as they crested a hill and looked down into Tacoma.

"That the ocean?" Tremont asked.

"No," Russell answered. He had to admit, it was an extremely beautiful sight. "That is Pew-jit sound," he read from the guide in his lap. At first he'd had no idea how to pronounce the name, but one of the brothers had spent some time in the area. Puget Sound was probably one of the easiest words he found. With names like Sammamish, Puyallup (pronounced PEW-wallup for some damn reason), and Issaquah, the whole area was a phonetic nightmare.

"So when you think we gonna see the first—" Tremont started to ask. A pair of police cruisers came in to view as they rounded a long, arcing bend in the interstate.

"Okay, gentlemen," Russell toggled his phone and brought the other cars up on a conference call, "time for talking is over. You all know what we are about. This is what you signed up for all those years ago. I want you to remember every single time you got pulled over just because you were driving through a neighborhood at night that the cops didn't think you belonged in. I want you to remember that it takes sacrifice to bring change. Our parents marched in Washington D.C., Selma, and Jackson. They took those first steps, now it is up to us to finish their journey. We've tried for decades to play the game by the rules…and it ain't got us a damn thing. This isn't about the violence and the killing to come, it is about the opportunity and equality in the future."

There was silence for a few seconds, then a series of confirmations. The men were ready. As they approached the roadblock, Russell set the sawed-off Mossberg in his lap. Everybody in the car stuffed in their earplugs as their car slowed and joined in the queue.

Tremont looked over his shoulder. He could see three of the other nine cars, trucks, or vans they had loaded into for the trip. His eyes returned to the front, and he tried to remind himself that what was about to happen *had* to happen. It was just that, after so many years since the South Central riots, that fire of injustice had gone a bit cold. He wasn't a kid fresh out of college anymore. He had a house and, while somewhat on the shady side, he had a job that made him a good living.

The car in front of them stopped and the police officer stepped up to the window. Of course, the occupants were white and the officer was really only giving them a cursory look; his attentions were already on the next car in line. Theirs. He placed the Beretta 93 in his lap and fingered the trigger.

Russell's eyes scanned the scene. The two officers checking vehicles were both looking fairly bored. The two that were supposed to be providing backup were sitting in their vehicle. That would be the problem, and that is where he would focus his firepower. He would rely on Tremont and Al "Panama" Hylton to deal with the exposed cops.

The car ahead was waved through, and they were signaled to approach, and then stop. The officer on the driver's side glanced at the license plate. Of course, they'd swapped out the last of the plates in the parking lot of a grocery store right after they crossed in to Vancouver. Since reaching Oregon, they had made periodic stops to find Washington plates and managed to acquire a set for each of their vehicles.

Tremont rolled down his window as he came to a stop. The officer let his hand brush his weapon in what Tremont figured the man considered to be an intimidating manner. "Where you men head—" He never finished the sentence as Tremont angled his handgun up and fired. The bullet caught the policeman in the throat and blood came in a bright red gush.

Panama had rolled his window down in the back passenger's side when they were still a couple of cars back in the queue. He brought his own weapon up, a Remington shotgun, and fired into the chest of the still-frozen officer who was just making his way down the right side of the car.

Russell didn't pause, he threw open his door and began pumping armor-piercing rounds into the other squad car. The two officers inside jittered and jumped as Pete Sanders came out from the car directly behind and opened up with his H & K MP5. In seconds that seemed like minutes, it was over.

Several cars in the queue started doing everything they could to get out of line and turn around. In their midst, other cars opened up and spilled their deadly cargo as the rest of Russell's men came out and brought weapons to shoulders. It only took sixty-eight seconds, but in that time, both squad cars on the northbound lane (apparently they weren't worried about anybody heading south) of Interstate 5 were in flames along with a dozen others.

"Okay!" Russell called after blowing his referee's whistle. "Let's get moving. In five minutes, the police will be flooded with calls. Some of these people driving away might have shot video on their phones. By the time we get to downtown Seattle, we will be wanted men."

The nine car convoy weaved its way through the carnage and sped away down a wide open interstate. Already the scanners were buzzing. The police knew something bad had happened; they just didn't know exactly what. It was very possible that they would encounter another roadblock before they reached downtown. As they sped by the on- and off-ramps along the way, they could see many of them had barricades set up to prevent anybody from reaching the most direct route in to Seattle.

So far, Russell thought as he watched the looming skyline grow out in front of them, *this is going almost as planned.* He cast another uncertain glance over at Tremont. He'd been correct. The man had tears rolling down his cheeks. He would need to watch his old friend. A chain being only as strong as its weakest link was an axiom he'd heard in sports. It certainly carried over to this situation. He didn't think he could kill his friend, but he could certainly disable him if it came to such a thing

MAY DECEMBER
Publications

**The growing voice in horror
and speculative fiction.**

Find us at www.maydecemberpublications.com
Or
Email us at contact@maydecemberpublications.com

TW Brown is the author of the *Zomblog* series, his horror comedy romp, ***That Ghoul Ava***, and, of course, the ***DEAD*** series. Safely tucked away in the beautiful Pacific Northwest, he moves away from his desk only at the urging of his Border Collie, Aoife. (Pronounced Eye-fa)

He plays a little guitar on the side...just for fun...and makes up any excuse to either go trail hiking or strolling along his favorite place...Cannon Beach. He answers all his emails sent to twbrown.maydecpub @gmail.com and tries to thank everybody personally when they take the time to leave a review of one of his works.

His blog can be found at:http://twbrown.blogspot.com

The best way to find everything he has out is to start at his Amazon Author Page:

http://www.amazon.com/TW-Brown/e/B00363NQI6

You can follow him on twitter @maydecpub and on Facebook under Todd Brown, Author TW Brown, and also under May December Publications.

CPSIA information can be obtained
at www.ICGtesting.com
Printed in the USA
BVHW041143170419
545798BV00012B/60/P

9 781940 734538